The Edge of Winter

Also by Luanne Rice

LUANNE RICE

The Edge of Winter

DOUBLEDAY LARGE PRINT HOME LIBRARY EDITION

BANTAM BOOKS

THE EDGE OF WINTER
A Bantam Book / March 2007

Published by Bantam Dell
A Division of Random House, Inc.
New York, New York

ISBN-13: 978-0-7394-7879-0

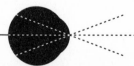

This Large Print Book carries the
Seal of Approval of N.A.V.H.

For Audrey and Robert Loggia,
with love

Acknowledgments

With love and thanks to Commander L. Paul James, USN (Ret.), for his constant friendship, his generosity in helping with my research, and for telling me about being at sea in the North Atlantic, especially the amazing detail of dawn arriving on the bridge.

Much love to William Twigg Crawford, for all the time we've spent on and near the sea.

Thank you forever to Mim, my grandmother, and to her nieces and nephews: Barbara and Mary Lou Beaudry; Lucille Kennedy; Bob Kennedy and Mary Keenan; Mary Beth and Brian Holland; Howard and Mimi Logee; and Arthur and Gail McCormack; and in memory of Florence, Josie, George, Arthur, Ida, Eva, and Gladys, for all the love, stories, and wonderful times in Rhode Island.

I'm so grateful to everyone at Bantam: Irwyn Applebaum, Nita Taublib, Tracy Devine, Betsy Hulsebosch, Carolyn Schwartz, Cynthia Lasky, Barb Burg, Susan Corcoran, Gina Wachtel, Melissa Lord, Kerri Buckley, Kenneth Wohlrob,

Igor Aronov, Paolo Pepe, Virginia Norey, Kathleen Baldonado, Ruth Toda, and Deb Dywer.

Thank you to my agent, Andrea Cirillo, and everyone at the Jane Rotrosen Agency: Jane Berkey, Don Cleary, Meg Ruley, Peggy Gordijn, Annelise Robey, Kelly Harms, Christina Hogrebe, Gillian Luongo, Trinity Boscardin, Lindsay Klemas, and Kathy Lee Hart.

Much gratitude to Ron Bernstein.

With love to Amelia Onorato and the BDG, and to Marianna Scandole, Monique Colarossi, and Ashley Elliott of Regis College.

Thank you to Mark Lonergan, Dore Dedrick, Riley, and Mattie, for their countless kindnesses to me and the girls.

Love to Colin McEnroe, who knows that all roads lead to a porch in Maine.

My appreciation to Dan Walsh for his knowledge and insight regarding U-boats.

My father, Thomas F. Rice Jr., flew during World War II as navigator-bombardier with the 492nd and 44th Bomb Groups. His bravery knew no bounds. Many thanks to my cousin, Thomas Brielmann; Norma and Bill Beasley, of the 492nd Bomb Group Association; and Paul Arnett, for Paul and Dave Arnett; Charles and Anna Arnett; Ed Alexander; Ernest Haar; Robert Dubowsky; Patrick Byrne; Allan Blue; Robin Janton; Brian Mahoney; and to the many other wonderful people I met in Dayton, for keeping the memories and stories alive.

The Edge
of Winter

Prologue

The day the world ended started out crystal clear, the sky so sharply, heart-stoppingly blue, it seemed it might crack. Although it was near the end of February, and freezing cold, Mickey and Jenna rode their bikes down the windswept road toward the barrier beach. They did this all spring, summer, and fall, but this was their first bike outing since the winter snows had receded.

Jenna's favorite bird was the black-throated blue warbler, although it was too early in the season to see one. Mickey's favorite bird—unseen by either her or Jenna, but loved for its mystery and elusiveness—

was the snowy owl, and the rare-bird group had sent out an e-mail that one had been spotted on Refuge Beach. Such e-mails came every day, but this was the first snowy sighting that Mickey could remember.

"It's freezing," Jenna said as they pedaled south.

"I know," Mickey said. "But just think— we're going to see a snowy owl."

"The e-mail didn't even say where it was!"

"That's because birders always protect owls. They're so shy and timid," Mickey said. "But don't worry. The poster gave it all away when he mentioned cranberry bogs and holly."

"There are bogs all along here!"

"I know," Mickey said. "But only one that has a thicket of holly, too. Come on, it's only another half mile." They passed the information center, where the Refuge Beach park ranger lived. Mickey had seen the lights on late at night, when she and her mother came down on summer nights to have starlight picnics. Mickey saw his green truck and wondered what he was doing on such a cold, quiet day at the park.

"I can't wait until we have our licenses," Jenna said. "One more year. Do you think we're being hopelessly immature, riding our bikes to Refuge Beach to see a stupid bird?"

"You didn't think it was stupid last summer," Mickey murmured, but Jenna didn't hear; the wind took Mickey's voice and whirled it over the dunes, out to sea. Her face stung from the cold, and her gloved hands seemed frozen to the handlebars. Jenna didn't know how much Mickey needed to do this today. Her chest burned—with exertion, but even more from an aching heart. Her parents were back in court this morning.

"We're getting too old to be birding," Jenna said warningly. "I do want to see a snowy owl, but that's it. Birds were one thing when we were younger, Mick. But frankly, I just don't care about them the same way."

Mickey nodded. She didn't reply. Did Jenna have any idea what she was saying? Did she really want to join the ranks of all the other teenagers in their class, who seemed to be losing their spirits drop by drop, suddenly obsessed with stuff like makeup and iPods, clunky boots, and the perfect, cool bike-messenger book bag?

Blowing sand grains whipped her cheeks as she pedaled harder.

Just before they got to the thicket, she noticed a construction truck parked on the sandy road. The truck bed contained a small bulldozer, lashed down by a thick chain. Wondering what it was doing there, she skidded and almost wiped out as she turned to look. But she righted her bike, signaled, and turned off the paved road into the small sandy parking lot.

They leaned their bikes up against a split rail fence, went running down the winding trail into the thicket. Mickey's heart had been pounding, but it relaxed in here. The path was just two-tenths of a mile long, but it seemed to bring her into an enchanted realm.

The thicket was magic. Only the hardiest shore plants could survive in this harsh environment between the dunes and the road. The wind was so relentless, it kept all the bushes low and leaning away from the sea. Pitch pine, blueberry bushes, red maple, shadbush, bayberry, black cherry, red cedars, cranberry bogs, and—in this stretch alone, of the entire ten-mile-long barrier beach—many American holly bushes. The thicket was a haven for migratory and year-round birds, and Mickey had been coming here with her mother since she was a baby. She knew every inch of it by heart, and loved it nearly as much as her own home.

When she and Jenna reached the far end of the path, just over the narrow boardwalk that crossed the marshiest part of the bog—frozen now, from the long winter—Mickey motioned for Jenna to start watching.

They emerged from the shady thicket—all branches bare of leaves, but thick enough to have blocked the sky—into dazzling blue. The white dunes were topped with graceful windblown beach grass. The beach was endless, pristine. Not a house was to be seen for miles either up or down the strand—Refuge Beach had never been developed, due to its combination of wetlands and nesting habitats.

Mickey felt ghosts here. A U-boat had sunk just offshore during World War II, and sometimes she imagined she heard the spirits of the sailors who had drowned. She thought she heard them now, and a sudden shudder went through her body.

It might have been the cold. Taking a few more steps, she gazed over the beach. Her face froze in the sharp sea wind. Beach grasses bent flat sketched circles in the hard sand. A crooked old wooden jetty, battered by storms and covered with barnacles, meandered into the sea. Long waves flowed in. There was a legendary break off this beach, and surfers loved it here, even in winter. But today was too cold even for them.

Mickey's heart kicked. She looked around. She had a sixth sense about birds, and she could feel the owl even before she saw it. Her eyes were drawn instantly: round and white, the snowy owl resembled a soccer ball sitting in the middle of the beach, just this side of the jetty, several feet from a silver, wind-blasted driftwood log.

"There," she whispered, her hand on Jenna's arm.

"Oh my God," Jenna whispered back.

They stood perfectly still for several minutes. The snowy owl didn't move. It was regal, elegant, pure white, the tips of some feathers flecked with grayish brown. Because it was midday, Mickey knew the owl was probably sleeping. The girls held their breath, not wanting to even breathe. Waves broke along the shore, the sea brilliant blue and fairly calm, despite the steady breeze.

Presently Jenna nodded; she was ready to leave. The friends backed away from the owl. Mickey stared at it as long as she could. She would have liked to stay in the dunes, waiting for dusk and the bird's fly-out. To see a snowy owl hunting low along this stretch of Mickey's beloved beach, so far south of its normal habitat, would feel almost miraculous to Mickey—and she knew she needed a miracle today.

"That was so cool," Jenna said, once they were well into the thicket and unlikely to disturb the owl. "I can't believe I finally saw one. Okay, check it off the list."

"It was amazing," Mickey said, pricked by Jenna's attitude.

By the time she and Jenna got onto their bikes, she felt anger and frustration building in her chest. How could Jenna not want to wait a little longer? How could she be so cavalier about seeing a snowy owl—the bird she knew was Mickey's favorite—for the first time in her whole life?

Something made Mickey turn around; she felt a flutter inside, and she was sure the owl was about to fly over. She saw that the footprints they had made on their walk into the thicket and over the dunes were already gone—erased by the relentless wind. There was no sign of the owl, but again she spotted the bulldozer and flatbed truck.

"I wonder what that's for," Mickey said to Jenna, gesturing at the equipment.

"It belongs to Josh's father," Jenna said, mentioning her boyfriend Tripp's close friend. Josh Landry's family had recently moved to the state, and his father was a well-known businessman who was always involved in controversial projects. Mickey had been so preoccupied with her parents lately, she hadn't been keeping up on local news.

"What's he going to do here?" she asked.

"Oh, something to do with that sunken submarine. Didn't you see it in the paper? I guess it's been snagging fishing nets, so they're going to try moving it, or removing the periscope and stuff like that. Mr. Landry wants to help by getting it out of here. He's going to take it somewhere so it can be turned into a museum." Jenna was glowing as she spoke, as if she thought he was a local hero.

"Help our community?" Mickey asked.

"By moving the U-boat? That's not possible!" Incredulous, she spun her head around to look.

This time she noticed a young man standing beside the truck. He held fire—tall flames shooting up from his fingertips. Mickey's mind whirled; having just seen the snowy owl, she thought he must be a sorcerer, about to do wild magic. Her eyes met his, and in that instant she recognized him as one of the surfers from her high school. His expression was dark, his hand blazing as he tried to duck back, out of view.

"We have to help him," she gasped, realizing that he was burning.

As Mickey charged toward him, her bike skidded on the sand. She felt herself lose control—not in a bad way, but as if she had suddenly grown wings. She was a snowy owl, lifting, rising above the road, almost high enough to see over the dunes and out to sea. She'd swoop down, put the fire out, save him.

"Mickey, watch out!" Jenna screamed.

"Whoa!" the fire boy yelled.

Mickey let go of the handlebars. She felt her arms go up over her head, up into the air, trying to steady herself, grab on to something solid in the sky. She heard the bike tumble and crash on the pavement beneath her, and then she heard Jenna scream again, and then she felt herself come crashing down like a bird with broken wings onto the cold, sandy tar.

1

Shane West held the flamethrower, stunned when he realized he wasn't alone. He'd come to the deserted beach to make his stand. His teachers were always saying he wasn't working up to potential, but this was just a different kind of potential.

Two girls rode by on their bikes just then—perfect but terrible timing. He recognized Mickey Halloran as she turned to stare at him, saw the fire. She looked panicked, and she must have thought he needed help, because suddenly she came charging at him on her bike. He tried to gesture "go away," but she flew at him like a two-wheeled missile, and he had to admire her for it. He knew single-minded purpose when he saw it. But just then she went into a skid and took a header over her handlebars.

Dousing the fire in a sand dune, he ran across the road, as the other girl—Jenna Carlson, he thought—jumped off her bike, ran back, and dropped to her knees next to Mickey. Shane pushed past her and crouched, leaning over to look into Mickey's eyes. He had never talked to her, but he'd noticed her around school. Her face was pretty, pale, lightly freckled; her enormous eyes were light green. Two long brown braids hung from beneath her dark blue knit cap. He could tell in one glance that it wasn't good. She had hit her head when she landed, and blood was pooling on the pavement. But her eyes were still open.

"Mickey, why'd you turn like that? Oh God!" Jenna was crying, almost hysterical.

"Don't move," Shane said to Mickey.

"They're going to move the U-boat," she said. "And they're acting like it's a public service." Her lips were blue; Shane knew she might be going into shock.

"Not if I can help it," he said.

"You were on fire," she said.

"Shhh," he said. "Pretend you didn't see that."

Her eyes rolled back, and her eyelids flickered.

"Whoa," he said, panicking. His heart accelerated, full blast. He hadn't been there for his father, but he was here now. Back then, things had gone so wrong. This time he'd make sure they went right. He stared down at the girl. They were in the same class, but different crowds. "No going to sleep. Talk to me. Your name's Mickey, right?"

"Yes, that's her name," the friend said. "And I'm Jenna, and she's right, you were holding fire in your hand. What was that?"

"Mickey, hey," Shane said, ignoring her friend. "Stay with me here. Dismantling the U-boat, taking it away? Changing the surf, and the way the beach is formed? How badly would that suck? Mickey?"

"Terrible," she said, coming back from the brink, those green eyes bright again, full of life. "Can't happen. The birds . . . snowy owl . . . need the beach the way it is . . ."

"Yeah," Shane said, thinking how sweet she looked, seeing how hard she was trying to stay alert. "And surfers need that U-boat.

Birds and surfers. Fly by air, fly by sea. Come on, Mickey. Stay awake." He looked up at her friend. "We have to get her an ambulance."

"Where? How?" Jenna asked, starting to cry again. She might not know exactly what was wrong with Mickey, but she could see the blood, and like Shane she knew it was bad. She was willowy and blond, and Shane took note of her pretty powder-puff looks and hoped she could be tough right now. "We're five miles from the main road, and cell phones don't work down here," she said.

Shane had come the back way, through the frozen bog. His car was broken down, and he had no money to fix it. His mother was out of town, so he couldn't borrow hers. Besides, cars left tire marks, and any idiot with a TV had seen enough forensics shows to know that treads could be traced. So he'd fit everything he needed into his pockets, carried the rest, and come to do what needed to be done.

"I'll run for help," he said, peeling off his parka. It was old, patched in places by silver duct tape. "You keep her awake and talking no matter what—you hear me?"

"Yes," Jenna said.

"Don't move her," he said. "Not even an inch."

Mickey was trembling. As he tucked his coat around her, careful not to jostle her, Shane touched her face; it was ice cold. She gazed up at him as if he was some kind of savior. The look in her eyes caught him like a fishhook because he knew he held her life in his hands.

"Does it hurt?" he asked.

Her mouth moved, but no sound came out.

"Think of that snowy owl," he said. "Just stay wide awake, and wish, and the owl will fly overhead. Just keep your eyes open so you don't miss it."

"You saw it?" Mickey managed to whisper.

"Of course," Shane said, staring into Mickey's green eyes. "Every time I surf. It's been here all winter." Then, to her friend, "Remember what I said—keep her awake."

"Okay. Hurry!" Jenna said.

Shane jumped up. "Watch for the owl," he said to Mickey, and then took off running. In another phase of his life, he'd been on the track team. His event had been the hundred-yard dash, but he wasn't a bad distance runner. Right now, although he had five miles to cover before reaching the state road, he ran as if it were a sprint—flat out, as fast as he could go.

He'd been young when his father had died, but if he could have run for help like now, he would have. Today, he knew failure was not an option. Surfing all winter, powering through the Atlantic cross-chop, kept him lean and mean, and he used the look in Mickey's eyes to make him run faster than he ever had.

He headed up the road, the dunes at his right. The thicket had thinned out here, and an icy wind blew full force off the ocean. Sand had drifted right onto the pavement; he saw the drifty remains of the girls' bike tire marks and admired them for riding down here on such a day. Hardly anyone loved this remote winter beach the way he did, not even most of his surfing buddies. They went for easy access, at the town beach. Mickey had mentioned the snowy owl. Was the bird the reason she'd come all the way out here in twenty-degree weather?

When he got to the ranger station, his stomach tightened. This wasn't going to be pretty. He saw O'Casey's green truck parked outside the low one-story building. Painted gray-blue, the color of the February sea, the ranger station blended into the sea and sky, into the beach itself.

Shane tore up the steps, into the office. O'Casey sat at his desk, dressed in his khaki uniform, glancing up over his reading glasses, looking just like the hard-ass authority figure that he was. Ex-Marine, people said. Shane wouldn't be surprised, and he thought of his mother down at Camp Lejeune. Jerks. Standing there, not wanting the ranger to see how out of breath he was, Shane glared down. He watched O'Casey tense up, his hand inching toward the desk drawer. Did he keep a sidearm in there? Jesus Christ, *Semper Fi.*

"What brings you back here?" O'Casey asked.

"Call 911," Shane said to his old enemy.

"What are you talking about?"

"There's a hurt girl," Shane said. "Hurry up."

All at once the ranger was on his feet. One hand reaching for the radio—static cracking, the police dispatcher taking the information as Shane relayed it: "Injured girl, bike wipeout, Beach Road, mile marker 3, near the jetty"—other hand grabbing his jacket, a bulky green government-issue job, just about as beat-up as the one Shane had left covering Mickey.

In that second, registering that Shane didn't have a coat, O'Casey thrust his at him. Shane refused to take it. He backed toward the door, hating to stand by the ranger. At six foot four, O'Casey towered over him. His shoulders were huge, but he somehow managed to look fit and trim for an old guy. His skin was weathered and lined, his hair nearly all gray. The way his eyes looked behind those reading glasses: like he'd spent most of his life either in battle or looking for one. That look sent a shiver down Shane's spine.

Locking the door behind him, O'Casey followed Shane down the steps. They climbed into the beach truck. The bench seat was cluttered up with coiled lines, binoculars, gnarly old leather gloves, and a printer's box of new Refuge Beach brochures—ready for next summer.

"What's that smell?" O'Casey asked as he backed out of the sandy lot.

Shane knew he reeked of kerosene, but

he just stayed silent, staring at O'Casey. It was a combination of disbelief and dare: disbelief the ranger could ask that when a girl was lying hurt in the road up ahead, and daring him to figure out what Shane was planning next.

"You're on probation," O'Casey said. "As far as I'm concerned, they should have taken your board away."

"Just for surfing the tail end of a hurricane?" Shane asked.

"Try thinking about the rescue workers who would have had to go in after you," O'Casey said, and that shut Shane right up. He felt himself go red, as if he'd suddenly gotten a sunburn. "Mile marker 3, you said?" the ranger asked, staring down the road.

"Right there!" Shane said, pointing.

But everything was different than he'd left it. The road was empty: the broken bike had been hauled off to the side, and Mickey and Jenna sat huddled together under Shane's jacket. Shane wasn't sure he'd ever felt this relieved: she wasn't paralyzed.

Jumping out of the truck, Shane ran to her. Her brown braids and the side of her face were streaked with blood from a scrape along her hairline. Her face was nearly blue-white, and she cradled her left arm with her right hand. At the sight of Shane—or maybe the ranger—she began to cry like a little girl.

"Let me see, sweetheart," O'Casey said, crouching down beside her, first-aid kit tucked under his elbow, tenderly pushing her hair back to see the wound. He must have jostled her arm, because she moaned in pain.

"Hey, watch it," Shane said. "Can't you see she has a broken arm?"

"Is that right?" O'Casey asked.

"My wrist, I think," she said.

"It's just hanging there, limp!" her friend said. "She can't even move it!"

Mickey pulled back Shane's jacket so O'Casey could see. Shane noticed that she'd bled all over the nylon, and he felt glad he'd been able to keep her warm. She wasn't in shock, and she was sitting upright: two great signs.

"I moved," she said, looking up at Shane.

"As long as you did it yourself, it's okay," he said, looking into her green eyes. "It's when other people move you that it can be a problem."

O'Casey had the first-aid kit open now. He eased Shane out of the way, pressed gauze to the still-bleeding wound on Mickey's head. Shane watched the way he stared steadily into Mickey's eyes as he gently applied more pressure. Mickey gazed up at the ranger as if he were her father, or the best doctor in the world. The trust in her eyes did something inside to Shane, made his heart tumble over, like a stone falling off a cliff.

"Can we get out of here?" Jenna asked. "It's freezing, and we have to get Mickey to the emergency room."

"We'll take her there right now," O'Casey said, and when they looked up the road, they saw the convoy: an ambulance and two cop cars.

"I don't need them," Mickey said, panic in her eyes. Shane wasn't sure whether she meant the ambulance or the police.

Two officers and the EMTs walked over. One of the policemen gazed down with recognition. Shane's stomach flipped, but the cop wasn't looking at him—he was staring at Mickey.

"Hello there," he said to her. "Are you okay?"

"I'm fine," she whispered.

Shane concentrated on the spark in her eyes. He wanted to put his arm around her, help her into the ambulance. Were they just going to let her sit here on the cold ground?

The EMTs began doing their thing, with O'Casey giving them his take on her head wound and broken wrist. Suddenly they had her up and into the ambulance; they wrapped her in blankets and handed Shane his jacket back. Jenna was led to a squad car, their bikes loaded into the back of O'Casey's truck. The ranger said something to the second cop. Shane saw their eyes flick over to him.

His blood was on fire. He knew he should run—start now and never stop until he got to California. There were places to surf out there that made the waves here look like they belonged in a bathtub. He could find his dad's friends, and they'd hide him in dune shacks till he was older and grayer than O'Casey.

But he had a mission here on this beach, and he had to say one last thing to Mickey. Make her a promise that would help her get well fast. Something made him know that was necessary—the fear in her eyes was too familiar to him to let her just drive away without speaking to her.

He pushed past the EMTs, crawled right into the ambulance. She was already strapped onto a stretcher, orange straps tight across her chest. She was staring at him, eyes focused on his jacket.

"I bled on your jacket," she said. "I'm sorry."

"That's okay," he said. "It'll remind me . . ."

"Of what?" she asked.

"Of the owl," he said. "The snowy owl . . ."

"I won't let them chase it away," he said. "If it's the last thing I do."

"Thank you," she whispered.

Shane touched her face, and then he felt himself being hauled out from behind. The ambulance rear door was slammed shut, but he could still see her face through the window as the vehicle began pulling away. She'd seemed really shy when he'd seen her around school. And Shane had stayed back in grammar school—he'd had "adjustment problems" that they attributed to his father's death. Whatever the reason, it had always made him feel like an outsider and he'd never approached her.

"The last thing you do," one of the cops said. "Interesting choice of words."

"Ranger O'Casey told us he smelled kerosene on you," the other cop said. "So we looked around and found these." He held up the Nerf pump-action ball launcher. Unfortunately, Shane had already soaked the Nerf in kerosene—he'd been seconds away from applying flame when Mickey had had her wipeout.

"Yeah, what about it?" Shane asked.

"You think acting like a moron, destroying Cole Landry's heavy equipment, is really the best way to stop them from dismantling the U-boat?" O'Casey asked.

"What's a surf slacker care about that?" Cop Number One asked. "It's just a tin can full of dead krauts."

Shane opened his mouth to let loose on him, tell him that the sunken U-boat was responsible for the most reliable swells on this stretch of shore, that its length, and the height of its conning tower, and the periscope and every other bit of barnacle-encrusted metal, caused a vortex, pulling so much water from below, creating waves that moved straight and fast, folding back on themselves and erupting in terrible, elegant explosions craved by surfers everywhere.

But O'Casey beat him to it.

"It's a grave, Officer," O'Casey said.

"Excuse me?"

"It's not a 'tin can,'" O'Casey said. "It's U-823, and there are fifty-five dead men aboard."

"Hey, Tim—your father's Joe O'Casey, right?" the other cop asked.

Ranger O'Casey nodded, and nothing more was said. Even with his jacket back on, Shane was freezing. He tried to hold the shivers inside, under his skin, so the cops and O'Casey wouldn't see. Not that the cops cared. One of them pulled out hand-cuffs, yanked his hands behind his back.

"You're under arrest," he said. "For the un-lawful use of hazardous materials, destruc-tion of property, and we'll see what else. You have the right to remain silent . . ."

Shane listened as, for the second time that month, he was read his rights. He glanced up and met O'Casey's eye. He nearly scowled out of habit, but then it hit him: O'Casey, while not exactly defending him, had pretty much just argued his case for not disturbing the U-823 wreck. He and O'Casey were, sort of, on the same side.

Strange, Shane thought. Very strange.

Then he let the cops lead him to the squad car—the one not occupied by Mickey's friend—cover the back of his head, as if they cared whether he whacked it on the car roof, push him inside, and drive him to the station.

2

Neve Halloran was pretty sure the tenth circle of hell was family court. The imposing stone building with massive granite columns, the marble floors, the individual courtrooms with their rows of dark wood seats, the judges in their black robes sitting above it all on the bench, gazing out at this local, hopeful sea of humanity—deciding fate with one blow of the gavel.

The problem was, the fates being decided affected not only the adults divorcing each other, but also the children of their marriages. Every time Neve walked through the heavy doors to the courthouse, she imagined herself holding Mickey's hand—not that Mickey would ever let her! But the image guided her, kept her from giving up before it started, kept her focused on what she had to do.

She had a team: her friend Christine Brody, and her lawyer, Nicola Cerruti. They had been here for her countless times before—and now, although the divorce was final two years ago, they were back again. Today they had a hearing for Richard's failure to pay child support. His thought process had become a great mystery to her, nearly as unfathomable as the mystery of how she had once loved him with her entire heart and soul in the first place.

She wore a blue suit, white blouse, sensible black pumps. Her auburn hair hung to her shoulders; behind wire-rim glasses, her eyes were soft blue. Her gold necklace had been her grandfather's watch chain. She also wore the sapphire birthstone ring her parents had given her for her thirteenth birthday: talismans blessed by her family saints.

"Why am I even here?" she asked her lawyer, standing in the hall and waiting to be called into the courtroom. "Who needs him and his money? I work, I support Mickey."

"You're here because of him," Nicola reminded her. "He's defying a court order."

"We're here because it's right," Chris said. "The court ordered him to pay, and he's not paying. Mickey needs things that cost money. It's that simple."

Just then the elevator doors opened, and James Swenson, Richard's lawyer, stepped out. Neve felt the ground shift beneath her feet. It was just like being in seventh grade. She felt a cold rush of nervousness, in anticipation of seeing Richard right behind him. Would they speak? Would he explain to her what he was doing? Would he have his girlfriend with him? Would Neve be able to keep from attacking him?

But the elevator doors closed behind the lawyer—no Richard. Swenson was tall and thin, with the same basketball build he'd had in college, when he and Richard had played against each other. He glanced in Neve's direction, turned away quickly. Not a smile, not a nod: no recognition at all.

"Oh man," Nicola said.

"What?" Neve asked.

"I smell blood in the water. . . ."

Nicola headed across the large hall, now

filling up with other lawyers and their clients. Neve watched as she made her way over to Swenson, and felt gratified that she seemed all-business, with none of the collegial banter she sometimes saw between other members of the bar. Swenson had pulled some papers from his briefcase, stood erect as Nicola got in his face—or as close as she could, considering the top of her head wasn't much higher than his elbow.

"Whoa, what's going on?" Christine asked, huddled with Neve, watching the scene.

"Swenson does not look happy," Neve replied.

"Good," Chris said. "He shouldn't look happy, considering what a creep he has for a client. Where do you think Richard is?"

Neve didn't reply. Thinking of Mickey, she felt her heart sink.

"Let's see," Chris said. "He could be any number of places. Selling someone swampland in Florida. Courtside at the Final Four. Cruising the Mexican Riviera with Alyssa. Schmoozing with Senator Sheridan. Or somewhere on a bender . . ." Chris shook her head at all the scenarios that added up to the prize that was Richard.

Neve knew that Chris meant well—Neve had railed and vented to her through it all. But at the same time, what gripped Neve today was the wish that Richard could get it together, show up for Mickey the way she knew he wanted to. Loving Mickey had never been hard for him—it was holding himself together that had been the problem. Why couldn't he just pay child support the way he was supposed to?

As Nicola turned from Swenson and began walking toward Neve with a satisfied smile on her face, the courtroom door opened and the sheriff beckoned them in before Nicola could fill her in. By now the procedure was routine: Neve and Nicola went to the table on their side of the courtroom, Christine sitting one row behind the wood rail, Swenson went to the other table, and all that was missing was Richard.

"Parties ready?" the sheriff asked.

"Yes," Nicola said quickly, before Swenson had the chance to say anything.

"All rise!" the sheriff barked out. "Court is in session, the Honorable Dennis J. Garrett presiding."

The judge entered from his chambers: black robes, salt-and-pepper hair, crooked glasses, bristly mustache. Neve had run the gamut of emotions with him during the divorce: elation when he'd given her sole custody of Mickey, outrage when he'd given Richard a share of her grandfather's estate, and everything in between. Why did they call this place "family court," when it was all about war and the aftermath, about families who had already torn each other apart?

Judge Garrett peered across his bench, frowned at Swenson.

"Well, Mr. Swenson. Where's your client?"

"Your Honor, I'd like to request a continuance . . ."

"Objection," Nicola said. "Mr. Swenson and his client had ample notice about today's hearing, and meanwhile Mr. Halloran's failure to pay child—"

Judge Garrett waved his hand, silencing her.

"Where is Mr. Halloran?" he asked, staring at Swenson with hard eyes. He reminded Neve of a strict father who'd heard one excuse too many.

"I . . . I don't know," Swenson admitted.

"He knew about today's hearing?" the judge asked.

"Yes."

"Then I'm issuing a bench warrant for his arrest. Failure to appear, failure to pay child support. His wages are about to be garnished."

"Your Honor," Nicola said, jumping to her feet, "since Mr. Halloran is self-employed, and claims that his real estate business is making no money, there are no wages to garnish. Meanwhile, as you see in our motion, he has made no payments on his daughter's health insurance, has failed to—"

"Enough, Ms. Cerruti. I get the picture. Mr. Swenson, I suggest you encourage your client to come in voluntarily. We're done here." He gathered the papers together, pushed back his chair.

"All rise," the sheriff called, and Neve and everyone in the court stood.

With a crack of the gavel, the judge left the bench. Neve looked at Nicola, saw the triumph in her eyes. Turning around, she saw Chris nodding with satisfaction.

They filed out of the courtroom, stood together in the hall. Swenson strode past them, already dialing his cell phone. Nicola could barely hold back her glee.

"They're both toast," she said. "Jim Swenson's in trouble with the judge—did you see the way Garrett looked at him? He hates lawyers who can't control their clients. And Richard's in so deep, he might never get out of it. If he's not paying child support, you want to bet he's also behind on his legal fees?"

"What kind of man abandons one family for another?" Chris asked. "He certainly lives in a nice house, drives a big car, takes enough trips. He has money—he's just hiding it from Neve. And now, with a new baby coming . . ."

Neve felt her lawyer and friend looking at her. Chris had seen Alyssa at the grocery store, reported that she was pregnant. Neve didn't mind that he was getting on with his life; she was glad he'd stopped drinking almost the minute she'd kicked him out, that he was now thriving. But why was he acting like this now? It gave her no pleasure to think he was back in the bottle again. Her worst fear was that Mickey would be hurt even more than she already was. Mickey had felt discarded by Richard during his drinking years, and again during the divorce—it must have seemed that her father had traded his time with her to spend every

minute with his new girlfriend. Now that
he'd stopped paying child support, it was
as if she no longer existed. Money was
strange currency for a young girl's self-
esteem, but there it was.

While Nicola and Chris kept talking, Neve
pulled out her cell phone. She had told
Mickey she'd call her when she got out of
court. Today was teachers' conferences, so
Mickey had the day off from school. She
and Jenna had planned to go to the beach,
searching for the snowy owl. If they found it,
Neve was going to drive down so they could
show her.

She had three messages. Three seconds
into the first one, her stomach dropped. It
was Jenna, crying hysterically.

"Mrs. Halloran, Mickey fell! She wiped out
on her bike, oh, she's hurt! We're on our way
to the hospital; come now, please!"

"Oh God," Neve said, grabbing her bag,
tugging Chris's sleeve, running toward the
elevator before the next message could
even start. Her brain was on fire, and she
pushed the elevator button, and it lit up and
she thought she'd scream because the elevator wasn't there yet.

"What's wrong?" Chris asked, eyes wide at the sight of Neve's panic.

"Mickey's hurt," Neve said, listening to a new voice, a man speaking calmly, telling her that Mickey had been taken to South Shore Medical Center. The elevator doors closed, and the phone connection was lost, and Neve felt her heart fly out of her body.

No ride had ever taken longer: the drive from Lambton to the hospital. Neve drove. Chris had offered, but ever since the start of the divorce, Neve had found strength and solace with her hands on the wheel, taking control of the car even as life spun out around her. Driving her own car to court, she felt a certain power. But right now it was gone. She hardly felt the pavement beneath the wheels.

"Whoa, watch it," Chris said as a pickup truck passed them.

"I see it," Neve said.

"Pull over and let me drive."

"I'm fine," Neve said. "It's just a few more miles."

The third message had been from the same man—he identified himself, but the connection was garbled, and he had a voice Neve didn't recognize—still calm, quietly reassuring, telling Neve that Mickey had a broken wrist and a possible concussion, that she was at the ER and asking for her mother and father, but wasn't in terrible danger.

It was as if Neve were connected to Mickey by fine, invisible threads—in spite of their delicacy, they had always felt so strong and unbreakable. But right now, driving south, Neve called up the image of her daughter in the emergency room, a stranger using her cell phone to leave Neve a message, and she felt everything was fragile, precarious, falling apart.

Her eyes blurred, and she slashed the tears away. Her thoughts went to Richard— where was he? The stranger had said Mickey was asking for her father; how would Neve tell her that no one knew where he was? The judge had issued a warrant for his arrest; Mickey would find out about that. She already knew he wasn't paying child support; Neve tried never to talk badly about Richard in front of her, but she wasn't a saint, and the last few months had been so hard financially. Little bits had slipped out, during conversations with Chris and with Nicola.

"Everything's going to be okay," Chris said now.

"I know," Neve said.

"No, I mean it really will. The message said Mickey's going to be fine. And the court is going after Richard. Do you know how much I'd like to be there when they cuff him?"

"Chris . . ." Neve said, feeling tears well up again, "I have to call him, to tell him about Mickey. Here, dial for me, will you?" She handed Chris her cell phone.

"Well, he couldn't be bothered to get himself to court, so he should at least meet you at the hospital," Chris said, scrolling through names, finding "R," hitting Dial. Even from the driver's seat, Neve heard it go straight to voice mail.

"Where is he?" she asked. "God, he's going to be so upset."

"You think he's drinking again? He must be!"

"I hope not; I really hope he still remembers how to find AA."

"I can't believe you're still so tender-hearted about him! After what he's done!"

"I'm not," Neve said, driving through the intersection, taking the next right. "Believe

me . . . it's just Mickey I'm thinking of."
Neve's love for Richard was long gone, but
what remained was a ridiculous, unshak-
able pity for him, mingled with occasional
wild rage. Like right now: where was he
when Mickey obviously needed him?

Flying down the exit ramp, she homed in
on the sign: a big blue "H" for "hospital."
She turned left at the stop sign, drove along
the marina road a quarter mile, past the
wide harbor and all the empty docks, then
into the South Shore Medical Center parking lot. She pulled up in front of the emergency room, parking in the first open spot
she saw, and ran through the big glass
doors.

She gave her name to the nurse at the
desk and was immediately led through the
inner doors—thrusting her insurance card at
Chris and leaving her to deal with the paperwork. The nurse led her along a row of exam
cubicles, most with curtains open. Neve
glanced in every one, looking for Mickey. Finally they stopped, and Neve burst through
the curtains—but there was no sign of
Mickey: just a tall man in a khaki uniform sitting in a chair, as if he were guarding the
empty space.

"Where is she?" the nurse asked.

"Still in X-ray," the man said, and Neve instantly recognized his voice: the stranger on the phone.

"Tim, why don't you head out now?" the nurse said. Then, turning to Neve, "And why don't you come back out to the waiting room? You'll be more comfortable, and we can take care of the paperwork."

"Let her stay here," the man said. "Her daughter will be back any minute. She needs to see her."

Neve looked at him, unsure of whether he meant that she, Neve, needed to see Mickey or the other way around. Either way, he had it right. His gray-blue eyes were cool, his gaze detached, but his tone somehow insistent, as if the world's balance hung on the nurse allowing Neve to stay.

"That's fine," the nurse said, walking away.

Neve glanced around the cubicle. A pile of Mickey's things lay on the counter: her light blue sweater, knit hat, fleece mittens. The sweater was streaked with blood, its left sleeve sliced open.

"She has a broken wrist," the man said.

"They cut her sleeve, to make it easier to get off."

"Are you the one who called me?" Neve asked.

"Yes," he said. "I'm Tim O'Casey, from the ranger station at Refuge Beach."

"I'm Neve Halloran," she said, shaking his hand. "Thank you. How did you find me?"

"Mickey gave me her cell phone," he said, reaching into his pocket, handing it back to Neve. "All she wanted was you and her father. She just kept saying so. . . ."

Neve nodded. And she wasn't there. She was in court, fighting over money. The sad stupidity of it made her weak in the knees. Their daughter was in the emergency room, and for the first time in her entire life, Neve had let her go through something like this alone—or at least without her parents.

"Thank you for being with her," Neve said. "Did she come to the ranger station for help?"

"No," Tim said. "She was with her friend Jenna—she was very upset, so her parents took her home. A . . . a young man actually came to get me, to let me know that someone was hurt."

"Young man?" Neve asked, thinking she'd like to thank him, too.

"Yes," Tim said. "A high school kid. He's not here."

"Oh," Neve said.

She walked over to Mickey's clothes, picked up her hat. It was made of midnight blue yarn, hand-knit by Neve's mother. But as she held it in her hands, she realized it felt stiff but sticky, and when she looked down at her fingers, they were reddish brown.

"Oh God!" she cried, realizing that it was Mickey's blood, that she hadn't noticed it before because the wool was so dark.

"Yes, she cut her head," Tim said. "She went over her handlebars. They did a CT scan first thing, but there's no fracture, no concussion. She broke her fall with her wrist."

Neve shuddered, holding Mickey's hat, hearing a strange man tell her what had happened. He was so tall, he seemed to tower over her. His hair was brown, nearly all gray at the temples. His narrow face was weathered, almost gaunt, with deeply scored lines around his mouth and slate-colored eyes. She looked into his eyes and felt shocked by the darkness and intensity she saw there. He had seemed so gentle

and kind, but suddenly something shifted—
she felt as if he were looking straight into
her soul, judging what he saw there.

"What is it?" she asked.

"Mickey told me that you and her father
were in court," he said.

"Yes," she said, leaving it at that.

"She wanted her father here, too."

"I can imagine that she wants that very
much."

"Can you call him?" he asked, his tone
sharp.

Neve tensed. She felt this stranger stepping over a huge boundary, straight into her
family's problems. His eyes were practically
blazing, and she felt criticism pouring from
him. For what? Because she was divorced,
or because she was fighting her husband in
court?

"I tried," she said. "He didn't answer."

"But you just saw him," he said. "You were
in court." He accented the word "court"—
Neve was right; he *was* judging her.

"I was," Neve said. "He didn't show."

"Then I'm sure he's in more trouble."

"*More* trouble?" she asked.

Tim O'Casey narrowed his gaze. He ran
his hand through his hair, staring at Neve as

if trying to decide what to say. She felt her blood boiling—in the time she'd been divorced, she'd realized that not only did people take sides—usually it was men siding with men, feeling the women were out to get them, to soak them for all they could. She could barely look at him.

"When we first got Mickey here, she was crying and in pain, and she told me that you and her father don't speak, that the only times you do is when you go to court or drop her off at his house. She's got a broken wrist, but that hurts her a whole lot worse."

"Do you have kids?" she asked, seething.

"A son," he said. "And I'm divorced. I know what that did to him."

Neve felt blood rush to her face. She stood there holding her daughter's bloody cap, feeling the derision of a man she didn't even know. She felt tricked by the fact he had at first seemed so sympathetic.

"You don't know me. You don't know *us,*" she said. "So don't try to tell me what I should do when it comes to Mickey and her father. She—"

Just then a doctor came in. He was young and in a hurry, and he looked straight at Neve.

"Mrs. Halloran?" he asked. "I'm Dr. Freeman. The nurse told me I could find you here." He stared at her in a way that made Neve's heart freeze, made Tim O'Casey disappear.

"Where's Mickey?" she asked.

"Asking for you," he said, smiling. "She has a broken wrist, a few cuts and bruises, but she's going to be fine. Come with me; I'll take you to her."

Neve followed him without a look back. O'Casey's words, and the way he'd looked at her and spoken to her, still stung, but walking down the hall, she shook it off. He'd probably been burned in a divorce and wanted to strike out at ex-wives in general. The doctor opened a door, and there was Mickey, sitting on an exam table, her left arm in a cast.

"Mom!" she said.

"Oh, Mickey," Neve said, throwing her arms around her. They held on to each other, and Neve felt herself trembling. When she pulled back, she saw the scrapes on Mickey's forehead, the bruise on her temple, dry blood stuck to her hair. But her green eyes were bright, her smile as quick as ever.

"I have a cast," Mickey said, holding it up.

"I noticed," Neve said. "What happened?"

"Where's Dad?" Mickey asked, looking around.

"Um, I left him a message. . . . Mickey, what happened?"

"Well, I wiped out on the sandy road . . . there might have been some ice, too. Jenna and I rode down to look for the snowy owl, and we found it, Mom! It was so beautiful, you wouldn't believe it . . . sitting right in the dunes, next to a driftwood log, just like in the Arctic!"

"Wow, honey," Neve said, excited for her daughter, seeing such an amazing creature. It seemed like the first bit of good news she'd heard all day, and Mickey's enthusiasm made her want to go see the owl for herself. They'd always shared a love of nature, birds in particular.

"I'll take you to see," Mickey said.

"That's a date," Neve said. "Maybe we should get you home right now, though. Can she leave?" she asked, turning to the doctor.

"Yes, she's free to go. I'll be at the desk, signing her out of the ER," Dr. Freeman said, walking out of the room.

"Yay!" Mickey said. She glanced down at her blue johnny. "Where are my clothes?"

"They're in the other room. I'll go get them," Neve said.

"Mom, there was a boy from school, a surfer, who helped me. He ran to get the ranger, Mr. O'Casey, who's been so nice! He came to the hospital with me, to make sure I wasn't alone."

"I know, I met him," Neve said, making sure her tone gave nothing away.

"He looks after the beach, Mom, and all the birds and animals that land there. He said that same snowy owl comes back every year, and he makes sure the bird-list people never divulge the exact location— because he doesn't want crowds coming to scare it away. Snowy owls are very timid, he said."

"Sounds as if Mr. O'Casey knows a lot," Neve said steadily.

"Mom, Jenna didn't even care. Not really. It was weird; I mean, there was the snowy owl, and she didn't even want to stay to watch it!"

"Well, it's so cold out," Neve said. "Maybe Jenna wanted to get home and get warm." She touched Mickey's head. Lately she'd noticed the two best friends growing apart; Jenna was maturing faster. She had a boyfriend, and she'd started wanting to hang out with other kids, go to the movies and the mall, do more teenage things, while Mickey still wanted to be outside in nature.

Mickey shrugged, frowning. "Shane, the boy who helped me, said they're doing something to the beach. Jenna already knew, and she didn't even tell me. I don't get her. She never used to be like this. Oh, Mom—I told Mr. O'Casey to call both you and Dad. Did you see him in court? Is everything okay?"

"There's nothing for you to worry about," Neve said.

"That's not the same thing as everything being okay," Mickey said ominously. "I want Dad to be here. Is he in trouble or something? You have to tell me, Mom!"

"One thing at a time, Mickey. Let's get you out of here. I'll go get your clothes, and we can get you home."

"If you see Mr. O'Casey, tell him I say thank you," Mickey said, and in spite of whatever she was thinking about her father, she smiled again.

"I will," Neve said.

And she would have, too. She swore to herself, as she walked down the hall to the ER exam cubicle, that she would hold her personal feelings inside and thank the beach ranger profusely for what he'd done for Mickey. On the way, the desk nurse came to meet her and told her that her insurance card was invalid, that she'd have to pay for Mickey's treatment out-of-pocket.

Neve was beyond being shocked by anything today. By the time she reached the cubicle, it was empty. Ranger O'Casey was nowhere in sight. Mickey's clothes were still on the counter. And there, resting on the top of the pile, was a business card. Neve picked it up. It bore the seal of Rhode Island, and said *Timothy J. O'Casey, Park Ranger, Salt Marsh Nature Refuge, Secret Harbor, RI.* On the back, he had written, "Take care of yourself, Mickey. I hope you'll bring your mother back to see the snowy owl."

"Thanks anyway," Neve muttered. But she picked up Mickey's clothes and hurried back along the hall, wondering where she was going to find the money to pay for everything, knowing how happy Mickey would be to see what the ranger had written.

3

Getting dressed in the cold early morn- ing, Mickey knew that today was the deadline to bring the check for her school trip. Everyone was going to Washington, staying in a hotel on Capitol Hill during spring vacation, going to the Smithsonian, Lincoln Memorial, Supreme Court, and to see the cherry blossoms, and Mickey was supposed to bring a check for two hundred and fifty dollars.

At breakfast, she practiced doing everything with one hand. She was right-handed, and she'd never before noticed how much her left hand did to help. Pouring cereal, positioning the bowl, reaching for her spoon, grabbing her orange juice glass—it took intense concentration, and getting used to.

Her mother hovered around, trying to help. Mickey knew that she was going to be late for work—she'd missed the last two days, the first going to court, and the second because Mickey had stayed home from school yesterday, sick to her stomach from the medication and the shock of the accident. Staying home had upset her almost as much as breaking her wrist; until yesterday, she'd had perfect attendance.

Being quiet all day yesterday had given Mickey a lot of time to think and worry. No one knew where her father was. He hadn't shown up for work, and he was in huge trouble. This wasn't the first time.

Lying on her bed, feeling the room spinning around, Mickey pictured him in all sorts of terrible situations: hiding, scared, even kidnapped. Or—and this was almost the worst—on a secret vacation with the woman he now loved more than Mickey and her mother. Was he drinking again? The thought was a knife in her back. Not only that, but Mickey now had to worry about the owl and the U-boat, and what it all meant.

"Hurry, honey," her mother said. "We have to go."

"Mom, you don't have to wait," Mickey said. "I can get on the bus myself."

"I'm going to drive you," her mother said.

"No. Jenna's meeting me on the bus," Mickey said.

Her mother hesitated. Mickey's stomach was a hard knot. She had heard her mother on the phone with Chris, and also with Nicola. There was a warrant out for Mickey's father's arrest—just because he hadn't been able to pay child support. Mickey swallowed hard—why couldn't she get everyone to understand she didn't need money, didn't need that kind of support? Her father was a wanted man, and Mickey felt that the world was ending. Her mother and the court were giving him reasons to keep running, drinking, staying away. Mickey didn't want to add to that.

"Mickey, I know you're upset," her mother said.

"Just tell the judge we don't need the money," Mickey begged. "You work—and I'll get an after-school job."

"Honey, aside from the fact that we do need the money, it's out of my hands right now. The problem is, your father defied a court order. . . ."

"But if you hadn't taken him to court in the first place, none of this would have happened!"

"Mickey, I know you're upset, but you don't understand. Divorce is hard on everyone—hardest on you, I know. I'm sure your father will explain when he comes back from wherever he is. . . ."

"He could be hurt! He could have amnesia!" Mickey shook, all the awful scenarios coming back now. She had called her father's house, cell, and office numbers many times in the last two days. She had even tried his girlfriend's cell phone, but it was turned off, and all she'd gotten was Alyssa's soft voice saying "I'm not here right now, you know what to do. . . ."

"I think he's fine," her mother said. Something about her tone made Mickey even more upset: it was as if her mother was trying to reassure her while not letting her father off the hook.

"He can't be fine. Otherwise he'd have called me. I left him messages about my wrist—he wouldn't ignore those. He must be hiding, so scared about being arrested.

Mom, you have to tell the judge you've changed your mind, you don't need the money anymore. Please!"

"Mickey. He missed some payments on our insurance, so now we're not covered. Do you know how much that hospital visit cost? I don't like to talk about the details of this with you, but I want you to understand—I'm not happy that your father is in trouble. It makes me sad. . . ."

Just hearing those words made Mickey's heart feel as if *it* were flooding with tears. They were trapped there, in her chest, unable to make it to her eyes. She thought back just three years, to when her father had still lived at home. They had been such a good family. Yes, he drank, but they had all loved each other. She looked at his spot at the table; even now, she never stopped hoping he'd sit there again.

"I'm late, I have to get to the bus," Mickey said, closing her eyes because she couldn't look anymore, and she couldn't listen either. Her broken wrist throbbed, and she felt worried about the beach, but those things were nothing compared to this.

"Do you need money?"

"No," she said, thinking of the school trip. "I don't need anything at all."

Her mother helped her bundle up against the cold, kissed her as she walked out the door. Mickey could feel her eyes on her back as she hurried down the sidewalk, could almost feel her mother's concern enveloping her like a big wool blanket. She both needed it and wanted to shake it off. In a way she wished she'd let her mother drive her, and in a way she wanted to just disappear from sight and go searching for her father—get to him before the police did.

The yellow bus rumbled into sight, rounding the shady snow-banked wooded corner, stopping for Mickey. She climbed on, feeling a blast of heat. Saying hi to the driver, she made her way up the aisle. She wished Shane took her bus, but he lived on another route. Kids greeted her, commenting on her cast. She walked all the way to the back, looking for Jenna.

But when she got to the seat where they usually sat, Jenna was there with Tripp Livingston. Mickey stared, startled, took the empty seat across the aisle. She glanced over, saw them holding hands.

"Hey, Mick," Jenna said. "You made it to-day."

"How's it going?" Tripp asked.

"Fine," Mickey said, stung. How could her best friend not have told her she'd made it to the holding-hands stage? She'd long known that Jenna pined for Tripp from afar, texted with him a couple of times, had even hung out with him at the beach—where juniors and seniors went to drink—one Saturday night. But holding hands on the bus? And letting him sit in Mickey's spot? She felt as if she'd swallowed a hot coal, and it didn't help that Tripp was best friends with the kid whose father was trying to remove the U-boat.

She sat alone, gazing out the window. The ground was still covered with snow from last week; the beach pines slanted in the winter wind. She heard Jenna and Tripp softly whispering across the aisle. They were talking about Washington, what they'd do on the school trip. Mickey pictured clouds of pink-white cherry blossoms, shimmering around the alabaster monuments. Her eyes blurred with tears. She had been to Washington with her parents once;

they had held hands, climbing the steps of the Lincoln Memorial.

When the bus passed the narrow road that led to Refuge Beach—the site of Mickey's accident and the location of the snowy owl—Mickey's heart bumped. In spite of all the awful stuff going on, and the fact that she was going to miss going to Washington, she dried her eyes and took comfort in thinking of the owl—just as Shane had told her to do the day she'd fallen off her bike.

Mickey and Jenna had seen it together. It was the best bird either of them had on their life lists. Turning toward Jenna, to smile and lock gazes and share that amazing memory, she saw her best friend looking away.

"Jenna," Mickey said. "Remember—the dunes?"

"Huh," Jenna said.

"What about the dunes?" Tripp asked. "What's there?"

"Oh, nothing much," Jenna said. "Just an owl."

Just an owl? Mickey stared at her, but Jenna wouldn't meet her eyes.

"Aren't you a little old for bird-watching?" Tripp chuckled.

"We weren't bird-watching," Jenna said. "We just happened to be taking a bike ride."

Mickey turned away, shocked. She stared out the window as the bus rambled along the coast road, watching the blue Atlantic flash through the thick scrub pines. She caught a glimpse of one perfect wave breaking, and she imagined she saw a surfer riding its crest, in toward the beach and the owl that lived in the dunes. She thought of her father, somewhere far from home, in a world that had already fallen apart, and the tears came back.

Tim O'Casey sat at his desk, trying to get through all the postings that had come in from rangers at other parks during the night. Caffeine from the big cup of coffee he'd picked up at the twenty-four-hour gas station after his dawn patrol kicked through his veins. He felt wide awake in some ways, dead numb in others.

Driving Mickey Halloran to the hospital, meeting her mother, had brought him more alive than he'd been in a long time. He knew he'd screwed up with Neve, coming on too strong with his opinions. It was a trait he'd learned here at the beach—fighting for what he believed in, what he knew to be important. He was probably ten years older than Neve, ten years ahead of her on the continuum of life, and as a parent.

He glanced over at the book he'd bought. Filled with beautiful photographs of snowy owls on the Manitoba tundra, it reminded him of a book he'd known and loved as a boy. He'd received it from his father, the man who had taught him to love nature with a burning passion. Tim's father and uncle had grown up loving the Rhode Island woods and shore, and they'd passed that on. Tim was a ranger because of them, and—he had to admit, when he faced facts in the middle of the night—in spite of the long silence between him and his father, the reason he had requested being right here, at Refuge Beach.

The book was for Mickey. Well, he wanted to give it to both of them—as a get-well gift for Mickey, and a peace offering for her mother. No time like the present, he thought, standing up. He had the info he needed, could drive over to the Hallorans' house right now. Mickey probably wasn't back to school yet, and he wasn't sure of

Neve's employment situation. He had just started wrapping the book in some leftover Christmas bird-motif paper when the door opened.

"Hey." Shane West, the surfer vandal, stood there, hands in his pockets. Tim stared at him, taking in the windblown hair, the winter sunburn, his cracked lower lip, the surfer T-shirt under a heavy black jacket. The kid reminded him so much of Frank, he almost couldn't speak.

"What are you doing here?" Tim asked. "I thought I told you to stay out of the refuge. Two offenses and you're out. Didn't the cops tell you this is off-limits?"

"Um, you might not like this," Shane said.

"Like what?"

"Well, after the cops took me away—in handcuffs, in case you didn't see . . ."

"I saw," Tim said.

"Did that make you happy?" Shane asked. "The police hauling me in as if I was a murderer? Perp-walking me in front of that girl, jamming me into the squad car?"

"What's the difference whether it made me happy or not? We found you with a home-made flamethrower, right there by the truck. You got arrested all on your own, kid."

"You're telling me you like the idea of raising the U-boat, messing up the ecosystems, all those fish and crabs and stuff that congregate down below? You're the park ranger, man—you're supposed to be fighting for the wild things. Not caving in to jerks who think every place should be a pretty, pristine park, with everything safe and sanitized."

Tim had his own way of fighting to keep things wild, and his own reasons for caring about U-823, and he didn't need this scruffy surfer telling him his business. Besides, he wanted to get to the Hallorans' house before Neve left for work, so he took a menacing step toward Shane West, hoping to back him out the door.

"I don't need a lecture from you on how to do my job," he said. "Now, why don't you go home, go to school, do whatever you're supposed to be doing. Okay?"

"Uh, that's why I'm here," he said.

"This isn't school," he said.

"No, I know. I'm suspended—the principal didn't like hearing I got arrested again, so I'm out. I'm court-ordered to community service."

"Then go do it."

"Yeah—I am."

Tim met the young man's stare. The kid's eyes were huge, unblinking. They were assessing Tim, almost more than the other way around, and Tim felt himself getting red in the face.

"No," he said. "They didn't assign you—"

"Yep. Right here. I'm ordered to do community service for you and the Salt Marsh Refuge. Ninety days of it. Since I'm suspended for the rest of the week, I figured I'd report for duty now. So, what do you want me to do?"

"Jesus Christ," Tim said.

Shane shrugged. His gaze traveled to the owl book on the desk, and he looked up, smiling. "That's cool! You should show it to Mickey. She was pretty crazy about seeing the owl on the beach. Is it still here?"

"Look," Tim said, thrown off base by Shane's announcement. He realized that he'd been too busy checking e-mails from other rangers to have read the one in his inbox from the county—official e-mails were usually just stuff about requisition forms, or paving the parking lot, or, lately, unwelcome news about the progress of the plan to raise the U-boat. He generally ignored them as long as possible. Today's bulletin had prob-ably contained news about Shane West be-ing sent here for community service. "I have some things I have to do. Why don't you go home, and come back tomorrow?"

Shane looked shaken—Tim saw emotions just below the surface, watched the boy try-ing to control them.

"So you can call the court and get me re-assigned?" Shane asked after a minute.

"I won't lie to you—yes," Tim said.

"Why? You think I'll try to sabotage things?"

Tim nodded. "I don't trust people who re-sort to violence," he said. "And I only work with people I trust."

"I care about this place," Shane said huskily. "I'm sorry about the flamethrower. I won't do it again."

Tim stared at him. He didn't know the kid well enough to know whether he would keep his word or not, but with at least two arrests under his belt at such a young age, he wasn't betting on it.

"I hope you mean that," Tim said. "But I can't take the chance. Check in with the court later—they'll give you a different as-

signment. Now excuse me—there's somewhere I have to go."

He finished wrapping the book, then
locked the door behind him. Shane stood in
the parking lot, staring at Tim as he drove
off—just as Frank used to do after some of
their fights. The memory gave Tim a lump in
his throat, and as he watched him recede in
the rearview mirror, he wondered whether
maybe he was selling this kid short without
giving him a proper chance.

Screw that, he thought. He's someone
else's son—let them take care of him.

He put Shane West out of his mind as he
left the beach road, driving slowly through a
small neighborhood behind the elementary
school. He looked for house numbers on
the mailboxes, specifically, 640 Bittersweet
Lane.

This was a real family area—the evidence
was everywhere. Basketball hoops nailed
above garage doors, birdhouses hanging
from tree branches, white picket fences
bordering small yards. Lots of hopes and
dreams contained within those white picket
fences . . .

He had looked the address up in the
phone book, and there it was: N. Halloran.

The number 640 had been hand-painted on a metal mailbox out by the street; he pulled up to the curb and peered toward the house, a small Cape Cod with salt-silvered white-cedar shingles and blue shutters. Birch, pine, and oak trees filled the front yard; instead of a white picket fence, there was a wild hedge running from the street back to dense woods behind the house.

The sight of the house struck him hard, and he realized that it reminded him of his beach office. The place his ex-wife called "the shack." This wasn't quite what he had expected. Hearing that Neve Halloran was in court, he'd figured she was fighting for more money. He'd pictured a big house with a big mortgage, lots of expensive landscaping, a fancy car in the driveway. Instead, there was an old 245 Volvo station wagon.

He climbed out of his truck, tucked the package under his arm, and walked toward the house. The yard was February-brown, with patches of snow lingering in the shadows of tall trees. He followed a winding walk of chipped blue flagstones embedded in the hard earth to a shallow stoop. Taking the steps in two long strides, he knocked on the door.

Footsteps sounded inside; curtains moved, and he felt her eyes on him. He could almost feel her deciding to not answer the door. A moment later he heard the lock clicking, saw the door being opened. Neve Halloran stood there, staring at him.

"Hello," she said.

"Hi," he said. Her blue eyes were enormous, and she just stared at him so directly, waiting for him to speak, that he felt a shiver run down his back and couldn't remember what he wanted to say.

"Is there something I can do for you?" she asked after a long moment. He noticed that she was wearing black slacks and a soft gray sweater, and he figured she had to get to work.

"I brought something for Mickey," he said. "Is she here?"

"She's gone to school," she said.

"Really?" he asked, surprised. "I thought she'd be laid up for a few more days—that was a pretty bad break."

"It was," she said. "But Mickey wanted to go. She never misses school—if it weren't for this, she'd be on her way to another perfect attendance award. She's had them almost every year since first grade . . . except twice—when she had the chicken pox, and when her grandmother died."

"Conscientious girl," Tim said.

"Oh, extremely," Neve said, smiling, softening slightly for the first time since she'd opened the door—in fact, since the first time Tim had met her. The sight of her smile caught him off guard. He took it in, wondering why he felt so rocked. Was it because most of the people he encountered lately were so serious? Winter beach aficionados were a moody and contemplative lot—Tim among them. And the kid, too—Shane West.

Neve stood there, arms folded across her chest, as if she was trying to give herself warmth. Her smile lingered, touching her lips and the corners of her bright eyes, then shifted to puzzlement.

"The reason I'm here," he said, pulling the package out from under his arm. "Right." He handed the bird-paper–wrapped book to her. "Just something for Mickey, to tell her I hope she heals quickly, and comes back to the beach."

"Thank you for thinking of her," Neve said. "I'm sure she'll love whatever this is."

"She told me you taught her to love the beach and nature," he said.

"It's in our blood," she said. "My mother taught me—Mickey, too. We used to go all together, when Mickey was young. She and I go still. I keep waiting for her to outgrow it, but it hasn't happened yet."

"Some kids hold on to loving nature their whole lives," Tim said, his chest feeling heavy.

"It's a gift," Neve said. Although her expression was serious, her eyes twinkled, as if she held the gift inside, close to her heart. It showed in her expression, her bearing.

"Yes, it is," Tim said. "I'm surprised I've never seen you down at the beach. I've been working there a long time—I thought I knew all the winter regulars."

Neve shook her head. "No," she said. "We have our own spots . . . even more remote than the places you patrol."

Tim nodded. He thought of Neve and Mickey exploring the beach, just as he and Frank had done. They had walked the tide line too many times to count, every year, until the summer Frank left. Memories of Frank were intense, made him feel he was passing through the sound barrier and shook him to the core. He felt himself frowning, and no matter how hard he tried, he couldn't stop it.

"What's wrong?" she asked.

"Nothing," he said. He tried to hold the words in—this was none of his business, no two families were the same. But he cared about this woman and Mickey—he'd bonded with the child on the spot, there on the frozen beach road, seeing her broken wrist and hearing her talk about the snowy owl.

"Is it about the beach?" she asked. "You're the ranger there—are there places we shouldn't go?"

"It's not the beach," he said. He squinted. "Stay out of court. Whatever differences you and your husband are having, work them out on your own—for Mickey's sake. There's so much to lose. . . ."

Her face changed in an instant. He watched her cheeks turn bright red—she looked embarrassed first, then furious, and he knew he'd done it again. He wanted to touch her arm, tell what had happened, return that gentle look to her eyes. But she was too angry; clutching the package, she backed away.

"I'll see Mickey gets this," she said, starting to close the door in his face. He stepped forward, stopping her.

"I . . ." he began. The next words stuck in his throat, and he couldn't get them out.

"This is the second time you've tried to tell me what to do regarding my 'husband,' as you call him. He's my ex-husband, Mr. O'Casey, and he's abandoning my daughter. She's called him twenty times, to tell him she has a broken wrist, and he hasn't called her back once. Okay? Do you understand now?" Her eyes were wild, staring straight into his. "I don't know what makes you think you know what I should do, I don't know if all divorced men stick together, but I'm telling you—leave me alone. Leave us alone."

The door slammed in his face.

Tim O'Casey stood on the step for a long time, staring at his own reflection in the small window. He saw an old man—face lined, hair gray. But staring deeper into the shadowy reflection, he saw Frank. His son standing there, staring at him with cold, judgmental eyes.

Tim touched the glass. He stood there for a few seconds as the cold traveled through his fingertips, straight into his core. The curtain moved, as if Neve Halloran had checked to see if he was still there. In case she was watching, he nodded—full of regret and apology—and then he left.

4

By the time Neve got to the Dominic di Tibor Gallery, she was still boiling over Tim O'Casey's comment. She tried to calm down, concentrate on everything she'd let build up during the last few days. Her desk was piled high with slides, sent in by artists hoping to be considered for the gallery's big summer show. There was a stack of phone messages from collectors and artists, all needing to be called back.

The gallery was located in a beautiful restored boathouse on Front Street, overlooking the protected harbor. It specialized in contemporary and nineteenth-century American art, with a focus on marine and wildlife paintings. Neve's job was doing research, primarily on the many older works done by illustrious bird artists from the last two centuries.

Although the gallery owner, Dominic di Tibor, was very wealthy, and stinted at nothing in terms of the space—climate control, security, enormous thermopane windows, highly polished pumpkin-pine floors—Neve's position wasn't very high paying. She loved her work, felt really lucky to have such an interesting job, but it always came back to money.

Sitting at her desk, she felt anger starting to simmer again. How dare Tim O'Casey tell her to stay out of court? Did he think she *wanted* to be there? He had no idea what her life was like. She had married Richard thinking it was forever. She'd fallen in love with him . . . well, at a low ebb in his life. While he built a career in real estate, she had gotten a master's degree in art history. She had dreamed of becoming a conservator—the person who restores old paintings and other works of art, gently repairing the damage done by time, weather, or, sometimes, violence.

Her expertise was in paintings of wildlife.

Having grown up loving birds so much, she'd transferred that passion to an interest in paintings by the great bird artists John James Audubon and Louis Agassiz Fuertes. When Neve was a child, her mother had taken her into Manhattan to see the Audubon prints at the New York Historical Society. She had attended Cornell because of its collection of Fuertes' papers, as well as the famous Cornell Lab of Ornithology.

So here she was, pursuing her dream of researching bird artists, getting paid next to nothing, fighting her ex-husband in court. Trembling, she thought of Tim O'Casey. Would he have her quit doing work that mattered to her, get a higher-paying job— maybe selling real estate, like Richard? That way she could pay her bills by selling her soul.

Just then the phone rang, and she reached for it.

"Dominic di Tibor Gallery," she said.

"Neve."

"Richard?" she asked, shocked to hear his voice. "Where are you?"

"Never mind that. How's Mickey?"

"She has a broken wrist—didn't you get our messages?"

"Yes, I got them," he said. "I've been going crazy, worried about her."

"Then why didn't you call?" Neve asked.

"Because of *you*," he said. "And this insanity—I told you, I'll pay you when I can. Jesus, Neve. I'm strapped right now. The market is tight, I've got more going out than coming in, and you've got the goddamn court all over my ass."

"What am I supposed to do?" she asked, trying to stay calm. "You say you'll pay me when you can . . . but when will that be? I'm not trying to make things hard on you—I just want you to take care of your share. You agreed to the terms of the divorce—it's not as if I was unreasonable. . . ."

"But you're being unreasonable now!" he exploded. "My lawyer says there's a warrant out for my arrest!"

"Because you didn't show up in court," Neve said, wondering how it was possible he was making her feel guilty for this.

"So, tell them we're working it out—get the judge to call it off. Christ sakes!"

"How can I get him to call it off when Mickey's health insurance has lapsed? Richard, I have to pay all her hospital costs out-of-pocket now. X-rays, exams, medication, the doctor. I need your help with that . . . and I want you to start paying the premium again. It was part of the agreement!"

"Well, I don't have it," he said. "I don't have the money, okay? To hell with the agreement. You don't understand, you never did. Alyssa, I swear . . ."

Had he just called her by his girlfriend's name? "This is Neve," she said.

"I know that," he said. "Christ, you think I don't know my own wife?"

"Your own . . ." she started, and then she knew. Suddenly everything fell into place. His erratic behavior, his irresponsibility, letting the insurance payments drop, his refusal to see Mickey: Richard *was* drinking again.

They first dated when she was in college and he had just dropped out. His father had died, and Richard was in a tailspin. He didn't call it that; he loved bars and parties, wanted people to think he was outrageous and fun. Neve, who loved wildlife and studied nature, saw him more like a wounded bird. Grounded, unable to fly, finding it hard to survive. He had found a job, selling cars to make money—and making a lot of it. But

Neve knew that the most important things in life weren't things, and she saw a young man who was dying inside.

Still, he had an undeniably attractive charm, a sense of fun and adventure, and a tendency to take life right to the edge. More comfortable in libraries or standing quietly with binoculars, watching birds, Neve sometimes felt overwhelmed by the excitement of being with Richard. They went to parties, enjoyed spur-of-the-moment trips to New York or Boston, drives to Vermont, sails to Block Island. He'd take her skinny-dipping in the moonlight after romantic picnics on the beach.

Often those nights were fueled with wine, or scotch, or after-dinner drinks. Richard claimed to love the finer things in life; he told her that drinking was just part of it. But after a few too many, he'd plunge into despair. He'd start missing his father. He'd talk about missed opportunities—dropping out of school, the law career he could have had, the chances other guys got instead of him.

By the time Neve was pregnant with Mickey, the fun was gone, and desperation was a way of life. Richard would drink until he passed out on the sofa, in front of the TV, leaving Neve to cover him with a blanket and go to bed alone. Or he wouldn't come home at all—he'd stay out all night, stumbling in the next morning, bleary-eyed, reeking of scotch, telling her "nothing happened," even when his shirt smelled of another woman's perfume.

What was supposed to be the happiest time of their lives, awaiting the birth of their first child, had become a nightmare. One night, coming upon her sobbing in bed, Richard had fallen to his knees, taken her hand.

"I'm sorry," he'd said, starting to cry himself.

"What is it?" she'd asked. "Why are you doing this? Don't you love me anymore? Aren't you happy about the baby?"

"I'm scared," he'd whispered. She could still remember how strangled his voice had sounded, how terrified his eyes had looked.

"Scared of what?" she'd asked.

"Of screwing up. Of not being able to take care of you both—of being a bad father."

"But you'll be a wonderful father," she'd said, thinking of his incredible zest for life, his spontaneity, wanting that for their child, wanting everything to go back to the way it was.

"How do you know?" he'd implored, searching her eyes.

"Because you're a good man," she'd said, gazing right back at him, steadily and with all the love she had, believing with all her heart that she was telling the truth, that all they had to do was believe in each other to make it all right again. "With a good heart."

"My father died too young," he said. "I don't have any role models."

"Then you have to be a role model for yourself," she'd said sternly. "We have a baby coming, Richard—and she needs a father."

"I know. I'll try to be a good one," he'd promised. "I swear to you, Neve. I'll really try."

And he had. He'd stopped drinking that same night, and she'd never seen him have another drop, not even one. No beer at baseball games, no wine at dinner, nothing . . . Until eight years ago. He'd started up on his thirty-eighth birthday. It was as if the crush of middle age, of approaching forty, had added up to more than he could handle, and he'd begun having a cocktail before dinner again—"just to smooth out the rough edges," he would say.

The rough edges must have included Neve and Mickey, because soon he stopped coming home. Or, he'd come home when he felt like it. Mickey's schoolwork and soccer games and birthdays lost their appeal for him; instead he gravitated more toward the bars and his own social life.

Finally Neve kicked him out, and he moved into a condo with Alyssa—a woman he'd met showing her houses after her divorce. Mickey would see him on weekends, and she reported back that he'd stopped drinking. He was working out; he and Alyssa went running every morning, and she was getting him into yoga. He was eating health food. Suddenly he started paying more attention to Mickey. It had hurt Neve, but she'd never let on' to Mickey: that Richard had become a better father to their child when he was living with someone else.

But now Alyssa was expecting a baby, and the pattern was repeating itself. Richard drank when he was stressed, when he couldn't handle the intensity and surprises of everyday life.

"Richard," Neve said now, "come back

from wherever you are. We'll work it out, okay? For Mickey's sake?"

"Everything's going down the drain," he said, his voice hollow, as if he hadn't heard her.

"It doesn't have to," she said. "We can figure something—"

But he hung up. She heard the fumbled click, then the sound of a dial tone. Cradling the phone, she felt her heart pounding. Richard wasn't her husband—wasn't her problem—anymore. But he was, and always would be, Mickey's father.

She found herself wondering what was in the package Tim O'Casey had brought by. In spite of what Neve felt about him, she knew that Mickey would be happy to know he'd thought of her.

Mickey knew, as soon as her mother came home from work, that something was up. It might have been that her smile was too bright, or the way she went straight to the kitchen to begin cooking—without even sitting down to talk for a few minutes.

"What is it?" Mickey asked.

Her mother looked over, and Mickey saw

her face instantly fall. Mickey and her mother could always read each other. They had the hardest time keeping secrets. From the time she was little, Mickey knew she could ask her mother anything and get the truth. The problem was, sometimes Mickey didn't want to know.

"Is it Dad?"

"Yes, honey," her mother said. "I talked to him today. . . ."

"Why hasn't he called me?"

"Mickey, he's drinking."

It felt like a punch in the stomach. Mickey walked over to the kitchen table and sat down. She stared at the salt and pepper shakers, standing together next to the napkin holder. Her eyes burned, scalding with tears. Why did it have to be this way? Other fathers could drink, and they stayed the same. When Mickey's did, the whole world fell apart.

"He doesn't care about me anymore," she said.

"That's not true," her mother said.

"He has a new baby coming, and I just don't matter."

"Oh, Mickey—you matter more than anything."

How could her mother say that? Didn't she see? Mickey bowed her head so her mother couldn't look into her eyes and see how lost she felt. Her father was with Alyssa now, and they were starting a new family. Both Mickey and her mother had been thrown out—he had walked out their door, out of their lives, and he really wasn't coming back.

"What he's doing has nothing to do with you. . . ."

"How can you say that?" she asked, looking down at her cast. She remembered other times she'd gotten hurt, and her father had been right there—when she'd fallen and cut her chin and he'd taken her for stitches, when she'd skinned her knee and he'd so tenderly cleaned and bandaged it himself.

Sitting at the kitchen table, she waited for her mother to reply. The silence ticked on, and no words came out of her mother's mouth—as if she herself were bewildered, unable to understand how it could be like this. Instead of replying, her mother came around the table, put her arms around Mickey.

"I love you," her mother said.

"I love you, too," Mickey said, burying her face in her mother's shoulder.

"Someone brought you a present," her mother said after a minute.

Mickey looked up, watched as her mother went to the sideboard, came back with a package wrapped in pretty paper. Tearing it open, Mickey found a big book of photographs: *White Night: Snowy Owls in Flight*. She paged through, and the photographs were sharp, brilliant, almost magic. Someone had written on the title page, and she leaned closer to see:

To Mickey,

Thanks for loving birds so much.

Ranger Timothy O'Casey

"Wow," Mickey said. "That's so nice."

"He dropped it off this morning, just after you left for school. It's giving me an idea. . . ."

"Mom," Mickey said, looking out the kitchen window, starting to smile. The weather had warmed up a little today; the icicles hanging from the gutters had melted, and more of the snow was gone. How much longer would the snowy owl be here on the beach before flying home, north to the tundra?

"Are you thinking what I'm thinking?" her mother asked.

"Beach picnic?" Mickey said.

"I really want to see that owl," her mother said, grinning. They put everything together: her mother heated up tomato soup, poured it into a thermos. Mickey grabbed bread, and with one hand managed to make two cheese and tomato sandwiches. Her mother threw in apples and cookies, they put on their warmest coats and hats, and hurried out to the station wagon.

Although their house was just a five-minute walk from the town beach, the snowy owl was all the way at the end of Salt Marsh Refuge, and they had to drive quite a ways along the deserted coast road.

The days were getting longer. The setting sun hovered, a red ball trapped in drifts of cloud. Pink light spread over the dunes, across the slate-colored sea. Waves broke just offshore, and Mickey imagined the U-boat down below, causing the spectacular wave break. She had always wondered about the men on board, at war so far from home, trapped underwater forever.

It made her think of her own father—sometimes it seemed that he was caught underwater, unable to swim up or away, at the mercy of whatever currents or waves held him down. Her throat choked up, and she opened the car window, just to breathe in the sea air. It felt cold, but smelled of salt and beach pines, and made her feel that things would be okay.

They passed the ranger station—there was Mr. O'Casey's big truck parked in the lot. Lights were on, and Mickey was tempted to ask her mother to stop so they could thank him for the book and for coming to the emergency room, maybe invite him to join their picnic. But when she turned to look, the expression in her mother's eyes was so faraway, Mickey decided not to say anything.

Once they drove past the heavy machinery—still there, in spite of Shane's trying to chase it away—Mickey signaled for her mother to pull over. They grabbed the food and two heavy blankets from the back seat, hurried through the thicket toward the beach. They passed the high-bush blueberries, silvery bayberry, gnarled red cedar, and scrub oaks. Crossing the small wooden bridge over the creek, they came out just behind the dunes.

Low sand hills rolled north and south, as far as the eye could see, facing the open Atlantic. The dunes were wind-sculpted, tufted with dry beach grass. A low, steady wind blew off the sea, rustling the grass and whistling into the thicket. Following a narrow path over the lowest dune, they crouched down.

Mickey saw the owl right away. It sat on the beach, above the tide line, in the lee of an enormous driftwood log. Her heart kicked over—it was just a few feet from where she and Jenna had seen it the other day. One hand on her mother's shoulder, she pointed with her cast. Her mother turned her head, scanned the dunes, saw the owl—Mickey could tell by the wild delight that crossed her face.

They sat very still, watched without saying a word. They stared at the snowy owl, a round white mass of glossy feathers with a sharp, dark beak. Every so often the breeze would lift the feathers along the owl's wings, making them ripple. Each time, Mickey's heart clutched, as she anticipated the bird taking flight. It was almost dusk, the time owls began to hunt.

How many times had Mickey and her mother taken nature walks together—looking for warblers in the woods each spring, climbing Lovecraft Hill every fall to gaze up for migrating raptors? Mickey tried to breathe as quietly as she could, feeling the chilly air on her cheeks and lips. She nestled closer to her mother, both of them crouched down as low as they could get, so the wind wouldn't carry their scent to the owl.

Gazing out over the sea, she saw the moon rising from the waves. Enormous and glimmering, it looked like an almost-round peach. Gesturing to her mother, she whispered, "Look . . ."

"Just a few more days," her mother whispered back.

"Wish on . . ." Mickey started to say, but stopped herself. She knew that most people wished on the first star, but she had always wished on the moon. It had started when she was little, and she and her family would take walks on moonlit nights. Mickey had always looked up at the moon, felt it smiling down on them, keeping her family together.

It was too late for that, so why bother wishing anymore? Mickey turned back to the owl, narrowed her eyes and concentrated.

"What were you about to say?" her mother asked.

"Nothing," Mickey said.

"I think I know."

"It's nothing, Mom."

"Wish on the moon," her mother said, putting her arm around Mickey's shoulders. "Go ahead, Mickey . . . wish."

Mickey closed her eyes tight. She thought of her father, so far away that he might as well have been in another life. The biggest shock in the world had been the divorce— learning that a family that had lived together for so long, had loved each other through hurricanes, blizzards, sunsets, moonrises, summers, winters, the chicken pox, the flu, headaches, spring concerts, fender benders, fallen trees, the death of grandparents, and so many other life-shaking things, could just cease to exist. Mickey and her mother were still together, but her father had moved to another world.

"Wish, Mickey," her mother whispered. "Anything you want . . ."

Mickey closed her eyes tight. She knew her mother probably expected her to wish her father would stop drinking, or would come home, but tonight Mickey felt something shift in her chest, as if her heart had just broken in a new way. She took her mother's hand, and when she opened her eyes and saw the snowy owl so brave and still, its white feathers glowing in the rising moonlight, she whispered, "I wish we could see the fly-out."

And her wish came true.

Ten minutes later, they watched as the snowy owl swiveled its head, looking all around; its yellow eyes glowed like stars. It shifted position, ruffled its feathers, shook its shoulders as if preparing for a great feat. Mickey knew that the owl was waking up after a long day's sleep, that its nocturnal rhythms were pulling it into night.

The owl flapped once, twice, and, on enormous white wings, soared straight over Mickey and her mother. Mickey caught sight of those terrible gold eyes, that wicked beak, its killing talons—she felt the rush of air from its flapping wings, moving over her like a cold cloak, and she jumped to her feet to watch the owl disappear over the pine trees.

"Did you see that?" she gasped.

"How wonderful," her mother said, standing at her side.

"The most incredible thing I've ever seen!" Mickey said.

And when she turned to look into her mother's eyes, she saw that two other people were standing there as well—had emerged from their own separate hiding places along the beach: Ranger O'Casey had come out of the old abandoned duck blind, just this side of the thicket, and Shane West had jumped up from behind the dune. They each stood there, completely still, watching the trees for the owl.

After a few minutes, they all noticed each other. It was almost funny, a little awkward, that they would all wind up at the same secret place, watching for the owl to begin its night hunt. When Mickey looked up to see what her mother thought about it, she saw her staring straight at Ranger O'Casey— and he was staring back.

Mickey blinked and looked away. Her stomach growled. She was hungry, and she knew the beach picnic would taste so good. She felt like asking her mother if they could invite Shane and the ranger to join them, but her mother was gazing again with such rapture at the sky where the snowy owl had been, Mickey just turned toward the low pine forest, waiting for it to emerge once more.

5

At school, Mickey kept her eyes open for Shane West. But the morning passed without seeing him in the hall or classrooms, or even while she was getting lunch—she scanned the noisy and crowded cafeteria as she pushed her tray along the metal rails with her good hand.

"Who are you looking for?" Jenna asked when they reached their table and Mickey was still looking.

"That kid," Mickey said. "Shane. The one who was there at the beach when I fell off my bike."

"Shane West?" Tripp Livingston asked. "Surfer-slacker-loser? He's suspended."

"For what?" Mickey asked.

"He's a criminal," Tripp said. "He got caught screwing with the wrong guy, and now he has to pay for it." He laughed, shaking his head, looking across the table at Josh Landry. "I wouldn't want to mess with your dad."

"Yeah," Josh Landry said. "You're right about that."

"What did he do?" Isabella Janus asked.

"Nothing. He just *thought* about doing something, and my dad pressed charges," Josh said. "He's out of school for the rest of the week, and they're making him do community service. My father wasn't about to let him skate."

Mickey ate her sandwich, not saying anything. She knew that Josh's father was a famous golf course and real estate mogul. They had lived in San Diego until last year, when the family had moved to Rhode Island. Mr. Landry had tried to buy a lot of land near Kingston, with the idea of building a new country club and fancy houses. When that fell through, he'd gotten interested in the U-boat. Mickey knew all this because every time Mr. Landry did something, he seemed to call the local paper. She knew that the heavy equipment parked by the beach belonged to him—she just wasn't sure exactly why he was involved with a project concerning a U-boat that had sunk so long ago.

"What's your father doing that for?" Mickey asked.

The whole table looked at her as if she'd asked something terrible. It made her nervous—even Jenna seemed horrified. Josh was the richest kid in school. He lived in a mansion on the water, and famous people who golfed visited—Mr. Landry had his picture taken with Tiger Woods just last week; it had run on the front page of the sports section.

"Doing? Other than teaching a little shit criminal a lesson? What's the problem?"

"Nothing," Mickey said. "Except Shane didn't actually do anything. He was . . . just trying to make a point, that the U-boat should be allowed to stay at the bottom of the ocean."

"What good's it doing there?" Josh asked. "Besides, it's a fucking German U-boat. We're Americans, get it?"

"Yeah, my grandfather fought in World War II," Tripp said. "He'd be the first to say 'good riddance' to that thing. They were here to bomb our coastline!"

"It's part of our history," Mickey said, looking at Jenna for help.

"That's true," Jenna agreed.

Last year, Mickey and Jenna had made care packages for soldiers overseas. They'd also attended the peace rally in Providence. Mickey cared about the world so much, every person and creature, and sometimes it seemed that Jenna was the only other person who got it. If the U-boat left, people might forget how horrible war was. She looked at Jenna, hoping for solidarity, but Jenna laughed.

"Part of our history fighting Germans," Jenna said. "Nazis right here on our shores!"

"Damn straight," Tripp said.

"Besides," Josh said to Mickey, his voice soft and his eyes looking as if they wanted to melt her, "it's just an old wreck covered with barnacles, snagging fishing nets, attracting sharks. All those surfers who claim it creates a great surf break? They'll thank us when it's gone and the sharks leave the area. Bad news: there won't be any big waves. Good news: there won't be any fins either."

"I hate sharks," Jenna said, giving a pretend shiver. "They're so scary."

Scary? Mickey tried not to react. She felt sad her best friend was acting this way, all damsel-in-distress in front of her boyfriend, who just happened to be Josh's best friend.

"What do you mean, 'when it's gone'?" Mickey asked. There'd been rumors, but suddenly this sounded real. "You're talking about a U-boat—it's not going anywhere. The periscope and hardware, maybe, but not the submarine itself . . ."

Josh chuckled. He was small and compact, and he wore clothes that looked as if they belonged in a magazine: designer jeans that didn't come from anywhere in Rhode Island, a blue shirt with an Italian name across the back.

"Whoa, dude," Tripp said. "What's going on?"

"No comment," Josh said.

Jenna giggled. "You sound just like your father when that golf course thing was happening, and the papers kept trying to get him to talk. Every time I read the front page, there was Mr. Landry saying 'No comment.' "

"You learn to say it," Josh said, "when you live a high-profile life."

Mickey wanted to gag, but she had to find out what he had meant, so she asked again. "You said 'when it's gone.' Do you mean your father *really* plans to take it away?"

"Which part of 'No comment' don't you understand?" Isabella asked.

"Look, Mickey," Josh said, his gaze softening again. "This is going to be huge. The whole world will be watching. I want you to come down to the beach, and I'll make sure you're on camera."

"On camera, woo-hoo!" Jenna said.

Mickey felt the ground shift beneath her, but she steeled herself to hear what Josh was about to say. "Why will there be a camera?"

"Because we're going to raise the dead."

"The dead?" Mickey asked.

"That's just a saying. . . . Listen, I shouldn't be talking about this. My father would kill me. You guys have to swear to keep this secret. An announcement will be made any day, but my father wants to control the way the media handles it."

"Okay, we swear," Tripp said. "Now tell."

"My father's going to raise the U-boat," Josh said.

"I thought that was just a story," Mickey said, her skin prickling.

"No. It's the truth. We leaked some stuff to the press, to get a reaction. Mostly, it seems as if people don't care. We didn't want the natives getting restless before, but now I can tell you for sure. My dad has access to heavy equipment you can't believe. There's this crane he's bringing over from France— it works on the Chunnel . . . the tunnel that goes under the English Channel. Man, this crane would take up an entire city block in New York. And he's bringing it to Rhode Island."

"How's he getting it here?" Tripp asked.

Josh smiled. "One of his divisions is a shipping line. So, by freighter, then by barge. I mean, this barge will be so big—to hold the crane—you'll think Block Island has somehow floated into the harbor. My father's company can do anything."

"And what's he going to do with the really big crane?" Mickey asked, thinking he sounded like a brat, bragging that his toys were bigger than anyone else's.

"He's going to haul the U-boat up and out."

"Cool, man," Tripp said, and Jenna smiled. Mickey felt hollow inside.

"He's going to televise the whole thing, and when he's finished, he's going to take the rusty old wreck to Cape Cod and turn it into a museum. There's one like it in Chicago, and one in England—U-boats open to the public—but nothing here on the East Coast. He says it'll be the biggest tourist attraction since the *Intrepid*, in New York City," Josh said.

"What's the *Intrepid*?" Jenna asked.

"A big fucking aircraft carrier where you charge admission and let corporations throw huge parties."

"He can't disturb it," Mickey whispered, feeling the others staring at her. "Not the U-boat."

"Why not?"

"Because . . ." she began. *Because it's ours; because it's here; because your father doesn't understand why it matters so much.* Those were Mickey's thoughts, but she couldn't say any of them out loud.

"Who cares about it, anyway? This is America—it's not as if the sub was one of ours," Josh said. He had bright golden-brown eyes and short curly hair, a smile that curved up just at the outside corners; his look should have been cute, but Mickey saw a shadow of meanness, right behind his eyes and smile.

"Yeah," Tripp said. "Good riddance to it. Hey—let's go down to the beach and have a send-off party. Our navy sank it, and now Josh's dad is going to raise it. Party on the beach Saturday night?"

"Definitely," Josh said. "We have to get into shape for Washington—that trip will be one big party."

"I'm in," Jenna said.

"Me too," Isabella said.

They all looked at Mickey. She cradled her broken wrist and thought of the snowy owl. It was roosting right on the beach that fronted the sea where the U-boat had gone down. She closed her eyes, thinking of how the party would disturb the owl, hoping maybe the bird would have flown north by Saturday. If it hadn't, she had to be there to protect it.

"Mickey?" Josh asked, looking straight into her eyes.

"Sure," she said, holding her arms close

so her friends wouldn't see she was shaking. "I'll be there."

Operation Drumbeat began after the Japanese surprise attack on Pearl Harbor on December 7, 1941, when German U-boats were sent across the Atlantic to attack American ships. Admiral Karl Dönitz had been planning this assault for years, turning his sea wolves loose on the east coast. His U-boats were manned by expert, veteran crews, patrolling the eastern seaboard from Cape Hatteras to the Gulf of St. Lawrence. During the first two weeks alone, five U-boats sank twenty merchant ships, giving the United States a hint of the massacre Dönitz had planned.

Tim O'Casey had volumes of history books and journals on the subject, and he sat at his desk reading one now, trying to figure out the best way to deal with what was going on. He knew that Cole Landry had U-823 in his entrepreneurial sights, with a plan that seemed a combination of *Raise the Titanic!* and "U-Boat Theme Park." Landry had set up a foundation to raise money to fund the project, and his board was a who's who of retired senators, current members of Congress, and U.S. naval officers.

As ranger of the Salt Marsh Refuge, Tim's duties included protecting all wildlife along the barrier beach. But he also held himself accountable for other aspects of the beach, including the reefs and rock formations, the salt marsh itself, the intertidal zone, and the several shipwrecks just offshore—U-823 first among them. He and Frank had dived on the U-boat countless times.

He had a pen and legal pad out, carefully making notes to aid in his presentation, and was so distracted, he didn't even see the car pull into the parking lot. He heard footsteps on the porch and looked up—totally shocked to see Neve Halloran coming through the door.

"Hello," he said, pushing his chair back, standing up. She looked hesitant, mistrustful—but as beautiful as ever, with translucent skin and dusky blue eyes. She wore jeans and a thin navy parka over a sage green cashmere sweater, a camera case slung over her shoulder. He was fifty-five, and although she had to be about ten years younger, her bright eyes and enthusiastic spirit made her seem like a college kid.

"Hi," she said, glancing at the paperwork. "Sorry to disturb you."

"You're not, I promise," he said. "It's a relief to see you."

"A relief?" she asked.

"Yes—I was drowning in textbooks," he said, but that wasn't what he'd meant. And as he stared at her now, he wanted to tell her that he knew he'd said the wrong thing again when he'd brought the book to Mickey; he wanted to explain everything to her. Yet he found himself unable to go into it—he was trapped in a memory of last night, gazing at her across the beach, both of them watching for the owl. Their eyes had locked and held, and in that moment, he'd felt something for her that went beyond explanations or apologies. "What brings you here?" he asked.

"I closed the gallery for an hour," she said, "to come down and try to get some pictures of the snowy owl—but it seems to have relocated."

"Really?" he said. "You looked by the log? Just beyond the jetty?"

"Where we saw it last night," she said,

nodding. A few seconds passed, and in the silence, Tim sensed her remembering the moment as he was: twilight, soft red sky, silver stars just starting to emerge, the rugged old jetty, the owl taking flight. "I saw you there. But the owl's gone now."

"It was there this morning," he said. "I watched it fly in, after a night of hunting. We could go look for it. . . ."

"I don't want to bother you," she said. "I see you're really busy. I really just wanted to get some shots before the owl disappeared for good."

"You're a photographer?"

"Not really," she said. "But Mickey is so excited about that owl. She loved that book you gave her, by the way. So much so, I thought she'd really like a picture of 'her' snowy owl. That's how she thinks of it . . . as if it flew down from the Arctic just for her."

"Maybe it did," Tim said, smiling, closing the history book he'd been reading from. "Come on—let's go find it so you can get a picture."

Neve hesitated.

"Come on. I promise not to say anything about court or lawyers."

"Really?"

"Yes. I swear. Let's go get a picture for Mickey."

Neve finally nodded, and Tim guessed it was the "for Mickey" that convinced her. Tim grabbed his jacket, and they walked out to his truck. She climbed in, and he handed her the binoculars to hold. Backing out of the sandy lot, he drove southeast, toward the stretch of beach the owl favored.

They passed the interpretive center, closed for the winter, and Tim glanced over to see Shane West nailing new boards over one of the windows. The last nor'easter had torn the shutters and some shingles off. Cole Landry's trailer and equipment were parked alongside. As much as Tim had resisted the idea of having the kid assigned for community service to the very area he'd planned to vandalize, it was a big help to have him helping. He was glad he'd reconsidered the idea of having Shane reassigned.

"What are you researching?" Neve asked.

"Excuse me?"

"Back at your office. Your desk looks just like mine when I'm trying to research paintings for a new catalogue, so I assume it's a big project."

"I'm just trying to come up with ways to stop Cole Landry from going forward with plans to move the U-boat."

Neve glanced across the seat. "I've read about that in the paper . . . they can't possibly do such a thing, can they?"

"Cole Landry can do just about anything—at least that's what he'll tell you. I hear he wants to do it this spring. He has an enormous crane with steel slings to lift the vessel from the sea bottom; he's got a location picked out on Cape Cod where he plans to put it."

"I wasn't talking about technology," Neve said quietly. "I mean, it's just wrong for him to even try."

Tim drove in silence. She had no idea of how much he agreed with her, and why. "Why do you think that?" he asked after a minute.

"At this point, it's such a part of our lives," she said. "Part of Rhode Island. I grew up here, and it's always been part of our legends and lore."

He thought of those words, *legends and lore*. They seemed so magical, out of a fairy tale. But the U-boat was real, a warship that had come across the sea to attack and sink American ships. It had been manned with a top-notch crew, the very best that Dönitz had under his command. They were hunting American ships, and many lives had been at stake. Tensing up, hands on the wheel, Tim stared at the road ahead as his mind spun with how he was going to make his case.

"Now *I've* said something wrong," she said, watching him.

"No," he said. "I'm just thinking."

"About the U-boat?"

"Yes. It's not a legend at all. It's an IXC-class submarine, 252 feet long, 23 feet abeam. She's made of steel, displaced over a thousand gross tons, carried three antiaircraft guns as well as a deck gun, and has six torpedo tubes, nearly brand-new at the time she was patrolling our coast. She crossed the Atlantic to attack us."

"I know that," Neve said.

"She's more than a legend."

"It's just a figure of *speech*."

By the tone of her voice, Tim could tell he'd offended her. He glanced over, wanting to tell her that as tender a subject as divorce was for her, the U-boat was equally sensi-

tive for him. How much would he have to divulge to get her to understand? He tensed
up, getting ready to try, when just then they
reached a wide-open stretch; the beach
and open ocean were visible out the left
side. When he turned his head to look,
straight out at the old jetty, he saw the owl
right there, nestled beside the log.

"We're in luck," he said, pointing.

"Good," she said, following his gaze, and
she opened the truck door so fast, he could
tell how eager she was to get away from
him. He didn't even blame her. He'd heard
the bitterness in his own voice, just as he'd
heard it the other times he'd met her. First
about court, now about the U-boat. The details of each situation were completely distinct, but they blended together in his heart
and emotions—because they were so connected. The past and the future colliding
right here, right now.

He followed her to the beach, where she
was already snapping pictures. Staying a
good thirty yards away from the owl, she
used a long telephoto lens. The sun was behind her, and she was a lean, dark silhouette, perfectly still. Somehow he could tell,
with just a glance, that she was more than

competent—she was an artist. He found himself wanting to see the pictures.

He stood close beside her, but she worked as if he weren't even there. A gust of wind blew across the stretch of sugary white sand, furrowing the owl's feathers. The owl moved slightly, shifting position by just an inch or so. The small movement delighted Neve, and she turned to see if Tim had seen. He nodded that he had, taken off balance by her radiant smile.

Two minutes ago she'd been upset with him, but right now she was glowing. Her smile relaxed something in his chest, and he stood a little closer. Watching wildlife was a serious, intimate act. You couldn't do it with just anyone.

Tim remembered times, early in his marriage, when he'd taken Beth to some of his favorite places: Hanging Rock, the Monninger Ravine, Mount Lovejoy, and right here at Salt Marsh Refuge. He had wanted to share with her his love of not just birds and animals themselves, but the beautiful habitats in which they lived. Even in their charged silence, his father and uncle had instilled it in him—and Tim had wanted to share it with Beth.

Turned out Beth didn't like being outdoors much. He'd dug her a garden, and it never really took hold. He hung a bird feeder from the maple tree, but she never seemed to watch the birds. He'd loved her so much it shouldn't have mattered, but it sort of did. He knew that now, but only after a long struggle with himself. People who don't like doing things together probably . . . well, probably shouldn't be married.

Gazing at the owl, winter sun in his eyes, he felt his heart pounding in his chest. Caring for nature was his job now—he got paid for it. But standing here beside another human being—inches away from Neve—felt like more than he had signed on for. It felt like too much to figure out, so he did what Beth had always told him he did: shut down. After a few seconds more, he turned and walked back toward the truck.

His attention was drawn out to sea, and he looked over his shoulder, at the spot where so much of his life had been formed. Out of the corner of his eye, he saw Neve swivel toward him, heard the camera beep. She'd taken his picture.

Tim climbed into the frigid cab. Instead of watching Neve and the owl, he turned his gaze seaward again, toward where the breakers were rolling in, over U-823. He knew exactly where it was—he could tell by where the waves broke—where they reared out of the sea in perfect, transparent sheets of water, then curled and smashed in on themselves in a single long, furious streak of white foam.

The U-boat had been stationed just off the coast, waiting for a convoy of merchant ships heading out of Long Island Sound from New York City. It would have followed them into the deeper Atlantic, joined by other German U-boats, if not for one man. They'd called him the Gray Goose, and even now he had more to do with air and flight than water and submarines. Staring at the surf break, Tim wondered what he would have to say about all this.

A few minutes later, he saw Neve cross in front of the truck, climb in on the other side. He'd been sitting in the cold, so the engine wouldn't disturb either the owl or her in her work, but he turned the key now, fired her up.

"Looks as if you might have gotten some nice shots," he said.

"I did," she said. "I even got one of you."

"That's one you'll want to delete."

"Thank you for bringing me here."

"Well, you said it was for Mickey," he said.

She nodded. "It is. You've been very nice to her—thank you. . . ."

Tim started to back out of the sandy lot, but she put her hand on his arm, and he looked at her. The weight of her hand was so light, but he felt electricity running from her fingers into the tendons of his arm.

"You don't like me very much," she said.

"It's not that," he said. "Not that at all."

"Then what?"

"Nothing," he said. Then, because it seemed rude to just stop there, he cleared his throat. "Just, did you ever make a mistake that was so bad, you want to keep everyone else from ever doing the same thing?"

"What did you do?" she asked.

"I followed in my father's footsteps," he said.

And then, because there was nothing more to say, he shifted into reverse and pulled out of the parking lot. The waves kept crashing in, one line of breakers after another, without beginning, and without end.

6

When she got back to the gallery, Neve put the kettle on to boil and stood as close as she could to the space heater, trying to warm up. The cold had gotten right into her bones at the beach; Tim had blasted the heat in the truck on the way back, but her fingertips and toes were still slightly frozen, tingling. Or maybe that had more to do with the way he'd looked at her, long and hard, when she'd said he didn't like her much. An expression had flashed across his eyes, it had made her shiver, and she couldn't get that sensation out of her body.

She tried to concentrate on writing cata-logue copy for an upcoming exhibit on a local bird artist who had lived and painted in the area during the late 1930s. He was a single-name artist, from a time when that was unheard of: Berkeley. Born in Newport, Berkeley had grown up in Rhode Island. There were rumors that he'd dropped out of high school to study at the Art Students League in New York, then almost instantly moved to Paris. He'd done fieldwork around Barbizon, Fontainebleau, and Honfleur; notes found in his sketchpad revealed that while overseas, he was filled with longing for his family and the birds of the northeastern United States.

During his time in France, the world was a powder keg, the fuse of Pearl Harbor about to be lit. Neve read through the scant biographical material available, looking for evidence of the effect the war may have had on his work; did he ever return from Europe? Had he perhaps been killed over there?

Berkeley's adopted name was thought to be an homage to the Irish philosopher Bishop George Berkeley, who had lived in Newport and done some of his most inspired thinking on Hanging Rock, overlooking the Atlantic in what was now the

Norman Bird Sanctuary. Neve had taken Mickey there for bird walks from the time she was a baby, strolling through the woods and wetlands, enchanted by all the species.

Now, sitting at her desk, she started to feel warm again. The kettle whistled, and as she got up to make tea, still thinking of Berkeley and the mystery of what had happened to him, the front door opened. A blast of cold air whirled in, scattering papers, and Chris Brody closed the door behind herself.

"You're just in time!" Neve called as she entered the tiny kitchen alcove.

"In time for what?" Chris asked.

"Tea!"

"Oh, good," Chris said, throwing her wool coat over the armchair by Neve's desk, walking into the back to give her a hug. "I am so ready for spring, it's not funny. Is it my imagination, or is this winter lasting forever? Don't we usually see the light at the end of the tunnel by now? Now I hear that snow is forecast for the weekend!"

"Really?" Neve asked. Maybe that would keep the snowy owl here a little longer. She measured Earl Grey into a silver strainer, filled the china teapot with hot water, and placed some biscuits on a plate, pushing thoughts of Berkeley and the war from her mind.

"You seem suspiciously happy," Chris said, peering at Neve. "Since when does more snow make you smile?"

"Oh, it's just that Mickey's been watching a snowy owl down at Refuge Beach, and I want it to stay as long as possible." She poured two cups of tea, handed one to Chris.

"You Hallorans and your birds," Chris said. "I don't quite get it, but that's just me."

Neve held the thin china teacup in her hands, blowing on it to cool it down, and she shook her head, smiling. Chris was such a good friend, but she was right: she didn't understand Neve's love of birds. Over the years, Neve had tried to introduce her to the simple pleasures of watching blue herons stand in shallow coves, humming-birds dart in and out of red trumpet vines. Lowering her teacup, she reached for her camera.

"No pictures, please," Chris said. "I'm a mess!"

"I'm not taking one of you," Neve said, scrolling through the digital images she'd shot at the beach. "I want to show you one—of the owl."

The two friends stood still, gazing at the one-inch screen on the back of the camera, and Chris acted politely interested when Neve came to the pictures of the snowy owl. Then an image of Tim O'Casey filled the screen, and Chris put her hand on Neve's wrist.

"Isn't that . . . ?" Chris began.

"It's Tim O'Casey—the park ranger."

"The guy you said was such a jerk at the hospital?"

"Yes," Neve said, staring at his picture. She'd surprised herself, snapping the shot. He'd thought she did it by accident, but the fact was she'd framed the picture, focused on his face, clicked the shutter—completely on purpose.

"Funny," Chris said, staring more intently at the screen. "I recognize him."

"From where?" Neve asked.

"Oh, a story that was in the Sunday paper a few weeks back. It was about his father— but *his* picture was in it, the ranger. Didn't you see it?"

"If it was a few weeks back, I was probably wrapped up in the court mess and didn't get to the Sunday paper," Neve said. She clicked the lens cover closed, heard the camera turn off. "What did it say? What did his father do?"

"He's sort of a hermit," Chris said. "Lives in the woods near Kingston somewhere. He's got a cabin and an aviary . . . takes care of wounded hawks, other birds. He's a wildlife rehabilitator."

"He loves nature," Neve said, thinking of what Tim had said, that he took after his father. She thought of her own mother and wondered what could be so bad about inheriting a love of the outdoors. "Is that what the story was about?"

"Not really," Chris said. "I can't remember the whole thing, but I know it had something to do with the plans Cole Landry has to raise the submarine."

"I suppose Tim's father opposes that for environmental reasons," Neve said, imagining an old man living in the woods, caring for injured birds.

"That wasn't the impression I had," Chris said, sipping her tea.

"What then?"

"Well, they called him the Gray Goose, and the story had more to do with the fact that he was in the Navy during World War II. A commander, or something, aboard the ship that sank the U-boat. Something in the story made me think they're estranged—father and son."

Hearing Chris's words, Neve felt the hair on the back of her neck stand up. Almost absently, she turned the camera back on, began to scroll through the pictures. She passed the shots of the snowy owl, each one more magical than the next, but she didn't stop until she came to the photo of Tim O'Casey.

He stood halfway between her and the truck, dressed in his khaki uniform and thick jacket, and she'd caught him staring out to sea. It had struck her as odd at the time—but only slightly—that with such a rare bird right there on the beach, so white and pure, the park ranger was looking out at the broad and endless ocean—always there, never really changing.

What had Tim said to her? *I followed in my father's footsteps. . . .*

He said that as if it was a bad thing, the worst in the world. How had an old Navy man come to live in a cabin in the woods, taking care of creatures that fell from the sky? Surely following in such footsteps had led Tim straight to the park service, a career as steward of Rhode Island's beaches and wildlife. So why would they be estranged?

"The Gray Goose," Neve said. "That's his nickname?"

"That's what the reporter called him."

"How did he go from the U.S. Navy to where he is now?"

"I gather there was some bitterness," Chris said. "The story might have said, but it didn't stick in my mind."

"Why was Tim in the article?"

"Oh, they were both weighing in on Cole Landry. They're both completely against raising the sub, but for different reasons. Now it's coming back to me," Chris said, picking up the teapot, refilling her cup. "Tim was talking about habitat, how the fish swim around the wreck, and how it serves as a natural breakwater, keeping the beach intact, the sand from washing out in big storms."

"And his father?"

Chris shook her head. "He didn't say much, and he wouldn't let anyone take his picture. I gather he's proud of what he did for the Navy, and he doesn't want the site to be disturbed. I can certainly understand that! . . . I remember visiting France on my honeymoon; Jeff and I went to Normandy, to Omaha Beach . . . you can feel the ghosts of the dead there. Jeff's father fought there on D-Day, and somehow survived—when I looked up, there were tears rolling down Jeff's face. My big old baby crying for his dad! Battlefields are pretty much holy ground."

Neve nodded. Her thoughts turned back to Berkeley. So many of his French paintings were of shorebirds on the Norman coast; had he been captured by the Germans, or killed by the Allies in massive air strikes before D-Day?

Now her gaze returned to the pictures she'd taken of the snowy owl, sitting so peacefully beside the driftwood log. Miles of white sand stretched along the coast, punctuated by small coves and inlets, by the Refuge Breachway—that tidal torrent that rushed from the salt marshes straight into the ocean.

Neve thought of all the times she and Mickey had walked that beach, collecting shells and sea glass, feeling their bare feet in the sand and shallow water, of how those walks had healed her from the sorrow of the divorce.

It seemed like the farthest thing from a battlefield she could imagine. But she thought of Tim's harsh words at the hospital, and the dark expression in his eyes; and she imagined an old man called the Gray Goose, living deep in the woods, estranged from his son.

The man who had followed in his footsteps . . .

"What are you going to tell your mother?" Jenna asked, leaning over the back of Mickey's seat on the bus.

"I don't know," Mickey murmured, not wanting to think about it yet.

"You have to think of something good. She won't let you go if you tell her it's a party. She's so *strict*."

"Yeah," Tripp said. "What's your curfew? Like, ten o'clock?"

"I can stay out later than that," Mickey said.

Jenna giggled, sliding back into the crook of Tripp's elbow. He latched on, and started to kiss her. Mickey could hear their lips brushing each other's, and she wished she could disappear. When had Jenna become a make-out person? On the bus home from school, no less.

The miles slipped by, but not fast enough. Every few miles the bus would stop, and some kid—or a group of kids—would have to gather up their things, zip up their coats, shuffle their way down the aisle.

Outside, the sky stayed light. It was late February, and every day was longer than the one before. Still, the air was so cold. Snow seemed poised to fall. The clouds were heavy with silver, and Mickey was sure that if they opened up, it would be a blizzard. Bare trees raked the sky, a canopy of interlocking branches over the winding country road. In this late-day light the tips of the branches looked pink, and Mickey felt as if she were tipping on a fulcrum, a seesaw of winter and spring.

Mickey sank lower in her seat, listening to the soft kissing sounds. She heard the sleeves of Jenna's nylon jacket singing against Tripp's. That party they had mentioned—why would Mickey even want to go? It was going to be all the cool kids, Jenna's new friends. Not just sophomores—some of them were juniors and seniors, and they'd be drinking and making out, acting cool and crazy, right in the spot where the snowy owl was.

Turning slightly, Mickey tried to catch Jenna's eye. She wanted time to stop and, in fact, rewind. She wanted to go back, back, to when they were best friends without complications, when Jenna had made Mickey laugh during the divorce, and Mickey had consoled Jenna after the death of her grandmother. She wanted the months to unspool, all the way back to last winter, to these weeks when the days were getting longer, when the anticipation of spring migration grabbed hold of their hearts and made them know they could endure divorce and death.

Tears warmed Mickey's eyes, and even though she didn't want Jenna and Tripp to see her crying, she wanted to will her old best friend to look at her, to feel how important it was to think of the snowy owl—and not just that, but also the black-throated blue warbler: their two favorite birds.

Some things were bigger than fun. The party would be great, Mickey was sure—if you liked things like that. But couldn't they have it somewhere else other than Refuge Beach, where—it seemed to Mickey—so much was at stake? Why did getting older have to mean getting stupider about things worth loving and caring for?

"Hey, are you spying on us?" Tripp asked.

Mickey shook her head. "I was just . . ."

"She's upset about the party," Jenna said, making Mickey's heart jump—even with everything that had come between them, she could still read Mickey's mind. "Right?"

Mickey blinked.

"Upset about what?" Tripp asked.

"Mick's upset that we're having it on the beach," Jenna said, gazing straight into Mickey's eyes—knowing her so well, reading her thoughts, translating feelings about the owl, almost as if white wings had spread over their heads. "Right?"

Mickey nodded.

"What about the beach?" Tripp asked. "What's wrong with it? It's perfect for everything we want to do there . . . a keg, music, a whole lot of darkness to hide what needs to be hidden." He squeezed Jenna, gave her a suggestive look.

Emotions flickered in Jenna's eyes. Mickey concentrated, trying to read them—

she was torn between her boyfriend and her best friend. But Jenna had to be true to herself, too, to her love of birds, to all the years when she and Mickey would dream of seeing their favorites—the snowy owl and the black-throated blue.

And for a minute, Mickey thought it was going to be okay—Jenna would smooth it over, get Tripp to move the party to Senior Field, behind the gym; or even to the bridge, that hidden spot behind the library, out of sight of the road.

"What's wrong with the beach?" Tripp asked again.

"I'm not allowed to say," Jenna said.

"Who's stopping you?"

Jenna shot Mickey a look.

"What, her? Come on, we don't have secrets here." Then Tripp turned toward Mickey. He smirked, as if he didn't believe she could withstand his will and charm. Touching the back of her head, he let his hand trail down her neck, onto her shoulders. Mickey caught Jenna's eye and saw that her friend didn't like Tripp doing that.

"It's that owl!" Jenna said. "Mickey doesn't want it disturbed. . . ."

"Fuck, who cares about an owl?" Tripp

asked, laughing. "Disturb it? We won't even go near it. Owls are spooky."

"See?" Jenna asked, softening her gaze, giving Mickey one of her old best-friend looks, cajoling now, touching her head in the same spot Tripp had. "See? No one's going to bother the owl . . . so come on, Mick. Think up a good story to tell your mother—otherwise we both know she'll say no—and let's plan for a great Saturday night!"

And then, as if Tripp couldn't wait to get started, he wrapped his arms around Jenna, and the squishy kisses started again, and Mickey looked out the window at the tree branches—black against the sky, the pinkness fading with the sunset. "A story" to tell her mother, Jenna had said, but she meant a lie. Mickey thought of her father, and how he lied—and felt the seesaw tilting away from spring, straight back to winter.

7

The night was wicked cold, the party loud and raucous. Someone had brought a CD player, and it blasted music straight into the face of the sea wind. Kids talked, laughing and fooling around, huddled around a crackling bonfire. It blazed and sparked—but some of the logs must have been damp, because the eerie low-pitched whistle of wet wood underscored the jubilant party noise.

Driving through the refuge with Jenna and Tripp—in his Jeep, taking the unpaved fire road to avoid being seen—Mickey had seen the ranger's lights on through the scrub pine trees and almost wished he'd see the kids and stop them. Everyone had blankets. Some couples were lying down, lost in closeness, not even paying attention to the party. Others were standing in small groups around the keg and fire, wrapped up against the wind. Partying at the refuge wasn't allowed, but they weren't likely to be discovered on such a cold night. Mickey leaned on the old jetty, just outside the fire's circle of light.

"Hey, are you having fun?" Jenna asked, coming over to stand with her, beer sloshing in a big plastic cup.

"It's okay," Mickey said, trying to hide the fact, even from her best friend, that she felt like a different breed among the partyers.

"It's *great*," Jenna corrected her. "C'mon, Mick. We have to grow up sometime, don't we?"

"Yeah, I know."

"Your mom knows you're sleeping over at my house—don't worry, you won't get in trouble. Here—have some beer. She won't smell it on your breath, my parents don't care, and you'll feel more relaxed."

"That's okay," Mickey said, shaking her head.

Jenna shrugged, took a long drink.

Mickey watched her, wondered why she felt so strange—when Jenna was the one drinking. She was surrounded by friends and classmates, here on the beach she loved so much. They were at least fifty yards from where the owl had been roosting, so she didn't really have to worry. But her stomach kept flipping, as if she were on a roller coaster.

She had lied to her mother. Well, not a flat-out lie, but a definite lack of truth.

What do you and Jenna have planned tonight? her mother had asked.

Oh, I don't know, Mickey had said. *Finishing homework. After that, who knows?* When all the time she had known about this party. Her heart pinched, thinking of some of the fights she used to overhear between her parents; her father would say he was going to be somewhere, and her mother would find out he'd been somewhere else. It had been so unfair, and had hurt her mother so much; and now here was Mickey, doing the same thing.

"Come on, have some!" Jenna urged, pushing the beer toward her.

Mickey hesitated, then took a big sip while Jenna held the cup, and just one sip made her body feel light and her head feel free, and she hated it because she thought of her dad and wondered if he was drunk.

"You know you want to talk to him," Jenna said, licking beer foam from her upper lip.

"What are you talking about?"

"Shane. Duh!"

Mickey felt her face turn red, and was glad it was too dark to see. Her gaze slid up the beach, to a shadowy figure sitting on top of the dunes. He was silhouetted by starlight, and Mickey saw his strong shoulders, his lean arms, the way he was completely comfortable on a beach—even on a cold February night.

"Look, just because Tripp and Josh say he's a freak, you and I know he's not," Jenna said, slipping her hand into Mickey's. "He helped you when you had your bike accident. Go talk to him!"

"I don't know," Mickey said, never taking her eyes off him. Even though Shane had been in her class for years, there was something about him that had always seemed so apart. He was older, for one thing; he should be a junior, but he'd stayed back in Woodland Elementary. Mickey had always figured that because he was a year older, and a surfer, he was way out of her league.

"Here, give him this—" She tried to thrust the beer into Mickey's hand, but Mickey backed away without taking it. "Goody-goody," Jenna said, but she grinned and kissed Mickey's forehead as she gave her a gentle shove toward Shane.

Mickey began to walk up the beach, following the jetty to the top. The sand felt soft and deep under her green rubber boots. Her heart was racing, and her mind was filled with the words she would say; she felt tongue-tied before she'd even opened her mouth. She saw him lying back on the sand, propped up on one elbow. When he turned slowly, to look at her, his gaze felt like a laser beam, filling her body—all her bones—with scalding white light.

"Hi," she said, climbing the dune, standing over him, looking down into his eyes.

"Hi," he said.

"I just . . ." she began, but lost track. "What are you doing here?"

"Oh, I found out about the party," he said. "And I came to keep an eye on things."

"You do that a lot," she said. Standing high on the dune, she felt colder than she had down below, by the sad little fire. A strong sea wind was blowing, and it tossed her hair all around. She tried to peel it out of her eyes and mouth, but the wind wouldn't let her.

"Sit down," he said. "It's warmer down here." He reached up to give her his hand, to guide her down, and she took it. They sat still, pressed close together, directly on the sand, slightly in the jetty's lee. She held her left arm up slightly so she wouldn't get sand in her cast. The dune still held some of the sun's heat, but what made Mickey feel warmest was the pressure of Shane's arm and hip against hers. She felt liquid inside, as if she were made of mercury.

"I haven't seen you at school lately," she said.

"Well, I haven't been there. I figured every-one knew the whole story—I'm suspended till Monday."

"You don't deserve it," Mickey murmured. "You helped me. And you were just trying to save the U-boat, and the beach, and the owl. . . ."

"People don't care about those things," Shane said. "Not when there's money to be made."

"Money?"

"Yeah," Shane said. "That's why Josh's father is famous. For making money, being rich. He'll open a U-boat museum and get richer." He pointed down at the party.

Mickey stared down from the top of the dune. People were clustered around the keg and the fire. Josh was telling everyone to fill their cups. The waves crashed in, and spray carried all the way up the beach, misting Mickey's face. Music blasted, but Josh's voice was louder. He raised his plastic cup high, facing the sea.

"To the U.S. Navy!" he shouted. "Who blasted the shit out of U-823. And to my dad, for getting it the fuck out of here. To-morrow there'll be a film crew right here, when he makes his announcement. You'll all get to be on TV."

Everyone raised their plastic glasses in a toast. Mickey stared past them, out at the waves. The sea looked so wide open, the white wave crests as bright as snowcapped mountains. The jetty pointed seaward; Mickey knew the sub lay submerged in sev-enty feet of water, partly covered with sand, a few hundred yards out. Even using the jetty as a marker, there was no way to tell by looking exactly where the U-boat lay. Its invisibility didn't matter; it was part of the landscape, part of who they all were.

"What are you doing with them?" Shane asked, gesturing at the kids.

"They're my friends," she said defensively.

"You know that's not true," he said.

"Jenna is. She's been my best friend since kindergarten."

"Well, she's hanging around with jerks. Getting excited about being on TV—in what? A reality show about ruining the coastline? If they thought about it for ten seconds instead of just jumping on the nearest bandwagon, maybe they'd realize he's making them into suckers."

"Not everyone loves the beach the way we do," Mickey said. She glanced past Shane, at his upright board stuck into the sand. "Did you surf today?"

"After I finished community service. Until dark," he said proudly. "That's how I figured out about the party. Josh and his friends showed up early to build the 'bonfire.' You should have seen them, dragging up driftwood from the tide line. Half of it is soaked through—he was putting the fire out before he got it started."

Mickey laughed in spite of herself. She watched some kids refilling their cups from the keg, then saw Jenna and Tripp holding hands, standing just outside the circle of firelight, starting to kiss. Somehow the sight of her friend's passion combined with the touch of Shane's arm against hers made Mickey feel hot. What was she even think-ing? He was older and so much cooler, probably just thought of her as a little kid who'd fallen off her bike.

She turned toward Shane, caught him looking at her. His face was just inches away from hers, so close she felt his warm breath on her forehead. The wind was still blowing hard; he reached over to push the hair out of her eyes. The feeling shocked her, made her heart pound. His fingers lin-gered longer than they had to, and she real-ized he wasn't wearing gloves.

"Aren't your hands cold?" she asked, her voice sounding almost like a croak.

"Not now," he said, touching the side of her face with his palm.

"You should be freezing," she said. "Sit-ting out here—no blanket, no gloves . . . how do you do it?"

"I'm used to surfing in the winter sea," he

said. "I just don't think about it. Warm, cold, what's the difference? We're alive—we're here for a short time, the shortest time you can imagine." His words sounded harsh, but they were also filled with grief. Something in them made Mickey think of everything her family had lost—their old closeness, the comfort of having all three of them under the same roof—and she leaned a little closer.

"What do you mean, 'the shortest time'?"

"My father died when I was three," Shane said. He stopped there, as if that was all that he needed to say. Then he cleared his throat, looked at Mickey. "He was only twenty-two. Just a few years older than I am now."

"How did he die?" Mickey asked.

"He drowned," Shane said. He stared out over the breaking waves, then glanced down at Mickey. "He was a surfer."

"He drowned surfing?"

Shane nodded. "Right here," he said. "On this beach."

"During the winter?" Mickey asked. She took in Shane's bare head and hands, his open collar, with no scarf to block the wind—he didn't even bother zipping his jacket up to the top.

Shane shook his head. "The first day of spring," he said.

"Who was with him?" she asked, because somehow she already knew.

"We were," he said. "My mother and I."

"I'm sorry," she said.

He shook his head. "Don't be," he said. "I'm just glad he didn't die alone. We saw him catch the perfect wave, and then we saw him go under. And not come up. My mother swam out, looking for him."

"Did she . . . ?"

Shane stared out at the sea, his eyes hot. "No, she didn't find him. We never did."

"Shane, that's so sad."

"Yeah," he said. "It is. When I was a little kid, the year I was old enough to ride my bike to school, I used to skip school. My mother would watch me head off, and she'd think I was going to Woodland. Instead, I'd double back around and come down here, looking for my father. That's the year I stayed back."

"I remember," she said. "The year you were suddenly in my class."

"That's why," he said. "My mother took my bike away, so I wouldn't stay back again."

"You stopped looking for him?"

Shane nodded. "I told myself the wave had taken him to California; he always used to talk about moving to Half Moon Bay, surfing Maverick's."

"Maverick's?" she asked.

"A big-wave surfing place," Shane said. "Named for someone's dog. I've always wanted to get a dog, call him Maverick. My dad would like that."

Mickey nodded. She thought of her own dad, how he'd always promised they'd get a dog. They'd go to a farm he knew, pick out a puppy from the litter, and it would be their dog. Mickey had imagined father-daughter walks on the beach, their dog running up ahead, exploring the tide line. It had never happened.

Glancing up at Shane, she watched him hold back a shiver.

"The first day of spring," she said. "It must have still been cold."

"It was," he said. "But the sun was out. I remember that, and I still love that combination—a chill in the air when the sun's shining."

"You kept me warm that day on the road, when I had my bike accident," Mickey said. Very gently—completely by instinct, certainly not thinking, because if she was she couldn't have done it—she slid her arm around him. "You were cold the day your father drowned, but you don't have to be cold now. You don't . . ."

Shane felt stiff, almost as if he wanted to pull away. But he didn't—he moved closer, turning toward her, putting his arms around her. Mickey felt her heart beating so hard, almost as if it wanted to break out of her chest. She even heard wings and felt the rush of something flying overhead, but when she tilted her head back to look up, all she saw was a white blur, just clearing the jetty.

"Was that . . . ?" she asked

"The snowy owl," he said.

They held each other, watching the owl's long, low flight over the beach. Shane clasped fingers with Mickey's good hand. They sat perfectly still on the dune, watching the owl soar out of sight.

The kids at the party had seen it, too: "Hey, what the fuck?" Josh asked.

"That was a freaking big seagull," Declan said.

"Seagulls don't fly at night," Isabella said.

"It's a snowy owl," Tripp laughed. "Sssh—don't tell Mickey."

"A snowy owl—no way!" Martine said.

"Hey, it's coming back," Josh said, peering down the beach. And he was right; the owl was making another pass along the dunes. Shane and Mickey were sitting so still, huddled into the tall grass, no one saw them there. Everything happened so fast, Mickey couldn't have moved if she wanted to—watching the owl, pressed against Shane's body, she was almost paralyzed with happiness.

Josh grabbed a long driftwood log from the fire. One end was unburned; the other was charred and smoldering: it was one of the wet pieces Shane had seen him throw onto the pile. He wound his arm back.

"What are you doing?" Jenna asked.

"It's just a stupid bird," Josh said, and he released the driftwood.

Shane let go of Mickey and jumped up, but he was too late: the log clipped the owl's wing, and the snowy owl fell to earth. Mickey heard a shriek and the rustle of feathers. She felt Shane fly across the dune to where it had landed.

"I'm going to stuff and mount it," Josh said, striding over. "It's mine."

"You idiot," Shane said.

"What did you do?" Jenna cried.

"Hey, it'll be like one of his dad's trophies," Martine said. "All those big-game heads out in the trophy room. Rhino, lion, snowy owl!"

Shane pushed the others away, went back to the bird. Mickey stared in horror: the owl was on its feet, one wing straight and dragging on the sand, trying to fly. In the darkness, its yellow eyes were like beacons, and in them she saw terrible pain, fear, and intelligence. Josh went straight for the owl, and Mickey jumped onto his back.

"What the hell are you doing?" he asked.

"Get away!" she screamed. "Leave it alone."

"Get off my back!" Josh said, slamming her onto the beach in one motion.

"Mickey!" Shane said. He'd been leaning over the owl, trying to figure out how to help it. But at the sight of Mickey on the ground, he took a giant step toward Josh and smashed his fist into his gut. The sound was a thunder crack, and Josh went down, clutching his stomach.

"You freak!" Josh shouted, when he got his wind back. He picked up a rock as he rose to his feet, glaring at both Mickey and Shane, as if unsure of who to attack first. Then he looked at the owl and brought the rock up over his head.

Shane seemed very calm. He stood still, his chest heaving. Without breaking a sweat or seeming to exert much effort, he just reached over and took the rock out of Josh's hands.

"Don't be more of an idiot than you already are," Shane said. He flung the rock across the beach into the water, then turned to Mickey. She was shaking. Her cast was filled with sand, and the irritation chafed her skin raw. Her ribs ached from where Josh had thrown her onto the ground. Shane helped her up. He stroked her face with his bare hand, and the look in his eyes made her tremble. In that flash of an instant, she knew that they had to save the owl, that they had to get away from the beach, that she had fallen in love.

She and Shane crouched by the owl; its golden eyes were less bright, one white wing was flapping madly, the other dead and useless, and it was crying. That's just how it sounded to Mickey: like human cries of anguish. Her heart, completely in love with Shane, was breaking for the owl.

"What can we do for it?" she asked, holding back tears.

"We'll take it to the ranger," Shane said. "He'll know . . ."

In that second Mickey saw the log coming down—she tried to pull Shane out of the way, but it hit his head with a thump. Shane tottered and fell, blood flowing from a gash in his temple. Mickey cried out, but just then she felt a blanket come over her head.

"No!" Jenna shrieked. "Let her alone!"

Mickey fought against the blanket. It bundled around her and the owl, sweeping them both up. The owl fought hard: thinking Mickey was its enemy, it attacked her with its claws and beak. She closed her eyes, feeling knives tear at her flesh. The blanket felt harsh and rough, and suddenly she felt herself being lifted—pressed against the owl so tight, neither one could move. She felt the softness of feathers against her cheek; when she opened her eyes, she saw nothing but blackness.

"Stop," she tried to say. "Please!"

Jenna's voice sounded right outside the blanket, and so did some of the others. She heard them pleading with Josh, but he didn't answer. He carried her, thumping across the sand. She could feel his footfalls, hard and full of purpose. The sea air came through the woolen blanket. The owl had stopped moving, but in the pitch dark she saw its eyes gleaming dully yellow, just inches away from her own.

Mickey felt Josh wind up—just as he had done with the driftwood log. Once, twice, and then release—he sent the blanket with Mickey and the owl bundled inside flying into the air. For a moment she thought it would be okay; she would land on her feet, catch the owl, keep them both from crashing onto the sand. Somehow, in that last moment, the owl spread its one good wing and broke free.

Mickey felt an instant of joy—the owl would be all right. But there was no place for her own feet to land: she felt the shock of cold water, more frigid than anything she had ever known. It took her breath away, and suddenly there was no breath to take. She swallowed icy salt water. Her heavy

boots filled, dragging her down. She strug-
gled against the blanket weighting her like a
sea anchor, dragging her straight down to
the sea bottom. She tried to kick her boots
off, but they were stuck—the water had
formed a seal, a vacuum against her skin,
and they were dead weights.

Mickey held her breath. She was dying,
plummeting downward. She looked around
wildly. The storm out at sea had pushed
enormous waves toward the shore, and she
was caught in them now. The action
pounded her deeper and deeper, down into
the sand. She looked into the depths, saw
the sub—she was sure of it, a dark hulk
right there, bright white faces of German
sailors peering out of the conning tower,
beckoning her closer.

Real faces, each one distinct; she looked
from one to the next, praying for help—were
they going to attack her? Suddenly she saw
a new shape diving toward her—a shark, a
black blur. It swam so fast, rocketing down.
She felt arms wrap around her—she flailed
around, disoriented, trying to find the owl,
struggling against the force. Something was
trying to drown her faster than the blanket
and the sea itself. She fought wildly, and

staring into the salty murk, she saw familiar eyes.

They were like Shane's: they were his father's! His father had come to be with her now, to help her be less afraid. She shuddered, tried to stop fighting. She could go with him. Her lungs were on fire, ready to explode. This was it. She opened her mouth, letting the last of her air go, bubbles escaping from her mouth.

And suddenly she felt Shane's lips on hers. Kissing her back to life, giving her strength, making her know she had to hold on. He wrapped her in his arms, holding her tight and gently guiding her up to the surface. They broke free, and she gulped water and air. Underwater had been calm compared to this: they were caught in the surf, in the inshore violence of breaking storm waves.

"Hold on," he said. "Don't let go of me for anything."

"The men, down below . . ." White, advancing toward her, making her remember something else: white, flying, soaring, falling.

"The owl!" she cried, sinking again.

"It's on land," he said, boosting her up,

stroking through the frigid water. "That's where we have to get to. . . ."

Mickey coughed, choking on the water she had swallowed.

"Stay with me, Mickey," Shane shouted.

"He killed it," she wept, gulping water.

"Mickey," he said, and his voice was tender even while his grip was pure iron. He let her sob as he swam her into the beach. Her broken wrist was numb, and her legs felt as if they were filled with sand. The waves battered Mickey and Shane, but he swam through them, straight and true. Her lost strength kicked in with a blast of adrenaline, and she began to swim. Her stroke grew stronger, and she felt the spray sting her eyes, but her own tears and a will to live washed it away.

When they got to the shore, kids surrounded them, helping them out of the surf. Tripp placed a blanket around Mickey's and Shane's shoulders. She felt Shane holding her, making sure she could make it above the tide line, easing her down because her legs suddenly wouldn't work anymore.

Mickey heard soft weeping, almost like the sea wind blowing through the thicket at the top of the beach, behind the dunes. She clutched Shane, realized it was coming from him.

"I thought I'd lost you, too," he said, staring into her eyes, and she knew he was thinking of his father. "I thought you were drowning . . ."

"I was," she whispered. "But you saved me."

They held each other while the other kids stood around. Josh was nowhere to be seen, but Jenna came running over.

"Mickey, thank God you're okay!" she gasped. "Shane, thank you for saving her."

Shane just slashed tears from his eyes and kept staring at Mickey. Jenna tapped Mickey's shoulder, made her look over.

"The owl," Jenna said. "It's still alive."

And then—as if he knew that for Mickey to really be saved, for everything to be all right—Shane nodded once, hard. He stared Mickey straight in the eyes, making sure she was alert, awake, not in shock. German faces swam into her vision—were they here? Had they climbed out of the sea behind her? She shivered, blinked, sent them away. Then she nodded at Shane to let him know she was fine.

"We have to get it to the ranger," Shane said.

"Mr. O'Casey," Mickey said, already getting to her feet.

8

Tim was stretched out on the narrow bed, reading. He was fully dressed—in his ranger uniform, right down to his boots— and he had one eye on the clock. It was ten-thirty, and the wind was dying. He'd seen the kids driving through the scrub two hours ago; he'd give them until eleven, then go break up the party. He wondered whether Mickey Halloran was down there; he wondered whether her mother had gone to winter beach parties as a teenager.

It had always been the same: when Tim was young, they'd partied on the beach. Frank and his friends: same thing, the way of the world. When Tim was new to the job, he used to bust up every gathering before it even got started. Now he was too tired—or maybe this was the beginning of wisdom. He was learning to let kids be kids, go their own way. He'd learned the hardest way of all: they would anyway.

Maybe he should call Neve Halloran and talk to her about it, ask what she thought. These thoughts had to do with her, but he wasn't exactly sure how. They had started that day he'd seen her at the hospital, waiting for Mickey to get out of X-ray. Something to do with family—parents, kids, and tenderness—that had been gone from his life for a long time. Three generations of O'Casey men—Joe, Tim, and Frank—had really missed the boat with each other.

Just then he heard a car heading out of the refuge—maybe the party had ended early. With the wind dropping, so was the mercury. A cold front was moving in, with more snow behind it. The high school kids weren't as hardy as Tim had been—except for Shane. As much as Tim didn't want to like the troublemaker, he had to admire his tenacity—he'd seen him out surfing earlier, even as the sun was setting into the pine trees.

The car stopped in Tim's parking lot—he heard sand crunching under tires, car doors slamming, and then the sound of worried voices. Then he heard the car peeling out. Someone banged on the door, and he heard Shane's voice: "Hey, open up! Hurry! Shit, I know you're in there. . . ."

"What the hell now?" Tim asked, pushing himself up from the bed. Just when he'd decided to be a nice guy instead of a ball-buster, Shane was going to make him regret it. Three long strides across the room, and he pulled the door open. What he saw there made him stop dead.

Shane, dripping wet, blood streaming down the side of his face, starting to freeze.

Mickey, soaked through and pure white, water pooling around her feet.

And held between them, the snowy owl, wrapped tightly in a blanket, yellow eyes fierce.

"What's going on?" Tim asked, pulling them inside.

"There was a party," Shane said. "A bunch of assholes, down on the beach. Didn't you see them? Why didn't you stop it? What kind of ranger are you?"

"What happened to your head?" Tim said,

staring at the cut, reaching toward Shane to examine it. But the boy flinched back, shook his head wildly—like a golden retriever who'd just come out of the surf, spraying water all over.

"Never mind that! Mickey's freezing cold, she's practically in shock, and we've got to help the owl."

"Mickey, come here," Tim said, thinking *First things first,* walking her over to the easy chair beside the radiator. She relinquished her grasp of the owl and let Tim help her down, pull the covers off his bed, press them around her. She was shivering hard, and he gazed into her eyes to see if she was going into shock.

"Shane saved my life," she said. "Again."

"You were going to be fine," Shane said, looking over at her, his gaze matching the owl's for ferocity. "You're a strong swimmer—even with your cast."

"Look, will someone tell me what happened?" Tim asked.

"We will, I promise," Mickey said, eyes welling up. "But first, can you help us? The owl's hurt. Please?"

"What's wrong with it?" Tim asked, standing slightly back from Shane, too concerned about the gash in his head to have really questioned how he came to be holding a snowy owl in his arms.

"Hurt, maybe broken wing, I think," Shane said. "Someone threw—look, never mind how it happened. It's just, the owl is badly injured. Can you help or not?" His tone was sharp and rude, but Tim didn't stop to register that. What he really heard was panic— Shane was holding the snowy owl, and he was aware of Mickey crying in the chair, and he wanted to make everything okay.

Tim took a deep breath. He had grown up with a man who knew how to help injured raptors, who had made a study of it. There was something terrible about a guy who'd rather tend to birds, who'd rather give his love—or what passed for it—to things with wings, than to people. Tim had sworn he'd never make that mistake, and he wasn't going to make it now.

But the fact was, he did know something of what to do—so he went into action. Rushing out of the room, he headed toward a shed out back, behind the building.

"Where are you going?" Shane yelled behind him.

Tim didn't reply. His thumb turned the

combination lock—0621—June 21, his son's birthday. The shed door opened, and Tim flipped on the overhead light. The first thing he saw was the scuba equipment; his wetsuit hung on a hanger, right beside Frank's. The masks and fins were on a shelf, and the air tanks stood in the corner. Seeing them stopped Tim in his tracks.

But Shane was yelling from the house, so Tim just shook his head and moved quickly. There in back—behind the wheelbarrow and bags of topsoil for the small garden out front, under a life ring and spare CPR kit and other summer lifeguard equipment—he saw the big metal cage.

It was standard park issue—for loose dogs, or aggressive raccoons, or any of the other problems that fell under the aegis of "animal control." Grabbing it, he hauled the cage out of the shed and into the house.

"What's that?" Shane asked, still holding the owl wrapped in the blanket.

"The main thing we have to do," Tim said, setting the cage down with a metallic rattle, "is immobilize the owl the best we can. Keep it from moving, injuring itself further."

"That's bullshit," Shane said. "We have to

do more than that, man! It has a broken wing! You have to—"

"My first priority isn't the owl," Tim said. He opened the cage door, swept out an entire winter's worth of spider webs. Entwined in the silk were dead flies, moths, wasps, and a few tiny peach-colored balls of unhatched spider eggs.

"What are you talking about?" Shane asked.

Tim quickly finished brushing out the cage. He tried to catch his breath, but something was pressing hard on his heart and lungs. Just trying to remember what to do, he couldn't help thinking of the care and precision with which the older man had done his work—the attention to detail, the tremendous tenderness with which he'd handled raptors: almost as if he loved them even more for their murderous beaks and claws, their warrior spirit.

"Give me the owl," Tim said, rising to face Shane.

"You just said it's not your first priority," the young man said. His lips were blue; his eyes were filled with rage and hurt. He held the owl just as if it were an infant—he cradled it in his arms. Tim saw him shaking, the small muscles just under his skin working like crazy, trying to keep himself warm, from going into shock.

"Give it to him, Shane," Mickey said, sounding alarmed.

"We'll take the owl to someone who cares," Shane said. "Come on, Mickey—"

"We don't have a car," Mickey said. "Tripp dropped us off, remember?"

"My bike," Shane said, his voice cracking.

Tim took a step toward him, placed a hand on his shoulder. He felt Shane's tension flood through his palm, straight into his own heart. Shane flinched, pulling back.

"You can't ride both Mickey and the owl on your bike," Tim said.

"I can if I have to," Shane said.

Tim shook his head, didn't even bother answering. He pried the owl out of his arms. Shane was past resisting, and Tim felt the situation decompress. Crouching down, he moved closer to the cage. Aware of the kids watching him, Tim tried to block out the past and concentrate on the present. Forget the old man and do what had to be done.

He looked into the owl's eyes—and in that second his attitude shifted. This had nothing to do with his father. This was a magnificent bird, a snowy owl, far from the arctic tundra. He thought of Neve, of how they had stood at the beach staring in awe and wonder. What would she think, to know the bird had been injured?

"A broken wing?" he asked now.

"Yes," Shane said.

"His left wing," Mickey said.

"Like your left wrist," Shane said.

"I hadn't thought of that."

Knowing which wing was injured helped Tim. He half crawled into the cage, still holding the bird. The cage was big enough to hold a golden retriever, large enough to accommodate the owl's wingspan. Tim questioned whether it was the right size, but he knew he didn't have a choice. Gently laying the owl down on its right side—disabling its good wing—he quickly unwrapped the blanket and got out of there before the owl began flailing.

The cries were sharp, visceral, terrible to hear.

Tim looked over his shoulder, saw Mickey sobbing, burying her head in Shane's side as he held her.

"Help it, please," Shane said, meeting Tim's eyes.

"It needs a chance to heal," Tim said, putting the blanket over the cage, to block the light.

"It needs—" Shane began, but Tim cut him off.

"Come on," he said, helping Mickey to her feet, marshaling both kids toward the door. "We're going to the emergency room—again."

"Getting him stitches," Mickey said, looking up at Shane. "That's your top priority, right?"

"You guessed it," Tim said, pulling on his jacket. "Now both of you—get in the truck."

The phone call woke her up.

It was Tim calling from the ER, and before she was totally awake, Neve heard him say Mickey's name and nearly had a heart attack.

"Is she okay?" Neve asked, already getting dressed.

"She's fine," Tim said. "It's just—you'd better come and get her."

Twenty minutes later, after driving way too fast, Neve flew through the double glass doors and smashed straight into Tim, standing in the waiting room. He grabbed her, held her steady, looked calmly into her eyes.

"We have to stop meeting like this," he said.

"Don't joke with me while my daughter's in the hospital."

"She's fine, Neve."

"Then where is she?" Neve asked, looking around.

"She's in there, with her friend," Tim said, gesturing past the triage station.

"Jenna? What happened? They were at her house . . ."

"Um," Tim said, leading her over to a chair, "they were at the beach."

"No," Neve said. "Mickey is sleeping over at Jenna's . . ."

"Maybe that's true, but before the sleep-over, there was a beach party. You remember beach parties, right? Kids, music, blankets? Well, this one went a little off course. Mickey got thrown in the water—"

"Oh my God!"

"She's fine," Tim said hurriedly, trying to set Neve at ease. His hand was on her arm, as if he could hold her down, keep her from jumping out of her skin. Oddly, and unexpectedly, it worked. Neve felt herself settling down a little.

"She's not hurt?" Neve asked.

"No. She was cold—you can imagine—and the doctors checked her for shock and replaced her cast—it was wet. Mostly she's worried about her friend."

"Jenna," Neve said again.

"Shane," Tim corrected.

"Wait a second . . . that boy, the one who helped her the last time?" Neve asked, and Tim nodded. Neve glanced around the waiting room. "Where are his parents?"

Tim shrugged. "We called his house, but there wasn't any answer. Getting the number out of him was a trial in itself. The kid's been doing community service with me all this past week, and learning anything about his life is more than a whole day's work. According to the court papers, his father died a long time ago. Do you know his mother?"

"Not really," Neve said. Shane had started school a year ahead of Mickey; his mother was much younger than the other mothers, and she'd never gotten involved in school things. Neve had the impression she'd had Shane very young, and she'd heard that

Shane's father had died when he was just a toddler.

"Well, she's missing in action," Tim said. "Shane's going to need someone with him when he's released."

"What?" Neve asked. "What *happened* at this beach party?"

At that instant, Mickey came running past the nurse's station. Neve jumped up, held her tight. "Mom!" Mickey said. "I'm fine, don't worry, but Shane got hurt trying to help me, and the owl! Oh, Mom . . ."

Neve held her at arm's length. Her head was spinning, and she couldn't even hear. The second emergency room—for Mickey!—in less than a week. This had been her life with Richard. Getting called to pick him up at bars, from the scene of accidents, from the police station. His drinking and lies had turned their marriage, their family, into chaos.

"Mickey, you lied to me," she said. "You told me you were staying at Jenna's."

"I was, Mom! I swear! But there was a party . . ."

"A beach party—in February?"

"Yes. They had a fire, to stay warm. But—"

"A fire on the beach?" Neve asked, turning toward Tim. "You allowed that?"

"I didn't know about it," he said. "It couldn't have been much of one—I didn't see any flames or smoke."

"The wood was wet," Mickey said, sounding as if she wanted to be helpful. Neve held her, wanting to shake her instead.

"Was there drinking?"

"Yes, Mom—but I didn't," Mickey said, blushing so fast and hard, Neve knew she had to be lying.

Neve just stared at her, and Mickey caved.

"Mom, I only had a sip. I swear—don't be mad. Especially now, because that's not what matters. We have to help Shane, and we have to—"

"Don't tell me what matters, and if Shane had anything to do with you getting thrown into the water, I don't even want to hear his name."

Mickey wrenched herself away. Her eyes looked sad and reproachful. "You don't listen," she said. "I told you Shane got hurt trying to help me. He saved my life, Mom."

"He did," Tim said.

"Then who did it?" When Mickey didn't reply, Neve shook her shoulders. "Tell me!"

Still silent, her lips tight together, Mickey wouldn't budge, and Neve knew what she had to do, how to get to her loyal, emotional child. "If you won't tell me for yourself, then tell me for Shane."

"What do you mean?"

"Your friend is in the ER because someone attacked you. Now I want to know who did it. Give me the name—for Shane."

"For Shane?" Mickey whispered.

Neve nodded.

"Josh Landry," Mickey said, turning to run back toward the cubicle where Shane was being seen to. Watching her go, Neve's blood started to boil.

"I want him arrested," Neve said to Tim.

"We called the police," Tim said. "They're investigating."

"Investigating? What are you talking about? Why aren't they here right now?"

Tim shook his head and shrugged. "They wanted to arrest Shane," he said. "He's been in so much trouble lately, they wanted to blame tonight on him—instead of Landry's kid."

"Why would they do that if it wasn't his fault?"

"I wasn't there," Tim said. "But supposedly Shane punched Josh first, when he saw him pushing Mickey. Who do you think the cops are going to focus on? A surfer who's already suspended from school, or a rich kid whose father is famous for spreading his money around?"

"I don't want Mickey involved with kids like that," Neve said—and she wasn't even sure whether she meant Josh or Shane. She felt everything slipping away. Her good daughter, so careful and self-protective; she had always avoided trouble, seemed to have great instincts for keeping herself safe. Mickey loved nature, did well in school, had learned from the painful situations in her own life to stay away from bad kids. Even if Shane wasn't completely responsible, it sounded as if he had played a part.

"Weren't you ever a teenager?" Tim asked.

"Yes," Neve said, looking up.

"And didn't you ever go to beach parties?"

"Yes," she said, filled with more than a few dangerous memories. "And I liked bad boys."

"Like mother, like daughter," he said, smiling.

"I want to save her from the same mistakes I made."

"You really think that's possible?"

"I have to think it," she said. "Or I'm not sure I could get through some of what I have to get through."

"Like being called to the ER to pick up your daughter."

Neve nodded. "There was one time in particular," she said, remembering one post–beach party night, sitting in a seat right across the room, waiting for Richard to get stitched up. Gazing at the chair, she could almost see the ghost of her younger self: so wild, exuberant, in love. . . . The thought made her look up, fast, at Tim. Was Mickey in love with Shane?

"Tell me exactly what happened," she said, calming down. "How did Shane get hurt? What did Mickey mean—that he saved her?"

"From what I can gather, the other kids were partying. Cole Landry's son, Josh, put it on. Celebrating the plans Landry has for the U-boat, something like that. Mickey and Shane were there to watch over the snowy owl, make sure they didn't disturb it."

"The owl," Neve said, remembering that Mickey had mentioned it first thing.

Tim nodded. "Josh attacked the owl, and Mickey went to help it. I'm not sure about the sequence here—both Mickey and Shane were too worried about the owl to tell it straight. All I know is, Mickey tried to stop Josh, and when Shane went to help her, a fight broke out—and someone, Josh I think, threw Mickey in."

"I need to see Josh Landry," Neve said. "So I can kill him. He threw her into the water—in February? She could have drowned."

"Yeah," Tim said, nodding. "I know. I'm glad Shane was there." His gaze slid toward the cubicles. "Just when I'm ready to throw that kid out, he does something like this."

"Surfer-slacker. That's what Mickey's friend Jenna says about him. Did she have some part in all this?"

"She and her boyfriend dropped Mickey and Shane off with the owl. From what I gather, Jenna's pretty upset at the other kids. Mickey said Jenna would have waited, but her boyfriend wanted to get her home."

Neve nodded, reassured to hear that. Jenna and Mickey had been friends since

they were five. They had learned to read together. Richard had built them a tree house
in the backyard, and they'd called it "The
Up-in-the-Sky Club." That's where they had
learned their love of birds, hiding in the tree
house as if it were a nest, observing birds as
they landed on branches or flew through the
sky.

"The owl," she said again, finally ready to
focus on something other than the here-
and-now of Mickey.

"It has an injured wing," Tim said. "At
least. I didn't spend much time examining it,
but I think part of its beak is torn, too. I'm
not sure what else."

"Oh no," Neve said. Looking up into Tim's
blue eyes, she remembered being with him
at twilight, watching the owl's fly-out.
She thought of the beautiful pictures she'd
captured—of the magnificent raptor, pure
white, flying through the violet sky, into
the dark pines. And of the park ranger, so
tall and hard, both in his posture and the
cast of his eyes. "No wonder Mickey's so
upset."

"Well, I think that has at least as much to
do with Shane being hurt."

"Where's he going to stay tonight? If they can't locate his mother?"

"He could stay with me," Tim said.

Something in the way he hesitated made Neve look up. "Do you have enough room down there?" she asked.

"Not really," he admitted. "There's just one bed. But I could sleep on the floor."

Neve shook her head, made up her mind. It wasn't ideal, but she couldn't think of another solution. "He can stay with us. On the couch. Just for tonight; I can't have him going home alone."

"That's nice of you."

She shrugged. "I don't like the idea of her spending a lot of time with him . . . but he did save her, and I'll never forget that. He can stay tonight, just until we find his mother."

"After having him work with me these last days, I'm not sure how easy that will be," Tim said.

Neve met his eyes. Was he warning her—telling her that Shane came from a bad family, that she shouldn't get involved? Neve swallowed. She wanted to teach Mickey to respect herself, choose wisely—in what she did and said, and in whom she befriended.

Neve had always taken in strays: dogs, cats, birds fallen out of their nests. Richard. When she'd met him, he had just dropped out of college. His father had died, and he couldn't afford tuition. He'd gotten a job, and he'd become a wild partyer, drinking so he wouldn't have to feel his loss. Neve had wanted to save him.

"What should I do?" she asked now.

"Let Shane sleep on your couch," Tim said.

"He's a good kid?"

"I'm beginning to think so," Tim said.

Neve nodded. Decision made; she always felt better once she'd made up her mind. She still had doubts about Shane, but letting him stay this one night wouldn't hurt. Meanwhile, she hoped the cops would do the right thing, and arrest Josh Landry.

"I'm just so glad they got the owl to you in time," she said.

"In time?" he asked.

"To save its life," she said.

He shook his head. The expression in his eyes was grave—right on the edge of something close to grief. The lines around his eyes and mouth had never looked deeper to her, and she saw the light go out of his face.

"Its life wasn't saved," he said. "Not for long, anyway. The injuries are too severe. The owl will be dead by morning."

9

But the next morning, the owl was still alive. Tim hadn't slept much during the night, listening to the rustling in the cage beneath the blanket. He kept expecting the sound to stop, and he came to dread every stretch of seconds without movement, without the owl shrieking. Silence would have meant death, so he stayed vigilant, hoping for noise.

He waited until dawn. He didn't want to keep checking—knew he shouldn't get attached to the bird in the cage. He'd learned the hard way, early on, that things he loved died—or left. Remembering the barn—out behind the house, where his father had taken up his brother's early work, taking care of raptors—Tim thought of the baby screech owls. He didn't think of them often, but right now the memories came flooding back.

He climbed out of bed at first light, walked over to the cage, and pushed the blanket back. The bird sat erect, tilting to one side. Tim crouched beside the cage, looking it straight in the eye. The owl returned his gaze with yellow eyes, glaring like two suns. The directness sent a jolt down Tim's spine.

"Are you hungry?" he asked.

The owl didn't flinch.

Trying to remember what to do, Tim left the living room, went to the sink, and filled a bowl with water. He rummaged through the refrigerator, took out the winter flounder he hadn't yet cleaned. When he returned to the cage, the owl had changed position, just slightly, as if to watch what Tim was doing in the kitchen.

Tim opened the cage door. He reached in slowly, expecting aggression. But the owl stayed still, letting him put his hand close, holding the bowl of water. He kept his arm rock solid, waiting for the owl to drink. Keeping still so long, his arm began to ache, but he didn't move. He had seen his father doing this—wanting an injured hawk to drink, the older man had held the bowl of water still for so long, Tim had begun to wonder if he'd turned into a tree. Or if he wanted the hawk to think that he had . . .

It had been a red-tailed hawk, who'd gotten caught in electrical wires. The bird had a broken wing, and Tim's father had been determined that it would survive. Even then he'd started getting a reputation as someone who could help raptors. And Tim had learned that if he wanted to be close to his father, he had to get close to the hawks, eagles, and owls, too.

Now, so many years later, he had his father's water-holding technique down to a science. Still, the owl wouldn't drink. After a few more minutes, Tim put the dish down on the cage floor. He offered the fresh flounder, but the owl ignored that, too.

Tim took the opportunity to assess its injuries: last night he'd thought the outer bone of the left wing had been shattered, that he could see the bone's jagged edge protruding through the skin, narrow and delicate and hollow, like the shaft of a feather. But in fact, that's what he was seeing—broken feathers. He couldn't tell whether the bones were intact or not, but its flesh had definitely been cut by the impact. The owl's plumage was pure white—this was a mature male—its luminous surface streaked with blood.

And the terrible beak that had killed so many moles and voles and mice and who knew what else—the food necessary to keep this magnificent raptor alive on his transcendent journeys to the north pole and back—was crooked, more hooked than it should have been, separating slightly from the owl's fierce white face, and this was even worse for Tim to see than the injured wing.

This time when he heard the knock on the door, he was past knowing what to expect. An injured boy, nearly drowned girl, broken-winged owl—what next? He walked through the kitchen barefoot, opened the door in the T-shirt and sweatpants he'd slept in.

Four men stood there—three obviously workmen, dressed in jeans and Carhartt jackets, the fourth in a black cashmere top-coat.

"What the fuck?" asked the topcoat guy.

"Excuse me?"

"You're the park ranger here?"

"Yeah, and good morning to you, too," Tim said.

"I've got a film crew arriving at noon. That's less than four hours from now. Didn't you get the communication about the shoot?"

"The what?"

"The communication about the shoot?"

"By 'communication' are you talking about a letter?"

"I don't know how the fuck they told you, but they told you. The network! We're going live tonight. Don't say you weren't aware of it, because I was assured you were told! You were to have your beach in order, looking good, for the camera."

The owl squawked behind him, and it sounded so much as if he were laughing at Landry, Tim joined in.

"What do you think is so funny?"

Tim stared at the topcoat idiot and knew he'd never understand in a million years. "Get the beach looking good for the camera?" he asked. "You mean, like without any seaweed or driftwood? Would you like the jetty varnished? Maybe you'd like the waves breaking just so . . ." He made a smooth motion with his right hand. If he straightened out his shoulder fast, he could break the guy's nose in one quick motion.

"Don't think you're so smart, asshole."

"Cole Landry, right?" Tim asked, not attempting to shake his hand.

"That's right," Landry said, with the self-satisfaction of a man who knew his face was known worldwide. Tim stared at him, slightly distracted by the fact that his dark brown hair was immobile. The wind was blowing a good fifteen knots, and the guy's hair wasn't moving.

"So, what's the problem with the beach?"

"There's a huge pile of charred wood—a bonfire from the looks of it. Plus tire tracks everywhere, and a bunch of empty plastic cups blowing all over. I told my people to make sure you had this place looking great today."

"There was a party on the beach last night."

"What are you talking about?"

"Ask your son," Tim said.

"My son? You don't know what you're talking about."

"Did the cops get to your house yet?" Tim asked.

From the hot anger in Landry's eyes, Tim

knew that he knew exactly what was going on. Just then the owl cried again, and Tim's anger began to boil.

"He assaulted two people last night. Here on 'my' beach, as you call it. He's got a mean streak, and I wonder where he got it from."

Landry went pure white. His eyes narrowed, and Tim knew he'd just made an enemy. "Shut up about my son," Landry said. "You don't know shit."

"How was it to have the police visit your house, the night before your big announcement?"

"That's between me and them. They knew my son was just having good, clean fun, and that derelict decided to make trouble."

"Did they arrest Josh?"

Landry laughed. "Of course not. Now, I'll give you two hours to get the beach cleaned up, or I'll take back my contribution."

"What contribution?"

"Two million dollars to the Refuge Beach Foundation. You really think the board wants to lose that kind of money? You fuck this up, and I can guarantee you'll be out of a job."

Tim took a step outside. The top step felt like ice under his bare feet, and the wind hit his face and bare arms, but he hardly registered the cold. He was over a head taller than Cole Landry, and he stared down and had to hold himself back from lifting the guy up by the collar of his black cashmere coat. He hated the thought of local cops backing down from Landry, but that's what had happened.

"You might know about boardrooms and tourist attractions and TV shows," Tim said, "but you don't know the beach. If you want to get rid of the tire tracks, either wait for high tide to smooth them down, or go grab a rake and do it yourself."

"You'll regret this conversation," Landry said.

"I already do," Tim said. He leaned back against the porch rail—as if it were a hot August day instead of late winter, with the mercury falling—folded his arms, and watched Cole Landry climb into the back seat of his big black Mercedes. The driver looked to be wearing an identical black coat; he met Tim's eyes with a paid-for dirty look, and backed out.

"Don't let the sand scratch your paint job,"

Tim called, thinking of what Frank would think of the sand blowing right now. *Beach tunes . . .*

The three workmen—not locals, but obviously regular guys just the same—climbed into a shiny red truck. They each gave Tim a grin and a thumbs-up. They nearly collided with the Volvo wagon driving into the parking lot.

Tim stared at who was behind the wheel: Neve Halloran. Mickey sat beside her, and Shane was in the back seat. So he'd slept on the Hallorans' couch after all.

"Not even nine o'clock," he said as the three of them climbed out of the car, "and already I've had two sets of visitors."

"None of us could sleep," Neve said.

"We came to see about the owl," Mickey said.

"Yeah," Shane said, watching the Mercedes drive down the beach road. "What was Landry doing here?"

"Giving me grief about the beach being a mess for the cameras. I told him he'd be better off worrying about the cops arresting his son."

"They didn't seem too interested in doing that," Neve said. "Especially after Shane told them he threw the first punch. I called them myself—I know you said they were investigating, but I couldn't let it go."

"Shane was defending the owl, Mom," Mickey said, and Neve didn't reply.

"You know the reason they didn't arrest Josh had nothing to do with Shane, don't you?" Tim asked.

Neve didn't reply; she just looked down the beach as if she was simmering over what had been done to her daughter.

"Neve?" he pressed.

"I know," she said quietly.

"How are you two doing today?" Tim asked, looking at Shane's stitched head, Mickey's new cast.

"Never mind us," Shane said. "How's the owl?"

"Still alive," Tim said, meeting Neve's eyes. He watched the words register—she had been so worried; he saw it in her eyes and mouth, in the almost imperceptible way tension drifted away when she heard the word "alive." She glanced over at Mickey, saw her daughter smile widely. Then, as if smiles could be contagious, Neve turned on Tim the most radiant, illuminated, beautiful smile he'd ever seen.

"Can we see?" Mickey asked.

"Sure," Tim said, opening the door. The two kids hurried inside, but Neve paused. She was dressed in a navy blue down jacket and hand-knit green hat. The colors reminded him of the winter sea: clear, clean, filled with the currents of life. "I'm glad you came," he said.

"Like I said, none of us slept much," Neve said.

"Worried about the owl?"

"And about Shane and Mickey. I'm seeing the danger signs."

"Young love," he said, and he had to force himself from leaning closer, touching her arm, smelling her hair.

"Love with a dangerous boy," she said.

"Don't jump to conclusions," he said.

"About which part?" she asked. "The 'love' or the 'dangerous'?"

He couldn't answer that. They went together, and both words were as loaded for him as they seemed to be for Neve. In some ways, facing Cole Landry had been a whole lot easier than this: he felt heat in his core, and he felt the winter wind blowing his hair.

"What are you doing, standing out here in

a T-shirt?" she asked, lightly touching his left bicep with one gloved hand.

"It's what I slept in," he said, then wondered why he'd said it.

She stared at his chest. The shirt was old, faded, fraying at the collar and sleeves. It had once been bright blue, but now was something closer to gray. The white insignia had once said USS *James*, but it had nearly washed away.

"You really should keep yourself warmer," she said softly, making him shiver more than the sea wind had. He nodded, letting her know he would take her words to heart. Then, holding the door for her, he followed her inside.

Mickey knelt by the cage, eye to eye with the owl. She was so close, it took her breath away. Last night she had held him after he'd plunged, stunned, onto the beach. Today he was locked in a cage. The sight of his injured, dangling wing made her wrist start to throb. She had two long scratches on her face, from where he had attacked her last night. She didn't care; he was the most beautiful bird she'd ever seen.

"I was just trying to help you," she whispered.

The owl stared back, unblinking.

A bowl of water and a piece of raw fish sat in one corner of the cage. Mickey glanced back, over her shoulder, at Mr. O'Casey.

"Has he eaten anything?"

"No," he said.

"He's not going to get better like *this,*" Shane said.

"What do you mean?" Mickey asked. Shane stood right beside her; except for the time he'd spent in the ER, getting stitches in his head, and several hours last night, when he'd slept on their couch, he had stayed so close. Almost as if he was Mickey's self-appointed bodyguard.

"He's badly hurt. Keeping him in a cage won't magically fix his wing. Or his beak. Look, he's not eating, probably not even drinking—right?" Shane asked, glaring at Mr. O'Casey.

"Right," Mr. O'Casey said.

Mickey felt hot tears fill her eyes. Terrible things were happening. Last night was both a blur and a collection of super-clear, indelible memories. When she tried to remember the sequence of everything, she couldn't. But certain moments stood out in stark relief, and she knew she would never be able to wipe them from her mind: the smell and feel of damp scratchy wool as the blanket was thrown around her; the shock of icy seawater; the sight of the U-boat and the white faces; the sound of Shane crying. And still—after all the messages she'd left for him—her father hadn't called.

No one spoke for a few seconds. Mickey just kept staring at the owl, and Shane dropped down beside her. It felt so good to have him here. He leaned into her slightly, his side touching hers.

Last night, after falling asleep, Mickey had had nightmares. She'd dreamed that her bedclothes were the blanket, tangled around her, taking her down to the sea bottom. She'd screamed out, and when she'd woken up, her mother was holding her, and Shane was looking over her shoulder—he'd run up from downstairs, where he'd been sleeping on the couch.

"I saw it," she said out loud now.

"What?" Shane asked.

"The U-boat. When I was underwater."

"Were you that far offshore?" Mr. O'Casey asked. "Because it's a good hundred yards out."

"I couldn't have been," she said, drifting

back, flashes of memory: she and Shane hadn't even been out past the surf break. She remembered coming up for air, having a huge wave crash over her head. "But I saw it anyway. . . ."

"You said you saw the U-boat," Shane said. "And its crew. When I pulled you out."

"I was a little out of my mind, I guess," she said, her gaze returning to the bird. "Worried about the owl and all."

"You had nightmares last night," Mickey's mother said quietly.

"I know," she said.

"I went in to check on you," her mother said. "And I met Shane at the door."

"Sorry," Shane said, and Mickey felt him tensing up, as if he was afraid he was in trouble. "The only reason I went to her room, Mrs. Halloran, was because I heard her yelling."

"Mickey has herself a protector," Mr. O'Casey said. And Mickey could tell from Shane's quick exhalation of breath that he was surprised to hear the ranger sticking up for him.

"Well . . . ," Mickey's mother started.

"We all need protectors," Mr. O'Casey said softly.

Something was going on between the two
adults; Mickey watched tension crackling
between them, as palpable as lightning in a
summer storm. The funny thing was, it
seemed like *good* tension—not like the fighting that went on between her parents, or the
rage she'd felt blazing from Josh last night
after Shane had shamed him by taking the
rock from his hands.

No, if she didn't know any better, Mickey
would say that it was electricity very like
what she was feeling for Shane at this
minute: wildfire pouring off their skin, pushing them apart, pulling them together.

"What are we going to do about the owl?"
her mother asked, still staring at Mr.
O'Casey in that crackling sort of way.

"We're going to let him rest, and hope that
he starts to eat and drink," he said.

"Shane says he won't," Mickey said quietly. "Not if we don't do something else to
help."

"I don't know what else we can do," he
said.

"I know something," Mickey's mother
said.

"What?" Mr. O'Casey asked.

Mickey waited for her mother to reply.

When she didn't, and the silence stretched out, Mickey saw that her mother was gazing at Mr. O'Casey with that weird, annoying infinite patience she had—like when she was waiting for Mickey to come up with the answer herself. Right now she was looking at Mr. O'Casey as if she wanted him to realize something he'd known all along.

"What?" Mr. O'Casey asked again.

"There's a wildlife rehab near Kingston," she said, "that specializes in raptors."

"No," he said. The word sounded like a door shutting hard.

"Yes," she said.

"How do you even know about that?" he asked. "I didn't say anything. Who told you?"

Mickey glanced at Shane. He seemed to be as much in the dark as she was. Her mother and Mr. O'Casey were having a completely over-their-heads conversation that neither one of them understood. But it was loaded; Mickey could tell by the way Mr. O'Casey was backing away, out of the circle around the cage, going to stand all by himself near the window.

"Does it matter who told me?" Mickey's

mother asked. "The point is, the owl needs more help than we can give it."

"Jesus Christ!" Mr. O'Casey exploded.

"You said we all need protectors," Shane said, his tone full of challenge, standing up, leaving Mickey to go stand by Mr. O'Casey.

"Not him," Mr. O'Casey said. "He's not what I had in mind."

Mickey met her mother's eyes, wanting her to explain what was going on. But her mother looked away, her attention caught by something out the window where Shane and Mr. O'Casey were standing. Mickey stood up, looked for herself.

A whole crew of people were spread out over the beach near the jetty—from here they looked like small, dark toy figures. But they were raking the tire tracks from last night, removing the remains of the bonfire, setting up cameras and lights and a tent that even from this distance looked as if it might blow away in the steady February wind.

"Landry's getting ready to make his announcement about the U-boat," Shane said.

"Yeah," Mr. O'Casey said, glaring out.

"If you let the owl die, it's like saying that

everything he does is fine," Shane said. "Him and his son."

"I'm doing my best to keep the owl alive," Mr. O'Casey said, matching Shane's belligerent tone.

"Mrs. Halloran just said there's a better place—a wildlife rehab place. Right?" Shane asked, turning toward Mickey's mother, who nodded. Mickey's heart bumped as she watched them turn into allies.

"Right," Mickey's mother said.

Mr. O'Casey shook his head hard. "You don't know what you're talking about. We're not taking the owl there."

"I will if I have to ride him there on my bike," Shane said, leaving no doubt that he was serious.

"That's okay, Shane," Mickey's mother said. "We'll use my station wagon." Mickey noticed the way Mr. O'Casey kept his back turned, just staring out the window. Staring at the blowing sand, as if Mickey, her mother, and Shane had already left, as if he just wanted to be alone with the sandstorm.

10

Sometimes it had seemed to Joe O'Casey as if the entire world existed on and under the sea; the only part that mattered, anyway. For his brother, the realm of existence had been the sky. Two such different elements—and two such close brothers.

But Damien was dead now, and had been for a long time.

Joe thought of him now, wondered what he would think of the modern technology that was making it possible for one very rich man to raise U-823, haul it to Cape Cod, and turn it into a museum. The man claimed he was doing a public service—removing

the rusty old wreck that snagged fishing
nets and endangered divers and surfers,
opening it so the public could enter and ex-
plore a slice of history. But Joe was too old
to believe PR; the man was doing it to make
a profit, never mind that it was on the bones
of drowned German sailors, and on the
pride of a dying generation of American vet-
erans.

Standing in the barn, he listened to the radio. He knew that the whole thing was being televised. He had a TV in the house. But
he'd grown up on radio, listening to Red
Sox games with his brother. He liked the
way announcers described things, letting
the listener use his imagination to bring the
events alive.

Right now he wished the events would
just cease. How could the United States let
this happen, sell history to the highest bid-
der? The announcer described the scene on
Refuge Beach: the governor was there, one
U.S. senator, an admiral or two, some Coast
Guard commanders . . . Joe pictured the
uniforms, imagined them giving gravity and
a military stamp of approval to the operation.

Townspeople were spread out, all bundled

up against the cold February wind. There were family members—and several of the USS *James*'s crew were on hand. Joe was willing to bet there were no family members of U-823 present. He wondered whether Tim was there. Probably he was. Refuge Beach was a state park, and Tim was the park ranger.

Joe knew how his son felt about U-823. Probably he would be very glad to see it go—good riddance to the wreck Tim blamed for just about everything that had ever gone wrong in his life. Joe glanced over at his workbench. There, above some small cages and a bunch of scattered bird bands, he saw the picture of his grandson, Frank. Tim's only child. There he was in his Marine uniform, a snapshot taken outside of Baghdad. Joe knew that Tim probably blamed Frank's being in Baghdad on U-823.

And maybe he was even partly right. . . .

But that didn't make it okay for Cole Landry to raise the dead, move them to a tidy little berth on Cape Cod, flanked by a clam shack and a bunch of tourist motels.

Joe stood still, looking around the barn. Eyes stared out at him from all the enclosures, and he saw his own breath hanging in the cold air. He felt closer to Damien here than anywhere else, among the birds. Damien had become a flyboy, and Joe had become a sailor—but in some ways, both of them had gone down in flames.

Making his way around the big space, Joe did his work. There weren't enough people trained to keep injured birds alive; Joe had gained a reputation through the years, and people brought him the ones they found. He had a cardinal that had slammed into a wall of glass—the homeowner had hung a feeder of sunflower seeds right by the huge window, for prime viewing—a seagull that had swallowed a fishhook, and a robin that had had a broken wing last summer and now refused to leave Joe's barn, long after the wing had healed.

But mainly he dealt with raptors. That was his specialty—probably because they had been Damien's favorite. As boys they had made it their mission to locate every eagle's aerie in Rhode Island, every fish hawk's nest along the Atlantic coast.

So now Joe had a red-tailed hawk that had eaten rat poison, a great horned owl that had been shot with a bow and arrow, a kestrel that had flown into the window of a passing semi on I-95, a young orphaned long-eared owl, a Cooper's hawk that had lost most of its tail feathers in a beef with a black bear, a turkey vulture that had flown into high-tension electrical wires, a barn owl that had become entangled in a barbed wire fence, and a gray morph screech owl with two broken wings.

At the sound of a car pulling into the yard, he went to the barn door. There was a station wagon with three people and, yep, a cage. Another wounded bird. Joe took a deep breath. He wasn't good at turning people away, but if he didn't draw the line somewhere, he wouldn't be able to give good care to the hurt birds that were already in his barn.

So he walked out into the yard, waving his arms.

"Go away," he said.

They had their car windows rolled up— heat probably blaring out, keeping them warm, but hurting the bird in back. People wanted to help, but they had no idea.

"Go away," he said louder. "No room at the inn."

There were two women—well, one woman and a girl. They looked surprised by his lack of welcome. Maybe even a little offended, hurt. Don't take it personally, he wanted to tell them. But there was a young man in the back seat—all fired up. Joe could see it in his face even before the back door opened.

"What do you mean, 'go away'?" the boy asked, jumping out.

"I mean what I just said. There's no room at the inn."

"This isn't a joke," the boy said.

"I don't mean it to be one."

The boy was about seventeen, eighteen. Tall, lanky, something irreverent about him. Long brown hair, a jacket with some surfboard insignia on it. He didn't have a hat or gloves on; there was a row of fresh stitches along the side of his head. Joe felt the kid taking his measure, knew that he was seeing an old man, pushing eighty-six, six foot four but stooped over, short gray hair, serious frown. Joe knew his frown could scare off even the bravest men, and this kid didn't look all that brave. Tough, maybe—but how brave could a surfer be?

"Think you can find your way out?" Joe asked.

"I told you, we have an injured bird."

"And I told you—no room—"

"At the inn. I know." The kid shook his head—more in disappointment, it seemed, than anger. He turned, shrugged to the girl and woman still waiting in the car.

"What's your problem?" Joe asked.

"You're not what I expected."

"What the hell would you expect? You don't know me."

"I thought I knew something about the guy who sank the U-boat."

"You're a surfer, aren't you?" Joe asked, nodding toward the patch on the kid's jacket. "Surfers and old Navy men don't have much in common."

"Yeah. Turns out you're right about that. I had some other idea."

At that, the kid whipped around, started walking back toward the car. Joe saw the woman register whatever was showing on the kid's face—sulking probably—and she opened her door. Jesus, Joe thought. He really didn't want to have to go through the whole thing again, especially not with someone as pretty as her. She had straight hair that fell across high cheekbones, soft blue eyes, and a huge dose of hope in her smile.

"Mr. O'Casey?" she asked.

"Yes," he said, suspicious. Did he know her? Had his forgetfulness—usually confined to whether or not he'd taken his pills, where he'd put his reading glasses, whether he'd fed the birds or not—spread to the point where he was forgetting that he'd met a beautiful woman?

"The Gray Goose?" she asked, smiling wider.

"That's me," he said, straightening with pride at his nickname.

"We've brought you a new patient," she said. "My daughter and her friend rescued it from the beach last night."

"As I just told your young surfer friend, there's no—"

She took a step closer. He looked into those eyes and saw the smile disappear. For a moment, he saw an expression he remembered from war—the kind of desperation that came from defeat, death, losing that which mattered most.

"Please," she said. "Mr. O'Casey."

He hesitated, aware of the young man stepping a little closer to her, just in case she needed him. That one step did something to Joe, but he didn't let on.

"It's a snowy owl," the woman said, giving

Joe just the out he needed—to avoid the sentimentality he always felt when he saw something that reminded him of Tim when he was younger, back when they were father and son.

"A snowy owl," he said, standing still, looking toward the back of the station wagon. "Such a rare bird for our area. I've only seen one other."

"Please help this one," the woman said.

Joe hesitated, then nodded—in ways this woman and the two kids could never understand, this was exactly what he'd been waiting for. He didn't speak, but followed her to the car, to carry the cage into his barn.

The barn was long and tall, and painted dull red. Inside, the roof rose to a sharp peak paneled with silvery, unpainted pine. A radio was playing, and Neve heard the announcer's low voice talking about Refuge Beach. She also heard the rustling and calling of what sounded like hundreds of birds. Mickey and Shane were already looking around; both walls were lined with tall, deep cages—some so large, they seemed almost to be rooms made of wire mesh.

Each space was occupied by one or more birds. The light was all natural, coming through the cages' far sides—which opened to the outside—as well as a row of clerestory windows along the top of one wall. Hearing wing beats, she looked up and saw a hawk flying along a mesh corridor from one enclosure to another. Neve followed Joe, carrying the snowy owl, to a cage at the far end. It seemed to be the most distant from his work area, and she felt alarmed. She fell back slightly, and he looked over his shoulder.

"What is it?" he asked.

"Shouldn't you keep him closer to your work area? He's so badly hurt. . . ."

"Snowy owls are very shy birds," he said. "I want to put him as far from most of the others as possible, not to traumatize him more than he already is. There's an empty spot down this end."

Neve watched as he opened the door to one enclosure, walked right in with the cage, and set it down on the floor. He opened the door, and right away the owl escaped. Trying to fly, he toppled over, then scuttled into the corner. Joe seemed unfazed, and left the owl, bolting the wire mesh door behind him.

Standing back, Neve met the man's eyes. "Is he going to make it?" she asked.

"Too soon to tell," he said. "But most of these other birds were as badly hurt or worse. That great horned owl"—he pointed up at an owl perched on a tree—a live pine tree—growing out of a pot in an enclosure— "came to me with an arrow sticking out of its chest. Missed the heart by an inch, broke the owl's wing as it went in. The minute I put him in there, he climbed up to the top branch. They're resilient."

"Why didn't you put the snowy owl into a cage that has a tree?" Shane asked.

"He wouldn't use it. Snowy owls don't roost up high," Mickey said softly.

"That's right," the man said, smiling at her. "Where do they roost?"

"On the ground, because the arctic tundra is so flat, and trees don't grow there. That's why they like beaches and airport runways, when they come south."

"You're a smart young woman," he said. "And you know a thing or two about snowy

owls. Here at the rehab we use furniture—
that's what we call trees, branches, cavity
nest sites—for many species, and it all de-
pends on the bird. Forest owls need height
to feel secure. That's why some of these
cages are eighteen feet high."

"You built them?" Shane asked, looking
up.

"My grandson and I," he said. "Long ago,
in a different location, I built the first cages
myself. That was years ago. But the enclosures were too small, I needed more room
because people kept bringing me wounded
birds—from all over New England. So I
moved here—and my grandson helped
me."

"Your grandson?" Neve asked, but the
man didn't respond.

"Are you a veterinarian?" Shane asked,
making even the simplest question sound
like a challenge.

The old man shook his head. "Nope.
Never even finished college."

"Then how can you help the snowy owl?"
Shane asked. "It's so badly hurt, and it
won't eat or drink. . . ."

Neve wanted to put her hand on his shoulder, remind him to be polite. She knew that

he was upset—they'd been unable to locate his mother, and even though he was nearly a grown man, he'd had stitches last night. Kids needed their parents after a visit to the ER—at any age. She glanced at Mickey and Shane, knew they were bonding, partly, over missing parents. But the old man seemed barely to notice Shane's rude tone.

"The most important part of caring for hurt birds is mostly about helping to mend their broken spirits," the man said.

"But . . ."

"That's why these enclosures are so big," the man explained. "Frank helped me build them tall and wide, and we put those flight corridors in overhead, because birds need to make their own choices. As often as possible . . . They need to choose their own territories, select their own roost, choose what height suits them, decide whether they want seclusion or exposure, whether they want to be alone or have company."

"Company?" Neve asked.

"There are several breeding pairs here," he said.

"Really?" she asked.

"Yep," he said. "We've raised a bunch of families in this barn. Another reason for the large spaces—they have to be suitable for young raptors learning to fly. They have to be big enough for the adult males to catch live prey, and for the babies to learn that food moves and fights back."

"That's amazing," Neve said. She felt wonder and admiration, and looked into the old man's blue eyes for signs of Tim. They were there, too. Not just the color, but the spirit—bright, intelligent, in love with nature, wanting to help. What had happened between them?

"Is that why they call you the Gray Goose?" Mickey asked. "Because you know so much about birds, because you've rescued so many?"

He shook his head. "No, I got that nickname long before I started this rehab." He began to walk over toward a long workbench set up in the middle of the barn. "Did you know snowy owls feed on lemmings? That's their—"

"You got it when you were in the Navy, right?" Shane asked. "The nickname?"

"Yep," he said. "A long time ago. I don't like it much anymore."

"Why not?" Shane asked.

"Because the Silver Shark isn't here anymore. He was the one who started it, but what did he know? War nicknames are stupid. They take the curse off what's really going on."

"I thought you were a big war hero," Shane said. "You sank U-823."

"That I did," he said.

"Are you sorry you did it?" Shane asked.

"Sorry I sank an enemy U-boat? That was trying to sink our ships?"

"Yeah," Shane said.

Neve watched Joseph O'Casey frown, go to the workbench, start filling out a sheet of paper. It looked like a standard form; he beckoned Mickey over, and she helped him fill in the blanks. *Where was the bird found? When? Identifying marks? Species?* Neve heard the radio broadcast coming from Refuge Beach, and so did Shane.

"I'm sorry about a lot of things," he said. "That's my right as an old man. Maybe you'll understand when you're my age, and maybe you won't." With that, Cole Landry's voice said, *". . . and we are proud to announce that we will raise U-823 this spring. Even now the crane is en route, on schedule to arrive in Secret Harbor. On April seven-*

teenth, the anniversary of the day the USS James *so bravely fought back the enemy, our team will be in place to hoist the U-boat from the sea bottom and transport it to . . ."*

"April seventeenth," Joe O'Casey muttered, turning off the radio. "God almighty."

Shane opened his mouth as if to protest, but then he just shook his head and backed away, down the row of cages, toward the snowy owl. Mickey followed him, leaving Neve and Tim's father alone.

"I'm sorry about what Cole Landry is doing," Neve said.

"So am I."

"We had blackout shades in my house, when I was growing up," she said. "Left over from World War II."

Joe stared at the silent radio. "All the houses along the coastline did. Lights shining from the houses and town could silhouette ships, making it easier for the U-boats to see and attack them. Kids now can't imagine what it was like. There was no eerier sound than the sirens going off—right here in Rhode Island—telling people to black out their lights and go inside."

"I always wondered why my parents and

grandparents left the shades up so long after the war was over."

"Maybe because it was such an important
event in their lives," he said. "It was, in all of
ours. It affected every single person who
lived in Rhode Island, Connecticut—all
along the eastern seaboard, really."

"And you were patrolling the coast?"

"Yes. I was in the Navy; my brother was in
the Air Corps. We joined up right after Pearl
Harbor."

"Your brother was the Silver Shark?"

Joseph O'Casey nodded. "We sort of
switched nicknames—he wanted to be
called something that reminded him of me,
on the sea, and I was called Gray Goose to
remind me of him in the sky."

"Did your brother die in the war?"

Joe shook his head. "He might as well
have. He came home from the war a different man. I guess I did, too. Just ask my
son." He looked over at Neve, as if willing
her to tell him the truth. "That's who sent
you here, right? Tim?"

"He actually . . ." Neve began, not wanting
to hurt the old man's feelings by telling him
that Tim had tried to stop her from coming.

"Oh, I know he wouldn't come himself,"

Joe said, waving his hand. "Don't try to shield him. He's made it clear how he feels. Not that I don't agree with him, most of the time. He thinks I'm better suited for life with hawks and owls than people."

"I don't know," Neve said, smiling. "You seem okay to me."

Joe gave her a grizzled smile, then went back to filling out the paperwork. As curator of a gallery, Neve knew about logging things in. In her case, it was paintings or drawings or photographs. In Joe's case, it was wildlife. She drifted closer to the workbench, saw that Joe had hung two pictures on the wall behind it. One was a painting of an osprey soaring over a long white beach—and it took her breath away.

"That's an original Berkeley!" she said.

"I collect him," he said. "Or I used to, before his stuff got so expensive."

"I work at the Dominic di Tibor Gallery," she said. "And we're doing a retrospective on him. I'm just writing the catalogue copy now . . . there's so little known about him."

"Yes," Joe said. "He was a man of mystery. But he sure knew how to paint birds."

"That he did," Neve said.

Joe glanced over at her. "What came first?

Your love of his paintings or your love of birds?"

She thought. "Birds first," she said. "That's how I discovered his work. How about you?"

"Same thing," Joe said, glancing up at the small oil. "My brother and I used to run wild through the woods and marshes of South County; when we got older, we'd take the long journey across Jamestown to Newport. We'd hike through the woods that became the Norman Bird Sanctuary. . . ."

"That's where Berkeley painted!"

"Yep," Joe said. "I remember seeing him there, his easel set up, looking out from Hanging Rock, painting a whole flock of sandpipers running along the sand flats below. Pretty inspiring sight."

"What was he like?" Neve asked, knowing she'd just come upon a gold mine.

"Strange," Joe said. "He wore a cape, and a hat pulled low over his eyes. Looked more as if he belonged in Paris than out in the woods."

"Did you talk to him?"

Joe laughed. "Try to talk to Berkeley when he was painting, and he'd go at you with his knife—I knew better than to get between him and his easel. Just made my way around him, and looked for birds on my own. I remember how weird it seemed—to be lost in the woods, listening for thrushes, and suddenly smelling oil paint. You ever heard a thrush? They have the most beautiful song of any bird. . . ."

But Neve was lost in the amazement of hearing about Berkeley. "There's so little information about him. All I know is, he was a Rhode Island native, and he painted birds better—in my opinion—than Audubon and Fuertes . . . and then he suddenly stopped. There were no new paintings after 1942."

"Who knows?" Joe asked. "I guess he just disappeared."

"I always wondered whether he stayed in Europe, maybe even got killed during the war."

"Well, there were plenty of war casualties, that's for sure."

"Yes, you're right," Neve said. She waited for Joe to say more, but he suddenly seemed intent on stowing the snowy owl form in the top drawer of an old wooden file cabinet.

"Hey," Shane called from the other end of the barn. "There's another snowy owl here!"

"A female," Mickey said, sounding excited. "Her plumage is so much darker."

"Like I said," Joe responded, "I've only seen one other snowy owl here in Rhode Island, and that's her. She was wing-crippled a year ago, found on Mansion Beach on Block Island."

"You put our owl in the cage right next to her," Mickey said.

Joe nodded. "Yep," he said. "Snowy owls are shy, but they form bonds with each other. I'm hoping those two will help each other out."

"How will it help?" Mickey asked, her voice thin and full of longing. Neve hung on Joe O'Casey's reply, waiting for what he would say, wanting it to ease Mickey's mind.

Joe stared at Mickey. He looked stern and demanding, his brow furrowed. "You're a smart girl. Don't you know?"

"Because of love," Mickey whispered.

Joe nodded. "Love's what counts in this world," he said. "Even for snowy owls."

Neve's throat tightened, aching so much, she turned away. She faced Joe's workbench; right beside the Berkeley painting hung the picture of a young man in uniform. Short brown hair, wide grin, the same bright blue eyes as Joe and Tim.

"That's my grandson Frank," Joe said, noticing her gaze.

"He looks just like Tim," Neve said. "And they both have your eyes."

"Big family resemblance," Joe said.

"He's in a uniform," Mickey said.

"Yep," Joe said. "Marine. Just like his father . . ."

"Tim was a Marine?" Neve asked, surprised.

"Sure was. A medic in Vietnam. All three generations of O'Caseys served our country."

"He talks like a pacifist," Shane said. "While I'm doing my community service over there at the beach. He told me to move to Canada before going to war. He has some big quote about fathers and sons, and war being hell."

"That sounds like Tim," Joe said.

They all stood by the workbench, a draft of frigid air blowing in through a crack in the barn wall. Neve stared at the picture of Tim's son and felt the hair on her head start to stand up.

"When is Frank coming home?" she asked softly.

"He's not," Joe O'Casey said in a low voice as raptors cawed and called around them, as wings beat in flight through the corridors overhead. "He was killed right when he got to Iraq, drowned when his tank went into the Euphrates."

11

The announcement ceremony was over. April 17 was to be the day U-823 would leave Rhode Island. The choice of date—the anniversary of the battle between the USS *James* and U-823—felt like a kick in the stomach. Tim couldn't even imagine what his father must be thinking. He stared at the waves, knowing that the date was only a month and a half away.

He saw a line of big black cars driving out the beach road, followed by the TV trucks and trailers, imagined that a whole new level of preparations was now under way. The crane was on a ship from France; a work barge had been dispatched from New York;

a team of engineers was planning the operation. Houses were being rented, hotel
rooms booked.

The last of Landry's television crew left
just at twilight; Tim felt a little pressure lift,
his chest expanded, and he knew he had
the beach back again. Throwing on his
jacket, he headed along the sand to check
things out.

A steady breeze was blowing offshore; he
felt the grains of sand stinging his face.
They seared his eyes, and he didn't care. All
morning he'd heard the windstorm whipping the sand around, and he'd taken the
card out, read the letter. He tried not to do
that too often; he wanted to keep it as new
and fresh as possible. He wanted to hear
the voice as if it were actually speaking. And
he wanted to smell his son—or at least
imagine that he could—as he touched the
paper he knew Frank had touched.

Tim had spent the time lying on his bed,
trying to make up for the sleep he hadn't
gotten last night. Easy to blame that on the
snowy owl, on sharing his space with another creature—the first living, breathing
roommate he'd had in quite some time. But
the real reason he couldn't sleep was Neve.

Walking along the tide line now, Tim took huge breaths of salt air. Sometimes a sandstorm made him feel as if he could dissolve—he'd imagine the sand blowing all the way across the world. He'd think of that hot wind, the relentless sun. Tim kept his jacket unzipped, just so the New England cold could touch him and let him know he was still alive.

He looked up ahead, saw that the film crew had left the beach in decent order. The sand was clean; they'd taken all their trash with them. He saw footprints all over and little marks in the sand—from where the lights and cameras had been set. He climbed over the jetty and turned to look out to sea, saw the endless spread of slate-gray water, with waves rearing up and breaking right over the sunken U-boat.

Mickey thought she'd seen German sailors last night. Tim stared out, wondering whether that could be possible. To think that men killed in battle remained with their ships, with their buddies—not so much their bones, but their spirits. Frank was buried in Beth's family plot up in Cranston. But was his ghost still near Baghdad, with the ghosts of his unit, in the submerged ruins of their tank? Tim's heart ached; he didn't want that to be true. He wanted every bit of his son home.

He walked toward the jetty until he reached the beached driftwood log where the snowy owl had been roosting. Sitting down on it, he saw a white feather caught in the wood's silvered splinters. He took it out, smoothed it between his fingers. He was staring at it, wondering how the owl was doing, what Neve had thought of his father, when he heard footsteps in the sand behind him.

"Hi," she said.

"Hi," he replied, without turning around.

"I looked for you at the ranger station," she said. "When you weren't there, I thought I might find you here."

"Yeah," he said. "I came to check on the beach."

"They didn't ruin it?"

"Not yet."

She nodded, and sat down beside him on the log. They stayed there in silence, feeling the wind blow their hair back, listening to the waves crash. After a few minutes, Tim handed her the white feather. She started to take it, but he didn't let go. They held the feather between them, looking into each other's eyes—and suddenly Tim knew she knew. She had a new expression—her eyes were still so pretty, but they were deep and touched with despair. She knew about Frank.

"How's the owl?" he asked, sounding unintentionally harsh.

"Fine so far. Your father has quite an operation there."

"He sure does."

"Tim . . ." she started.

"Don't," he said, putting up his hand to stop her.

Her mouth was wide open, the unspoken words right there; he could almost hear them, could almost hear his own response. How many times had people tried to say they were sorry? How often had he heard expressions of sympathy? *He was such a good boy; he was such a great athlete; he loved the water, he was an accomplished diver, he loved nature, just like his father; he died serving his country; he was a hero.*

Neve stared at Tim. Her eyes were liquid, filled with pure shock—that's what it was. He knew that expression so well. He'd seen it in Beth's eyes a hundred times. All Beth had ever wanted to do was talk about their son, and Tim had just wanted her to shut up and go away. They'd been divorced for three years at the time of Frank's death; she'd been remarried for two. But when it came to Frank, she wanted only to talk to Tim. And he'd say he didn't want to—what was there to talk about? Frank was dead.

And Beth's eyes would fill with tears and shock, just like Neve's right now.

"The snowy owl," Tim said. "Why don't you just tell me what my father said about the bird? Is he going to survive or not?"

"He's not sure," Neve said.

"Well, it'll give him something to do," Tim said. "Trying to save a rare species. *Nyctea scandiaca.* Bet he's never had another of those in that barn of his."

"He has a female right now. She was found on Block Island."

Now it was Tim's turn to be shocked. And it was a good shock, too—the pure surprise, the unexpected thrill, of hearing about a bird you didn't expect to be around. It was nothing like the shock of having your ex-wife call to say there were two uniformed officers standing at her door, or of getting a letter from your son two days after his funeral.

"Well," Tim said, "that's great. He needs some good news, with what's going on with the U-boat. April seventeenth; of all the days to take it away. At least my father must be pretty happy about the owl. Especially the fact it's a male. I'm sure he's thinking about the brood of snowy owls that will be hatching this time next year."

"Tim . . ."

"Every day is Christmas morning when you're a birder. Did you ever notice that?" he asked, gazing up and down the beach, then out at the horizon. "Like now. Look at all these birds: common eider, two species of loon, three species of scoter, there's a merganser, two crested cormorants . . . you never know what to expect. Anything can happen."

"It's true," she agreed, holding the white feather. "You never know what you're going to see."

"Frank was a great birder," Tim said.

"He was?"

Tim nodded, squinting as he looked out over the waves, at a raft of buffleheads. "He birded in Iraq. We didn't get many letters—

he was over there such a short time. But the ones he wrote home were about birds. Crested larks, masked shrikes, European bee-eaters, Eurasian collared doves, house sparrows, common moorhens . . . He wrote about pygmy cormorants half the size of the cormorants he's used to here, at home."

"He sounds like a wonderful boy."

Tim nodded. "Yeah."

"Your father has his picture hanging over his desk."

"I bet he does," Tim said, tensing up. He stared out at the waves, at the cormorants swimming so sleekly along the surface. Their silhouettes were low and black, like small U-boats. When they dived below for fish, he wondered whether they'd see Mickey's ghosts. "I tried to get my father to talk," Tim said. "The whole time I was growing up. I'd tag along with him, trying to help him with the birds, wishing he'd tell me about what happened."

"What happened?"

"In the war. When he sank the U-boat. Kids want to hear about their fathers being war heroes. It was one of the biggest events of his life—and everyone knew about the U-boat. My friends would ask me, and I'd ask him. He told me part of the story once. But only part."

"Maybe the rest was too painful," Neve said quietly.

"Yeah."

They sat still, both staring down at the owl feather.

"He talked about it with Frank, though," Tim said after a minute.

"Why?" Neve asked.

Tim shrugged, as if he didn't know—but he did, and when his heart slowed down a little, he told her. "Time turns war into myth," he said.

"Myth?"

"History lessons. You stop smelling the blood, tasting your own fear, seeing your buddy die beside you, and you're able to tell it like a story. My father couldn't do it with me, because back then he was still living the war inside, every day. By the time Frank came along, time had smoothed out the edges."

Neve waited, listening.

"Frank ate it all up. He'd go over to that barn after school—helped my father build more enclosures, more flight cages. My father must have talked nonstop, all through the hours Frank spent there—because Frank would come home and tell me about what happened right here that cold April day."

"Things you must have wished your father could have told you himself," Neve said.

Tim shrugged as if it didn't matter.

"What did he tell Frank?" Neve asked.

"Oh, about how he and Damien had joined up on the same day, right after Pearl Harbor. About Damien in his silver plane, a B-24 Liberator, flying on daylight missions over Rostock, Karlsruhe, getting shot down on his way back from Dresden, getting rescued by three French sisters who hid him in a barn.

"And about himself aboard the USS *James*, being part of a hunter-killer group going after Dönitz's wolf pack, how U-823 sank the steamer *Fenwick* in the mouth of the Thames River, and how he commanded his men to chase it down and blast it with depth charges and sink it right here—off Frank's own beach, right off the tip of this jetty." He gestured at the crooked, ramshackle structure, sinking into the sand on rusted iron pilings. "My father made it all come alive for Frank, like a big Technicolor

movie of war, bravery, and being a pa-
triot. . . ."

"Your father told me you were in Vietnam."

"That's true," Tim said.

"Your father—" she began.

"Like I said, my father came to see things
differently as time went on," Tim said.
"When I was a kid, it was so obvious that
the war had left him a shell. He'd seen such
horror, and his brother had come back a
zombie. Talented, sweet man—and Damien
wound up having a breakdown. My father
never talked about it—he just . . ." He
paused, not wanting to air his family's dirty
laundry. "Anyway, by the time Frank came
along, my father had cleaned up his act.
The raw pain was gone, so he was able to
take the terrible stuff and turn it all into one
big heroic story. . . ."

"You blame your father for Frank enlist-
ing?"

Tim started to say "No," but he knew that
was a lie. He blamed everyone: himself,
Beth, and his father. If Tim had been a better father, if the divorce hadn't gotten so
ugly, if Frank hadn't taken refuge at the raptor barn, if the war stories hadn't started
rolling . . . Tim stared out at the crashing

waves, the enormous sea. He thought of the sailors Mickey had seen. His father's voice filled his ears.

"You know what my father told *me*?" he asked. "The only time he ever talked about his time in the war?"

"What?" she asked.

"He saw the *Fenwick* get torpedoed. It went down right off New London, its fuel blazing all around the wreck. He saw men swimming through the fire, heard them screaming. They were burning alive. Some of them dived underwater, choosing to drown instead of burn. He carried those screams his whole life. He said he never shut his eyes without hearing them. He told me when I was twenty-one, for one reason—to explain why he never talked, why he was so quiet, why we never had a good father-son relationship."

"By telling you that, he must have been trying to make up for everything. It sounds as if he had PTSD."

"Everyone who goes to war has it. In the Civil War they called it 'soldier's heart.' In World War I, it was 'shell shock.' It doesn't go away, but it gets better with time—if you survive, if you don't kill yourself when you get home."

"At least your father told you something. . . ."

"Yeah. Once." He paused, wondering whether he should tell her his theory. She was looking at him in such an open way, he decided to jump in. "It was Vietnam. We never talked about the war—but when he told me that story, I thought . . ."

"He didn't want you to go."

Tim nodded. "He never would have said that. He was all about patriotism, duty, serving the country, hated draft dodgers, guys who went to Canada or filed as conscientious objectors. But telling me about hearing those screams, I had to wonder."

"You signed up?"

"After college—I had 12 for a draft number. I was going, there was no way out. My father drove me to the train that took me to boot camp. He told me he was proud, that I was joining a family legacy of serving America, that I had to 'keep my eyes on the ball.' Whatever the hell that meant."

"Maybe it meant stay safe, stay alive."

"Yeah," Tim said, glancing over, wondering how Neve could so quickly decipher

O'Casey-speak. "I wonder whether he said the same thing to Frank. I doubt he had to—he could have come right out and talked straight about the war. Frank would come home from the barn, telling me about Grandpa's stories. All about World War II, the thrill of battle, and what happened right here, off the end of the jetty."

"With the U-boat?"

Tim nodded. "Frank said U-823 was personal for my father, because he'd seen what happened to the *Fenwick*. My son was sensitive and perceptive; he'd get that."

"What else did your father tell him?"

"Well, that he was commander of the USS *James*—a destroyer escort, part of a hunter-killer group with two Coast Guard frigates, another DE, and the destroyer *Crawford*. He'd assumed his command very young—that's how it was in wartime. He had an awesome responsibility. . . ."

Neve listened. Tim could almost feel her wanting to steer him back to Frank, to how Frank must have related to a grandfather who had become a naval commander when he wasn't much older than he was, to what had happened to Frank, but Tim couldn't let her. He had to keep talking about his father, because if he didn't, he'd think of his son. Neve being here had somehow brought Frank back, closer to home—and Tim almost couldn't stand it.

"The warships were on their way back to the Charlestown Naval Base, after escorting a convoy of merchant ships to New York City. The *James* just happened to be closest to the *Fenwick* when she was attacked, and right away my father picked up the U-boat on radar, at a distance of about fifteen hundred yards."

"So close," Neve said.

"Yes," Tim said. "He had her compass heading, and he looked at the chart, and he figured she had to be making southeast for a steep shoal, just off Block Island. My father explained to Frank—who explained to me—that typical U-boat strategy was to duck into deep holes and avoid sonar contact."

"So he wanted to head them off . . ."

"That's right. He called the other warships, and they formed a patrol line, three abreast, to start searching the sea. It was a race to keep them from getting to the shoal, getting away."

"Back to Germany," Neve said.

Tim nodded. "The *James* was in the lead, and my father and his crew used everything they had. They had code-breakers, and they used HF/DF—high-frequency direction finding, what they called 'huff-duff.' The *Cubzac,* the other DE, made first contact—sound contact—just a few miles west of here, off Watch Hill. They blasted it with hedgehogs."

"Hedgehogs?"

"Antisubmarine weapons. Small mortar bombs that exploded on contact—instead of working on a fuse, like depth charges. The spigots looked like hedgehog spines."

Neve nodded.

Tim watched her for a few seconds. She stared at the water, and seemed steeled to hear the rest of the story. "It's stupid," Tim said. "Cute names like 'huff-duff' and 'hedgehogs.' You know?"

She didn't reply, or take her eyes off the spot where the waves kept breaking.

"Anyway, after three attacks, the *Cubzac* lost the target. An hour later, my father picked it up—right here. The ships had been continuing their sweep, and my father reestablished sonar contact."

"Right here?"

"Yes. They must have been sitting on the bottom, trying to stay still and silent as long as they could. My father's ship passed too close, and the U-boat commander must have figured it was just a matter of time. U-823 came to the surface, fired ten rounds of three-inch fifty cal at the *James*."

"Was anyone hurt?"

Tim nodded. "Two crewmen. They died here, right off Refuge Beach. No refuge for U-823 after that."

"Your father fired back?"

"Yes, and the U-boat submerged again. My father started dropping a circular pattern of depth charges, all around the bubbles. It didn't take long; that's when oil began rising to the surface. Then charts, and pieces of wood. Finally a German officer's hat. They didn't stop attacking—my father kept it up all through the night, until dawn. Divers confirmed the kill."

Neve was silent, and so was Tim. He stared out at the open water where so many men had died.

"Snow was falling, he told Frank. My father stood on the bridge and looked over here at the beach, and it was all covered in white. It was spring, April. And there was a flock of swans. Hundreds of them, he said. Just huddled in the shallow water along the beach, waiting for the snow to stop."

"Frank told you?" Neve asked.

Tim nodded. He remembered his son recounting his father's moment of glory: his blue eyes shining, his fist pumping as he counted the depth charges. Frank had been so proud of his grandfather—and so had Tim. There were moments, growing up as a child of World War II, when Tim had honestly felt his father had saved the world.

"Your father noticed birds, even at a time like that," Neve said quietly.

"Just like Frank noticed them in Iraq," Tim said, staring at the cormorants.

"Did you . . ." she began.

"In Vietnam?" he asked. But he couldn't reply. Suddenly his throat was too tight, aching. He couldn't tell her about the beautiful marshes, so watery and green, filled with more herons and egrets than he had ever seen. It had seemed horrific to him, ghoulish dissociation, a nightmare, watching birds while people died. But to think of Frank doing it seemed so beautiful. . . .

Neve seemed to understand. She didn't

finish her question, or ask again. She just sat there on the log beside him, holding the white feather. He'd been positive it came from the snowy owl, but suddenly he wasn't so sure. What if it had lasted here all this time, a remnant of that flock of swans here on the beach that snowy spring day in 1944?

"You said you don't like words like 'huff-duff' and 'hedgehogs,' " she said softly.

"I don't," he said. "They fool you."

"They hide the brutality of war," she said.

"Exactly," he said, looking down at her, meeting her clear blue eyes.

"That's what your father said about war nicknames," she said. "Gray Goose, Silver Shark . . ."

"I don't believe it," Tim said. "He and his brother gave those names to each other. He loves them. I'm sure he has one for Frank." Tim stood up, backing away from the log, staring at Neve with narrowed eyes. "And if he told you what it is, I don't want to know. You hear me?"

"Tim," she began.

"I told you—I don't want to know."

"I doubt he has one for Frank," she said in a voice so soft Tim barely heard. Especially because he was running down the beach as fast as he could—away from Neve, the white feather, the jetty, U-823, its crew of drowned sailors, and the memory of his beautiful son.

12

Shane's mother came home that night.
She had been visiting her sister in North
Carolina, and she brought him an American
flag T-shirt from a shop on the base. She
noticed his stitches right away and stiffened
up at the sight of them.

"Got hit by your board again, didn't you?"
she asked, and he could tell she was trying
to control her voice.

Shane was sitting at the table, eating
Cheerios. Mrs. Halloran had fed him well—
dinner last night and breakfast that morning—but he hadn't eaten anything since
then, and cereal was all he could find in the
house. And he felt strange—shaky and

light-headed, from getting hit in the head and learning that the U-boat would be gone by mid-April . . . and from having spent the night in Mickey's house.

"No, Ma," he said. "I didn't."

"You want to surf all winter, fine. But don't expect me to like it! You're all alone down on that beach until summer comes, and what if something happens? Who would help you?"

"The ranger," he said. "Mr. O'Casey."

"Well, he can't be very happy with you. Not after what you tried to do to that trailer. . . ."

"It was a truck."

His mother shook her head, waved her hand. "Whatever it was. You're on probation, doing community service. . . . Are you trying to break *every* law in Rhode Island? Surfing on Refuge Beach is forbidden, and you know it."

"They're not going to arrest me—it's a stupid law, never been enforced."

"It's a law for a reason."

"Everyone does it."

"Everyone is not on probation! Oh, I wish Aunt Corrie and Uncle Brad lived closer. If Uncle Brad got his hands on you . . ."

"He'd make me cut my hair, I know. He'd probably burn my surfboard and walk me down to the recruitment office. I'd be doing push-ups in boot camp if he had his way."

"Well, it's better than getting hit in the head with your board—in the middle of winter, my God, Shane! You of all people should know what can happen—I think it's horrible of you to make me worry about you. I should put you on a bus down to Camp Lejeune right now."

Shane stirred his cereal, took another bite. He tried to read the Cheerios box, just to keep himself sane. His mother was leaning over him now, touching his stitches with cool fingers.

"Why do you do it?" she asked. "Can't you imagine how it makes me feel, seeing you do the same thing your father did, tempting fate in the same way?"

"I'm doing what I love," he said.

"That's what your father used to say. The bigger the waves, the better—he surfed hurricanes, knowing the beaches were closed and South County was being evacuated. He was foolish, Shane. He thought he was so brave and cool, but he wasn't. He risked his life, and look at us now!"

Shane's skin tingled with the thrill of knowing his father had done that, wishing he had known his father better, knowing that he, too, would surf every storm surge that came his way.

"You went in after him," he said, looking up at his mother.

"I was foolish back then, too," she said. "If I'd drowned, you would have lost both parents."

"How come you married a surfer, and Aunt Corrie married a Marine?"

"Because only one of us had any sense," she said, whisking away from the table, opening the refrigerator, putting groceries inside. She must have stopped at the store on the way off the highway.

In spite of the mean way she'd been talking about his father lately, Shane didn't really mind. He knew how she'd felt about him: it was obvious from all the pictures she had of him, hung all over the house. Shane's dad on wave after wave—she must have spent most of their time together sitting on the beach with a camera, trying to catch him at that sweet spot, just as the wave started to curl, sun shining through the water as if it were a piece of perfectly blown blue glass, as if he had found true peace.

"Why didn't you tell me where you were going?" he asked, watching her over the top of the cereal box.

"I did tell you," she said. "What are you talking about?"

"Well, you said you were going to visit Aunt Corrie," he admitted. "But you didn't say you were staying so long, through the weekend."

"Things happen," she said.

"Like what?"

She grabbed a yogurt, slammed the refrigerator door behind her. Rummaging through the silverware drawer for a spoon, she frowned as if nothing had ever frustrated her more—and he knew it wasn't the spoon that was bothering her. It was Shane.

His mother wasn't like Mrs. Halloran. She wasn't . . . well, she wasn't really that mom-like. She was hardly old enough to be the mom of a high school kid, had gotten pregnant when she was only seventeen. She'd fallen in love with his father, eloped down to Cape Hatteras, where swells from a late summer storm were breaking on the Outer

Banks. They'd spent their honeymoon with her throwing up and him surfing monsters.

Now Shane's mother had a business selling jewelry over the Internet; she and her sister made it. Pretty stuff made of silver, glass beads, semiprecious stones, and seashells. Aunt Corrie promoted it down on the base, and it seemed all the military wives bought it for Christmas, birthday, wedding, and shower gifts for one other.

"So, what were you doing down there so long?" Shane pressed. "Something with your jewelry? Did someone have a shower or something?"

"Not exactly," his mother said. She looked over at him, really sharp, as if in defiance. She had blond hair, freckles on her nose and cheeks, wore clothes that came from the same stores his friends shopped in the mall—young stuff like bell-bottoms and peasant blouses. But tonight she was dressed differently—she wore her usual jeans, but she also had on a red sweater that made her look older, more sedate.

"Where'd you get the sweater?" he asked.

"Someone gave it to me. It's cashmere. . . ."

"Who?"

"That major I told you about, okay? One of Uncle Brad's friends. He's very nice, and he wants to meet you."

"Cashmere's expensive, right?" he asked.

"Very." She smiled.

"What do you mean, are you dating him?"

"Yes," she said, sounding defensive. "In fact, I'm going back down there next weekend. You're welcome to come, if you want."

"Is there surfing at Camp Lejeune?"

"It's not far from the Outer Banks," she said. "But for God's sake, Shane! There are other things to do."

"Ma," he began. He stared at her, not knowing what he wanted to say. It wasn't as if she hadn't ever dated before. But usually the guys didn't last. She'd meet them through friends, or on the Internet. She'd joined some dating site, and for a while she was going out nearly every weekend. Shane had never minded—he wanted her to be happy, so she'd stay busy and let him alone about surfing.

But this seemed different. She was traveling interstate. Something about the way she'd glowed when she said "that major." He'd given her a cashmere sweater. This seemed serious in a way Shane hadn't seen before. She looked excited. Her eyes darted toward her computer—he could feel her wanting to get on there and start IM-ing her boyfriend.

"You'll like him," she said.

"Yeah, whatever," he said.

"You will. Aunt Corrie said so, too."

Shane started out of the room. Let his mother go online, he didn't care. His head ached, and the stitches pulled. He'd been about to tell her about Josh hitting him with the log, but now he didn't want to. Let her think he'd gotten hurt surfing—she'd look at the scar and think of his father.

"You weren't foolish," he said, stopping short in the door to his room.

She was already booting up the computer. It made sounds like a whale singing and clicking. But she turned away to look him in the eyes, puzzled.

"What?" she asked.

"To dive into the water and try to save Dad," he said.

"I know," she said. "I didn't mean . . ."

"And it wasn't foolish to fall in love with a surfer."

"Okay, Shane," she said, sounding funny—as if she was past even thinking about it, beyond thinking it was dumb or not. She was wearing cashmere, and she had someone waiting to hear from her.

Well, so did Shane. He grabbed the phone, went into his room, closed the door behind him. Even through the closed door he could hear his mother's fingers clicking on the computer keys. Shane turned on his stereo, blasted the Pixies, dialed the phone. When Mrs. Halloran answered, he turned the music down.

"Hi," he said. "It's Shane."

"Are you home?" she asked. "Did you find your mother?"

"Yeah," he said. "She was visiting her sister. I just . . . forgot."

Mrs. Halloran didn't reply right away. In her silence, Shane could hear her thinking what a loser he was, for forgetting something like that, for having a mother who'd leave him alone for days at a time. She'd never do that to Mickey. But when she spoke again, her voice was quiet and kind, and there was no hint at all that she thought he was a loser.

"I'm glad she's back," Mrs. Halloran said. "It must be nice for her, having a sister."

"Yeah," Shane said. "I guess it is. They have a business."

"What is it?"

"Jewelry," Shane said. "They make it and sell it."

"That sounds really good," Mrs. Halloran said. "Well, I guess you're calling for Mickey. Take care, Shane . . ."

"You too," he said.

He held the phone, listening more to Mrs. Halloran calling Mickey than to *Surfer Rosa*, and stared up at the pictures on his wall. There were shots of his father everywhere. Hotdogging it on a short board; proving twin fins were a viable option in Misquamicut surf; getting spit out of a wave on Refuge Beach. Shane stared at them all, knowing his mother had taken them, knowing that he—their little kid—was probably sitting right there beside her on the blanket as she pointed and shot.

"Hey," he said when he heard Mickey come on the line.

"Hey," she said.

"What're you doing?"

"Homework," she said. "How about you?"

"Nothing much."

"Shouldn't *you* be doing homework?"

Shane didn't reply. He half wished his mother had asked him that question before going online with the major. He stared at a photo of his father smiling into the sun—king of the waves—and wondered whether he'd be giving him grief about schoolwork if he were still alive.

"You're coming back to school tomorrow, right?" Mickey asked.

"Yeah," Shane said. "My suspension's up."

"That's good."

"I guess," he said. "Sometimes I think I should just drop out, spend the rest of the year surfing. The beach and the waves won't be the same once they take the U-boat away."

"April seventeenth," she said, sounding empty.

Shane closed his eyes. It was terrible, knowing the exact date his world would change, the waves would die.

"They can't take it away," she said. "They can't."

"Just because we don't want them to?" he asked.

"Because of the men," she said.

"Why?"

"Because where would their spirits go? They were real, Shane."

What if she was right? he thought. What would happen to his father if the wreck was taken away?

"Don't give up hope," she said.

As he stared at his father's pictures and listened to his mother IM-ing in the kitchen, Shane's chest ached as if he'd just swallowed a wave, and he wondered how Mickey just held on, always believing in the best, expecting the good.

"What do you mean?" he asked. "What's there to hope for? It's a done deal."

"We can fight," she said.

"But how?" he asked.

Mickey was silent, but he could almost hear her thoughts turning.

"Fight a rich guy like Cole Landry?" he asked. "Look at Josh—he's not even going to get in trouble for what he did to you."

"What he did to you, too," Mickey said. "They think everything belongs to them, and they think they're right, even when they're so wrong. That's why we have to stop them."

"Mickey," Shane said tenderly; she sounded so positive and earnest, and she was so optimistic. He wished he could hold her now, soothe her, because he knew how disappointed she would be.

"I keep thinking of Mr. O'Casey—of how he must feel about Frank. Knowing he'll never see him again . . ."

"It's the worst thing in the world," Shane said.

"I know."

"You know what's weird?" he asked, thinking of the strange day they'd had, visiting the old guy at the raptor rehab. "All those broken birds. Some of them will never fly again, and some of them are winging it around the cages as if they're in the middle of the woods. But it's where they all belong; they have their place."

"They do," Mickey said.

"What's our place?" he asked.

"South County, Rhode Island," she said. "Refuge Beach."

"Yeah," he said, nodding. "That's mine."

"Mine, too. I'm glad it's . . ." she began, but stopped as if she couldn't quite finish.

But Shane knew what Mickey meant, even without saying the words: the same place for both of them. She didn't have her father, and Shane didn't have his.

"We're going to fight for it," she whispered.

"How?" he asked, knowing he'd do whatever it took.

She didn't answer, and he closed his eyes, listening to his mother's fingertips dance over the computer keys. He pictured Mickey's green eyes and remembered how she'd felt in his arms. Maybe a place wasn't so much a spot on a map as it was the people who were there with each other.

People and ghosts.

And Shane and Mickey were going to fight for them.

At school the next day, everyone was talking about the TV broadcast. Many kids from their class had shown up on the beach, standing in the background while Mr. Landry and politicians from both Rhode Island and Massachusetts made the big announcement: April 17. It was such a symbolic date—the day the U.S. had nailed the enemy. Also, it worked in terms of the weather; mid-April marked the time when the danger of winter storms had passed and the threat of hurricanes had not yet begun.

It was coming soon. U-823 would be moved to a new location, where it would become a museum for the education and pleasure of millions.

As Mickey walked through the halls, she heard kids talking about it. She tried to block it all out, concentrate on getting to her next class, keeping her eyes open for Shane. But as everyone kept buzzing, she felt the tension build: they were right. April 17 was just around the corner.

After French class, Jenna walked over to find her. Mickey's heart flipped at the sight of her friend; they'd been inseparable since kindergarten, but lately Mickey had felt she hardly knew her anymore. Their last sight of each other had been when Jenna and Tripp had dropped Mickey, Shane, and the owl off at the ranger station.

"How are you?" Jenna asked.

"I'm fine," Mickey said.

"You look good," Jenna said, glancing at Mickey's short green kilt and navy blue sweater, brown boots and green tights.

Mickey didn't reply. That was such a high school girl thing to say—"You look good." It wasn't the way best friends talked to each other, especially after what had happened.

Mickey and Jenna had learned to read together. They had learned to ride bikes,
watch birds, and knit together.

"I have to get to the library," Mickey said.

"No—" Jenna said, grabbing her arm.
"Don't go."

"How was the big TV announcement?"
Mickey asked, her voice shaking.

"It was okay," Jenna said.

"I guess you must have had fun, getting
on TV and all."

Jenna shook her head. As she did, her
eyes filled with tears. She was staring at
Mickey as if she wanted to jump into her
arms, but was afraid she'd be pushed away.

"It wasn't fun at all," she said. "Not without you there. I looked down the beach, and
all I could think about was you not being
there. I kept seeing you getting thrown into
the water that night. It was horrible."

"It was," Mickey said.

"Josh—he shouldn't have done that."

"No, that's for sure," Mickey said, trembling because Jenna sounded like her best
friend again.

"It's just," Jenna said, grabbing Mickey's
arm, "why are you causing trouble,
Mickey?"

"Causing trouble?"

"I know you were upset about the owl and all—but it's more than that. Josh was out of line—he knows it and feels terrible. He'll tell you, if you give him a chance. But Mickey—it's so obvious you're against Josh's dad and his plans."

Mickey closed her eyes. She felt the rush of water all around her, saw the white shapes of German sailors surging out of the wreck.

"You are, aren't you?" Jenna pressed.

"Of course I am," Mickey said. "How can I not be? Jenna!"

"He's doing good—for everybody! Why can't you see that?" Jenna asked.

Mickey held her books more tightly with her good arm. She stared at her friend, wondering why she sounded like an automaton. When had Jenna lost herself, stopped thinking for herself?

"You haven't asked about the owl," Mickey said.

"Will it be all right?"

"I don't know," Mickey said. "We took it to an aviary, behind the university in Kingston. There's this really amazing man who helps wounded birds. The whole barn is full of flight cages. You would have loved it, Jenna. . . ." Or at least the *old* Jenna would have, Mickey thought.

Mickey remembered when they were young, the time they had found a robin's nest in the woods behind Mickey's house— the nest itself was no bigger than a teacup, woven of soft, fragrant pine needles and meadow grass. They'd climbed a tree nearby to look down from a higher branch, and saw three perfect blue eggs inside. Three days later, they heard peeping, climbed the same tree, and saw three tiny chicks.

Soon afterward, they went to the tree and found the nest on the ground, the three baby robins gone. Some predator had gotten to them, and Mickey remembered standing there with Jenna, the two of them holding each other in shock and disbelief. She watched Jenna battling with herself now; she still cared about the old things that had bound her to Mickey, but she was pushing them away. Everything had changed between them.

"Come to Washington," Jenna said, gripping Mickey's good hand, making her almost drop her books.

"I can't," she said.

"It's our class trip," Jenna said. "We'll stay in a hotel—it'll be one big party."

"Who cares?" Mickey asked. "There are things to take care of up here!"

"Like what? The owl? The stupid submarine? Mickey, come with us—see the cherry blossoms, see the Smithsonian—I'm sure there'll be birds, too. You can see the migration."

"You still care about the migration?" Mickey asked, feeling love for the old Jenna.

"I don't know. I guess," Jenna said. "But the important thing is, we'll have fun. You need to get away from here—you're all upset about everything that's been going on. . . . And Mick, I don't think hanging around with Shane is very good for you."

"What are you talking about?"

"He's just an antisocial misfit."

Mickey stared at her, remembering the feeling of Shane's strong arms around her, dragging her out of the surf; the sight of blood pouring from his head after he'd defended her against Josh.

"He's my friend," Mickey said.

"I love you, Mick," Jenna said. "I always

will—you know that. But you've been changing. Shane West's a bad influence on you. To be honest with you, I don't think your dad would approve of you hanging out with a guy like that."

"A guy like what?" Mickey asked. "A guy who'd stand up to the rest of the school for something he believes in?"

"Tell yourself that, Mickey. But he's just one step away from being a dropout. Josh was wrong to get so angry that night. But at least he has a future—and parents who care about him. He made a mistake, but he'll be fine. Shane won't. He stayed back once. Now he's just treading water to make it through school, and then he'll be lost to the beach. I just hope he doesn't take you with him. . . ." She paused, glaring at Mickey. "You know why Josh got so upset that night?"

"Why?" Mickey asked, shaking.

"Because he wants you to think the U-boat museum is cool."

"What are you talking about?" Mickey asked.

"Think about it. Josh threw you in, right? You know what it's like around here—why do boys throw girls into the water?"

"You're kidding," Mickey said.

Jenna shook her head. "No, I'm not."

Glancing across the room, Mickey saw Josh Landry leaning against a desk, giving her a long look. Jenna had asked: *Why do boys throw girls into the water?* She and Mickey had a lifetime of playing on long, pristine Rhode Island beaches, tussling with boys at the water's edge, pretending to fight back as the boys dragged them into the surf, and Mickey knew the answer:

Boys threw girls into the water when they liked them.

"That's ridiculous," Mickey said softly. "Not in February. It wasn't just throwing me in; he could have killed me."

"He didn't mean to, Mickey. Talk to him."

Mickey shook her head. "That'll never happen. If Shane hadn't been there, I would have drowned."

"I know what Josh told Tripp; if you showed any interest at all, he'd break up with his girlfriend so fast . . ."

"I have no interest in him at all, Jenna," Mickey said. She gazed into her friend's eyes, and felt that maybe this was the saddest part of what was happening to their friendship: didn't Jenna know who she was? "After all this time, how can you think I'd like Josh Landry?"

"You should talk to him sometime. You'd find out what he's really like. . . ."

"He showed me what he's like that night," Mickey said quietly. Josh was staring at her right now, as boldly as if she were an object, a car, as if she didn't have eyes or feelings, as if he didn't care whether he was making her uncomfortable. He was probably used to getting whatever he wanted. She thought of the arrogance of his father setting a date for taking the U-boat away. Mickey stared back at him, turned to Jenna.

"You can tell him something for me," Mickey said.

"Sure—what?"

"That he's a creep," Mickey said, trembling. "For what he did to me and Shane, and to the owl. And for moving into our town, him and his father . . . and just thinking that our history doesn't matter."

Jenna didn't reply, and Mickey ran down the hall to leave her to decide whether or not to pass the message on to Josh. Mickey didn't really care if she did; her words had been more for Jenna, anyway.

When she got to her locker, she found

Shane waiting there. He stood still, leaning against the wall, grinning as she approached. Shane had a shy, mysterious smile that he didn't use very much, so seeing it made her feel special. He was tall, lanky, with that messy brown hair looking windblown even here in the school corridor. His face was tan, windburned, with a track of dark stitches beside his right eye.

"Hi," she said. "You're back in school."

He nodded, gazing down at her. His eyes were dark blue, the color of ocean waves at night. They sparkled with secret light. She wanted to stand on tiptoes, just to get a better look at his eyes.

"You're shaking," he said, touching her arm.

"I'm fine," she said.

People walked by, staring at them. Mickey saw a few kids who'd been at the beach Saturday night—but even those who hadn't been seemed to have heard about it. She blushed, turning away so they couldn't see her face.

"Everyone's whispering," he said.

"I know," she said.

"I should just walk out," he said. "Go back to the beach . . ."

"No," she said, shaking her head. "You should stay right here."

"I don't know," he said, looking around.

"There's something we have to do," she said, taking his hand.

He looked down at her, surprised. "What is it?"

"Remember I said we have to fight?"

"Yeah," he said. "It's all I've been thinking about."

"Come on—let's go to the library. I know what we're going to do, and I'll tell you when we get there."

13

Tim had a dream of Neve. They were sit-ting on the beach, right on the driftwood log where they'd been side-by-side two days ago. Tim could feel the frigid cold air swirling around them, blowing off the sea. He put his arm around her, drew her closer, wanting to kiss her. His lips brushed hers, and he felt such hot, imperative yearning, he thought he might melt through his skin into her. Just then, he saw the feather: the white feather he'd given her to hold.

"He flew so far from home," Neve said.

"From the Arctic," he said.

"Not the owl," she said, holding his gaze. "I mean Frank."

"We don't say his name," Tim said.

"Then you must write it," Neve said. Suddenly, the way things do in dreams, the white feather morphed into a quill. He took it from her, knelt down in the powdery sand, and began to write over and over: *Francis Joseph O'Casey, Francis Joseph O'Casey, Francis Joseph O'Casey . . .*

Tim filled the beach with his son's name. He concentrated on every letter, writing with perfect penmanship. He didn't want the quill to slip, didn't want to make a mistake. If he did it right, would it bring Frank back?

He wanted to look up, to ask Neve, but he was afraid that if he did, the wind would blow and erase what he'd written. Then all would be lost. As he continued writing he saw shapes out of the corner of his eyes, behind him, down by the water. The shapes were bright white, but ephemeral, like whitecaps, like sea foam being blown off wave tops by the offshore breeze.

But deep down he knew they were the spirits Mickey had seen. It was broad daylight, and the crew of U-823 were coming out of the water—leaving their grave, advancing toward him. April was approaching, the time was short; they needed his help, but he couldn't stop writing. If he paused, even for a second, the wind would erase Frank's name. Just then the sand began to blow, and he heard the music of the beach. Still, he kept writing.

Francis Joseph O'Casey, Francis Joseph O'Casey . . .

Tim moaned, and woke himself up. He sat bolt upright in bed, sweating. He glanced toward the drawer, couldn't open it. He covered his eyes—the sun was already up, bouncing off the waves. He climbed out of the bed, ran to the front of the house. He threw open the door, stood on the porch.

The beach spread out, miles in either direction. Tim's heart was pounding as he ran down onto the sand. It felt ice cold on his bare feet, but he didn't even notice. He looked left and right, up and down the whole length of barrier beach. Frank's name wasn't there. He stood there dumbly, knowing it couldn't have been, feeling shocked all the same. In the dream it had felt as if he could bring Frank back . . . if he only did the right thing, if he covered the beach with his son's name . . . His wonderful boy, the best swimmer Tim had ever known—drowned in his tank, unable to escape.

Walking inside, he felt numb. That was nothing new. Feeling alive these last days, since meeting Neve—that had been strange. This was familiar. He made coffee, took a mug over to the window. Looking out, he saw a fishing boat beating in slow circles over the wreck site. He didn't recognize the trawler, assumed she wasn't one of the regulars, had gotten her nets tangled on the periscope, the conning tower, the deck guns. Didn't fishermen read their charts? Another loss of fishing equipment, adding up to who knew how much: more ammunition for the U-boat museum people to fight the battle they'd already won. Supposedly the big crane was already on the way to Secret Harbor.

What did it matter, anyway? Who cared what happened? How could a great swimmer drown? Tim imagined him trapped, just knowing that if he had been able to get out, he'd have found a way to swim free. . . . Tim held his coffee mug, felt the heat warming his fingers. They'd gotten so cold—not just now, outside on the beach, but in his dream . . . holding on to that quill pen, writing in the sand for so long. It was as if his body didn't know the difference between a dream and reality.

Tim had lost track.

"Mickey, you're going to miss the bus," Neve said, calling down the hall, rushing to get ready for work. The catalogue had to go to the printer's that morning, and she still had a few details to straighten out. She'd been awake until late last night, polishing the text, laying out the photos of Berkeley's work, noticing that several of his blue heron, sandpiper, and plover paintings looked as if they might have been set in the Salt Marsh Refuge.

"I know," Mickey said, walking into the kitchen. She wore jeans and a blue sweater, and she carried her ski fleece and winter hat. Neve glanced over, wondering why her daughter looked more ready for a nature walk than school.

"Hurry up," Neve said, opening the refrigerator door to hand Mickey her lunch—leftover chicken, fresh cranberry sauce, and sprouts on seven-grain bread, one of Mickey's favorites.

"Thanks," Mickey said, stuffing the brown

bag into her lightweight backpack—not her regular school bag. Still, she wasn't moving fast, didn't make any moves to pull on her coat, kiss Neve, run for the door.

"What's going on?" Neve asked.

"I'm waiting for Shane," she said.

"Shane? Why is he coming over now? Mickey, go get on the bus and tell him you'll meet him at school!"

Mickey shook her head, rummaging in the closet, coming out with her bike helmet. "We have a plan," she said.

The words stopped Neve dead in her tracks. When Mickey had a plan, nothing could deter her. Just then the school bus came around the corner; Neve heard its brakes as it slowed down, paused for Mickey, then took off again without her.

"Don't worry," Mickey said. "I have two free periods first thing this morning. I won't miss anything, and I'll be there in time for English."

Shane came wheeling into the driveway, kicked his bike over, and ran up the kitchen steps. Mickey had the door open even before he could knock, and even though he was sweaty and out of breath from riding, he looked so relaxed and relieved to be in her presence. Neve watched them standing there, six inches apart, each glowing at the sight of the other.

"Sorry if I'm late," he said. "I had to put air in my tires—"

"That's okay," Mickey said, smiling as if he'd just said he'd planted her a secret garden.

"Good morning, Mrs. Halloran," he said, spotting her.

"Hi, Shane. You rode your bike all the way here from your house—before school?"

"I'm going to get my car back on the road," he said. "It's just that it never runs right in the winter—the battery keeps going dead. So I thought I'd wait till spring, then get it fixed once and for all. The surf shop reopens then, and that's where I work, so . . ."

"Great plan," Mickey said, pulling her coat on, handing Shane a corn muffin, hurrying over to kiss Neve goodbye.

"Where are you going?" Neve asked.

"We have an important errand," Mickey said. "It can't wait, which is why we're doing it before school. But don't worry—we'll get there in time for class. . . ."

"I asked you where you're going," Neve

said, knowing she was being railroaded. Knowing Mickey the way she did, she had the feeling this had to do with the owl. Did they plan to visit the rehab barn? "You can't ride up to Kingston. For one thing, it will take too long, and for another, those back roads are too dangerous—with all the sand and salt, your bikes could skid, or . . ."

Mickey's eyes looked desperate, as if she really thought her mother was going to stop her from what mattered most in the world. Neve watched her start to turn away. She had heard Mickey on the phone last night, leaving another message for Richard. Neve had even called Alyssa, seeing if she could track him down, but he was still missing in action.

"We're not going to see the owl, Mrs. Halloran," Shane said. "Tell her, Mickey."

"We have something for Mr. O'Casey."

"Honey, I just said I don't want you going to the barn."

"Not *that* Mr. O'Casey! His son—at the beach. The ranger . . ."

"What do you have for him?" Neve asked, feeling surprised. Why hadn't Mickey mentioned anything to her about this? Her last sight of Tim O'Casey had been of his back, running away from the driftwood log.

"Something about the beach, and the U-boat," she said. "That he needs to know, to stop the Landrys."

"Mickey," Neve said gently, knowing that her ghost dreams had continued. "I know it's all been so upsetting. But honey, the deal is done; Cole Landry is bringing the crane here to take the U-boat away."

"No," Mickey said stubbornly. "We're going to stop it."

"Mickey—"

"With Mr. O'Casey."

"Well, he's the park ranger—he's taking care of things the best he can."

"He needs our help," Mickey said. "And we need his. If we don't leave right now, we *will* end up being late for class. . . ."

Neve glanced at her desk, in a corner of the kitchen. She was worried about the catalogue. It would contain many beautiful images of Berkeley's work, but so little biographical information on the artist himself. She had to accept that—spending a few extra minutes right now wouldn't make his life story suddenly appear. Bundling what she had into her briefcase, she grabbed her coat from the closet.

"Come on, I'll drive you," she said.

"You don't have to," Mickey said.

"I want to," Neve said.

The kids climbed into the station wagon, Mickey in front, next to her mother, and Shane in the back. Neve waited for Shane to load his bike into the way-back; when he didn't, she realized that he wanted to come back for it later. She hesitated. That meant Shane would come back with Mickey on the bus, be here with her alone while Neve was at work.

"Your bike, Shane," she said, staring into the rearview mirror, meeting his eyes.

"Mom, he'll pick it up after school!" Mickey said, sounding outraged.

"That's okay," Shane said, climbing out of the back seat, going around to get his bike. In the two seconds Neve had looked into his eyes, she knew that she and Shane had come to an understanding. She had put him on notice, and he had accepted the terms.

Mickey was furious, and she really had no idea of what had just gone on. Neve sat there, the car idling, while Mickey shook her head angrily.

"I don't know why you're acting like this," she said to Neve.

"No boys at the house while I'm not home," Neve said, knowing they were at a milestone: the first time they'd had this conversation. It wouldn't be the last, she thought, glancing over at her daughter.

"Nothing's going to happen!" Mickey said.

"That's right," Neve said mildly as Mickey exhaled with frustration. She waited for Shane to climb back in before putting the car in gear, driving toward the beach.

They headed south on the winding country road, past bare tree branches tossing in the wind. Morning sun shone through them, throwing patches of light on the road. Neve mentally reviewed the papers she'd thrown into her briefcase, hoping there was enough material for a good catalogue. She wanted Dominic di Tibor to be impressed enough to give her a raise; it had been over a year since her last, and without Richard's child support, she was getting worried about bills.

The kids were passing papers back and forth to each other, obviously getting a sheaf together. It reminded her of what she'd been trying to do with the catalogue.

"What do you have there?" Neve asked.

"Just something we found for Mr. O'Casey," Mickey said enigmatically, her cool tone suggesting payback for Neve's being strict about Shane.

"I know, you mentioned that it's to help him with the beach and the U-boat. What's it for, though?" Neve asked.

"I told you—we're going to stop Mr. Landry."

"We want the U-boat to stay where it is," Shane said from the back seat.

"And we think this will help Mr. O'Casey persuade the state that it should," Mickey said.

Neve gave Mickey a look, letting her know that her patience was wearing out, and was rewarded with an excited smile; Mickey had never been able to hold things inside for very long.

"Okay, it's names of the U-823 crew," Mickey said. "We figured that if we could make everyone realize that they were real people, with real families, that it would make everyone think twice."

Neve glanced over, catching her daughter's emotion. "What do you think that knowing their names will do?" she asked.

"It will make people think," Mickey said quietly, staring at the papers in her lap, "that real lives were lost."

Neve felt a rush of pride for her sensitive daughter. She drove across Route 1, down the shore road that led to Refuge Beach, past all the closed-up summer houses. The kids talked quietly with each other, leaving Neve out. She didn't really mind; she was always touched by the way her daughter's heart and mind worked. Especially now, with how worried she was about Richard, Mickey's thoughts were for others.

She pulled into the parking lot and had barely stopped the car before the kids jumped out, ran up the steps to knock on the ranger station door. She kept the car running, the heat on. Her hands were on the wheel, and she watched the door with as much anticipation as she imagined the kids felt. In spite of Tim O'Casey's unpredictable demeanor toward Neve, he'd been completely kind and attentive to Mickey. But it was early—would he be up? Would he mind being disturbed without a call first?

The door opened, and she saw him standing there—in T-shirt and sweatpants, just like last time. His hair was tousled, as if he'd already been out in the wind. He broke into a grin at the sight of the kids, and Neve was shocked to see it getting even bigger as he gazed across the parking lot, spotting her. He waved.

Neve waved back.

He motioned her to come to the door, but she shook her head.

She held on to the wheel, watching Mickey and Shane handing him the papers they'd put together, pointing enthusiastically at one sheet in particular, seeing him bend closer to read. He seemed completely absorbed in what he was looking at; Neve was mesmerized by his shoulders. They filled his navy blue T-shirt, were so lean and muscular, and the longer she stared at them, the more she forgot about the fact she was going to be late for the printer.

Glancing up from the folder, Tim put his hand on Shane's shoulder, said something to both him and Mickey, and started toward Neve's car. She sat up straighter, met his eyes as he walked over. He moved slowly, almost laconically, which struck her as odd, considering he had bare feet and the temperature outside was hovering around thirty-eight degrees. She rolled down her window.

"They missed the bus so they could deliver that to you," Neve said.

"I'm glad they did," he said.

"Mickey really wants to stop Landry."

"I know."

"Do you think there's a chance?"

He shrugged, then shook his head. "How can there be? There's not enough time. The crane is on its way already."

"Will you look at what they brought?"

"Of course," he said, glancing over his shoulder at Mickey and Shane. Then, leaning on the door, he turned back to look at her through the open window.

"Aren't your feet freezing?" she asked. "Why did you walk over here barefoot?"

"I wanted to see you."

Why did those words hit her so hard? She felt a lump in her throat, blinked against the stinging wind. When she didn't reply, he went on.

"I dreamed about you last night," he said.

"You did?" she asked, surprised. "After our last time together, I thought you'd probably never want to speak to me again."

"Because you brought up Frank," he said.

"My dream . . . well, it sort of addressed that. I'm sorry for running off the other day."

"That's okay," she said. Then, because he wasn't moving, and because the kids were still standing at his kitchen door, organizing their folder, not even looking over, she glanced up, stared right into his eyes—they were the color of the winter sea, and the expression was just as turbulent. "What was your dream?" she asked.

"I'll tell you about it," he said. "If you'll have dinner with me."

"Dinner? I—"

"Tonight?" he asked.

"I . . . I have to finish a catalogue for work," she said. "It has to get to the printer, and there's a deadline. . . ."

He stared at her hard, with those stormy-sea eyes of his, and somehow she knew he knew she was lying—by tonight the catalogue would be put to bed, she'd have finished her work, there would be no better time to kick back and have dinner with a friend.

"Maybe another time, then," he said.

"Yes," she said, blushing as he stared at her. He saw right through her, she was sure. His gaze softened, and his mouth turned up

slightly. Was he amused by her nervousness? What was wrong with her? Why
couldn't she just tell him she'd made a mistake, she could do it after all?

"I should get the kids to school," she said
instead.

"Okay then," he said, waving Mickey and
Shane over to the car. They tore across the
lot, and Neve saw the way Mickey looked
up at Tim, her eyes glowing.

"Do you think it will help?" she asked,
breathless.

"I don't know. I wish I could say yes, but
the permits have already been granted,
everything's in motion, and the time is getting really short."

"Please just look at it?" she asked.

He smiled gently, and Neve could see him
not wanting to get Mickey's hopes up. "I
will," he said, tucking the folder under his
arm.

"It was Mickey's idea," Shane said. "But if
it works out, do you think we could count it
toward my community service here at the
refuge?" He broke into a grin.

"We'll discuss that later," Tim said. He
turned back to Neve. "I have a question—
what's your catalogue about?"

"Berkeley," she said. "The bird artist. He was . . ."

But Tim just nodded, a slow smile tugging the corners of his mouth. While the kids were busy getting into the car, he said softly, "You sure you don't want to reconsider dinner? I could tell you some things about his bird paintings you might not know. . . ."

"Really?" she asked, feeling excited. "Refuge Beach—this is where he did his blue heron and least sandpiper paintings, right?"

"Maybe," he said. But he smiled, and she knew she'd guessed correctly. Berkeley had painted right *here.*

"I'll take a rain check," Neve said, giving him one last look, then starting to back out of the lot. As tempted as she was to hear what he might say, her real deadline was in about thirty minutes. She had to have everything at Drummond Printers by nine, so they could get started and have the catalogue back in time for the show opening.

"Did Mr. O'Casey just ask you out to dinner?" Mickey asked, sounding surprised and slightly disapproving.

"Yes," Neve said, giving Mickey a glance. She hadn't dated since the divorce, so neither one of them had ever had to react to something like this. "But I'm not going."

"Mom, I just heard you give him a rain check," Mickey said.

"You should have dinner with him," Shane said from the back seat.

"I don't think she should!" Mickey blurted out.

"That's because you don't know the joys of Internet dating, the Marines, and having your mother tell you she's moving to Camp Lejeune."

"Your mother's moving to North Carolina?" Neve asked, looking at Shane in the rearview mirror.

"Looks like she might," he said.

"Really?" Mickey asked.

"Seems that way," Shane said.

Neve just drove faster, anxious to drop the kids off so she could get to Drummond in time, wondering all the while what Shane's mother's move would mean for him. Glancing at her daughter's thoughtful face, she wondered whether Shane would go with his mother, and what that would mean for Mickey.

14

Neve made the deadline and opened the gallery right on time. Dominic di Tibor arrived several minutes later, bearing a small silver thermos and two porcelain demitasse cups. He pulled his black cape off with a flourish, left it draped on the back of a green leather armchair. But he left his beret on as he stood at Neve's desk, pouring strong black coffee for them.

"The Berkeley show will be a smash," he said.

"It will," she agreed, amused because only her boss could make a relatively small art exhibit sound like a Broadway musical.

"And we need it to be even more of a smash," he said.

"We do?"

He nodded enigmatically. "I have a good feeling about this exhibit, Neve. Berkeley's time is coming round," he said. "People love birds and bird art; that is undeniable. Look at Audubon. Even clods who would never set foot in an art gallery love his paintings of . . . robins, eagles, and the like."

"That is true," Neve said. "When 'Audubon's Aviary'—small segments of the watercolor collection—are shown at the New York Historical Society, our local nature groups sponsor bus tours down to the city."

"Bus tours," Dominic said, gritting his teeth, as if she'd said "flogging." Sipping his coffee, he recovered. "The point is, Berkeley inspires a cultlike devotion. From nature lovers, yes. But also from people who love miniatures, who revere delicacy, whose imaginations are captivated by flight . . . did you know Berkeley wore a cape because he thought it was the closest a human could get to having wings?"

"I know that's one theory," Neve said, wanting to gently dissuade him.

"Well, he *was* the local birdman," Dominic said.

"Yes, but he also spent time in New York and Paris. It's thought he started wearing a cape there, that someone, maybe a lover, gave it to him . . . and he brought it home to Rhode Island, and wore it on his painting sojourns before returning to France—more as inspiration than anything else."

"Oh, you little know-it-all," Dominic said with affection.

"It's in my essay . . ."

"Darling, I can't wait to read it. When will the printers have proofs?"

"In a day or so," Neve said.

"Excellent. You know, and you must never tell a soul, not even after I'm dead and my biographer comes scratching on your door—but he's the reason I wear a cape."

"Berkeley?"

"Of course. I want people to think I adopted it during my years in Rome, but no—it started right here, in my home state. Growing up in a backwater is never easy," Dominic said. "Trust me. Life in Central Falls was less than scintillating. Surrounded by mills and mill workers, all my aunts and uncles, when the biggest excitement was going to Federal Hill for Caserta's pizza on a Friday night—I took comfort in knowing that Berkeley had lived in our little state before I. Sweeping down Thayer Street, buying his painting supplies, wearing that cape . . ."

"It's as if he put it on and became someone else," Neve said. "Artist as superhero. He left whatever real life he was living to become 'Berkeley.' Do you know, I called every single person named Berkeley listed in any of the Rhode Island directories, and not one of them claimed him as a relative? Some had never even heard of him, and many told me their families had been here for generations."

"Well, darling—that's the other reason Berkeley has such a cult following. He's a mystery. So few artists are, these days. Everyone has a press agent. . . ."

"Not Berkeley."

"I hope you've accented the mystery— that will get people in the door. I've been talking to a producer from public television, and there's interest in doing a documentary with our show as the focus. You know, a sort of quest: who *was* Berkeley?"

"Anonymity as a marketing tool," she said quietly.

"It will up the prices of his work," Dominic said, all humor gone, a trace of worry in his eyes. "And that's what matters. To be honest, I would kill to know his true identity. If only we could unveil it here, at our show. Imagine!"

"Yes, you're right."

"The prices would skyrocket."

Neve stared at a tiny watercolor of a tern; beautifully framed, it was leaning against the wall, ready to go up for the exhibit. Dominic was right—after this show the value of Berkeley's work in private collections would increase dramatically. Thinking of money, she knew she had to make her move.

"Dominic," she said, "there's something I need to discuss with you."

"What might that be?"

"I've been working here for seven years now, and since last year, after Adele left, I've pretty much been doing everything— mounting the shows, preparing the catalogues, selling the work." She sat up straight, gazing at Dominic, but keeping sight of Mickey—the school photo propped on the corner of her desk, behind the piles of books and paper.

"Yes, love—you're a godsend," he said.

"Thank you," she said. "I was hoping—"

His cell phone went off; extracting it from the front pocket of his black jeans, he held up one finger. "*Un momento,*" he said.

Neve's heart was racing. Staring at Mickey's picture now, she wondered whether she should explain about Richard—Dominic had never liked him, thought he was slick and insincere. But Dominic never wanted to get too involved in his gallery employees' personal lives. Besides, Neve didn't want him to feel sorry for her; she wanted a raise because of her work, not because Mickey's father wasn't coming through.

Closing her eyes, listening to Dominic speaking to someone about renting a villa in the South of France next summer, she pushed his voice away. She kept Mickey's picture in her mind, but there was something else as well: Tim's voice. She could hear him—all the way back, right at the beginning, there with her at the hospital, caring about Mickey, caring about both of them. She could do this—she knew she could.

Her eyes flew open—what was this about? Leaning on Tim O'Casey for support while she asked for a raise, when she hadn't even wanted to have dinner with him? She shook her head, coming back to reality.

Dominic clicked his phone shut, stepped closer to the desk.

"Bastards," he said. "They promised me first refusal on a place in Beaulieu, and now they have given it to a skinny movie star— one of those girls with painfully little talent but an absolutely riveting love life. The priorities of people these days!"

"I need to ask you—"

"What I need is to get to the South of France," he said. "I have a line on a private collection of Cocteau's mermaid drawings, and I'll need the summer to make the deal. Frankly, we need the money."

"The money?"

"Yes, love. It takes money to make money. I have to spend so I can earn, acquire so I can sell, *comprends-tu*? That's why the success of this show is paramount. It has to finance my mission, so to speak."

"Dominic, the thing is—"

"Anyway, I'm sorry, darling. I must run. We'll talk more about whatever it is you want to talk about. Soon! Ciao, love!"

Leaving the thermos and cups for her to

wash, Dominic grabbed his cape and was already dialing a new number on his cell phone before he was out the door. Neve watched him cross the narrow, windblown street, climb into his ice blue Jaguar, and drive away.

Five minutes later, standing at the sink, Neve heard the bell over the door sound again. She leaned back, saw Chris Brody entering the gallery.

"Did I just see Dominic driving out of town?" Chris asked, coming back to kiss Neve.

"Yes," she said. "Escaping."

"Escaping what?"

"Me. I was right in the middle of asking him for a raise, and suddenly he had to take a call—his villa rental fell through. He has to spend to earn. Do you know, that place would have cost more for the summer than what I make in two years here?"

"How much?" Chris asked. "Enquiring minds want to know!"

Neve just shook her head—more with derision than discretion.

"How did a boy from Central Falls get so rich?" Chris asked.

"He married a countess," Neve said. "And she didn't have a prenup."

"Social-climbing gold digger!" Chris laughed.

"There are times I wonder—really ask myself—what the hell I'm doing here. It's like life in a cartoon. Berkeley's paintings are so ethereal, not of this world, yet so down to earth—and Dominic is such . . ."

"An asshole. Let's get him back here so you can kick his butt and make him pay you a decent wage."

"I was ready," Neve said. "I was completely inspired. You should have heard me . . ." She trailed off, and Chris noticed the look in her eyes.

"What inspired you?"

"Mickey," Neve said. "But something else, too . . ." She hesitated, not sure whether to mention it, even to her best friend.

"The sure knowledge that someone who would pay that much for his summer vacation could afford to pay you another two dollars an hour?"

"No," Neve said. "Tim O'Casey."

"Ranger man?" Chris asked, clapping her hands. "Thank you, God! My friend is coming out of her coma!"

"Coma?"

Chris nodded. "The one Richard put you in. You've been in love-seclusion ever since the divorce. And now this stuff with the child support . . . Why *would* you ever trust men again? That's why I'm so glad to hear this about the ranger."

"Don't get carried away," Neve said, drying the demitasse cups, placing them with the silver thermos on a shelf behind Dominic's large cherrywood desk, then heading over to her own.

"Tell me about the inspiration," Chris said, calming herself down, sitting in the chair beside Neve.

"He's very steady," Neve said, trying to bring back the feelings she'd had while facing Dominic. She'd thought of Tim's strength and reserve, his conviction, and the way he so quietly championed Mickey. The way his eyes had looked when they'd talked about his son . . .

"Steady: the opposite of Richard."

Neve nodded. "That's part of it, probably. I'm reacting to what's been going on there."

But Chris shook her head. "No," she said. "I don't believe this is just a reaction. Neve, when you were reacting, you were in shut-down mode. Richard would misbehave— his drinking, Alyssa, his debts, making you grovel for child support—and I'd watch you getting smaller and smaller. You stopped wanting to go out, even with me. The idea of some guy, any guy, inspiring you—yay! Tim's one special park ranger."

"Special?"

"He has to be, for you to even be talking about him."

"He asked me out to dinner," Neve said.

"Great! When are you going?"

"I'm not." At the look on Chris's face, Neve amended it. "At least, I'm not right now. I guess I want to think about it."

Chris shook her head. "All you should be thinking about is what you're going to order. That's it. You're going, girl."

"I know, but not yet. I—"

"You're going," Chris said stubbornly. "I watched you fall off, fall hard. It's been a long time, Neve. It's time. Get back on that horse, Neve."

"Horse?"

"The dating horse. Especially with some- one who actually seems slightly wonderful. Jeez! Don't you know what it's like out there? It's a whole world of websites and profiles—uploaded photos of poor hopeful guys, half of them taken at least five years ago, desperate to meet someone who won't notice or care. It's blind dates with your friends' divorced brothers. It's guys so set in their ways they expect you to spend the night watching *Law & Order* reruns, never mind that you both know the episodes by heart."

"How romantic," she said, thinking that Chris sounded like Shane talking about his mother.

"Honey, Tim doesn't seem like the reruns type. Maybe he's one of those nature guys who doesn't even have a TV. Perfect for you—you can commune with birds instead of Lenny Briscoe. Why don't you call Tim and ask? Tell him you've reconsidered about dinner."

Neve sat still, staring at the phone. She could tell him she wanted to hear about Berkeley after all.

"Come on," Chris said. "You can do it."

Neve gave her a loving look; Chris had always been her greatest cheerleader. They'd known each other for so long.

"You're always there for me," Neve said. "Through so many hard times. Thank you."

"It's my pleasure," Chris said. "Now let me be there through some good times, okay? It's the least you can do. . . ."

Neve laughed, and picked up the phone.

Tim had planned to spend the whole day on the beach, repairing and restaking snow fences. They were in such terrible repair from the winter's storms; the wind had torn up a stretch near the jetty and twisted it into a huge ball of wire and wood slats. It had caught bits of seaweed and driftwood, shells and skate egg cases—New England's version of a tumbleweed. Or an avant-garde sculpture—maybe Neve could do an exhibition.

But instead of hitting the beach, he started reading the material Mickey and Shane had brought him. Tim had expected it to be kids' stuff—grasping at straws, trying to keep the U-boat where it was. Shane had already taken a stand, and Tim knew he wasn't going to let the surf break go easily. Mickey and her sighting those drowned sailors was personally heart-wrenching for Tim, but he wasn't sure how far it would get them with the mid-April deadline.

So, sitting at his desk at eight-thirty, he turned to the folder expecting to spend five, maybe ten minutes checking it out. Three minutes in, the hair on his head stood on end. By nine-fifty, he hadn't moved. He'd gone through every bit of research they'd done, then gone on the Internet to double-check a few of their sources. They had come up with all fifty-five names of the drowned German sailors, as well as the two Americans. Not only that, they'd tracked down addresses on the Internet. At ten, he made a new pot of coffee, poured himself a big cup, and started to wonder whether any of the addresses could still be accurate.

By ten-thirty, he was pretty sure they'd have to get one, if not both, U.S. senators involved.

The whole time, one thought was drumming in his brain, just behind the others, a bass note that wouldn't go away. He tried to push it down, tell himself there were other ways to check things out—and there were. He could have gone to any history book covering the Navy, Operation Drumbeat, hunter-killer groups, U-823, and the USS *James.* Any history book covering World War II and Rhode Island—or even less specifically, the eastern seaboard—would contain documentation of the battle that had taken place just off the beach.

Mickey had already started writing letters. She'd enclosed copies of two. She only had fifty-three more to go. And that didn't count the two Americans. Real names, real young men, real families: not just abstract sailors lost in a long-ago battle.

At eleven-thirty, Tim picked up the phone, started to dial, got a ring tone. Hung up.

At eleven-forty, he picked up the phone again, dialed, actually heard the man answer. Hung up.

Eleven forty-five, there was no turning back. He dialed, let it ring, forced himself to stay with it.

"Who the hell keeps calling?" blasted the voice at the other end.

"Hi, Dad," he said.

Silence. Long silence. Then, "Tim?"

"Yeah."

"Tim . . ."

Now it was Tim's turn to be silent. He held on to the receiver, staring at his desk until the papers blurred. His mind was swimming with the last time he'd talked to his father, the yelling they'd both done, Frank's face front and center in his thoughts now as then. This is for Frank, he told himself right now. Where had that thought come from? He shook himself out of it, cleared his throat.

"Dad, I need to talk to you about something."

"The snowy owl," his father said. "You sent it over with those folks, calling to check up on it, are you?"

"Actually," he began, but his father interrupted.

"You were right to do what you did. He's seriously injured, as I'm sure you know. Injured wing. Not broken, as I'd first thought, but badly sprained."

"What about his beak?" Tim asked. Now that they were talking about the owl, it seemed easier than anything to do with the war—any war. Birds had always been uncomplicated, a way for him and his father to relate, to talk without the other stuff rising up to choke them.

"That's the really tough part. I trimmed the broken part—there was a lot of bleeding, and the beak was split all the way up. Didn't want to use silver nitrate or Quick Stop—

afraid it'd get in his eyes. But that nice lady who brought him in—"

"Neve Halloran?" he asked.

"Yes. She works at an art gallery, and she had the idea of using acrylic. Something she had plenty of on hand . . . Smart thinking—don't know why I didn't come up with it myself."

"You've been talking to her?"

"Seeing her, too. She brought the acrylic over. She wanted to check on the owl—her daughter's taking it very personally. And the boy."

"Shane."

"Yep, Shane. Nice people. Mrs. Halloran really helped me out with that acrylic. She's got a good head on her shoulders, that's for sure."

Tim kept staring at the papers. This call was a mistake. The dream came back to him: Frank's name in the sand, the panic Tim felt as he realized the wind would blow, erase Frank's name, erase Frank.

"Tim, you there?"

"Dad, I've got to ask you something. Not about the owl."

"What, then?"

"About U-823."

"Those bastards want to drag it up, out to Cape Cod, turn it into a goddamn museum," his father said. The friendly tone of his voice was gone; in its place was the bitterness Tim had always known, and hearing it now somehow set him feeling right—back on the solid footing of knowing he was speaking to his distant, bitter, military-loving father.

"That's what they want," Tim said.

"They're going to make money off the dead," his father said. "That jerk Cole Landry and the rest of them. Haul the U-boat up to the surface, no regard for the memory of the Battle of the Atlantic, what it all really meant. What a knife in the heart, taking it away on the anniversary."

"They think that turning it into a museum will make the battle come alive," Tim said.

"That's bullshit," his father said. "Put a memorial up on the beach, that's what needs to be done. Right off the end of the jetty. Let people use their imaginations— look out at the calm sea and imagine that day back in '44 when shots were fired, and charges exploded, and blood shed."

"I want to ask you about that," Tim said. "The bloodshed."

"Fifty-five Germans dead. All hands lost," his father said. "That's their grave. Their ship is their burial place."

Tim stared at the folder prepared by Mickey and Shane. They had acknowledged that very fact—their paper listed the fifty-five German casualties, ranging from the captain to the lowest-ranking crew member. But these two kids had also taken into account the patriotic state of mind fueling the raising of the U-boat, the anti-enemy fever that captivated so many—often including Tim. And they had asked a question that Tim knew just might be the one that could tip the balance.

"What about American casualties?" he asked.

"What do you mean?"

"The crewmen who died," he said. "Off Refuge Beach, when the U-boat fired on you."

"You mean my men," his father said sharply, as if he'd been momentarily stunned before. "Johnny Kinsella and Howard Cabral?"

"Yes."

"Well, I think of Refuge Beach as their burial place, too. I go down there and throw a wreath in the water every seventeenth of April."

"I know you used to."

"Never stopped."

Tim didn't respond to that, but it sent a shiver through him, to think his father had been doing that without his knowledge. The emotions were too big to handle, too numerous to count, and he couldn't even speak.

"You there?" his father asked.

"You come down to my beach to do that, and you don't even tell me?"

"I didn't think you'd want to know," his father said. "You haven't wanted much to do with me since—"

"I'm the ranger down here," Tim said, cutting him off before his father could say *since Frank was killed*. "You should have told me."

"Huh. Well, I'm telling you now, I guess. The seventeenth of April is coming up soon, and I'll be down there on the beach at first light. With a wreath."

"Before the crane lifts it away?" Tim asked.

"Yes."

"I'm sorry, Dad."

"Disgusting," his father growled. "Money-grubber, that's what Landry is. Nothing makes me sicker than idiots using the flag, the war, to advance their own agendas. Landry's exploiting our history, taking it away from us, all in the name of patriotism; and if he makes a nice pretty museum to the battle, that'll just glamorize war. Can't you stop him, Tim?"

"I'm trying," Tim said, wondering whether his father ever thought maybe he'd glamorized war to Frank.

"What?" his father asked, as if he'd just asked a rhetorical question, not expected a real answer. When it came to his father, Tim's heart was encased in iron—but right then, hearing the hope in his father's voice, he realized this meant more than Tim had been admitting to himself.

"I said I'm trying," Tim said.

"Let me help," his father said. "I'm up here in the woods, with nothing but hurt birds and Frank's picture for company. Tim, please let me help you."

"I've got to go," Tim said. "I'll call you if I think of anything." He hung up the phone, sweating, his heart pounding. He'd been about to give his father something to do—a task that no one could do better—but then his father had mentioned Frank's picture, and that was that.

The phone rang, and Tim was tempted to just let it go. Maybe it was his father calling back, wanting to talk more, wanting to make things right. Well, there was no making things right. Tim had photos of Frank, too. He also had the flag that had been draped over his coffin.

The telephone was as shrill as screaming, and Tim couldn't stand it anymore, not one second more.

"Hello," he shouted, grabbing the receiver.

"Tim?" a woman's voice.

"Yes," he said cautiously, his blood pressure still right up there.

"It's Neve," she said.

"Neve, hi," he said. He took a deep breath, tried to calm down.

"I was wondering something," she asked.

"Sure," he said. "What?"

"Is that dinner invitation still open?" she asked.

"Yes," he said, a slow smile spreading across his face, "it sure is."

"Because I was thinking, I'd really like to hear about Berkeley after all."

She was calling him for research? "Anything you want to know," he said, trying to keep his disappointment from showing in his voice. "Tonight?"

"Would tomorrow be okay?" she asked.

"I'll pick you up," he said. "Just tell me what time."

"Seven?" she asked.

"I'll be there," he said.

He hung up the phone, put Mickey and Shane's papers back in the folder, pulled on his jacket and went out onto the winter beach, into the cold sea air, to head toward the jetty and mend snow fences and try to block out the constant sound of the water and blowing sand.

15

Joe walked down to the far end of the flight cages and stood looking through the mesh at the wounded snowy owl. He claimed to like all birds, or at least all raptors, equally, but the truth was, he felt closest to the owls. They had a mystical quality that went along with their reputation for being wise—whenever he looked into their bright, still eyes, he felt as if they knew more than he did.

Staring at this bird huddled at the back of his cage, Joe crouched down so he could be at eye level. Mrs. Halloran had done him a great service, bringing him this owl. Not just because he hoped the bird, once healed, would become part of a breeding pair, but because the owl reminded him of his brother. He hadn't felt this close to Damien in many years. Right now, standing in the frigid barn and shaking, shivering with cold and something more, a feeling deep inside, Joe stared across the dark space and started talking.

"He called me," he said to the snowy owl. "Tim did. Said he had a question for me. It had to do with the U-boat, maybe it did. The reason doesn't matter, does it? The point is, my son called."

The owl stayed perfectly still. Joe wasn't crazy; it wasn't that he thought this bird was his brother. No, it wasn't that at all. Joe was nearly eighty-six years old, and he had his faculties intact. But he stared at the snowy owl and remembered the trip he and Damien had taken after they'd both come home from the war.

Oh, that time. Their first chance to see each other and spend time together. Their first chance to assess the damage. Joe had felt hungry for contact—for the easy brotherly times, the comfort of family, the rhythm of joking and storytelling and finishing each other's sentences.

They'd taken a train, then hitchhiked, then

bummed a ride from a Canadian Mountie to the tundra. Damien was shell-shocked, and the only thing Joe could think of, to bring him back, was to take him on a trip to see a bird, a rare bird, one they'd never seen before. The snowy owl.

They'd made it to the tundra, up by Hudson Bay. Joe had let the icy air and the northern lights leech the smell of gunpowder, diesel, and salt off his skin and out of his spirit. He'd let the long darkness lull him into dreams, away from nightmares. He'd look over at Damien, just to see him.

And he'd looked the same. But, equally, not the same. There was a certain darkness behind his eyes, but that wasn't necessarily it—Damien had always been deep, sensitive, a thinker. The biggest difference was that he looked older. And not just as if he'd aged in years—as if he'd hardened inside, as if he'd turned from a boy into a stone man.

Joe had needed his brother—his own experiences during the war had rocked him, shocked him. He'd seen things he'd never imagined before, heard sounds that haunted his sleep; these were events too terrible to talk about, at least with normal people, friends and family who'd never been to war. All he'd wanted to do was talk to Damien, exchange stories, pour it all out to each other up here on the tundra permafrost so they could leave it all on the ice, let it freeze over just like hell, forget the war forever and get back to their old lives.

So Joe had waited. He'd smiled at his brother, but no smiles came back. The stories got started, but they went nowhere. No finishing each other's sentences. He'd sat with his brother in endless silence for hours on end, in that black cube of a cabin they'd found, staring out at nothing.

No war, no death, no fallen buddies, and no talking about any of it. Just deeply frozen snow and ice. Sitting in the cabin, scanning the white landscape, Joe had heard insistent scrabbling beneath the frozen surface: lemmings. Food for snowy owls. There was hope, but Damien just stared, never once reaching for the binoculars or even his pencil and pad. And not talking, not telling stories, none of the brotherly banter or humor they'd always had. Just the sound of those lemmings scratching under the snow.

White arctic foxes came over the low hills, dug for the lemmings. The foxes stalked the prey, along underground corridors in the densely packed snow. Joe had a nightmare that night—that he was a white fox, hunting creatures that lived under the surface, fifty-five of them that would die there without ever breathing air again, without ever seeing sky.

"Damien," Joe said out loud now, and pretend as he might that he was fine and all was well, and that he wasn't losing his grip, he was directing his words at the injured snowy owl. "Tim wants a memorial. I'm pretty sure that's what it is. He asked about my men—Johnny and Howie, the ones who died there at the beach."

That dream—there had been fifty-five trapped creatures. Should have been fifty-seven, counting Johnny and Howard. What had he been doing in that dream—acknowledging the Germans, the enemy, while his own went uncounted? The snow was the sea, and beneath it lay the dead.

"Tim's making up for what's been left undone," Joe said to the owl.

Damien would appreciate that. Maybe if he'd lived longer, he'd have gone back to Alsace, to the spot where his B-24 had been shot down. Or to Helgoland, the island in the North Sea where his first crew had died. Joe thought back to that cabin on the tundra, how still Damien had sat for hours and hours, waiting for just a sight of one snowy owl, not speaking, barely even breathing. Ptarmigans and hares moved against the white hills, but Damien's gaze never wavered: he wanted only to see the snowy owls.

Joe had tried to ask him about other things. About his missions, flying by day so deeply into Germany, seeing so many planes go down in flames. Joe had wanted Damien to tell him what he had seen and heard. They were brothers—two Irish-American Catholic boys who'd been raised to believe in God and care about their fellow men. And they had both killed. Killed so many.

Did it make it less a sin, to take the life of another person, when it was done in the name of country? It wasn't that their war wasn't right, it wasn't that they weren't fighting on the side of good, it was just that Joe had to know. And he had needed Damien to tell him.

He'd imagined that trip to the tundra as a catharsis. They'd talk about things in that cabin that they'd never tell another soul. They'd pour it out to each other; Joe could tell Damien about that last sound, the one he'd never told and would never tell anyone else on this earth, the noise he'd heard coming from U-823 after the oil slicks, and the debris, and the German commander's hat came floating to the surface.

"See," he said to the snowy owl now, "you were always the kindest person I knew. Ma said you were too sensitive for war, but I told her no, you were tough. You could take it. That's what I said."

The tundra had been quiet. Not like the calm before battle—something Joe and Damien knew so well—but like the calm before heaven. Maybe this was heaven, Joe had thought, alone with his brother and the binoculars and the hope of seeing snowy owls. Dawn broke gently over the snow, a lot like sunrise at sea.

Oh, that most blessed time of day.

"So sensitive," he said to the owl now. "I'm not sure even I knew how much. Even I, Damien. Those sunrises on the tundra, when we'd open our eyes and see the day, I'd see your eyes all crusted over. Your tears had frozen to your lashes in the night. I started wondering whether you could take it, hearing about that last sound."

Joe swallowed, staring into the owl's yellow eyes. His brother's tears at dawn had been such stark contrast to Joe's joy. He'd wake up so glad to be alive, on solid ground, his brother beside him. He'd see that first arctic light and remember standing on the bridge of the *James*, the arrival of dawn signaling a new day, a night they'd made it through without getting killed—for nights were prime time for U-boats to attack.

"The smell of baking," he said to the owl. "Down below in the ship. The smell of fresh, sweet rolls and the slight warmth on my face of the sun just coming up, the pink of the eastern sky, it was wonderful. Wonderful. That's what those arctic dawns made me think of."

The owl shifted its injured wing, and Joe stopped pretending he didn't think he was talking to Damien. His brother, his beloved brother there in the cage.

"I was just so tired," he said. "All the time. For months I hadn't had four consecutive hours of sleep, never more than six in any twenty-four-hour period. I was young, Damien. Too young. You know when I saw that, realized it for sure? With Frank. With Tim's boy. We were his age. When I saw him go off to war, I thought my God—he's too young! And so were we."

The female snowy owl rustled behind the wall of mesh, and Joe saw the male blink and turn its head slightly. The sight filled Joe with emotion; he couldn't say why.

"To have all the doubts of any young person that age, but to have responsibility for my ship and crew—that was an awesome responsibility. Twenty-four, and a commander. Same age as the U-boat commander. I lost two; that was too much—but he lost everyone. Oberleutnant Kurt Lang. It was a battle, a fair fight. But Damien, that sound I heard. God, Damien . . ."

The broken bird flexed its damaged wing; in this dim light, Joe could see its splintered beak, the broken edges stark beneath the shine of Neve's epoxy. Joe closed his eyes, thought back to the Arctic. He and Damien had finally spotted a snowy owl—in its own battle.

Yes, what a triumphant moment it had been for Joe—to be in the frozen North with his brother, seeing a bird they'd only dreamed of, a chance for them to free themselves of the war and return to life, their love of birds. Joe had watched, spellbound, as if it were a movie:

A snowy owl hovered in flight just above

and behind an arctic fox. The fox leapt onto a snow mound, started digging, emerged with a lemming—and the owl swooped down, raking the fox with its talons. The fox bared its teeth, dropping the prey. The lemming must have been in shock—it ran in a tight circle, then stopped dead-still while the owl and fox battled it out. But you could see its whiskers quivering—alive, alert, looking for a chance to get away.

Just then the owl dove down, claws out. The lemming made a run for it, but the owl grabbed it by the back of the neck, white wings flapping, speed building, the lemming's legs pedaling air. Damien tore out of the cabin.

"No!" he yelled. "Let it go, drop it! Let it go! Don't kill it, don't kill it, don't kill it!"

Joe had had to run out after his brother, the two of them black shadows against the stark whiteness. He'd caught up with Damien, reaching into the sky, sobbing as he watched the snowy owl fly away with the writhing lemming. Joe had held Damien, and his brother's face froze to his, covered in tears.

Staring at the downed bird now, Joe saw his brother. They had both loved to fly, owl and man, flying killers. And they'd both been broken in flight, destroyed in more than just body. All those dead, all those dead. Joe's sensitive brother hadn't been tough enough at all. And neither had Joe. Joe's response to war had been bad enough, but his response to seeing Damien turned to stone had been even worse.

People always joked about the Irish loving to drink. Maybe there was something to that—a genetic predisposition. Certainly when the O'Caseys got together, beer and whiskey had always been part of the party. But after the war, both brothers had learned how to drink in a new way: to escape. From the memories of what they had done, and from each other. If they were drunk enough, they wouldn't have to notice that they were talking but not saying anything.

Joe had always taken seriously his status as older brother, and the more he saw Damien messing up, the worse he felt. Sometimes he'd go out to a bar with Damien just to keep him from getting into trouble— but that was really an excuse. By that time, Joe had his own reasons for being there, his own craving for escape. Their families had suffered. Joe's son and Damien's daughters.

Sometimes Joe thought about his own

wonderful father—how he'd always talked to Joe and Damien, taken them on hikes and fishing trips, taught them to be open to the world and the people they loved. When Joe thought of how he'd turned out as a father, he wanted to hang his head in shame.

The heat in the barn must have started going on, because suddenly Joe heard the first tap-tap in the pipes. He knew he had to get out of the barn before the sound got louder.

"Damien," Joe said, reaching toward the owl, "Tim's going to make it better."

The owl shifted in its cage.

"For all of us," Joe said. "He's going to make it better."

Tim. The war had done something to Joe and Damien, but even so, Tim was going to make it right. That's the kind of man he was.

And so Joe walked out of the barn, into the field, to breathe the fresh cold air and look into the wild blue sky and forget about the tundra and his brother and how both he and Damien had looked at that lemming and thought of the men they'd killed and the sound of someone tapping on the inside of a U-boat, trying to get out, begging to be set free, asking to be allowed to live.

Mickey got a message on her cell phone. It was from her father. He was drunk; or maybe not totally drunk, but his words were all slurry, and he sounded so sorry, that awful way he could sometimes sound when he'd really messed up and knew he was in bad trouble.

"Sweetheart, I miss you. Your dad has been busy, working, Mick. But that's not an excuse, is it? Not a very good excuse for not seeing my girl. You know I'm thinking of you, you know that, right? Selling houses like crazy, making money so I can get out of this hole . . . come back and see you. Miss you, Mickey. Never think I don't. I've made a lot of mistakes. But never think I don't love you."

And that was that. Mickey got the message when she turned her cell phone back on after history class, and she stood in the hall listening to it through twice. What was that catch in her father's voice? And how could he lie to her, say he was selling houses, when she knew he wasn't? She didn't care—the money was nothing to her.

If only he would come back, they could all talk about it. Everything would be fine.

"You're going to miss out on a good time," Martine said, walking over.

"Washington?" Mickey asked, because what else could it be? The trip to the nation's capital was all anyone in her class was talking about these days. "That's okay. Someone has to stay here and hold down the fort."

"We're even going to get to meet at least one of our senators," Martine said. "All because of Mr. Landry!"

"What's he got to do with it?"

"Well, because we're all from Secret Harbor . . . Refuge Beach, where the U-boat sank, and all. Josh's dad is making it so we all get to meet our legislators, and have our pictures taken in front of the White House— maybe even with the president!"

"Big deal," Mickey said.

Martine wasn't one of her closest friends, but she looked shocked, as if Mickey had just slapped her. "It *is* a big deal," she said. "They think we're special. Why are you ruining it?"

"Don't you get it?"

Martine shook her head. "Get what?"

"They don't think we're special," Mickey said. She held her cell phone in one hand. Her father's message was still on it, and she thought of how he had said that he missed her, loved her, and she knew the reason he wasn't coming home was money, that the reason she couldn't go to Washington was money, and that the reason Mr. Landry wanted to move U-823 was money.

"Then why are we getting to see one of our senators and maybe even the president?"

"Because Mr. Landry wants us to make him look good. Martine, they're taking away the thing that makes our beach special. Didn't you grow up hearing about how our grandparents had to pull blackout shades down at night? To block the light so U-boats couldn't see convoys of ships going by?"

"Yes. But—"

"Those shades were still up when my mother was a teenager; she asked about them, and her parents told her what they were for." Mickey paused. "Didn't your mom or dad used to walk you along the beach, point out the spot you couldn't even see— somewhere out in the waves—where the battle was fought, and where the U-boat still is now?"

"Yes," Martine said, looking doubtful.

"Didn't you imagine how scared they all had to be? Both the Americans, shooting at the sub, and the Germans, trapped down there underwater?"

"I did," Martine said, nodding. "My brother and I used to play ship, there on the beach. We'd keep lookout for periscopes. . . . Once we were swimming on a calm day, and we found some old shell casings."

"You could donate them to Mr. Landry's museum," Mickey said.

"We gave them to the town library," Martine said.

Mickey nodded. She had seen them—or casings like them—in the glass-front bookcases in their local library. There were also clippings about the battle, photographs of the USS *James*, pictures of the German crew, the commander's hat that had floated out of the wreck, German plates and cups brought up by divers. Mickey remembered going to the library with her father, holding his hand and listening to him try to explain to her how when he was a little boy the war had come to his own backyard.

"Everything to do with U-823 will end up going to the new museum," Mickey said.

"Not the shells Andy and I found on the beach," Martine said.

"Everything," Mickey said, still holding her phone, feeling her father's voice in her fingertips. "All our history."

"Huh," Martine said, frowning. "That's weird. Now I'm not so sure how I feel about it."

She started walking away just as Shane came over to see Mickey. He put his arm around her, bent down, brushed his lips across hers—right in the middle of school. Her knees turned to jelly, but she fought the feeling, stood up straight, and looked him in the eyes.

"It's working, isn't it?" he asked.

"Made her think, anyway . . ."

"They think the only people who care about the wreck are surfers and old WWII vets," he said. "The thing is, they care, too—but just don't know it."

"Everyone has a reason," Mickey said, still holding her cell phone, knowing her father's voice was captured there, that she could listen to it anytime she wanted. And even standing in the high school corridor, she could see the German crew, looking out from the wreck, white faces glowing in the murk, telling her their tales in a language she had never heard before but understood all the same.

"What are you doing after school?" Shane asked.

"Going home to study, I guess," she said.

"Come down to the beach," he said. "Watch me surf."

"It's so cold," she said, reaching up to touch the stitches in his head. "Won't it be dangerous?"

"Everything's dangerous, I think," he said, pressing his lips against her ear, so she felt the warmth of his breath on her skin, and her legs turned to mush again. "And I don't know how long the wreck will be there, and once it's gone, the break will be gone, too."

"Everything goes," she said, holding the cell phone and knowing that even though it contained the message, who knew where her father was now? People said things in messages that sometimes never came true.

"Don't think that," he said. "Some things last."

"Everything goes," she said stubbornly.

"I won't go," Shane said, holding her hand, looking so hard into her eyes that she felt shocked, and believed him.

16

Yesterday Mickey had gone to the beach to watch Shane surf, and today, with a break in the cold weather—sun actually shining, and snowdrops poking up out of the frozen ground, and only the lightest of breezes—she was going back.

She loved watching Shane in his black wetsuit, diving into the gray-green water, paddling out past the break, half on and half off his board. His legs looked so strong, pushing through the surf, and she loved the way he concentrated, just staring off toward the horizon at waves that hadn't even happened yet.

Walking the tide line in her green rubber

boots, she picked up blue mussel shells, silver oyster shells, and bits of green sea
glass. Every piece she gathered was a me-
mento of this day, of coming to Refuge
Beach to watch Shane surf. She wore a
white eyelet skirt—from last summer, and a
hope of more summer days to come—and a
long cream-colored fleece, open in front because the breeze felt so good.

Mickey held on to her cell phone, not
wanting to miss another call from her father.
Wherever he was, he had to call back.
Didn't he know he was in a race against
time? He was in such trouble with the
court—it almost killed Mickey to think that
he could be arrested for not paying child
support, when she didn't even care.

Or maybe she did care. Not because she
wanted the money, but because she wanted
him. It had been so hard, knowing he had
fallen in love with Alyssa and was starting a
new family with her. But he was still her
dad—he'd always said that nothing could
change that.

She watched as Shane waited for the right
wave, saw him jump up on the board, ride
the heavy swell until it turned as clear as
cellophane, rippled, and broke beneath him,

trailing off into tendrils of white lace. It seemed so precarious, the idea of a boy riding water. She hauled herself up on the jetty, the narrow, barnacle-encrusted wooden structure jutting out into the water, and tried to balance while Shane rode the waves.

It happened over and over: the wave looking so solid, then smashing into a million foamy pieces. And Mickey standing on the jetty with her heavy green boots, weaving in the sea breeze. Her cast felt heavy, but it gave her stability as she walked slowly, one foot in front of the other, along the narrow jetty.

Tonight Mickey's mother had a date. Yes, a date. The fact that it was with Mr. O'Casey meant something, but even so, Mickey's heart was heavy. It seemed as if today was the end of a dream—that her parents would one day get back together.

When Mickey had said goodbye to her mother this morning—before getting on the school bus—her mother had held her face between her hands. She'd looked Mickey straight in the eyes and said, "I love you more than anything."

"You don't have to say that," Mickey had said.

"But it's true."

"That's why you don't have to say it."

That had been the closest Mickey could come to giving her mother her blessing. Her mother had broken the news last night, before Mickey went to bed. She and Mr. O'Casey would be going out to dinner. They wouldn't stay out late. Mickey could wait home alone, or with a friend—no, not Shane. Jenna, maybe? Chris Brody had invited Mickey for dinner, if she'd prefer that.

No, Mickey had said. She'd be fine home alone. Her mother had let that stand for about five minutes, then said she'd really prefer it if Mickey had dinner with Chris— Chris could pick her up at the beach, if Mickey wanted to go watch Shane surf again.

Now, staring out at Shane on his board, Mickey pictured her mother at home, getting ready. Mickey had seen her mother get dressed to go out for dinner with her father a hundred times. She'd stand in front of the mirror, put on makeup, dab on a little perfume. Annick Goutal's Eau d'Hadrien, a gift brought back from Paris by her mother's boss. Mickey liked the way it smelled.

Her mother would probably wear a skirt.

That's what she had always picked out for the most special occasions with Mickey's father—for birthdays, or their anniversary. They had made it to their thirteenth; unlucky thirteen. A black skirt, a white silk blouse, maybe a silver necklace. Pearl earrings. High heels . . .

Mickey shook herself. Stop thinking about what her mother was wearing. The reason Mickey didn't want to be home right now was that she knew she couldn't bear to see her mother walk out the door, all beautiful and ready for a special evening, with a man who wasn't Mickey's father. Even Mr. O'Casey.

She gazed into the distance—at Shane on his surfboard, but also at the waves themselves. The way they reared up, turned into tubes, trembled beneath Shane's board, shattered. The white edge never stopped, just poured from one wave into the next.

Staring at the salt spray dissolving under the edge of Shane's surfboard, turning into mist, into vapor, she thought about how things disappeared. Here today, gone tomorrow. Kids waiting for parents to come home, parents who would never walk through the door again. Her parents had been fighting for so long; couldn't they make peace with each other?

After a long stretch, Shane paddled in to shore, pulled his board through the surf, ran with it under his arm to where Mickey stood on the jetty. The closer he got, the more her heart warmed up, so that by the time he got close, she jumped into his arms, wrapped him in a wet, salty kiss, and was hot all over. Her pocket was full of shells and glass, and her lips tasted of Shane and the sea.

"How was it?" she asked.

"It was great, because you were here," he said, holding her tight, his lips cold against her cheek.

"Really?"

"Yes," he said. "Massive swells, the occasional solo giant, the way the waves begin at the tip of the U-boat, roar up and start to boil, double up when they pass over the conning tower, and hollow out into long, empty tubes."

She nodded, holding him.

"I saw you standing over here on the jetty." He squeezed her tighter, kissed her, tilted his head back, looking straight into her eyes. "And I thought, I never want this to end."

"Neither do I," Mickey said. She thought about the letters she'd written. Thirty-seven so far, using every free moment she had. She glanced up at Shane; he was a year older, almost old enough to go to war. She scrambled out of his arms and back onto the jetty, pulling him up so he was standing behind her. They stood on the jetty, facing out to sea, listening to all the sounds around them: each other's breath, flocks of shorebirds flying overhead, the waves crashing over the wreck, the fresh breeze that felt like winter dying and spring coming on, and the unspoken voices of all the fathers and sons—under the sea, and above.

Tim pulled up right on schedule at six—not seven as they'd first said. He told Neve they needed extra daylight so he could show her something, and she'd agreed. Chris was all set to pick Mickey up at the beach, and as odd as it felt for Neve to not see her daughter first, she was almost relieved. It felt strange, going out on a date, and she was just as glad to not have to watch Mickey's reaction.

"You look great," Tim said, holding the

door to the truck open as she climbed in—wearing a slim black skirt, black cashmere sweater, and tall black boots.

"So do you," she said, and he did: khakis, blue oxford shirt, leather jacket filled out by very broad shoulders. He looked like a smart, rugged college professor with a penchant for working out.

"I thought we'd head to Newport," he said as they drove along. Through the trees, onto Route 1—but instead of toward the beach, heading north.

"Newport's great," she said, thinking of favorite restaurants on the wharf.

"With a short stop first," he said.

She nodded. The radio played quietly, and Neve felt a small jolt inside. Music on a car ride; it felt so fun and easy, such a reminder of being young and romantic. She hadn't had a thought like this in so long, she had to stare out the window so Tim wouldn't see her smile and wonder why such a small thing was making her feel so happy.

Over the Jamestown Bridge, across Conanicut Island, then to the Newport Bridge; Tim threw a token into the basket, and they drove up onto the bridge. It felt like liftoff to Neve—the sweeping climb over Narragansett Bay, the spectacular view south of town, wharves and houses and the white steeple of Trinity Church, Fort Adams, boats in the harbor, whitecaps, and there in the distance, out in the Atlantic, like a turtle on the horizon, Block Island.

"There's Block," she said.

"It's a clear evening," he said, "to get such a good view."

"Have you gone there much?" she asked.

"Yes," he said. "Quite a bit. When I was young, my father used to take me out there in our fishing boat. We'd moor in Old Harbor, go to Ballard's for shore dinners, spend the night. And then we'd always go out to East Ground. . . ."

"East Ground?" she asked.

"The shoal and trench," he said. "I know that's where he always believed U-823 was making for when he sank her."

"Is it deep there?" she asked.

"Very," he said. "The Ice Age scraped this whole region clean—when the glacier receded, the leading edge pushed up a whole line of rubble, glacial moraine from here out past Nantucket. The upper part forms the islands—Block Island, Martha's Vineyard . . . and the lower part forms the reefs and ledges, like East Ground, the nineteen-fathom bank."

"Did your father teach you all that?"

"No," Tim said, shaking his head as they drove off the bridge, past Newport, heading east. "For a Navy guy, everything he taught me had to do with the air. Birds and flight. For the sea, I had to go to college."

"So you have a background in oceanography?" she asked.

"Yes," he said. "I guess I studied it as a way of getting close to my father, understanding what drove him. I wanted to know what those trips to East Ground were all about, and I knew they had to do with a deep ocean trench."

"Deep enough for U-823 to hide."

"Yes," Tim said. "But the U-boat never made it that far. . . ."

"You said your father never talked about it," Neve said, thinking back to their time on the driftwood log, when Tim had cut her off. "Did he talk to your mother?"

Tim shook his head. "Communication wasn't very big in our house. Luckily, my mother came from a big family. She had four sisters, and they all lived nearby. Looking back, I feel bad for her. She had me and my father to deal with, and neither of us did too much talking. She never seemed un-happy, though—she had a great sense of humor, and she was always laughing. No thanks to us."

Neve thought of how a person's silence and unhappiness could use up all a family's oxygen, threaten to take over the house. Before Richard left, when he was the most miserable, days could go by without any real conversation. He'd sit at the dinner table, barely saying a word, both Neve and Mickey walking on eggshells, trying not to upset him.

"What are you thinking?" Tim asked her now.

"About my marriage; you're reminding me of what it was like to live that way," she said, and she felt almost disloyal, even though Richard had been long gone: she had been raised to keep things to herself, not talk about what went on under her family's roof.

"That way?" he said.

"With someone who never talked, kept all his feelings to himself. I never knew what my husband was thinking. In his case, there was drinking involved. . . ."

"My father, too," Tim said.

"Really?" Neve asked, glancing over.

"Yeah," Tim said. "Till he went to AA and got sober."

"It's bad enough, being married to someone with a problem," Neve said. "But it's so much worse for the kids. Mickey could never understand what was going on. I'd watch her trying to be so good—almost as if she thought that if she behaved a certain way, was smart enough, or funny enough, she could keep him from going out to the bar. It had nothing to do with her."

"I'm sorry you and Mickey went through that," Tim said. "Is that why your marriage broke up?"

Neve nodded. "At least partly," she said. "It's hard to separate out the causes at this point. All I know is, we were just so unhappy. I didn't want Mickey to grow up thinking that's how life should be—I wanted her to see joy and possibility."

"That's good," Tim said. "You both deserve that. . . ."

As they drove east the sky began to glow. The sun was setting behind them, and the peach-colored light was spreading all over the trees and landscape. Neve noticed the tips of the branches turning pink, and she felt spring in the air. Glancing over at Tim, she was almost afraid to ask what he was thinking. But something told her that this would be the time, so she went for it.

"What about you?" she asked. "What happened to your marriage?"

"Like father, like son," he said. "I learned how to be tough, fight my own battles, take care of business. Beth—my wife—never stopped trying to get inside. I thought I'd be burdening her to talk about things."

"Things that were worrying you?" Neve asked.

"Yes," he said.

She thought of what she knew about Frank. Had he still been married when Frank had joined up, gone overseas? Having seen the way Tim was with Mickey, the way he'd taken care of her and worried about her when she was in the hospital, she could only imagine how he must have felt about Frank, and how his silence and holding his feelings in must have frustrated Beth. Thinking about all that, she found herself reaching across the seat.

She found his hand. Took it, held it in hers, laced fingers with his.

He glanced over, surprised—but not half

as shocked as she felt herself. Her heart was beating so fast, right against her throat. The late winter sky surrounded them, so full of pink light and the promise of spring. She thought of their two failed marriages, their two beloved children, the damage that too much silence had done everyone. Yet riding along, she couldn't imagine a word that could make her feel closer to him than she did right now.

A few minutes later they came out behind St. George's School. Passed the road leading to Purgatory Chasm, down the hill past Second Beach, round the bend by Third Beach. The graceful curve of Hanging Rock dominated the scene, hovering over the marsh, just behind the beach and ocean. Neve stared over as Tim parked, facing the vista.

"Hanging Rock," he said. "Part of the same glacial moraine I mentioned earlier."

"This stretch of shore is so sandy," she said. "The rock really stands out."

"That's true," he said. "It's a spectacular landmark. Sometimes it's called 'Paradise Rocks.'"

She followed his gaze, which was riveted on the boulder itself. Was this what he had brought her here to see? If so, she was moved and impressed—by its natural beauty, and the sight of sunset light illuminating its surface, turning it fiery red. Glancing at the beach, she heard huge waves and saw clouds of silvery sandpipers skittering along the dark sand flats. She still held his hand, and music played on the truck radio, and she couldn't remember the last time she felt this way.

"You know that material Mickey and Shane brought me?" he asked.

"Yes," she said. "Although they didn't show me; I know they worked hard on it."

"It's very good," he said. "They're great kids. I sold Shane short at first, but he's really committed. The challenge is to help him figure out the best way—so he doesn't shoot himself in the foot."

"Mickey will help him with that," Neve said. "She's so careful and measured."

"You're proud of her," he said, looking at her straight on.

"I am," she said. She loved Mickey so much, and wore her feelings right on her sleeve. She couldn't have hidden them if she wanted to, but she looked over at Tim, feeling her heart in her throat. "As proud of her as you must have been of Frank."

He tried to pull his hand away, but she held on tight, wouldn't let him.

"Tim . . ." she said.

"I want to talk about him," he said. "I just can't. I haven't been able to."

"Tell me one thing about him," she whispered. "That's all."

Tim sat still, staring out the window. At first she thought he was just trying to make her stop—using the tried-and-true way of silence. But he squeezed her hand slightly, very gently, and nodded toward Hanging Rock. Paradise Rocks . . .

"Frank loved it there," he said. "It's part of the Norman Bird Sanctuary—that's where he worked for his summer jobs."

"He loved birds," she said, to help him along.

"Yes. And he loved that rock. He'd look out to sea; he told me that if he looked hard enough and far enough, he could see where the bottom dropped out at East Ground, where the U-boat was heading that last day. It always came back to his grandfather for Frank; he idolized him."

"Your father is a very interesting man," Neve said.

Tim nodded—neither agreeing nor disagreeing, and she knew he was focused on Frank. "The great glaciers came down across New England at least four times," Tim said. "No one knows exactly why. But they made the islands and trenches, and they made Hanging Rock. Frank once sat there all night—he wanted to figure out the answer, because he loved this area so much."

Neve stared up at the enormous rock. Darkness was starting to fall, and a few stars appeared in the soft, hazy sky. She thought of a young boy so passionate for this place that he'd stay up there all night.

"Didn't Bishop Berkeley used to sit up there?" she asked, thinking of the famous philosopher who had spent so much time here. "Thinking about life and existence?"

"Yes," Tim said. "That inspired Frank, too."

"Because he was a philosopher?"

"Because of another Berkeley—the bird artist. He used to come here to paint, and as your research probably told you, he took his name from the bishop."

"And of course Frank would be interested in him because he loved birds so much," Neve said, feeling excited by the connection, thinking of the Berkeley picture she'd seen at Joe's raptor barn, of the upcoming Berkeley exhibition, of the catalogue she'd just put to bed.

"And because he was Frank's great-uncle," Tim said.

"What?" Neve asked.

"Berkeley," Tim said, turning to look at Neve. "That's why I wanted to bring you here, to this spot—where he did so many of his paintings. He was my father's brother Damien. Damien O'Casey . . ."

"He stopped painting after the war," Tim told her later, over coffee. They had had dinner at the Black Pearl—both ordering the famous clam chowder, then sea bass for Neve, swordfish for Tim. Candlelight reflected by the dark, varnished wood, danced in Neve's blue eyes. The way she'd taken his hand in the truck had been electric—pure shock and power surging through his body—and he couldn't wait for dinner to be over so he could reciprocate.

"There was so much speculation," Neve said. "Some believed he was the right age to have fought in the war; some researchers thought he was killed."

"No, he survived," Tim said. "But he came back very changed. From the time Damien returned to the States from England, he never picked up his paintbrush again. Another thing my father doesn't talk about much."

"He was such a great talent," Neve said. "People in my field, who know about art and artists, think his bird paintings rival Audubon's."

"Ask my father, and he'll tell you they're ten times better," Tim said, watching the way her eyes shone, her lips turned up. He wanted to reach across the table, touch her face. She smiled so easily; that had struck him about her right away. She was ready for happiness.

"I think I'd agree with your father," Neve said.

"That would make him happy," Tim said. "He likes you."

"You've been talking to him?"

Tim nodded, tensing up. Talking was one thing; he wasn't sure he was ready to get into his current relationship with Joe O'Casey. "He told me you've been out to the raptor barn a few times."

"I brought him some acrylic," Neve said. "To help repair the snowy owl's broken beak. And, I have to admit, to look at that Berkeley he has hanging over his work-bench. He never said a word. . . ."

"About it being Damien? No, he wouldn't," Tim said. "He's made it his mission to pro-tect his brother's privacy. In fact, I probably shouldn't have even told you."

"I won't say a word," Neve promised. "But why keep it such a secret? Berkeley is beloved—everyone loves his work. And he's been such a mystery for so long. The state of Rhode Island has always claimed him as their own, but we've never really been sure. He hid his identity, so no one knew whether he was born here, or just moved here to paint—or even settled here. So many ques-tions . . ."

Tim nodded. He looked across the table, saw her wanting to ask. He could tell her, too—at least to the extent that he knew the answers. But as angry as he was at his father, and as much as he blamed him for certain things, he also respected his desire to control the information about his brother.

"Please?" Neve asked. "At least tell me—why did he wear that cape?"

"Before the war, he went to Paris. He was a prodigy—no one could hold him back, even though his mother worried he was too young to go. He loved it there, honed his art. He met a woman who became his model. She used to pose in his studio, and he gave her the cape to keep her warm. Then, one day, she was gone. Just disappeared. But she left the cape behind."

"How terrible for him," Neve said. "Did he ever find her again?"

Tim shrugged.

"Did he get married? Did he have a family?"

"I'd tell you more," he said to Neve, knowing that this part of the story was too painful for tonight. "But the rest is my father's to tell. Do you understand?"

"I think so," she said slowly.

"My father loved his brother a lot," Tim said. "Sometimes I think he loved him more than anyone."

"Not you," Neve said, shaking her head. "You should hear how he talks about you."

"I don't know about that," Tim said. "I disappointed him. He loved Frank as much as Damien—that I'd believe."

"And you too," Neve said stubbornly. Then, when he didn't relent, she smiled. "Our first argument!" she said, and he smiled even wider because that meant she was thinking there could be others—that there was something in the future for them. He had no idea what he was thinking about that, but it sent a long shiver all through his body.

"Yeah," he said.

"I won't even press you about Berkeley—even though I'm dying for you to tell me more."

"Maybe someday, okay?" he asked, and she nodded.

He smelled her faint perfume, even across the table, and it was driving him a little crazy. Getting the waitress's attention, he asked for the check. He knew she was ready to leave, too—he could tell by the way she gave him a secret smile as he signed, pushed back his chair. He pulled the table forward so she could slide out, slipped his arm around her waist as they walked to the door.

Her black cashmere sweater felt so soft; underneath, the curve of her body felt taut. When they stepped outside, the air had a chilly bite—but already, in just a few days, he felt it warming up. Overhead, stars were visible, even through the lights of Bannister's Wharf.

Instead of walking to the truck, he steered her out the wharf, beneath the archway over the path between the shingled shop buildings. Every summer, this spot was filled with people—sailors on boats, people staying in the rooms overhead, couples strolling after dinner. Right now, with a cool wind blowing off the harbor, Tim was alone with Neve.

He'd been so weary. So bone-tired. Breathing had been too much of an effort. Seeing the sun rise, knowing Frank couldn't see it, had made him want to sleep forever. Seeing all those families at Refuge Beach in the summer, watching them swim and knowing Frank would never swim again, had made every inch of his skin hurt. Thinking of how Frank had died. And that had made him feel so tired.

Right now he was wide awake. All the stars were out, blazing. He was on fire, from the inside out. His blood was so hot, moving so fast. Neve made him feel more alive than he'd ever felt in his life. He'd never believed he could feel this way, not after the grip of grief and exhaustion. Was this real?

He could feel his own nervousness pouring off him. His heart was racing; could she feel it? They were walking so close, his arm around her. Was that his heartbeat or hers? When he glanced down, he realized that she was nervous, too. This was new territory for both of them.

"Want to go back?" he asked.

He meant back to the truck—it was getting cold, and once they reached the other side of the buildings, they were standing right at the head of the dock, no big boats at this time of year to block the broad sweep of wind blowing off the harbor. But as he asked the question, he knew he meant something else—*Want to go back and pretend nothing is happening?*

"I don't want," she said, stepping closer to him, looking up into his face, "to go anywhere or be anywhere but here. With you."

"Neither do I," he said.

He kissed her; bent down, touched his lips to hers. He wasn't sure he'd even remember how to do it, thought maybe they'd be awkward—like kids, like anyone on a first date. But it was so natural, the way she reached up, touched the side of his face, leaned into his body as if she belonged there.

Her mouth was so warm, and at first she seemed so hesitant—or maybe it was him holding back; he wasn't sure, didn't stop to think. But suddenly there was no hesitation at all, just him and Neve and so much desire. He must have kept it pent up somewhere, because now it was flowing out—all he wanted was her.

There was nowhere to go, so they leaned up against the salt-weathered shingled building, feeling the dock sway beneath their feet, the rhythm of the waves a whole lot less intense than the beating of his heart, arms around each other, kissing hard, or maybe soft, he was sort of past thinking about it, just feeling as if he wanted it to go on forever.

Never wanted it to stop.

Never.

It did, eventually. He felt her shivering so hard—even with spring in the air, winter had hold of the harbor, had iced the northern bay and rivers so that even here, near the mouth of Narragansett Bay, the relatively warm sweep of the Atlantic couldn't do much to keep the temperature from dropping at night.

"Here," he said, taking his jacket off and sliding it over her shoulders.

"You'll be cold," she said.

He just shook his head; slid his arms under his own jacket, wrapped her in his arms. Hoped that maybe they could stand there a little longer.

But he was too polite for that, and he could really feel her shaking. She stood on tiptoes to put her arms around his neck again, start to kiss him . . . it was with the greatest regret he'd had in a long time that he pulled her hands down, stuck them into the pockets of his jacket, held her in a tight embrace and started walking her toward the parking lot.

When they got to the cobblestones, they stopped to steady themselves. He kissed her again, and in that moment, caught the look in her eyes.

It reflected streetlights, starlight, the fire in his own expression. She looked so beautiful and soft, as if in these last cold minutes she'd melted a little; and he felt the same way. Tim thought of those four glaciers

Frank had been so amazed by—plowing down from the Arctic. There were times Tim had thought he'd gotten trapped in the ice, that he would never thaw. The snowy owl on Refuge Beach had known—had come to find him, transport him to the land of ice, where he belonged.

Right now, looking into Neve's eyes, he knew that she had come to take him back.

"Thank you," he said, touching her face.

"For what?" she whispered.

"I was frozen," he whispered back.

"So was I."

"You . . ." he began, but the words wouldn't come. For once he didn't want to be silent—he wanted to tell her everything, tell her it all. But his throat was shut tight, and he couldn't speak.

She stood up on tiptoes, kissed his lips once more, looked him straight in the eyes.

"Spring is coming," she whispered.

And then she took his hand again, and together they walked across the cobblestones and through the shadows of the Newport waterfront, to his truck.

17

The next day, Neve was something just this side of useless. She went through the motions at the gallery: opening up, answering e-mail and phone calls, greeting customers. But she was lost.

It had been all she could do to pry herself loose when Tim dropped her off last night. They had sat in his truck until the last possible minute, there in her driveway, just being together. A movement behind the curtains let her know that Mickey was standing there, waiting for her, so their last kiss was quick and chaste.

Neve hung on to the feelings she'd had, standing at the end of Bannister's Wharf, the wind whipping off the water, Tim's arms around her. So cold and so warm. He had said he'd been frozen. For Neve, it had been almost worse: ever since the last year or so with Richard, she'd been like that line in the James Taylor song: "the sky won't snow and the sun won't shine."

She'd been stuck somewhere between seasons—in a gray, slushy, edge-of-winter neverland of disappointment and dashed hopes. She had grown up thinking that love was everything—and although she'd never quite stopped believing that, she'd found herself trying to redefine "everything."

Now, sitting at her desk, she could barely stop smiling. She wanted to maintain the connection with Tim, just keep the feeling of closeness going, so she found herself doing an online search for Berkeley, looking for any evidence that she might have missed in her catalogue research, that he was the alter ego of Damien O'Casey.

Then she started looking up Damien on his own, finding several mentions of him on World War II websites—one, the 492nd Bomb Group; the Caterpillar Club—airmen who'd been shot down; and the 44th Bomb Group, the one he'd joined after the 492nd had been disbanded. She found an old *Providence Journal* article about Joe O'Casey and his raptor rehab, with a quote: "When a creature loses its ability to fly, it affects every one of us. My brother Damien showed me that; he celebrated birds in every one of his paintings, showed us their beauty and pure poetry. Every bird I help, I think of Damien."

She stared at that quote for a long time. There was no mention of Damien as Berkeley, but there it was, between the lines, in black and white. The story continued with details about Damien having flown with the 492nd—the bomb group that had sustained heavier losses than any other in the Eighth Air Force, how according to his brother he had once been a promising painter, but how he'd stopped upon returning from war.

Just around noon, two things happened: the phone rang, and Chris walked through the gallery door. Waving hi and motioning Chris toward the chair beside her, she answered the call.

"Dominic di Tibor Gallery," Neve said.

"Hi, Neve—it's Tim."

"Oh," she said. Just hearing those four words, she was a little more gone. She tilted her chair slightly away from Chris. "Hi. I had a wonderful time last night."

"Me too," he said. "That's why I was calling. What are you doing later?"

"Probably just going home, making dinner for Mickey." She paused, aware that although Chris was pretending to read some printouts on her desk, she was listening acutely.

"Was she okay when you got home?" he asked.

"Yes," Neve said, although that wasn't the whole truth.

"She didn't mind that I took her mother out?"

"Well, it's complicated," Neve said, thinking of how quiet Mickey had been when she'd walked in, how Neve had heard her talking to Shane late, after she'd said she was going to bed, how she'd heard Mickey asking him if he believed love between humans could last forever—the way it did for swans.

"I hope she gets used to it," he said. "Because I want to see you again."

"Me too," she said, glancing over at Chris, seeing her absorbed in the printout of the article about Joe and Damien.

"Can we meet Friday night?" he asked.

"I think so," she said. "I'll have to see."

"Come to dinner at the beach," he said. "I'll cook."

"Okay," she said. "Friday night." Then they said goodbye, and Neve hung up.

"My, my," Chris said, gesturing at the phone with the article. "It's all O'Casey, all the time. Tell me everything!"

Neve smiled, felt quiet and still deep inside. When she was young, she had loved to talk about the boys she liked, sharing every detail with her best friend; it had been a way of feeding the fire, keeping the emotions revved up. The more she talked about them, the more she felt them. But this was different. The way she felt about Tim today was so intense and private, something she wanted so badly it almost scared her.

"We had a really good time," she said, in a way that didn't invite discussion.

Chris gazed at her face with such tender happiness. "You did? I'm glad, Neve. I'm really glad."

"He's . . ." She searched for the word. But she couldn't find one that fit Tim, at least not a word she'd want to say out loud. She just shook her head.

"I get it, honey."

"What did Mickey say about it last night?" Neve asked.

"She was basically quiet," Chris said. "I picked her up at the beach—she was sitting on the jetty with Shane, watching a whole flock of swans swimming just beyond the surf break. I offered him a ride, but he said he had his bike. Apparently he rides with his board under his arm . . . can you *imagine*?"

"He's devoted to surfing," Neve said, thinking of Mickey's words to Shane about swans. "I have to admit that."

"You don't like him?"

"It's not that," Neve said. "It's just . . . I see Mickey falling head over heels . . . it's her first time, and I think she's in love."

"And that's bad?"

Neve gazed at a Berkeley watercolor leaning against the wall, one of her favorites; it showed a female osprey feeding her young. She loved it for the subtlety of coloration, the familiarity of landscape, the mother-child connection. Before Tim, the picture had struck home for another reason—the mother was alone.

"Love is dangerous," she said.

"Oh, Neve," Chris said. "All men aren't Richard."

"I know," she said, thinking of Tim.

"Then what's wrong?"

"I just want Mickey to be happy," Neve said. "And safe. Shane seems so extreme. They're both so passionate about the beach, about keeping everything the same, saving the U-boat. The cause is pulling them together—it's as if they're magnetized. But what will happen after the U-boat is gone? After Shane's surfing spot is ruined, and they don't have the fight bonding them anymore?"

"Neve, why are you doing this?" Chris asked, smiling.

"Doing what?"

"Ruining it. I can tell you had an absolutely amazing time last night. You don't want to tell me about it, that's fine—but you're glowing, okay? Your eyes are shining, your cheeks are pink, you look as if you have the biggest secret in the world. *You're* the one falling in love, and you're scared out of your wits."

"No," Neve said, shaking her head.

"Richard ran you into the ground," Chris said. "You loved him so much—you had a storybook wedding. I was your maid of honor, remember? I was there. He was handsome and charming and so much fun, and we all looked at you and thought you had it all."

Neve closed her eyes, thinking of "it all." On good nights she got a call from the bartender, telling her Richard was too drunk to drive and suggesting she come to pick him up; on bad nights she had no idea where he was and lay in bed staring at the ceiling, picturing him with another woman, or imagining him dead in a ditch.

"So, how do you come back from that?" Chris asked. "Especially in a month that began with you in court, chasing him—yet again—for child support. Honey, forgive yourself for having lost your belief in love; just, please, don't pass that on to Mickey. Let her have it for herself."

"Shane reminds me of Richard," Neve said. "At least, the way Richard was at the beginning. There's something so wild and hopeful about him."

"What's wrong with wild and hopeful?" Chris asked, smiling. "They sound like pretty good qualities to me."

Neve smiled back. Chris had a point.

Disappointment was such a powerful emotion, and Neve had felt it for so long. Last night had sparked something she hadn't felt in ages—maybe years: desire. And desire, at least the way Neve felt it, was the wildest thing there was, wrapped up in hope.

"Speaking of court, though," Chris said. "We really do have to find Richard."

"What do you mean?"

Chris paused, staring down at the print-outs on Neve's desk, as if wrestling with herself over what she should say. "There's a class trip to Washington, D.C.," she said finally. "Mickey mentioned it last night."

"I haven't heard anything about it!" Neve said.

"I know. Mickey let it slip when we were leaving the diner after dinner, and Josh Landry was walking in; he asked her if she'd changed her mind about going. When I asked her the details, she said that you didn't have the money, and she didn't want to put more pressure on you—or her father."

"But she can't miss her class trip!" Neve said.

"If Richard would just come through the

way he's supposed to, there'd be no problem," Chris said.

"It kills me, Mickey worried about putting
pressure on her father."

"She made me promise not to tell you."

"Thanks," Neve said, shaking. "I'm glad
you did. She's going on that trip, if I have to
pawn my grandmother's cameo."

"You do and I'll kill you. I'll chip in for the
trip."

"I can't let you do that," Neve said, giving
her a grateful look. "Seriously, how much
can it be? A couple hundred dollars—she
couldn't ask me for that?" Her mind was
racing—how had Mickey kept such a big
secret? Why did she suddenly feel she
couldn't confide in her mother? They could
have figured it out together, found a way to
come up with the money. She was so absorbed with Mickey and the issue of secrets, she barely even noticed Chris tapping
the article.

"As I said earlier, all O'Casey, all the time.
What's this you're reading about two old
men? The raptor guy—that's obviously
Tim's father. But what about this other
one, Damien? He painted birds, like Berkeley?"

"He *is* Berkeley," Neve said without thinking. She'd been so lost in thoughts and emotion about Tim, rattled by the news about Mickey, that she just let it slip.

"You're kidding," Chris said, her eyes getting bigger, just as the door opened behind her. "Berkeley is Tim's *uncle*?"

"Oh my God," Neve said, bowing her head, shocked by what had just come out of her mouth. She wanted to call it back, pull the words right out of the air, make Chris forget she'd said them. "Chris, you can't tell a soul. I shouldn't have said anything."

"Is it true?"

"Chris, he was destroyed by the war; he never painted again. Tim told me everything, but he made me promise not to tell."

"This is incredible," said Dominic di Tibor, sweeping his cape off and fixing Neve with a razor gaze. "My genius, Neve Halloran—you've discovered the true identity of Berkeley? Let me kiss you!"

She bowed her head as Dominic grazed her lips, knowing that her own hope and wildness had just brought her to the edge, that she'd just broken a promise and made the mistake of her life, that she'd just spilled a secret that hadn't been hers to spill.

Something was wrong with her mother. Mickey had no idea what it was, but she knew it was bad.

Last night, after "the date," her mother had floated in, almost as if she had wings, trying to act as if nothing had happened, trying to focus on Mickey and whether she and Chris had had a good time, and whether she'd finished her homework. But Mickey had seen her just glistening—as if she were the princess in a fairy tale, as if she'd just fallen in love for the first time in her life.

What did that say about Mickey's father?

The thing was, Mickey was beginning to know about love. She knew about the feeling that started in her toes, traveled up her legs, all through her skin, right to the hair on her head. It felt the strongest when she was kissing Shane—or just thinking about kissing him, but ever since that first night on the beach, she'd felt it more or less all the time.

Looking at her mother last night, she could tell she was feeling it, too. Yet it couldn't be the same thing, not at all; for Mickey and Shane, it was the beginning, the very first time either of them had felt this way. For Mickey's mother . . . well, there were all those wedding photos in the album, and that white dress up in mothballs in the attic, and there was Mickey herself to prove that her mother had already felt this way once before.

So what did that say about love?

Maybe her mother was having the same thoughts. Because one thing for sure, the way she was acting tonight was nothing like last night. Mickey watched as she sat at the kitchen table, staring at more or less nothing. Just sitting there. No smiles like last night, no kissing Mickey and being solicitous, no glancing at the phone as if she wished from the bottom of her socks that it would ring.

Just, at one point, a bombshell:

"You're going to Washington," her mother said sternly.

"What?" Mickey asked, shocked.

"Just, please bring me everything the school sends home, Mickey. Wasn't there a permission slip or something?"

"Yes," Mickey said. "But I knew we couldn't afford it, so . . ."

Her mother held up a hand, very impatiently. "That's not for you to decide. I know what we can and can't afford. I'm your mother."

"Yes, no *kidding*. Wow, I really thought I could trust Chris. I won't make that mistake again!"

"Don't go blaming Chris," her mother said. "You're the one in trouble here. When the school gives you something to show your parents, I expect you to leave it right here on the kitchen table." She thumped the surface with her palm, for good measure.

"If I'm in trouble, why do you say I'm going on the trip?"

"Don't you want to?"

Mickey shrugged. The truth was, she would love to go: cherry blossoms, all those alabaster buildings, getting to meet one of Rhode Island's senators and maybe the president, staying in a hotel. But what good would it be if Shane couldn't go, too?

"Not really," she said.

Her mother peered at her, reading her mind. Mickey could tell—there was a little flicker of humor, and even understanding, there in her mother's smile. "Why? Because Shane's not going?"

"Maybe," Mickey said, blushing, wondering how her mother always seemed to know just what she was thinking.

"Young lady, that's not a good reason. He'll still be here when you get home."

"It's too late anyway," Mickey said. "The deadline already passed."

"I'll call the principal if I have to," her mother said. "You're going. And Mickey?"

"What?"

"I love you, honey. Just, please, don't keep things from me. Secrets . . ." Her mother trailed off, and Mickey saw her eyes fill with tears. "They hurt more often than they help."

"Love you, too," Mickey said, kissing her mother, giving her an extra-long hug—partly because Mickey was inwardly so excited about the idea about going to Washington, even more because she sensed her mother needed it. Her mother clutched her hard, kissing Mickey's hair. Mickey knew she smelled like salt air, from all the time she'd been spending on the beach with Shane.

And she knew how much her mother loved the smell of salt air.

Now she had to figure out a way for Shane to get the money so he could take the trip, too. But first, she had to help her mother. She saw the sadness in her eyes, and it felt like a nail in Mickey's heart. Last night, as confused as Mickey had felt about seeing her mother happy again, happy about another man, she had at least known that something wonderful was going on. Questions were questions, but there was nothing like seeing your mother happy.

"What's wrong, Mom?" Mickey asked.

"Nothing for you to worry about, honey."

"Please tell me."

But her mother just tried to smile, gave Mickey another hug, and went back to staring at the table. Mickey backed away, toward her room, where she was going to call Shane, but gazing at her mother, she felt that nail going deeper. Her mother looked so worried, and if Mickey didn't know her better, know that her mother was the best person in the world, she'd have thought her mother was being crushed by the weight of having done something awful.

Shane grabbed the phone the second it rang. His mother seemed to be on the line just about 24/7, talking to Major Dickweed down at Camp Lejeune, and Shane needed a few minutes of airtime himself. He'd expected it to be the major himself, but felt a thrill to hear Mickey's voice instead.

"Hey," he said.

"Guess what?" Mickey asked. "I'm going to Washington!"

"Yeah?" Shane asked, his heart falling. "I thought you said you weren't."

"Well, I didn't think I could—but my mother's friend Chris let the whole thing slip, and now my mother says I can."

"How did Chris hear about it?"

"From Josh, of all people," Mickey said. "When we were walking out of the diner last night, he was on his way in, and he said I should try to go. Or something. Big idiot."

"Yeah. Idiot," Shane said. But as he lay on his bed, staring at the ceiling, he could see the whole thing in his mind: Josh getting Mickey alone in Washington, showing her

how much better it was to hang out with a
guy who had money instead of one who
couldn't even afford to get his car fixed.
Mickey's mom's friend Chris had acted so
impressed about Shane riding his bike with
his board under one arm, but he had actually read her mind, seen her thinking "loser."

"Josh is such a jerk," Mickey said. "I don't
know why he even speaks to me, considering what I think of him."

"He speaks to you because he's hot for
you," Shane said.

"No he's not."

Shane saw no reason to argue with her.
Mickey was so modest, it was almost funny.
She was the prettiest girl in school, with the
liveliest mind and the most beautiful body,
but instead of acting as if she thought she
was all that, she seemed the opposite—as if
she didn't think about it at all.

Meanwhile, Shane got to watch Josh sali-
vating over her every chance he got. He
watched him watch her in the cafeteria, and
in the halls, and walking into class. Shane
saw Josh staring at her out the window of
his stupid Mercedes sports car—watching
Mickey climb onto the big yellow school
bus with Shane, or riding her bike with

Shane—as if he knew it was just a matter of time before Mickey figured out which guy would be better in the long run: the one with a rusted old Taurus parked behind his house, or the one with the outrageously en-gineered German automobile that ran fast and looked great.

Hmm, Shane thought. Tough choice.

"Never mind about Josh," Mickey said now. "The point is, we have to find a way for you to come, too."

"To Washington?" he asked. "Forget it."

"We have to!" Mickey said. "It's our class trip, and I'm not going without you."

"Look, Mick," he said. "I see the way your mom looks at me, and I don't blame her. When she first met me, I was on probation, doing community service. The fact she lets you hang out with me is amazing. You think I want to blow that by spoiling your chance to go to Washington?"

"But Shane . . ."

"Come on. The nation's capital! Don't you want to meet our senators, shake hands? I won't let you deprive our senators of the chance to have their pictures taken with you."

Mickey laughed, and he was glad. Steer

her away from this stupid topic; now Shane wished time would fly. Let her go to Washington as soon as possible, so she could return home. He'd use the time carefully, wisely, figure out a way to make her so proud she'd come flying back to him.

"Nice try," she said. "But I still don't want to go without you."

"Look, I don't even want to go to Washington," he said. "I hate politics and politicians. Besides, there's no surfing there, you know? The tidal pool—forget it. And the reflecting basin, whatever the hell it's called— dead calm and totally flat."

"But cherry blossoms; I want to see them with you. Clouds of beautiful white flowers, petals raining down from the trees," she said, her voice catching. He could hear the emotion even through the phone; he felt it himself, imagining seeing something that wonderful with her.

"I know," he said. "But spring will get to Rhode Island eventually. We'll see them here. You know I can't leave—I have to surf the wreck every chance I get. It might be gone by summer."

"You won't even *try* to come to Washington?" she asked, sounding hurt. She believed him, Shane realized—that he would rather stay home and surf than take the class trip—and that was good.

"Nah," he said. "It's not for me."

She fell silent. He could hear her breathing over the phone. Maybe it wouldn't be so bad for her to go away on the trip. Let Josh try to get her—give Mickey the chance to really decide. Being away from Shane might be good for her. *It might be*, he told himself, even though the thought made him hurt so much inside, he sat bolt upright on his bed.

"Tonight," Mickey whispered, swallowing hard, and Shane could hear she had started to cry. "What's wrong tonight?"

"Nothing," he said.

"Not just with you," she said. "My mother, too. She's upset. And you; I thought you'd be excited about Washington. About the idea of going together!"

"I don't know about your mother," he said. "But me—there's nothing wrong with me. I'm just . . . Sorry, Mickey. Washington's just not my thing."

Shane's mother poked her head into his room, motioned that she needed the line. Probably the major was going to call. For once, Shane didn't really mind. He knew that if he didn't get off the phone with Mickey, he'd lose it. He'd beg her not to go, or he'd promise he'd find a way to join her—but how? Sell his heap of a car?

Sell his bike, or his board? He probably *would* sell his board—as much as it was part of him. But it was old and patched—he'd bought it used for fifty bucks two years ago. What would it get him now? Twenty-five? That wouldn't even cover meals for a day.

"I gotta go," he said. "My mom needs the phone."

"Okay," she said, sounding hurt and hesitant.

"Sorry, Mickey," he said. "About Washington."

"It's okay," she whispered. "It's just . . . I know you say Washington's not your thing. I just thought that being together was. That being together with me was your thing."

"We'll be together when you get back," he said, hanging up fast. Because if he'd stayed on even one more second, he'd have told her something he'd never told anyone in his life—words that never got spoken here in his house, that hadn't been said under this roof since his father had gone into the waves and not come out: *I love you.*

"Shane!" his mother yelled. "Get off the phone."

"I am already!" he yelled back.

Shane loved Mickey so much, his hands were shaking. His heart was thudding as he thought of her sitting at home, wondering what was going on; she had sounded so hurt. And Shane wouldn't hurt her for the world. He pushed himself up off the bed, went over to his desk. It was covered with schoolbooks, none of which he had the remotest interest in opening.

It was also covered with pages and pages of notes for the materials that he and Mickey had given to Ranger O'Casey. Shane still had plenty of community service left at the beach. While Mickey was in Washington, he knew something he could do to make the time go by—it had to do with one angle his research had turned up, that he and Mickey hadn't included in the packet.

He might die trying to make this happen, but at that moment—standing in his room, listening to his mother's happy voice as she talked on the phone out in the kitchen, knowing that Mickey was going away—he didn't really care.

There was precedent in his family for dying for love. Turning his eyes to the pictures on the wall, he looked at his father and knew that's what he had done. Surfing that winter sea, Shane knew how filled with love his father had to have been.

That's what life on the waves was like: having an ocean under your board, the entire sea swelling and building, bearing you in one seismic crash after another back onto the beach. For Shane, there was no other way to express how he felt about the wildness of love, the fullness of life. He looked into his dad's eyes, knowing something no one else did. And the funny thing was, Mickey had given him the idea.

The right underwater photo would be one foolproof way to keep U-823 where it was, and if he could accomplish that, Mickey would be so proud of him.

And that would be worth everything.

18

Neve drove down the beach road at dusk, noticing that the sky was staying light a little longer each day. Right now the sun was setting behind the pines on the inland side of the road, spreading thin pink light across the wind-sculpted white sand dunes, into the darkening sea.

When she pulled up at the ranger station, she took a deep breath and stared at the water for a moment. Coming to the beach had always settled her, brought her back to herself. The sound of the waves came through the car windows. There must be a storm somewhere offshore, because the waves were enormous today. She felt churned up herself.

There on the water, fifty yards or so down the beach, she saw the shapes of surfers. Was one of them Shane? Mickey had seemed subdued earlier—Neve knew she was torn because Shane wasn't going to Washington and she was. In spite of feeling relieved that they wouldn't be in a hotel together, she felt sorry for Shane.

Climbing out of her car, she grabbed the things she'd brought, then hurried across the parking lot. Tim stood at the door, smiling as he watched her. She ran up the steps, stood facing him.

"You made it," he said, taking the bottle of wine and box of cookies she'd brought, placing them on the counter. Then he took her in his arms.

"I did," she said.

He kissed her, brushing the hair back from her face. He was both tender and clumsy in the most endearing way, trying to tuck the hair behind her ears, missing, kissing her anyway, arms around her, pulling her closer now.

They walked into the living room, and she sat down while he went to pour the wine.

He'd put out a plate of cheese and crackers—Brie, cheddar, chèvre. Dar Williams sang on the stereo—"Mercy of the Fallen." Neve leaned back and tried to let the music soothe her. Glancing nervously toward the kitchen door, she knew she had something to tell Tim, and she'd better do it soon.

"I hope you're in the mood for fish," he said as he walked in, handed her the glass.

"I am," she said. "Especially here—" She motioned toward the window, with its stark view of the beach and sea.

"Good. A friend of mine runs charters out of Galilee, and he brought me some winter flounder. Fresh this morning . . ."

"Sounds great. It must be almost the end of their run," she said.

"I didn't think spring was coming this year," he said, sitting beside her. "It hasn't in a long time, no matter what the calendar says." He put his arms around her, tilted her head back, kissed her gently. Then again, not gently.

Neve closed her eyes, feeling his body pressing against hers. She turned half into him, one leg crossing his. His body felt so hard, and she couldn't get enough of it. Thoughts flickered in her brain, but she pushed them away. She told herself there would be time to talk in a few minutes, or a few hours.

While they kissed, the sun went all the way down; it was the moon rising that got their attention, pulled them back from the brink. Or maybe it was the smell of good food coming from the kitchen.

Neve could feel how much he didn't want to pull away, and he didn't—he just took her hand, tugged her toward the kitchen when he had to go in there. She fell easily into the rhythm of helping out. Mixing the salad dressing, tossing the greens. Cutting French bread, placing it in a basket. He had set the table, so she lit the candles.

They sat down across the small table from each other. Crossing her legs, she bumped his foot; they smiled.

"Sorry," she said.

"No problem," he said.

The candlelight flickered in a draft coming through the window. It threw shadows across the table, but there was plenty of light from the moon rising over the beach. White-blue moonlight spilled across the table's oak grain, across their plates. They ate, and the food was delicious.

"You're a good cook," she said.

"Thanks," he said. "I like doing it. I guess I started right after the separation; my son would come spend weekends with me, and we were both sick of pizza."

"He'd stay with you?" she asked. "Here?"

"Well, before I was posted here, I was the ranger for a nature preserve up near the Massachusetts border. The cabin there made this one look palatial." He laughed, as if remembering the close quarters. "But yes, eventually he stayed with me here."

She nodded, glancing around. The place was so small; she imagined Frank sleeping on the couch. It didn't matter to him, she was sure, as long as he was near his dad.

"I wish Mickey's father were more . . ." she started to say.

"Doesn't she ever spend weekends with him?" Tim asked.

Neve shook her head. "Not at all anymore. She did, a few times at first. He made a big show of renting a fancy condo just outside of Providence, so she could have her own room, and there was a pool and a game room. . . . I wondered how he'd be able to afford it . . . but I did like the fact he was thinking of Mickey."

Tim didn't comment on that, but she saw an expression cross his face—maybe reflecting what she felt about Richard renting an expensive place supposedly for Mickey, and then never seeing her.

"What does he do on weekends if he's not seeing her?"

"Alyssa," she said. "At least at first. He fell in love." She shook her head. "And when Richard does that, stop the presses; everything else falls by the wayside. He tried to balance his two lives for a while—Mickey and Alyssa. Then Alyssa got pregnant."

"You can't tell me he loves the new baby more than Mickey?" Tim said, looking up with anger in his eyes.

"The baby hasn't even been born yet," Neve said. "Richard just . . . well, I guess he got scared. He let the condo go and bought a big house. The payments must have been something to behold. Mickey would be happy with anything—pizza, a walk, taking a ride—as long as she was with her father."

"And he can't handle that?" Tim asked.

"He can't handle anything," Neve said quietly. "How did we get started talking about Richard?"

"I'm sorry," he said. "I don't like talking

about Beth, either. It just must be so hard on you. Mickey has to know it's not her fault, right?"

"I hope so," she said. "But he's her father, you know? The other day, after my friend Chris took Mickey out when you and I went to Newport, she told me Mickey spilled the beans about a class trip—she hadn't even asked me to go, because she didn't want to get her father in trouble for not helping out financially."

"It must be hard on you," he said.

"We get by," Neve said. "I'm going to ask for a raise, though."

"You should," he said. "I'm sure you're doing a great job there—I can't wait to see the catalogue you did of my uncle's work."

Berkeley. Her stomach fell, and she looked into Tim's eyes, knowing she had to tell him that she'd slipped up, told Chris, and that Dominic knew, too. She had finished eating, laid her fork and knife down.

"There's something I have to tell you," she said.

"Come here," he said, pulling her up out of her seat, leading her into the living room. The moon had completely risen, and it looked like a disc of pure silver. The sight of it took everything away, especially because his arm was around her, drawing her closer. His breath felt warm on her cheek, and his arms felt so hard and strong, and her heart was racing so fast she could barely catch her breath.

"It's important," she said, just as he was about to kiss her.

"Okay," he said, backing off just slightly, easing her down onto the couch beside him. "Sure, what is it?"

"It's about your uncle," she said. And although her heart was still beating fast, now it was more from fear than passion—how would he react to what she was about to say?

"What about him?"

"I did something awful," she said quietly, holding his hand. "No one's ever known Berkeley's real identity, all this time. . . . I know you asked me to promise not to tell, and I never would have—there's no excuse, Tim. But I was so excited about it, I told someone. I just blurted it out."

He didn't drop her hand, didn't look away. He just nodded as if he wanted her to go on.

"My best friend," she said. "Chris Brody. It was yesterday, right after you'd told me.

She came to the gallery, and I was distracted—she had just told me about Mickey's school trip, and I was shocked because I didn't even know about it, and Mickey obviously hadn't told me. I can't even remember exactly how it happened, but I said it right out loud—that Berkeley was your uncle."

He hesitated, and in those few seconds, she felt the ground tilt. She wanted to take it all back, rewind time, retract her words.

"Okay," he said slowly. "That's not the end of the world."

"The worst part is, my boss walked in just as I was saying it. He heard, but I swore him to secrecy. Both of them—Chris and Dominic."

That worried him a little bit more. Even as she watched the doubt cross his face, she kicked herself a little harder for letting it slip.

"Why has your family kept it secret for so long?" she asked.

"Before he went to war, he kept the paintings to himself," Tim said. "They were just for his family, friends. . . . It wasn't until after he got back that he was 'discovered.' A collector got hold of some, I guess, and the word was out. Suddenly my uncle—who'd

just been this bird-loving guy who happened to paint—was sought after. But by
then, he was gone."

"Gone?"

"I don't mean dead—I just mean, so damaged. He'd stopped painting—which only
made the frenzy greater. His family was devastated; his wife and daughters."

"Daughters?" Neve asked, wondering
where they were now.

"My father wanted to protect him," he said
quietly. "From people asking questions,
wanting his work, wanting to know why he'd
stopped making art. To know that my uncle
had that kind of talent, and to know that the
war blasted it out of him. It was all lost."

"You don't lose talent," Neve said.

"You do if you stop using it," Tim said,
pulling her closer. "That's true of everything,
not just art. Things that come so naturally—
if you don't use them, they go away. Trauma
can do that. You lose the ability to talk, to
give, to care, to love."

"His wife and daughters?"

Tim nodded.

"That's what happened to me," she whispered, looking up at his eyes—dark blue in
the moonlight.

"To me, too," he said. "Until you."

He kissed her, and she knew everything was going to be okay. He'd forgiven her for the slip—she'd done damage control, and they'd manage to keep the secret. She closed her eyes, felt the moon's brightness penetrating her eyelids, felt Tim's mouth on hers and his arms tight around her body.

The beach behind them, out the window, was deserted. The surfers had gone home. Kissing Tim, Neve heard the waves crashing, couldn't tell the difference between the sea and her own heartbeat. He was right: she'd lost the ability to talk, to care, to love a man—she'd told herself that being Mickey's mom was enough. To think that she might have missed this, missed Tim, was almost too much to bear.

His kiss was insistent, and so was hers. The candles on the table flickered, and the moon's brightness poured in. She felt she was floating on it, just drifting with Tim on a sea of moonlight, feeling the air and water move beneath them. Nothing had been right for so long, and now it seemed as if nothing could ever be wrong.

Just then the phone rang.

Tim could have ignored it; Neve felt him

wanting to. The call would go to voice mail; they could keep kissing, keep holding each other. But suddenly she thought of Mickey—what if she was trying to get them? It could be something important— Mickey or someone else. Tim must have thought the same thing, because suddenly he kissed her gently, pushed up from the couch, went over to the small table that held the phone, weather station, and binoculars.

"Hello," he said.

Neve leaned back—not quite nervous, but unable to relax until he came back. She heard the ocean pounding, tried to breathe more slowly, listening to the sound.

"Oh—hi, Beth," he said, shrugging as he looked at Neve. What could she want? His ex-wife . . . did she call him often? They must have been bonded hard and fast by Frank, maybe even more by his loss. Neve turned away, not wanting to intrude. She swiveled on the couch, arm across the back, stared out the window at the moon on the water. The waves moved constantly, breaking the light into a million pieces.

The tone of his voice caught her attention—even more than the words.

"When?" he asked sharply. "What did they say?"

She couldn't keep looking away after that—she had to turn and face him. He wasn't meeting her eyes. That was her second clue, after the hard edge in his voice.

"Yeah, well, thanks for letting me know. Thanks for telling Dad."

He hung up the phone—and Neve knew.

"Oh, no . . . ," she began.

"Your boss called the press," he said. "He was on the six o'clock news, saying that he'd solved the mystery of Berkeley."

"Tim, no—"

"Beth heard it, and she called my father to warn him—one thing, after twenty years as my wife, she knows how O'Caseys feel about having their stories told. Privacy—secrecy—is a big deal with us. I guess you know that, too."

"But you said . . ." she began, feeling panic. She had arrived here feeling so nervous and upset, not wanting to admit to him what she'd done. But Tim had been so understanding, so forgiving.

"The funny thing is, I didn't think it would bother me," he said. "When you first told me, it was almost a relief."

"Then why is it so bad?" she asked, crossing the room, standing right in front of him, looking up into his eyes. "Don't let it be, Tim. Please don't . . ."

"You know why it's so bad?" he asked. "Because it will lead straight from my uncle to Frank."

"Frank?" she asked, confused.

"Even Beth said that. She's in shock—I could hear it in her voice. But your boss laid it all out for everyone; he said my uncle was 'destroyed by the war.' Already the reporter tracked down his service record, and my father's. They're putting it together, our family connection with war. U-823 is a hot topic, and they were on it—Beth said the TV showed footage of Landry's big announcement."

"But that's not about Frank. . . ."

"Not yet," Tim said. "But it won't take them long. His obituary mentioned my father and uncle. Some reporter will drag it up, put everything together."

Neve pulled back from him, dropped her hands to her sides. She felt sick. She felt like attacking Dominic, but the whole thing was her fault.

"I'm so sorry," she said.

Tim just shook his head, walked to the window. She reached out, wanting to touch his back; he was staring at the moonlight as if he wanted to disappear into it. It suddenly looked so cold—white light filling the night, coating the waves like spilled mercury.

Backing away, Neve picked up her bag and jacket. She took one last look at Tim, but he didn't turn around. Opening the kitchen door, she let herself out.

The air that had felt so full of spring and promise before, now felt cold and damp. Mist was rising from the sea, wrapping Neve in shame and grief. She had never meant to cause Tim and his family pain. But she had, and she couldn't think of any way to undo it. She climbed into her station wagon, started it up, backed out of the sandy lot. She had to wipe her eyes to see through the tears.

Some broken hearts really couldn't be fixed, she thought.

Especially because she'd just broken Tim's heart a little bit more.

19

One day the harbor was empty, and the next day the crane had arrived. Mickey saw it with a shock, coming around the corner on the school bus. The driver exclaimed, pointing it out to all the kids. He pulled the bus over, idling at the curb, so everyone could look.

The crane was bright yellow, gleaming in the sunlight, reflecting in the harbor's still water. It stood on the deck of a barge so enormous, it dominated the entire outer harbor, just inside the breakwater. Looming just offshore, it was a reminder of the job it had come to do, of the loss about to occur. As the bus driver pulled away, all the kids started buzzing, turning to stare. Only Mickey refused to look, huddled in her seat; the sight of the crane had made her stomach ache.

People drove from all over the state to see it. Cole Landry's announcement had piqued everyone's interest, because suddenly the process seemed unstoppable. Shops and restaurants in town were doing great business—better than on summer days, when crowds flocked to the beach. The local paper ran an editorial about how Landry's plan was good for the Secret Harbor economy in the short run—but what would happen after the wreck was gone for good? What about the divers who came to see it? And the World War II buffs?

Mickey had read that editorial thinking about the folder of material she and Shane had given Ranger O'Casey and the letters she was starting to receive in response to the ones she had sent out—fifty-five to Germany. She wondered whether more would come in time. The crane was a reminder that time was flying; they had less than four weeks. Would she and Shane be able to do everything they had to do before the crane went into action and the U-boat was taken away? And would Mr. O'Casey still want to help?

Her mother had been getting close to Mr. O'Casey, but ever since she'd gone down to the beach to have dinner with him, they hadn't even spoken. Mickey knew, because of how keyed in she and her mother were to each other. It wasn't that Mickey was trying to spy; it's just that she couldn't help noticing that her mother was spending all her time reading, avoiding the telephone—not even picking up when Chris called.

Her mother had always taught Mickey to be enthusiastic about work, to be eager to do a good job. But every morning, while Mickey was getting ready for school, she'd see her mother lagging behind—getting dressed slowly, drinking coffee and staring out at the bare trees, lost in thought, acting as if she didn't want to go to work.

"Mom, look—an eastern phoebe!" Mickey had said yesterday morning, looking out the kitchen window at their favorite harbinger of spring.

Her mother had nodded, saying nothing. She'd tried to smile, to drum up a tiny bit of enthusiasm for their first sight of that most

reliable early migrant—and right on schedule, too, the middle of March.

"We saw it together!" Mickey had said.

"I'm glad, honey," her mother had said,
but had gone back to sipping her coffee and
looking as if she was plotting a way—any
way—to avoid going to work.

Mickey wanted to ask her what was
wrong, what had happened between her
and Mr. O'Casey. After dreading any connection her mother might make with a man
who didn't happen to be Mickey's father,
Mickey had actually felt pretty good about
Mr. O'Casey. *Beyond* good; she had felt
content and easy and happy.

But Mickey couldn't really ask, because
she knew her mother might then turn things
around and ask what was going on between
her and Shane. And Mickey couldn't really
answer that, because she didn't exactly
know. Ever since the whole Washington trip
had arisen, he just seemed so quiet and
withdrawn. He surfed every day, and hardly
ever asked Mickey to come with him.
Mickey knew that he felt left out; she
wanted to reassure him that she didn't care
whether he had the money for Washington
or not.

But she knew how tender it was for him, especially with Josh flaunting his family's wealth, continually pointing out the crane to anyone who would listen, telling him that it was just one of his father's toys. Mickey could see Shane tensing up nearly every time Josh opened his mouth. The thing was, Josh could be useful. He was so busy bragging and showing off, but Mickey had figured out a way she could get him to help—without him knowing. Why couldn't Shane see that?

At least her father had called her again. He'd left another message—didn't say where he was calling from, but told her he was on the road. He said he had a business opportunity out west, in the Sunbelt, in Arizona—a really big deal that was going to bring in lots of money. He'd be flush, on easy street. He went on about how he was going to rent a great condo with a pool and a waterslide, and how he hoped Mickey would come visit him.

He didn't mention Alyssa or the baby.

One way Mickey knew that she was growing up was that this time she didn't believe her father. It made her sad to realize that he was probably just making something up to keep her from being mad. She used to be so special to him, but now he was treating her just like anyone else: his creditors, her mother, Alyssa . . . the people who wanted something from him.

So Mickey focused on her projects. She called the raptor rehab, to ask about the snowy owl, and old Mr. O'Casey gave her updates. She heard sadness in his voice, and realized it had something to do with what her mother had told Chris and Mr. di Tibor. That just made Mickey know she had to keep going—work on Josh, write the letters, get them out, wait for replies.

If only Josh or his father could pull strings in Washington—that would be amazing. They'd be doing good whether they meant to or not. If he could really use his father's connections to introduce Mickey to their senator, maybe she could really accomplish something. She was getting her cast off soon, before the trip. And that was good, because she was going to need her left hand, to hold the letters while she shook hands with the senators.

Life was changing. She had once heard that if a butterfly flutters its wings in the Amazon, it could affect an entire weather system in the United States. That's how she felt about the events of the last few days, right here in Rhode Island. Perhaps because it was such a tiny state, everything seemed to affect everything else. Maybe there were a *lot* of butterflies flapping—or at least two.

Mickey and Shane. Changing the world.

"So," Josh said, walking over to Shane's locker. "I hear Mickey paid her money in time for Washington. Also, and I couldn't be sorrier about this, I hear you're not coming on the trip. What a pity."

Shane ignored him. He was rummaging around inside, looking for his history assignment. A poetry book by Thomas Hardy tumbled out—Mickey had given it to him when they'd really started their campaign to save the U-boat. Shane picked it up, shoved it under his arm.

"Your girlfriend seems pretty excited about the trip," Josh continued.

Shane frowned, trying not to let that register. The inside of his locker's gray metal door was plastered with surf decals and pages torn from *Surfing Magazine*: endless blue waves about to break. He tried to think of his last strenuous session, riding sets of massive breakers over the conning tower, ultra-thick double-ups, feeling the ocean's majesty and knowing he was surfing in his father's footsteps.

"Didn't you hear me?" Josh asked.

"I heard you," Shane said.

"She's hot to meet Senator Sheridan, that's for sure. Actually, she said Senator House would be cool, too—but my dad's really closer to Sheridan. They belong to a few of the same clubs, you know?"

Shane burrowed through piles of stuff at the bottom of his locker. He'd had the paper just before last class. What was wrong with him? He was totally losing his shit right now. He knew what Mickey was doing; all he had to do was stay focused on not letting Josh get to him.

"Burning Tree, Manassas, Briar Hill . . ."

"Any of them in Rhode Island?" Shane asked.

"No. The Washington area, why?"

Shane just shook his head. Family of idiot carpetbaggers, coming to Rhode Island to take what they could, make money off the state's heritage, and then move on. Coast into some other unsuspecting community, take its treasures, and split—a whole lot richer.

"Anyway, Mickey's really going to enjoy some quality time with Senator Sheridan. He's going to meet and greet our whole class, but I'll make sure she gets to really talk to him. Because she asked, and that matters to me."

Shane was determined not to react. If only Josh knew what Mickey was really planning, he wouldn't be acting so pumped. Shane kept searching for his history paper; he'd written it over the weekend, late at night, after surfing was done for the day. With his mother back and forth to North Carolina so much, he could do homework in his own way, without her on his case to get to bed early. Up before dawn, surf a few sets, school, back to the beach, then homework. *Priorities . . .*

Mickey was in there, too. As in, he thought of her all the time. When he was on his board, when the drop was steep over the wreck, when the water was as blue as the sky, when a fifteen-foot rogue wave came out of nowhere, breaking out behind him and smashing him under—or when the wave lifted him up, curled over, turned into a tube, and spit him out on the beach—the whole time he'd be thinking of Mickey.

"She's growing up, our little Mickey," Josh said now. "Started the year off into birds and saving the world, and now she's coming around."

"What's wrong with saving the world?" Shane asked.

Josh laughed. "It's just . . . not possible."

"What do you know about it?"

"You sound like a little kid, you know that? My dad says all the do-gooders are just people who haven't grown up yet. 'Saving the world'—listen to yourself!"

Shane shrugged. "Better than listening to you," he said.

Josh's eyes turned mean. "At least Mickey's figured it out. She's finally given up on fighting a losing battle—she's joined the winning team."

"The what?"

"I'm talking about the U-boat. It *is* going to be a museum."

"Don't be so sure. It isn't yet."

"It was cute of her to want to keep it here, for whatever sentimental reasons, but she's a realist—a smart girl. She knows my dad has pulled all the strings necessary, and it's heading to Cape Cod. This summer. She's figuring out that power's what gets things done."

Shane found his paper. He stuffed it into his knapsack, still holding on to the book of poems.

"You want something done," Josh said, right in Shane's face, "you have to go for it. That's why we know senators—and that's why I'm going to make sure Mickey meets Sheridan. Hope you don't mind."

"If it makes her happy, I don't mind," Shane said.

Josh smiled. He had really, really white teeth. Also, he had a tan. Shane knew his family had a private jet, and kids talked about how the Landrys flew to St. Bart's just for the weekend whenever they wanted. They skied in Vail all winter—leaving after school on Friday, returning before class Monday morning.

"Yeah, I think it makes her happy," Josh said.

"That's good, then," Shane said, fighting the urge to knock out Josh's very white teeth. Dude was annoying. He was short— the top of his head came to the bottom of

Shane's chin. He had skinny shoulders and a pathetically narrow chest.

"You know," Josh said, "she talked about cherry blossoms, and how we might see a black-throated blue warbler or some bull-shit. It's kind of cute—she's holding on to those childish ways. But what really turns her on, and I can tell, is that I've promised we'll go to the Russell Office Building. Ever been there? The seat of power, man. It's where the senators run the country. Yeah, Mickey wants to meet them. Sorry you won't be able to make it."

"Have fun," Shane said. It was all he could do to walk away. His right hand was itching to punch Josh's lights out. Not because he'd gloated about the trip, or because Shane couldn't afford to go—not at all be-cause Josh's father knew senators and was going to introduce Mickey to them.

It was the part about the black-throated blue warbler that got to him. Josh didn't de-serve to know how she felt about birds. Shane thought of their times on the beach—when he'd come out of the water, she'd be standing there in her green boots, standing on the jetty, all excited because she'd just seen some kind of bird—a ruddy duck in the shallows, or some cedar waxwings in the thicket. She'd put her arms around his neck and he'd lift her down, feeling her strong body in his cold, wet hands. And she'd talk about the birds she'd seen, and he'd know how much she loved them, and that made him love them, too.

Walking down the hall, he wished Mickey would walk by; he wanted to talk to her, tell her what Josh had just said. He knew her schedule—she had biology for the next hour, and the science rooms were on a different floor. He was a few minutes early for history, so he put his paper on the teacher's desk, then took his seat. While the classroom started filling up, he pulled out the book Mickey had given him.

Josh had no idea who Mickey was; it made Shane feel solid, holding the book. He felt her steadiness, strength flowing into him, right from the pages. Still, it stung to think of her talking to Josh. Even for such a good cause.

Opening the book, he realized that his hands were shaking a little. Mickey had read this poem in her English class, and it had seemed so perfect for what they were trying to do, she had made Shane read it.

They'd copied it, stuck it in the folder they'd given to O'Casey.

The folder, filled with their most persuasive arguments. With thoughts about the war, about the battle that had taken place right here on the Rhode Island shore, about men who had died far from home, buried in a common grave.

That's what U-823 was, Shane and Mickey knew: a common grave. Shane had kept the book, and the Hardy poem, because it meant more to him than Mickey had even known. Staring down, he read it now:

> *They throw in Drummer Hodge, to rest*
> *Uncoffined—just as found:*
> *His landmark is a kopje-crest*
> *That breaks the veldt around;*
> *And foreign constellations west*
> *Each night above his mound.*
>
> *Young Hodge the Drummer never*
>   *knew—*
> *Fresh from his Wessex home—*
> *The meaning of the broad Karoo,*
> *The Bush, the dusty loam,*
> *And why uprose to nightly view*
> *Strange stars amid the gloam.*

Yet portion of that unknown plain
Will Hodge forever be;
His homely Northern breast and brain
Grow to some Southern tree,
And strange-eyed constellations reign
His stars eternally.

By the time Shane finished reading the poem through again, the teacher had walked in. Shane had to keep his head down, to hide the fact his cheeks were burning hot. Mickey had told him it was a war poem, that Drummer Hodge had been buried on the battlefield, under foreign constellations.

She had held Shane's hand on the beach, and together they'd stared out over the water. Before Mickey, he had valued the U-boat only because it created such a magnificent surf break. Since her, he cared about the men who were buried inside. They might have come here as German sailors to attack America, but now they were just the skeletons of men. That's all that mattered, that's all that lasted.

Mickey had taught him that.

Shane closed the book and looked up at the teacher. She was talking about tomorrow's quiz, but he was thinking of all those German sailors, buried in the Atlantic Ocean's unmarked grave, beneath the strange-eyed constellations. Shane stared at the teacher, thinking of Mickey.

He wished he could go to Washington with her, and he wished that she didn't have to talk to Josh anymore. Josh could never understand Mickey the way Shane could; and he closed his eyes, knowing that she was helping him understand himself.

20

Joe O'Casey made the rounds, feeding the birds. Spring had officially arrived, and the owls felt it. They all did, actually. Winter plumage molted, and mating behavior commenced. The air was warm, and the barn filled with mating calls. Joe opened the baffles and flight corridors between cages, to encourage bonding.

He hung back, watching the male snowy owl. This guy had made remarkable progress, but Joe could see that he was permanently damaged; it would be irresponsible to consider releasing him.

Staring at his gleaming white head, his piercing yellow eyes, his shattered beak,

Joe saw a great warrior. This owl had made countless migrations—probably had a wife somewhere out in the wild; it was almost inconceivable to imagine that such a fine bird would lack a mate.

Joe thought of Damien's wife and daughters. That was a subject almost more painful than Damien alone. The news about Berkeley had seemed the perfect opportunity for Joe to reach out—but Genevieve had gently declined. And Joe's nieces remained strangers to the uncle who had adored them as children.

Watching the male owl crane his neck, communicating with his female neighbor, Joe was grateful to have observed her flight last night; she'd flown up, through the corridors, swooping down to visit. He'd called to her, and she'd responded. It was happening again right now—the male vocalizing, and the female reacting. Joe almost held his breath—examples of bonding between middle-aged owls had taken place over the years, but none more astonishing than this.

"Joe?"

Hearing his name, he looked over at the barn door. Neve Halloran stood there, looking hesitant, even scared. He put a finger to his lips, motioned her over. She hurried, silently, worry in her eyes.

Joe pointed at the cage. She followed his gaze, saw the two snowy owls sitting together, the female quietly grooming the male, him allowing her solicitations. Sunlight came through the skylight, pouring down on Joe and Neve, on the owls. Joe pretended to be watching the birds, but he was quite conscious of Neve—breathing a little too hard, seeming as stressed as the male snowy owl had been when she'd first brought him to the barn.

"See what they're doing?" he asked.

"I don't understand," she said.

"You should," he said. "It's quite obvious; they're becoming a pair."

"Really?" she asked.

He nodded, but even such good news didn't erase the pain from her eyes. Placing a hand on her arm, he gestured for her to follow him into the office. Too much human contact could interrupt the owls' bonding process, and Joe didn't want that to happen. Also, he saw that Neve would burst if he didn't give her the chance to have her say; she was a few years younger than Damien's oldest daughter.

"Mr. O'Casey," she began the instant they stepped inside his office.

"I thought you called me Joe. Are we going backward?" he asked.

She looked stunned. "I didn't think you'd want me to call you Joe, or anything," she said. "I can understand you not wanting to have anything to do with me."

He stood at the counter. There was an old electric teakettle; battered and ancient, it had been rewired more than once. He'd gotten used to tea during the war, never quite given up the habit. Walking over to the sink—piled with water dishes and beakers and pipettes for giving medicine and feeding owl babies—he filled the kettle to the brim.

"Want tea?" he asked.

"Joe," she said. "I just want to—"

"Earl Grey or Irish breakfast?" he asked.

"Irish breakfast," she said.

"Good choice," he said, nodding. "Just what I'd expect from a Halloran. Wait, that's your married name, right? What was your maiden name?"

"Fallon."

"Tipperary, right?"

"That's where my grandparents are from, yes," she said.

"Ireland is like Rhode Island," he said. "Everyone knows where people are from, who's related to whom. The advantage of being from a relatively small island."

"Joe, I'm so sorry about what I did," she said. "For letting the secret out; I didn't mean to do it, but that's no excuse." He had his back to her, fiddling around with teacups. The teakettle worked fast—he plugged it in, and it started hissing right away.

"My brother had one of these in his Nissen hut," Joe said, tapping the metal lid. "He got hooked on tea over in England—East Anglia is where he was stationed. Those Brits loved their tea, and Damien knew a good thing when he tasted it. Kept him awake for those long flights, you know? He sent me a bunch of it back, and damn if I didn't start drinking it myself."

Neve didn't say anything. He could almost feel the emotion pouring off her, enveloping them both. Earlier, whenever she'd stopped by the barn, they'd stood out in the main section; she'd never been in his private office before.

The walls were covered with his brother's work. Not just finished paintings, but sketches and studies—the roughest, most rudimentary pencil drawings of herons standing in salt ponds, burrowing owls soaring over fields.

"This one's a favorite of mine," he said, gesturing at a sketch of a barn owl peeking out the vent of a church steeple. "Damien did it when we were supposed to be at mass. We hung out across the street instead. I smoked cigarettes and he drew the owl. We were fifteen and seventeen."

"Who was older?" Neve asked quietly.

"I was," Joe said.

"You didn't tell me," she said, sounding almost hurt. "I came here with the snowy owl, and I admired that painting you have hanging out in the barn, and I told you I was working on a Berkeley exhibition catalogue, and you never said a word."

"No," Joe said. "I didn't."

"You didn't want it known at all," she said. "That's why I'm so sorry."

Her face looked tense and drawn, but there was no dimming the wattage: she was still lovely, with those high cheekbones and intelligent blue eyes, with that high color in

her cheeks and lips. No wonder she'd gotten to Tim. Because she had—Joe had no
doubt.

"He wouldn't have told you if he didn't
want you to know," he said as the water
boiled.

"What do you mean?"

"Tim told you, right? That Berkeley is—
was—Damien?"

She hesitated; Joe saw her trying to protect his son, and it made him smile. He
turned his back, poured the hot water into
the brown china teapot, so she wouldn't
see.

"It's almost funny," he said.

She didn't reply, still holding it all inside.

"Look at all the trouble we're both in. I've
spent the last sixty years protecting my
brother; now you're protecting Tim. You
know—I think they're both big enough to
take care of themselves. Let me guess now:
Tim's shut himself off again, this time because you spilled the beans about Damien."

"He'll never speak to me again," she said.

Joe shook his head, staring at the teapot.
"That's ridiculous," he said. "What did you
do that was so bad?"

"I told my boss, and he called Channel 10.

You know—Beth called you. I was with Tim when she called him."

"Beth," he said. His heart filled with tenderness mixed with irritation for his troubled ex-daughter-in-law. She'd called him all right—full of something like malicious glee. "She and Tim had a very unpleasant divorce. I'll never speak ill of her—she was like a daughter to me—but I'll just tell you that she doesn't mind being the bearer of bad news when it comes to Tim."

"It wasn't her fault," Neve said. "It was mine."

"Neve," Joe said, "if you really want to put the blame somewhere, why not give it to Tim? He's the one with the big mouth. If you're thinking in terms of family secrets, that is. Because that was the whole motivation for keeping the Berkeley stuff to ourselves. Old, sad, bitter grief . . . That's what most family secrets are made of, don't you know?"

"I know," Neve whispered.

"So you've actually done us a favor," Joe said, pouring the tea, handing her a cup. "You've turned on the lights, so there's nowhere left to hide."

"Tim was afraid the story would become about Frank," Neve said.

Joe tensed up at that. But he sipped his tea, and he instantly felt better. Damien had known what he was doing with this stuff—better than the whiskey he'd preferred after the war.

"Well, the Berkeley story broke over a week ago," Joe said. "And yes, reporters have been coming around. But tell me, how bad would it be if a story ran about Frank O'Casey? You know what I think Tim was really upset about?"

"What?" Neve asked.

"That they *wouldn't* be asking about Frank. He's gone, and the silence just makes it worse," Joe said. "It's not the questions people ask, it's not the stories they tell—it's the questions they don't ask, the stories they don't tell that makes the hollowness worse, makes us miss them even more, makes us start to wonder if we ever had them at all."

"Do you really think that's it?" she asked, her voice so thin he could hardly hear it over the birds calling out in the barn.

"Yes. I do," Joe said. He opened his desk drawer, pulled out all the clippings he'd cut from the *Providence Journal, Boston Globe*, and *New York Times* in recent days. "Look at all these stories about Damien. This is the art-world story of the year, the fact that my brother was Berkeley. Everyone wants to hear how he started painting, why he loved birds so much, why he wore a cape, all of it. And they want to hear about the war, too. The timing, everything happening with U-823, is stirring them all up."

"I'm sorry about that," Neve said. "It must bring up horrible memories for you."

"They're painful, yes," Joe agreed, spreading the newspapers out on his desk. There were photos of Damien in his bomber's jacket, crouching with his crew by their B-24, of Joe standing on the bridge of the USS *James,* wearing sunglasses, scowling at the camera. "We look pretty tough, don't we?"

"You do."

"A couple of nature-loving kids from Rhode Island," he said. "One with a God-given talent."

"You both have a great talent," Neve said quietly. "Look at what you've done here, with the raptors. Your brother would be very proud."

"I'd like to think that," Joe said. "It makes me feel close to him, doing this work. I imagine the pictures he'd paint of all these owls and hawks. And I look at what Tim's doing down at the beach, keeping that sanctuary open and thriving."

"You passed it on," Neve said. "Your love of nature. Tim has it now, and so did Frank."

Joe nodded. He tried to drink his tea, but he suddenly felt too choked up. Like Tim, he couldn't bear to think about Frank. He gestured toward the barn, and Neve followed him. He wanted to tell her what it had been like, to come back from war and know that everything in Rhode Island had changed; not that the landscape was altered, or the birds had stopped migrating, or that Narragansett Bay had gone dry, or that the Arcade had moved from its spot between Weybosset and Westminster streets in downtown Providence. No, everything had changed because Joe and Damien had come back different.

"We wanted to be good fathers," Joe heard himself say, stopping in front of the snowy owl's cage.

"Who, Joe?"

"Damien and I," he said. "It meant everything to us, because we'd had such a good one ourselves. He showed us how to do things right. Talk to us, throw a ball back and forth, be there for the big things and the small things—didn't matter, just be there. Most of all—he talked to us."

Neve nodded, waiting.

"We didn't do that," Joe said quietly, staring at the male owl. "Couldn't, I guess. The stuff we'd seen in the war. Damien—my sweet, artist brother . . . he firebombed Dresden."

Neve let those words hang in the air, even as the birds squawked and called. Joe closed his eyes, picturing fire raining down from the sky. He had a pretty good idea of what it might have been like, because he'd seen the sea blazing—those men burning alive as they'd tried to swim away from the *Fenwick,* the ship torpedoed by U-823.

"Made my brother stop painting, start drinking," he said.

"I'm sorry," she said.

"It was a way of hiding out—from the people who loved him, from himself. I hated seeing him like that. Maybe I used my brother's desperation as an excuse for my own drinking. We did it together—we'd meet at the bar, just sit there, not talking. I told myself I was looking after him."

"Maybe you were," she said.

Joe shook his head. "Nah. I was just making excuses."

"Excuses?"

"Yes. I was scared. Scared of how I felt inside, of all the things I'd seen and done. And scared of losing my brother. He stopped taking care of himself—had pain in his side and ignored it. Didn't even go to the doctor until it was too late. I think he felt so guilty, he didn't think he deserved to get help."

"What was wrong with him?"

"Cancer," Joe said. "It ate him up. By the time he had surgery and radiation, it was much too late."

"What did his family do?"

Joe sat quietly, remembering Damien's last days. There had been love and forgiveness between him and Genevieve, but it had come too late. "They loved him," Joe said. "We all did—we always had."

"And what about you?" she asked.

"What about me?"

"Did you take care of yourself?"

He gave her a grateful look; from her tone

of voice, he honestly believed she cared. "I started to. Watching Damien slip away, I knew I didn't want to end up like that. I knew I had to . . . well, I stopped drinking."

"Tim must have been happy."

Joe shrugged. "I'd spent so much time turning to birds instead of my son, I'm not so sure he even noticed."

"I think he did," Neve said quietly.

Joe turned toward her. She had such wisdom in her eyes—she seemed so young to him, but in another way she seemed his own age. He had the feeling she'd been through some wars of her own. Battle scars, he thought. They didn't make her any less delicate, though.

"You're nice to say that," he said.

"Your son turned out well," she said.

Joe bowed his head. "But not happy." He couldn't look up. "He's honest, honorable, kind, and trustworthy. But he's not happy."

"Joe . . ."

"That's the thing a parent wants most for their child," he said. "You try to instill goodness, but basically that happens on its own. I don't take any credit for how fine a man Tim has turned out to be."

"Then you shouldn't take the blame for any of it either," Neve said.

"I thought . . ." Joe said, raising his eyes—not to look at her, but to gaze into the cage at the two snowy owls, sitting side by side. It was time for them to sleep, and that's what they were doing. Shoulders touching, two catastrophically wounded birds a thousand miles from home.

"What did you think, Joe?" she asked.

"I thought that you were a miracle," he said.

"Me?" she asked, her eyes widening. "What do you mean?"

"You and your daughter," he said. "You found Tim, and you gave him something to live for. He's been hiding out in that cabin on the beach for so long. Guarding that grave—that U-boat I bombed, those men I killed. Bones wash up on the beach now and then, did you know that? And Tim alerts the Navy each time. He makes sure those bones get a proper burial. He does that for Frank, you see."

"Because Frank drowned?"

Joe nodded; the sadness made the smallest movement feel almost impossibly difficult. "Yes. But he does it for me, too."

"For you?"

"Yes," Joe said. "We don't talk about it, because Tim and I still don't talk about much. But he knows how I feel. See, Neve—we go into battle for duty and honor, and we kill or are killed. But it doesn't end there. Marines, soldiers, airmen, and sailors are responsible for the lives we take. And Tim knows that."

"That's why he cares so much about the U-boat," Neve said.

"Yes," Joe said. "And for a while, when you first entered his life, I thought there was some hope."

"Hope for what?" she whispered.

"That you would bring some light to my son's calamitous life," Joe said as the two snowy owls rustled, edging closer, their white feathers merging in the quiet darkness of the cage. "And that he could be happy."

21

The silver Lexus was parked outside South County High, and if the repo man didn't come by during the next fifteen minutes, things would probably turn out okay. Well, not really okay—the situation otherwise known as "life" was an unmitigated disaster. But at least he'd still have wheels.

Wheels were paramount at the moment. Richard was a moving target. He was behind on child support, he hadn't paid the mortgages, he had bar tabs all over the state, Alyssa was a wreck, Neve was dragging him through court, and his leasing company had had enough. Richard had kept up the car payments as long as he

could, knowing that if all else went to hell—
which it seemed in the process of doing—
he could always sleep in the Lexus.

Being a deadbeat was hard work. It took
effort to send your life crumbling around
your ears. Really, it did. He had a top-ten list
of "Worst Moments." They rotated in and
out with each other, depending on circumstances, but right now, the number one
worst moment had to be that phone call
with Alyssa, hearing her voice screaming in
his ear, saying the sheriff had just been to
the door looking for him.

"You're wanted!" she'd shrieked.
"Wanted, like a common criminal! You
haven't paid child support for Mickey? For
your own daughter? How do you think she
feels? Is this what it's going to be like for me
and the baby? Chasing you around the
countryside while you piss everything away
in those tacky, disgusting bars you love so
much? That you love more than *me*?!"

Love so much? Is that what she thought?

Those bars were his foxholes. That's all—
nothing more, nothing less. Who in their
right mind loved a foxhole? They were bar-
ren dugouts, fortifications against the hundreds, thousands of ways the world was

cruel. September's was a foxhole against his money problems; the Hitching Post was where he hid to avoid the disappointment of love; Mike's Sports Bar was a last-stand kind of place, where he went to forget what a world-class shitty father he was.

He sat in the car now, shivering as his body went through detox. Hadn't had a drink in nearly twenty-four hours. Long time ago, Neve had gotten brochures from Edge-hill, a rehab just over the way in Newport. That's where Kitty Dukakis had gone to quit drinking. Lots of people had—she was just the most famous. The rehab wasn't there anymore—the big brick mansion had a new use. A resort or something.

Richard knew there were other places he could check out. Hazelden, in Minnesota. The Betty Ford Center, out in California. The Caron Foundation in Pennsylvania. Those were fine rehabs; celebrities went there to get their lives in order, and although he wasn't famous, Richard F. Halloran Jr., went first class or he didn't go at all.

The trouble was, he didn't have any money to pay for it. His insurance had lapsed as well—just ask Neve, who'd left him messages and sent registered letters to his lawyer informing him that Mickey hadn't been covered for her broken wrist. Richard had felt like a million bucks, hearing that—his little girl had needed medical help, and her time in the ER had had to come right out of her mother's pocket. Congratulations, Halloran—why not have a double vodka to celebrate?

So, no high-priced rehabs for Richard. He'd just hold on tight, knowing he had to muscle through this on his own. He just hoped his heart held out; his body was going through hell this time. The hangover was nothing compared to the tremors. He'd puked his guts out all night—right now he was in the full light of day.

And craving a drink with everything he had, but determined not to stop at the package store. Top-ten worst moments—they were haunting him big-time. Getting drunk just couldn't cut it anymore. Mickey's messages on his cell phone were numbers two, three, and four. Jesus, she'd broken her wrist, panicked about the U-boat, and gotten a boyfriend. Endless messages about the bad and the good in her life, and Richard wasn't there for any of it.

Shaking in the driver's seat, he stared at

the front door of her school. She'd walk out any minute. He'd let her know he was still alive, still loved her—and then he'd drop out of her life again. She was better off without him anyway.

Since he hadn't been drinking, he was okay to drive. He'd offer her a ride home. He could explain a little of what had been going on. The message he'd recorded the other day—purposely left in the middle of school, when he'd known she wouldn't answer— had laid the groundwork for his cover story.

"Mick," he'd tell her, "I've really fallen into a gold mine out in Arizona. Selling houses left and right! I'll start banking the money soon, but there's . . ." Here he would insert an explanation, indecipherable to anyone but a realtor, about lenders, lawyers, and escrow—"a thirty-day holdup until the funds are released."

"Then we'll be—on easy street—in the pink—in the money—riding high." *Insert bullshit phrase here . . .*

Staring at the high school, he wondered whether she'd buy it. Her mother never had. Neve had always been too smart for his crap. She'd seen right through the fear and the lies, wanted him to get help. She hadn't even gotten mad at the end—by then she was past yelling, even past crying. She was just sad.

"Mickey loves you," she'd said. "She needs a dad. And you love her so much, if you don't give that to her, if you don't stand up and act like a good father, you'll hate yourself."

"What about you?" he'd asked, trying to take her hand. "Don't you love me?"

That's when the sad look had kicked in. It had flooded her features—her wide, intelligent, sea blue eyes, her delicate mouth—it had made her look so regal, because she wasn't breaking down, but also so tragic, because her face revealed every last bit of grief he'd put her through over the years.

"I did," she said. "I loved you more than anything. But right now I don't like you very much. I barely even know you."

There it was—the fifth-worst memory. Neve Fallon Halloran, the love of his life, telling him she didn't like him. He couldn't blame her, either, because he couldn't stand himself. Who was this jerk who couldn't show up for his family, who came home reeking of booze, who slept with women and forgot their names, who fell behind on mortgage payments for his family's house because he had to have sharp clothes and a fancy car? Oh—it was him.

Kids had started pouring out the front door of the high school. Some ran to the yellow buses parked at the curb, others to the large parking lot around back. Richard's heart was beating so hard, he thought he might die. There was Jenna—Mickey's best friend. If Jenna was here, Mick couldn't be far behind.

Jenna holding hands with Tripp Livingston. Edmund P. Livingston III. They called him Tripp because he was third in line. Richard knew his father, Edmund Jr. They used to golf together at Newport Country Club, back when Richard could still afford the greens fees.

And the Landry kid—Jenna and Tripp were laughing, talking to the son of Cole Landry. Richard watched them—imagine, Cole Landry settling in this part of Rhode Island. This sleepy, quiet little area; it wasn't Vegas, it wasn't Miami, Landry's usual type of stomping grounds. A few years back, when Richard was more of a player—or at least thought he was—he'd met Cole Landry at a real estate convention in New York. They'd held it at the Landry Tower, a thousand realtors from all over the country—top producers every one of them.

The Landry Tower had been controversial, as so many of Landry's projects were. It stood on the West Side, rose seventy stories. Blocks of old neighborhood had been razed—old brownstones, coffee shops, grocery stores, vest-pocket parks, a church, and a synagogue. The taller it went, the more it blocked the light. Neighborhood residents used to a low skyline, to late-afternoon butterscotch light pouring over the streets, now lived in shadow.

But the Tower was spectacular. Yes, it blocked others' views of the river. But it was majestic. Made of limestone, reminiscent of the robber barons' palaces, it imposed itself on New York City. The lobby was all marble, crystal, and gilt, with a sailboat pond right in the middle. For fifty bucks a half hour, you could rent a miniature, remote-control twelve-meter yacht. The doormen dressed like members of the Royal Navy.

The convention had been held in the Commodore's Ballroom. A lot of Rolex watches had been in that gathering, Richard remembered now. Cole Landry had stood up in front at the podium, challenged the attendees all to build their own towers. "Doesn't matter whether you live in the dust bowl or your state capital," he'd said. "Doesn't matter whether there needs to be a tower—the point is, you *want* there to be one, right? You want to put your names on something. You can make your mark in this business, gentlemen."

Richard had eaten it up. He'd had visions of big developments from Westerly to Pawtucket. He'd develop a tower in Providence—taller than the Fleet Building, and with twice the style. He'd adopt the Landry method of real estate—don't take into account the needs of the community; don't worry about replacing sunlight with shadows; just bulldoze everything, put up something big, and stick your name on it.

Watching Jenna and Tripp with the Landry kid, he wondered whether the new generation was following that same credo. He figured it probably was; he'd been in a Cranston bar; not out west, as he'd told Mickey, the day Cole Landry had made his big announcement about U-823. Slouched at a table in back, Richard had stared up at the television, seeing familiar faces on the screen.

So many of Mickey's friends had been there, standing in a semicircle around the dignitaries: Cole Landry, Senator James House, Senator Sam Sheridan. The sight of Sam had given Richard a little kick—back when Richard had still had some stuff, he'd helped Sam find a new house. It was a beautiful place, too—a brick Georgian right on Rumstick Point, the nicest spot in Barrington, with a gorgeous lawn sloping down to the water.

Was Sam really behind this crazy plan to move the U-boat? Richard hated to think he'd fallen for Landry's deal. Landry had greased the wheels, spread money around—that was a given. But somehow Richard had always thought Sam Sheridan was above that. God knows, Richard's connection with him hadn't done any good when Richard had tried to push that condominium project through—over in Bristol, on the water, great views, mixed-use zoning— he'd envisioned a Starbucks in there, coffee for all the affluent condo buyers. But Sheridan had shot him down, said the town's character could be compromised, even the state's, that he wouldn't sell out Rhode Island.

Now, sitting in his car, Richard stared at young Landry charming Mickey's friends. He was so intent, he almost forgot that he was jonesing for Absolut, and he almost missed Mickey walking out of the school.

God, his baby. She was so pretty, small, smart, radiant. She had a cast on her wrist. Bright eyes, talking away, dressed like the tomboy she'd always been, in black pants and a jean jacket.

She was with a tall, rugged-looking kid—obvious to anyone who'd lived a lifetime in the Ocean State that he was a surfer. Shaggy sun-lightened brown hair, muscles from powering through the surf, a torn old blue windbreaker with a Rip Curl patch on it, looking as if it came out of some beach's lost-and-found. Mickey had mentioned in her message that the boy she was seeing surfed at Refuge Beach.

Richard sat still, watching them together. He noticed the way the boy—Shane, he thought Mickey had said—gazed down at her. Touched her shoulder, almost as if he was afraid she'd dissolve. He seemed gentle, respectful. And Mickey looked up at him

with stars in her eyes, green eyes, like
Richard's. He watched the smiles pass between them, and as Mickey backed away,
he saw Shane lean forward, as if pulled to
her.

Mickey must have told him to wait there,
though; he stood still, watching Mickey
walk over to where Jenna and Tripp were
standing with Landry. Not even a glance
back at Shane as she went to Landry,
touched his elbow.

Landry looked at her—lit up. Richard
watched the expression on his face—triumph mingled with something much more
innocent, something like delight. Well, what
high school boy wouldn't be delighted to
have Mickey talk to him? Richard looked at
Shane, saw him just standing there. *Go after her,* Richard wanted to tell him.

Jesus, Richard thought—she's inherited
more than the color of her father's eyes.
Had Mickey also inherited his foolproof way
of screwing up relationships? Shane had
sounded like such a nice guy; most of all,
Mickey had sounded so eager for Richard
to meet him. That had to mean she really
liked him, right? To want to introduce him to
her dad?

Watching Mickey talk to Landry now, Richard wondered whether everything was his fault. The Landrys were fancy cars, fancy houses, fancy watches: lessons Mickey had learned from her father. He'd spent so much time and effort chasing crap that didn't matter and didn't last, he'd dropped the ball on everything that mattered.

Shane would have been his idea of a loser, no doubt about it. A young man who wasted time at the beach—when there was money to be made, connections to be solidified, clubs to be joined. Richard would have preferred the idea of someone like Tripp Livingston for his little girl. But right now, shaking in the front seat of his leased and about-to-be-repo'd Lexus, Richard knew he'd had a sea change; nothing sounded better to him than warm sand, a sea breeze, and the cradle of ocean waves holding him up.

Opening the car door took all his effort. He wobbled on legs that nearly gave out from under him. Kids passing by on their way to the bus gave him looks of alarm—he knew he reeked of old gin and two nights without a shower. He hadn't shaved. And his eyes looked wild and haunted with all he'd lost and given away.

"Mickey," he said.

She didn't even turn around. So absorbed in young Landry—there she was, laughing and chucking him on the arm, seeming to hang on his every word as he told some big story, gesturing expansively, talking in a loud voice—Mickey didn't even see her father standing there.

"Mick," he said. "Hey . . ."

Shane saw him; their eyes met, and Richard knew instantly that Shane knew who he was. He'd been unlocking his bike, but he dropped the chain, walked over to Mickey, touched her shoulder. She wheeled around—the look in her eyes as she caught Shane's gaze was happy first, then hesitant, as if she didn't want him messing up whatever she had going on with Landry. But then Shane pointed, and Mickey looked.

"Dad."

She must have whispered it; he had to read her lips.

He steadied himself against the car door, lifted his hand to wave at her. Would she run away? Go tearing off in the opposite direction, get away from him as far and fast as she could? He wouldn't blame her if she did. Was she embarrassed by him? Did she hate him? The tremors were terrible, but he just held on, hand in the air in a stalled-out wave, letting her know he was here, wanting to get her away from Landry.

"Dad!"

This time he didn't have to read her lips. She shouted it, came running over at top speed—just the way she used to run toward him when she was little and he'd come home from work, throwing herself into the run with all she had, all her heart—that little heart of hers so big and brave.

"Mickey," he said, catching her.

She nearly knocked him down; sent him flying back against the car. If he thought he was shaking, he didn't know anything—because Mickey's chest was heaving, her body was quaking.

"Mickey," he said. "Oh, honey."

"I thought I'd never see you again," she said, unable to lift her head from his shoulder because she was weeping.

"I'm here," he said.

"I thought you were gone forever," she cried.

He couldn't quite answer that, because

he'd thought he was, too. Stroking her head, looking over at her friends, he made eye contact with Shane. It was almost impossible to read his gaze—it seemed stern, exacting, yet somehow unsure. Jenna whispered something to Tripp, and they turned their backs. Landry just looked annoyed that Mickey had left the circle.

"You okay, Mickey?" Shane asked, taking a few steps closer.

She nodded, not even turning around.

"She's fine," Richard said. "I'm her father."

"I know," Shane said.

Richard heard mistrust there; he tried to glare at Shane, but couldn't pull it off. His legs were about ready to give out. Gently easing Mickey away, he gestured for her to get into the car. Mickey was eager to do so, just about loped around the front, into the passenger's seat.

Shane took another step forward. He reminded Richard of a cop about to issue a field sobriety test.

"Are you all right to drive?" he asked.

"I'm fine," Richard said.

"Because I don't want anything to happen to her."

"Look, I just told you, didn't I?—I'm fine."

Then, relying on the fail-safe wit that had gotten him so far in life, Richard drew himself up, gave the kid his most imperious I'm-better-than-you look, and said, "Why don't you go find a nice big wave now. All right?"

Shane gave Richard a long look of assessment. He didn't flinch or act offended in any way. He just narrowed his eyes; Mickey was already in the car, so she couldn't hear him when he said, "You'd better not hurt her."

Richard didn't respond; he just climbed into the car, eyes on Shane, trying to act tougher than he was, showing pride for his classy behavior. Why shouldn't he feel proud of having one-upped his daughter's high school boyfriend? Jesus Christ.

Richard started up the car and drove slowly away. Shane just stood on the sidewalk, watching them pull out of the parking lot. Richard tried to block out the boy's look of alarm and derision, concentrate on the fact that Mickey was right here with him, grabbing for his hand with the fingers of her cast-encased hand, gazing at his drink-ravaged face and crying her eyes out.

22

As they drove slowly out of town, Mickey could hardly believe she was with her father. It was like all of her dreams coming true at the same time, all the stars coming out at once. The nights she'd worried about him, the messages she'd left, the calls unreturned, the sight of court documents on the dining room table: all disappeared in this wonderful moment.

"Dad," she said, "I thought you were in Arizona."

"I was, sweetheart," he said. "But I had to come back for . . ." He paused, swallowing. She watched, waiting for him to finish his sentence. "For a closing here in Rhode Island."

"On a real estate deal?" she asked.

"Yes," he said.

"Did you . . ." she began, not even knowing how to ask this. "Did you know that the, well, the police, were looking for you?"

"Honey, that's just a misunderstanding," her father said. "There was a big mix-up at court, a glitch—you know? I had the dates wrong. That's what happens when you're trying to juggle too many deals."

"Especially the one in Arizona, right?" Mickey asked, wanting to believe him.

"Mmm, yes," he said. "Exactly."

His teeth seemed to be chattering, but it wasn't cold. She smelled an old familiar odor of cigarettes and drinks. She'd grown up with that smell; it made her nostalgic for something she didn't even know how to define. It reminded her of him coming home late, of her parents fighting, of the hope she always had that they'd make up, that he would "get it" and stop going out at night. She glanced at him now—he looked so thin, hollows in his cheeks, the color of his skin too pale, sort of sallow.

"Are you okay, Dad?" she asked.

He chuckled, but the sound didn't accompany a smile. "Your friend Shane asked me that."

Her mouth dropped open. How did he know that was Shane? "I didn't introduce you," she said. "So how . . ."

"You left me that message," he said. "Told me about the wonderful boy you liked. I figured that if he's really wonderful, it had to mean he really liked you and respected you. And that boy I saw back at the high school did—Shane, right?"

"Right," she said.

Her father took a right off the school road, onto Route 1; from there he headed down the beach road, heading toward Refuge Beach. Mickey felt a little surprised; this was more a place she would expect to come with her mother. Her father usually took her to the mall, or to a restaurant— places where, as he put it, "the action is." Really places where he could get a drink.

"We're going to the beach?" she asked, a little confused.

"Yes," he said. "You like it here, right? Birds and nature and all? What was that you told me about a snowy owl?"

"We found one here!" she said, remembering the excitement of seeing it—first with Jenna, then her mother, then Shane.

"Can you show me?"

Her heart tumbled, sort of fell; she glanced over at him. Hadn't he listened to her messages? "It's hurt, Dad. We took it to a rehab up in Kingston."

"Oh," he said. But as if it didn't really matter to him anyway; he just fished a cigarette out of his jacket pocket and kept driving. Mickey watched the way his hand shook. The cigarette trembled in his lips. He couldn't hold the lighter steady enough to light it, so he just gave up trying.

They passed the ranger house; Mickey turned her head, saw Mr. O'Casey's green truck parked there. She wondered what had happened between him and her mother; he hadn't called the house in days. And her mother just seemed preoccupied. It seemed strange for Mickey to be riding with her father, wishing about her mother and Mr. O'Casey. It seemed disloyal.

When they got to the thicket, Mickey motioned for him to stop.

"I can show you where the snowy owl *was*," she said. "If you want to see."

"Sure," he said.

They got out of the car. Leaning against the door, he managed to light his cigarette. Mickey hated to see him smoke, worried that he'd get lung cancer and die. But it had been almost worse to see him shaking too hard to use his lighter. Everything seemed like a huge conflict, even such a simple, awful thing as her father smoking.

Walking through the brush, Mickey heard birdsong. The migration was under way! She thought back a month ago, when she and Jenna had come through here. The thicket had seemed absolutely dead—almost as if the brambles and branches were lifeless, instead of just dormant. Right now, walking through, she heard the unmistakable song of the white-throated sparrow: *peabody, peabody . . .* And there were green shoots coming out of the marshy ground, and tiny white buds on the branches of shadbush, and spring was here, or at least on its way.

Once they got to the other side, they stood at the top of the dunes—stretching up and down the beach like an endless moonscape—and felt the sea wind in their faces. Mickey glanced over at the jetty; her heart skipped, because she knew Shane would be here soon, and that's where she always stood to watch him surf.

"That's where the owl was," she said, pointing toward the gargantuan driftwood log.

"Where'd you say it is now?" he asked.

"At Joseph O'Casey's raptor rehabilitation center," she said. "Up near the University of Rhode Island."

"Funny," he said, as if he hadn't been listening, staring over at the big silvery log, just this side of the jetty. "That looks just like the spot where Cole Landry was standing when he cut the ribbon."

"What ribbon?"

"Oh, it's just an expression," her father said. "You know, when someone cuts the ribbon on a new project—it means an announcement, but one you need extra press and attention for. It's a loudmouth gesture."

"Well, he's a loudmouth," Mickey said.

Her father gave her an odd look.

"You think so?" he asked.

"Um, yeah," she said. The way he was staring at her made her blush. Had she said the wrong thing? Probably her father loved Cole Landry—he was a huge success in her father's field; he'd started off in real estate and turned into one of the most famous businessmen in the world. She felt herself panic, wanting to backpedal, to not hurt her father's feelings. "Why, do you know him?"

"I've met him," her dad said. He stood a little taller, puffed his chest out a little bit more; Mickey was almost glad to see his pride coming back, even over something as sad as having met Cole Landry. "I went to a convention down at the Landry Tower in New York, remember?"

Mickey shook her head. "No, I don't."

Her father's face fell. "I guess your mother didn't tell you about it," he said. "Maybe it was after we got separated. I forget, exactly."

Or maybe Mickey's mother hadn't believed him when he'd told her he was in New York. Mickey knew that her father used to lie about things like that; he'd say he was playing golf with the governor, but then they'd be on their way to the grocery store and see his car at the Hitching Post.

He'd say he was having lunch with Ted Turner at the New York Yacht Club in Newport, and someone would tell Mickey's mother that they'd just seen him in Providence, sitting on a barstool at Buddy's.

But right now, standing on Refuge Beach, watching the wind blow the white tops off waves breaking so beautifully and elegantly over the conning tower of U-823, Mickey had to know the truth.

"Did you really meet Cole Landry?" she asked.

"Of course I did, sweetheart," he said. "When I tell you something, you can take it to the bank. . . ."

The *riverbank*, she thought. The *piggy bank*.

"Dad," she said. "Were you really in Arizona?"

"Sweetheart! How can you . . ." he started. But then, as if the wind were coming at him at sixty knots, hurricane strength, instead of wafting over in cool early-spring gusts, he seemed unable to withstand the force. He sat down hard on the sand, and Mickey sat beside him.

"You weren't, were you?" she asked.

"No," he said.

"Why did you say you were?"

He stared out at the sea as if it were his mortal, avowed enemy. He looked as if he wanted to slaughter the sea. His chin trembled, as if the sea were about to make him cry. Mickey couldn't bear it. She couldn't look at her father, but she couldn't look away.

"Dad?" she asked.

"Because I'm a failure," he said in a very quiet, very still way.

"No," she whispered.

He nodded. "You asked if I'd really met Cole Landry."

"You don't have to explain," she said. "So you didn't go to New York that time—it doesn't make you . . ."

"I have met him. I've heard him speak. I've talked to him personally."

Was it true? Mickey wondered. And if it was, would her father now defend him, try to explain how progress sometimes bore an emotional price, that in this case the cost of raising the U-boat would be the pain it might cause the locals, but that it'd be worth it in the long run? She'd heard Josh saying all that, and if her father was a Cole Landry fan, he'd probably say it, too.

"I know his son Josh," Mickey said.

"I saw you talking to him."

"He . . . he's just like his father," Mickey said.

"Then he's a fool," her father said harshly, taking Mickey's hand.

"Dad," she said.

"You and your mother have always loved this beach," he said. "She used to ask me to come down here. I did a few times—but I always had something better to do. A deal I was trying to make, a house I was trying to sell. Your mother loved the peace of this place; I wanted everything but peace."

"You like excitement," she said, repeating the phrase he used to say to her when trying to explain why he needed to be out and about so many nights every week.

"Maybe," he admitted.

She glanced up at him, saw him taking in the beauty: the clouds scudding across the sky, the birds flitting through the thicket, sandpipers running along the hard sand at the water's edge, the waves breaking, breaking, breaking.

"Why do you say Josh Landry is a fool?" she asked.

"Because I saw him on television with his father," he said. "They want to haul the U-boat out of here as if it were nothing. And to them, it *is* nothing."

"I know," she said, staring out at the waves. "I hate them for it."

"You do?" he asked. "They why did I see you walk away from Shane, over to Landry? It looked as if you were friends—as if you were looking up to him."

She gazed up at him. He was her father, but he barely knew her. Did he really think that could be possible?

"Dad, that's ridiculous," she said. "I just want him to introduce me to Senator Sheridan on our class trip to Washington."

"Really?" her father asked, getting a funny gleam in his eyes. He had seemed weak, almost sick, and she'd been so worried about him since getting in the car. But suddenly, with that one look, he seemed like her old dad—shrewd, smart, a little devilish.

"What, Dad?" she asked.

"I think I can help you with that," he said. "Or at least put in a good word. Your dad knows a few people, Mickey. You want to see Senator Sheridan, leave it to me."

Mickey gazed back at the waves. She felt heat rising in her face; her father sounded so sure of himself, but could she believe him? Or was this another of his stories? He had a way of trying to make her feel better—

but then, when he couldn't follow through, she always seemed to feel worse.

"I'll make a call or two," he said. "Get someone from his staff on the line. Once he hears that Richard Halloran's daughter wants to see him—consider it a done deal! We're old golf buddies—he's loyal to his old friends and supporters, especially ones who've played a few eighteens with him, know what I mean?"

She swallowed.

"What do you want to see him for, sweetheart?"

"I don't know," she said, because she couldn't bear to tell him the truth. It was too important, and his lies made it seem trivial. "I guess just because it seems like a good thing to do on a class trip to Washington."

"Well, you can count on it, okay? You're meeting Sam Sheridan."

"Thanks, Dad," she said smiling, giving him a kiss on his cheek. She knew the promise would wash away, just like the tide. It would have been nice to think she could stop being nice to Josh, but she knew that he was a better bet for what she needed to accomplish. Her father took her hand and held it tight, and she felt how badly his was shaking.

"I'm going away," he said quietly.

"What do you mean?"

"Arizona," he said. "This time for real. There's opportunity, Mick. I have to get straight with your mother—Alyssa, too. I'm going to head down to the Sunbelt and sell up a storm. I'll send you a ticket out to visit, as soon as I get settled."

Mickey's chest felt tight, and her throat ached as the wind blew off the sea. It blew her hair straight back, made her eyes tear up. He was going away; it didn't matter whether it was to Arizona or the Hitching Post. They were together for this short time, and then he'd disappear again.

The wind was full of moisture from the waves, the steady, giant waves breaking over the conning tower of U-823. She thought of the men she had seen underwater; they'd died attacking Mickey's beloved shore. Some of them had been fathers back in Germany; she wondered what their children and grandchildren thought about them. She stared at the sea and understood, just a little, of how it felt to have a father disappear, not know if he was ever coming home.

That made her put her head on her father's shoulder, breathing in his smell of smoke and gin, and thinking *he's right here, he's right here, he's right here*, as the tears welled in her eyes, because she knew that soon he'd be going away.

And just then, the police arrived.

23

Getting ready for the Berkeley exhibit took all Neve's energy and effort. With all the news stories—not just in Rhode Island, but nationally—a large crowd was expected that night. The Dominic di Tibor Gallery was about to have its moment, in just a few hours. As Neve walked around the exhibit, she realized that this brilliant artist was on the verge of finally receiving the widespread acclaim he had so long deserved.

The paintings were all hung, and as she stopped in front of each one, examining the delicate brushstrokes delineating a little blue heron's feathers, and the sharp edge of an osprey's beak, she remembered why she had fallen in love with Berkeley in the first place, and she felt a moment of calm, a sense of being absolutely present and still, in the midst of chaos.

He had always made her appreciate the quiet magic of the birds she saw every day. His paintings didn't elevate or aggrandize any species; to look at Berkeley's work, one would realize that he loved all birds, loved the environment in which he found them. He depicted quick movement, and there was such joy in life apparent in his paintings, something so tender in the fact that he chose to paint the smallest of all creatures, those closest to pure spirit.

She wondered whether Tim or Joe would come to the opening. She had sent them both invitations, written personal notes on a separate piece of paper. Joe's had been easy—he'd made her feel so much better when she'd visited the owl. His words about Tim's "calamitous life" kept ringing in her ears, making the note she had to write to Tim so much harder.

"Please come," she'd written. "Your uncle's love of birds inspired my own, and, as you told me, yours. Please come celebrate his beautiful work and spirit with me." She'd written "I miss you," but then she'd thrown out that sheet and started all over, leaving out the last line.

There had been no response. What had she expected? Tim had been right that attention would be paid to Frank. The more the story unfolded, the more reporters who'd picked up the thread of Damien O'Casey's military service—the juxtaposition of the preternatural peace of his paintings and the fact that he'd flown over thirty missions aboard a heavy bomber during World War II.

The stories linked Damien to Joe, revered local war hero, responsible for destroying Rhode Island's own U-boat. But they really gained traction because of his connection to Frank—one of Rhode Island's casualties in Iraq. There were stories about "the O'Casey curse," patterned on the Kennedys; other reporters focused on "one family's courage." They all made Neve sad to read, and they all made her wonder how Tim was doing.

She started unpacking the boxes of catalogues, placing them on a long mahogany table against the wall, near the gallery's front door, reflecting on how her essay—

given the recent discovery of Berkeley's true identity—was already obsolete. Her anger at Dominic was tremendous, undiminished by the fact that she was also furious with herself. He had been studiously avoiding her when others weren't around, but she expected him any moment. She hoped he'd get here before the crowds so she could tell him what she thought, but just then the phone rang.

"Dominic di Tibor Gallery," she said, half expecting it to be another reporter asking for background for a story on Berkeley, or requesting directions to the gallery for that night's opening. But it wasn't a reporter.

"Mom?" Mickey said, and from her tone Neve knew in less than a second that something was wrong.

"Are you okay?" Neve asked.

"Mom, it's Dad," Mickey said, starting to cry. "We're at the Secret Harbor police station."

"I'll be right there," Neve said, forgetting about Dominic and the exhibition.

She grabbed her jacket and bag, locked the door, and ran outside to her car. Secret Harbor was such a small town, she could practically see the station from here. But she drove anyway, down Main Street, to the plain brick building situated just before the municipal tennis courts.

Mickey was sitting in the waiting room. She jumped up at the sight of her mother, and Neve ran right into her arms. Mickey's face was streaked with tears, but she seemed calm and strong, pulling her mother over to the corner of the room so they could talk without the desk sergeant listening.

"What happened?" Neve asked.

"Dad came to pick me up at school," Mickey said. "We went to the beach and talked. It . . . it was so nice, Mom! Just to be with him, talking like normal people. And then, just out of the blue, a police car pulled up."

"What did they want?"

"They said they'd had a report about a drunk driver. . . ."

Neve held Mickey's hand, thinking of how she must have felt. She remembered being in the car with Richard once, getting pulled over, watching as the cops made him walk the line.

"But he wasn't drunk, Mom. They gave him a Breathalyzer test, and he passed it."

"But they held him anyway?" Neve asked.

"Because of the child support," Mickey said, breaking down. "He's under arrest because the judge issued that warrant."

Neve tried to breathe. She kissed Mickey and then walked across the room to the desk. She recognized the sergeant sitting there from around town. He sometimes worked at the school, for big events. And she'd seen him at the grocery store, apprehending someone who'd been caught shoplifting. They'd never spoken before, but she knew that he recognized her, too.

"Hi, Sergeant," she said.

"Hi, Mrs. Halloran," he said.

"Would it be all right for me to see Richard?"

"He's in there." The sergeant gestured toward a closed door. "Being questioned."

"Does he have his lawyer with him?"

"No," the sergeant said. He was in his thirties, compact and trim, with salt-and-pepper hair and mustache. His brown eyes looked apologetic. "He used his phone call to call someone else."

Neve raised her eyebrows; who could he have called? Alyssa?

"He called Senator Sheridan," the sergeant said.

"He wanted the senator to get him out of jail?" Neve asked, lowering her voice so Mickey wouldn't hear, thinking that this took big-shotism to new heights.

"I guess," the sergeant said. "He made the call from a private booth. . . ."

"Well, I'd like you to stop the interrogation," Neve said.

"It's not exactly like that, ma'am. We're not trying to sweat him, believe me. The judge issued a bench warrant for his arrest, so we have to hold him. That's just the way it is. He's going to have to post some hefty bail before—"

"I just said, I want you to stop the interrogation," Neve said.

"Excuse me, ma'am?"

"Right now," Neve said. "Stop questioning him until his lawyer gets here."

"Mrs. Halloran, he hasn't asked for one."

"I'm asking for one on his behalf," Neve said.

The sergeant looked puzzled. "The warrant is for nonpayment of child support. I thought you'd be glad to have him in custody so we can collect it. That's a pretty nice Lexus he's driving—we'll seize it, and the proceeds can—"

"His lawyer is Jim Swenson—I don't have his number, but his office is in Westerly."

"Fine," the sergeant said, shaking his head as if he'd never understand the thinking of ex-wives. He used the intercom to tell whoever was speaking with Richard that an attorney was on the way; then he checked a directory, scrawled a phone number on a scrap of paper, and handed it and the phone to Neve.

She spoke with Jim's paralegal. At first the young man didn't want to take Neve's call— she was the opposing party, after all. But once Neve explained the situation, he thanked her and said he'd tell Jim right away.

Turning to Mickey, Neve gestured for her to stand up so they could head home.

"I'm not leaving," Mickey said. "Not without Dad."

"Honey, his lawyer's on the way."

"I don't care," Mickey said. "I'm staying until they let him go."

"Mickey, they will. His lawyer will straighten things out. . . . Come on, let's get you home. And I have to go back to work."

"You go ahead," Mickey said, crossing her

arms across her chest. "But I'm not leaving."

Neve sat down beside her, looked straight into her green eyes. She saw determination and anger there, a storm brewing deep inside. Neve wanted to put her arms around her, tell her that some battles weren't worth fighting. The trauma of Richard's drinking— the way he seemed determined to ruin his own life—was a very old war that Neve had once made her own. Now she saw their daughter doing the same thing.

"Mickey, you can't make Dad be different."

"I'm not trying to do that," she said.

"He has to make his own mistakes," Neve said.

"I know, Mom. But he wasn't drunk! Whoever called the cops on him said he was— but he passed the test. I think I know who did it, too!"

Did it matter who had called? Neve felt secretly grateful to whoever it was. Richard might have been sober today, but the idea of Mickey getting into a car with him still made her shudder.

"Mickey, we can talk about this at home," Neve said.

But Mickey just shook her head, wriggled more deeply into the chair, settled with her arms wrapped so tightly across her chest, it was almost as if she were trying to hold her heart in. Her eyes glittered with furious tears.

Neve took a deep breath. The show opening was in hours, and Dominic would kill her if everything wasn't perfect. She still had so much to do this afternoon—check the lighting, make sure it was directed properly at each painting; call the caterers to make sure they had doubled the usual order, to accommodate the extra crowd Dominic was expecting; field last-minute press inquiries.

Glancing down at Mickey, Neve removed the book bag from the seat beside her. She sat down; Mickey barely registered. The desk sergeant gave her a noncommittal look, then went back to his computer screen. Neve sat back, trying to summon up images of Berkeley's work, just so she could exhale.

She thought about calling Chris, then Nicola. What would her own lawyer think, to know that she was here at the Secret Harbor police station, standing up for Richard? *He's a deadbeat,* Nicola would say to her.

He won't even take care of his own daughter, so what do you care about him for?

Neve knew she'd have a hard time answering to Nicola. But she glanced down at her child, sitting there with such intense vigilance, and she knew why she was doing this, ignoring her own obligations at the gallery, why she still cared about him.

Neve thought of Tim's love for Frank, Joe's love for Tim. Fathers and children . . . Richard was Mickey's father, and always would be. And for that reason alone, for Mickey, Neve knew that this was a battle still worth fighting. And even the opening of the Berkeley show would have to wait.

Down at the beach, everything was quiet. Shane had arrived just as the cops had come to take Mr. Halloran away. He'd caught a glimpse of Mickey—she was in the Lexus, being driven behind the squad car by another cop—and the look of hatred in her eyes told him she knew he'd been the one to make the call.

Shane had nothing left. The last weeks of winter had brought him so close to Mickey, and now he'd probably thrown that away.

She'd invited him to her mother's art gallery, for a big party that night—but after what had just happened, once she'd realized his part in it, Shane figured he'd be the last person she wanted to see.

So he'd come to the beach with his father's old camera—a huge, clunky underwater job that his mother had bought him for their wedding present. Shane didn't know if it even still worked. He'd seen some pictures his dad had taken—fish swimming around the wreck, the old periscope, a white blur that looked like the underbelly of a shark.

He thought that if he could get some good pictures of U-823, maybe he could give them to Mickey, maybe she'd forgive him. She could give the pictures to whatever legislator she met with on the class trip to Washington. He'd seen her talking to Josh, knew that she was still focused on her goal. Shane glared out over the waves, desperately wishing he could make everything okay again.

A few minutes later, he saw someone walking down the beach. Just a dark figure, heading from the direction of the ranger's house. Shane peered over—it had to be a surfer. He was wearing a black wetsuit, but where was his board?

When he got close, Shane saw that it was the ranger. Tim O'Casey climbed over the jetty, carrying air tanks.

"What are you doing?" Shane asked. "Aren't you going to that art gallery thing?"

"I could ask you the same thing. How's Mickey?" he asked.

"She . . . she's with her father."

"Was that him in the squad car?" Tim asked.

Shane nodded. "You saw?"

"Yeah," he said dryly. "They drove past—I tend to notice things like cop cars down here at the beach. So I called the station, and they told me what happened."

"He smelled like booze," Shane said. "I didn't want her driving with him, but I couldn't stop them from leaving the school."

"You did the right thing," Mr. O'Casey said.

"I did?" Shane asked, looking up, surprised.

"Yes," he said. "You didn't want her to get hurt."

Shane took that in. It wasn't every day that

an adult understood him. Even now, with Ranger O'Casey getting half of it, he was missing the other part.

"Well, I didn't want him getting hurt, either," Shane said.

Ranger O'Casey looked at him, waiting for him to say more. Shane almost couldn't. It was like holy ground for him, talking about a father getting hurt, dying. He stared out at the waves.

Shane had surfed a lot of big breakers, and he knew that it only took one moment— you could surf a thousand monster waves, or drive drunk a hundred times. You might slip by time after time, might think you're invulnerable, might start to believe nothing bad will ever happen to you. And then that one time . . .

Shane knew better than anyone else what *that one time* meant. That last moment on his father's board—what had it been like? Whenever Shane paddled out, feeling the cold water on his hands and the spray on his face, he thought he knew. Exultation, man. The opposite of Mickey's father. Shane had looked into his gray face and seen death just hanging back, waiting.

"You didn't want her father to die in a

wreck, take her with him," Tim O'Casey said.

Death had visited Shane's family long ago. Looking up into Mr. O'Casey's eyes, he knew that it had visited his, too.

"You're right," Shane said.

"She'll understand someday," Tim said.

Shane's chest heaved. Why couldn't adults get it? *Someday* would be too late. Shane wanted her to realize it right now, know how he felt about her, understand that he'd just wanted to protect her from the loss he'd gone through with his father. He wanted to be with her at the party tonight.

"What's that camera?"

"It was my dad's," Shane said. "A Nikon Nikonos II, thirty-five millimeter."

"The best underwater camera there was," Mr. O'Casey said. He glanced at Shane for permission to pick it up, and Shane nodded.

He watched the older man examine the camera, noticed his gray hair and the lines on his windburned face. Park rangers and surfers: they both spent a lot of time out in the open air. Would Shane's father be gray, would he have such a weather-beaten face if he were still alive? Shane stared out to sea and knew that he'd never know.

"Really fine," Mr. O'Casey said, examining the camera, then looking up at Shane. "Does this have to do with the U-boat?"

"Yeah," Shane said. "Haven't you seen the crane, on the barge moored in the harbor?"

"How could I miss it?"

"Didn't you do anything with that stuff Mickey and I gave you?" Shane asked. "There were so many ideas in there—but you're not doing anything. That crane is going to come right over here to the beach, reach down and pull the U-boat up from the bottom, take it to freaking Cape Cod! And you're not even going to stop it!"

"I'm going to try," Mr. O'Casey said, his voice very still.

Mr. O'Casey looked down, still holding on to Shane's dad's camera. His hands were big and rough, but Shane noticed the way he held the camera so lightly, running his thumb over the smooth metal edges, as if he really appreciated it.

"May I borrow this?" Mr. O'Casey said, looking up.

"Well, I was going to use it," Shane said.

"You scuba dive?" Mr. O'Casey asked.

"Well, I have," Shane said. "I just don't have the tanks." He glared at Mr. O'Casey to hide his embarrassment. Surfing was cheap—anyone could do it. All you needed was a board and—if you wanted to go all winter—a wetsuit. The waves were free. Scuba diving was different, it was for rich people; everything cost money. A good mask and fins could run over a hundred bucks, easily, not to mention tanks.

"Are you certified?"

Shane nodded. "Yeah. I did it at camp one year. Big deal."

"It is a big deal," Mr. O'Casey said gruffly. Then, "So, if you're not planning to dive, how were you going to photograph the U-boat?"

"I didn't say I wasn't planning to dive—I'm just not going to scuba dive."

"Then how?"

"Hold my breath," Shane said.

"You know how deep the wreck is?" Mr. O'Casey asked. "Over seventy feet. You wouldn't have the air to get down there and back up; it would be too dangerous."

At the words "too dangerous," Shane suddenly focused on the fact Mr. O'Casey was wearing a wetsuit, carrying fins and tanks, had his mask slung over one arm.

"Wait a second," Shane said. "What are you planning to do? Dive alone?"

Mr. O'Casey hesitated—obviously not wanting to be a bad influence.

"You are, aren't you?" Shane said, his voice rising.

"Look, I'm a very experienced diver," Mr. O'Casey said. "My dive partner isn't here right now, and there's no time to wait—if we don't get documentation, as much as possible, right away, Landry's crane will come in and—like you said—take the U-boat away."

"What the hell are you talking about?" Shane asked, watching as the older man started to go to work: checking his gauges, strapping on his air tanks, slipping his mask over his head, letting it dangle around his neck, walking toward the water's edge. "You'd go in there alone, without a buddy?"

"Solo diving is sometimes preferable," Mr. O'Casey said, strapping the tanks on. "Especially on a deep dive."

"I know—getting tangled, getting disoriented, necrosis," Shane said. "I told you—I'm certified. But seventy feet isn't considered that deep a dive. Don't try to bullshit me when it comes to the water!"

"Okay, you're right," Mr. O'Casey said. "Technically, this isn't that deep."

"Besides, even if it was, and you decided to go without a buddy, you'd still need support on the surface," Shane said. "It's not like surfing, where it's better alone. It's basically suicide to dive on a wreck without someone watching."

Mr. O'Casey gave him a look, and it scared Shane. Not because it was menacing, but because it wasn't. Mr. O'Casey didn't care—that was it. He was going to go in, and he didn't care if he came out. Shane could tell by the slope of his shoulders, the slackness of his face.

"Don't worry about me, Shane," Mr. O'Casey said. "I know what I'm doing."

"Then give me back my camera!"

Mr. O'Casey handed it over, then reached into the knife sheath strapped to his calf— there, along with a ten-dollar dive knife, was a very expensive, tiny, flat, underwater digital camera. He checked it, put it back. He checked the buckle on his weight belt, adjusted the regulator, basically acted as if Shane wasn't there.

"Wait for your dive partner!"

Mr. O'Casey turned his back, started into the water. When he was knee-deep in foam and about to pull his mask on, Shane splashed in after him, grabbed his arm.

"I said, wait for your dive partner," Shane commanded.

"I can't, Shane," Mr. O'Casey said.

"But why?" Shane asked, gripping his arm. "You have to—it doesn't matter if he's not here right now. Wait for him, so you can dive safely together."

Mr. O'Casey shook his head. "That's not going to happen," he said.

"Why?" Shane yelled, holding on tighter as the ranger tried to pull away, barrel into the waves.

The sun was canting downward in an almost-end-of-the-day way, and the waves beat in relentlessly. Shane had a flashback: him and his mom on the beach blanket, his dad going into the water alone. He knew one thing for sure—he wasn't going to let Mr. O'Casey dive without someone going below with him.

"Jesus!" Shane shouted, hating to destroy equipment, knowing he would if that's what it took. He grabbed the back of Mr.

O'Casey's wetsuit, pulled so hard, the neoprene started to rip. Mr. O'Casey ducked, turned, pushed back.

"What the hell do you think you're doing!"

"You're not going to dive alone!" Shane yelled. He gripped the ranger's face mask, tried to pull it off. "God, what are you doing? Get out of the water, get out right now! Call your dive partner, he'll come help you. Don't you know that's how the buddy system works? Didn't you learn anything in dive school?" Shane had him in a death grip, trying to wrestle him out of the surf, and Mr. O'Casey must have had enough, because he twisted free, gave Shane one hard push to the chest, sent him flying backwards onto the sand.

"My dive partner can't come!" he shouted, staring down at Shane. "He can't come because he drowned. He's dead, all right?"

"Who . . ." Shane began.

"My son Frank is dead."

Shane stared up, shocked, the wind knocked out of him, the worst feeling he'd ever had flowing in like the foamy waves all around him.

"Mr. O'Casey," Shane said, "I didn't know . . ."

"You didn't know what?" the ranger asked. He was standing tall now, the slump gone, silhouetted against the glowing sea. Even in shadow, his face was a mask of grief—Shane saw it and recognized it. When he was only three years old, and had lost his father, he felt the exact same way Mr. O'Casey looked now.

"You didn't know I had a son?" Mr. O'Casey asked. "Or you didn't know he died? Don't you read the papers? Frank O'Casey. Lance Corporal Francis O'Casey, grandson of Commander Joseph O'Casey!"

"And Lieutenant Timothy O'Casey!" Shane shouted. "I read the papers!" And Mickey had shown him. They had pored over old clippings and new stories. They had found Frank's obituary. It had mentioned how much Frank had loved the beach, how he had learned to swim right here at Refuge Beach. And there, listed in the family left behind, was Timothy J. O'Casey, who had served as a medic in Vietnam.

"I know," Shane said, struggling to his feet. "I knew that you had a son, and that he'd died in the war. You were good to me, when I had to do community service.

Mickey and I found Frank's obituary. Why do you think we're doing this?"

"Doing what?" Mr. O'Casey asked.

"Trying so hard to keep U-823 here?"

"Because of the surf break."

Shane shook his head, and tears welled up. He hated that, didn't want Mr. O'Casey to see, but it was too late. They flooded out of his eyes, and he stared with helpless fury at the older man.

"For a memorial," he said. "For your son, and my father. And all the men who died in the battle."

"Shane," Mr. O'Casey said, looking shocked.

"So don't say I don't read the papers," Shane said. "The only part I didn't know about was that Frank was your dive partner. That's all."

"I understand. I'm sorry," Mr. O'Casey said. Shane stared at him, knowing he'd attack him again if he had to.

"You're not going in that water," Shane said.

"No," Mr. O'Casey said, walking back toward Shane, unclipping the weight belt, dropping it into the sand. Strangely, he looked a lot lighter. The lines were still in his face, but his eyes looked almost alive again.

"Good," Shane said.

"It's ironic," Mr. O'Casey said. "That you thought it would have been okay for you to dive down alone."

"Like you said," Shane said, "I probably wouldn't have gotten very far."

"Since you're certified, maybe we can dive together another time."

"Yeah?" Shane asked, feeling as if he'd just gone over a speed bump.

"Like *you* said," Mr. O'Casey said, "it's no good to dive alone." He looked at the sky, which was starting to glow with the twilight hues of pink, red, and purple. Shane wondered whether the ranger was thinking of the party—he'd been invited, too.

"She wants you to go," Shane said.

"Who—where?"

"Mrs. Halloran," he said. "She wants you to go to the opening thing. She's nice; I like her."

"Yeah, so do I," Mr. O'Casey said.

"That dude's your uncle or something?" Shane asked.

"Berkeley. Yes, he is. My uncle Damien."

He looked over at Shane. "You read about that in the papers, too, I guess."

"Yeah," he said. "It's all over the news. Kind of cool, because the stories all mention U-823. It's almost as if your uncle and Frank are trying to save it for us."

"What are you talking about?"

Shane looked down at the beach, scuffed the sand with his foot, making a circle. He tried to get his thoughts together. It wasn't easy; they were thrashing around, like seaweed in storm waves. He didn't have any men in his life—his dad had drowned, he had no uncles, his grandfathers were dead. But there'd been something about those news stories that had pulled him in, made him wish he'd come from a family like the O'Caseys, men who had influenced each other, who held each other up, who were all part of the same team.

"You know," he said, "the way they both fought in the war, different wars. And how your father was the commander who sunk U-823. It's as if Frank and Damien would never let Cole Landry take away your father's U-boat."

"But what can they do?"

"They can help," Shane said.

"They're dead," Tim said, his voice not much more than a whisper.

Shane looked at him as if he was a really sad case. Hadn't he been listening to Mickey when she'd talked about being thrown into the water, when she'd seen the U-boat and the white faces of German sailors? Shane believed his father's spirit had been there, too, had helped Shane rescue Mickey that night. He believed his father was with him when he surfed, when he caught a perfect emerald wave and rode it home.

"Maybe you're not paying attention," Shane said. "They're here."

"Frank is here?"

Shane nodded. He could practically see him, standing right there at Tim's elbow.

Mr. O'Casey turned away. He took a few steps toward the water, as if scanning the surface for a young man swimming. Shane wanted to tell him he was looking in the wrong direction, that Frank was right there beside him, standing on the beach. But Mr. O'Casey was new at this. He was old, and it took old people longer to get certain things. When he turned back, his face was lighter still.

"Thank you," he said.

"No big deal," Shane said.

"That opening tonight—you invited?"

"Yeah," Shane said. "But that thing with Mickey's father . . ."

"Like I told you," Mr. O'Casey said, "she'll understand."

"Right—*someday.*"

"Today's someday," Mr. O'Casey said. He picked up the weight belt, slipped out of the tanks. "Come on. I'll give you a ride so you can get changed. We'll go to the gallery together."

Shane nodded. He took the weight belt from Mr. O'Casey, also the fins and mask. He'd help him carry the stuff back up from the beach—it was really too heavy for one person to manage alone.

Besides, Shane knew it was what Mr. O'Casey's dive partner would want him to do.

24

The Dominic di Tibor Gallery was filled with people drinking champagne, eating smoked salmon canapés, and, especially, gazing with pure awe at the largest collection of Berkeley paintings ever amassed in one place. Neve circulated, answering questions of collectors and potential buyers, but mainly she kept her eye on Mickey.

Mickey sat at Neve's desk. She looked almost official, staring at the computer screen. Neve knew that she was working on a project—she could have stayed home, done it there, but Neve hadn't wanted to leave her alone tonight. Mickey was devastated about her father—and almost as much about Shane, for having turned him in.

"What a great show!" Chris said, slipping her arm around Neve. "Dominic is in his glory!"

Neve nodded, glancing over toward the wall of shorebirds. Dominic held court, dressed in black Armani, explaining each painting to the throng of press—some of whom had little interest in art, who had just come for the O'Casey family story.

"Listen to him talk about Damien and Joe as if he knows them personally," Chris said.

"I know," Neve said. "Close personal friends."

"You deserve a raise just for not gagging over that," Chris said, tightening her grip.

"Excuse me a moment," Neve said. She walked over to Dominic and stood looking at him long and hard—until he flinched and backed away from the group.

"Great crowd," he said.

She didn't reply, just stared at him.

"You seem upset," he said, sounding nervous.

"More than you can know," she said quietly. "To you, this is a big event. To other people, it's a huge betrayal."

He rolled his eyes, waved his hand. "Those relatives of Berkeley's?" he asked. "Darling, this is free publicity. The prices of the paintings they have hidden in the attic will skyrocket!"

"Is that all you think about?" she asked.

"The value of artwork? Yes. Yes, as a matter of fact, it is. And you should be glad of it—especially because I'm giving you a raise. A substantial raise—plus I'm throwing in benefits. You're a jewel."

"I feel sorry for you, Dominic," she said after a long moment. "The O'Caseys are friends of mine—I care about them so much. I learned about Berkeley in confidence; it was my mistake, telling you. But I never thought you'd call the press."

"I'm an art dealer, Neve. This is my business. I'm sorry for hurting you, but I'm not sorry for the *New York Times* being here— along with arts editors from nearly every other major paper and magazine. Do you understand?"

"No," she said. "I don't."

He shrugged, kissed her cheek, and returned to the group.

Walking away, she felt shaken. She'd said what she needed to say—and she'd been about to quit. But how could she leave her job, especially now that he'd just offered her a raise? She was a single mother—and with Richard in the bad shape he was in, she couldn't afford to stand on her principles.

"What just happened?" Chris asked when Neve walked back over to her.

"He just raised my salary."

"How inconsiderate—just when you were about to blast him."

"Well, I did, sort of," she said. "God, I wanted to quit on the spot, but I can't. Mickey and I need the money. Who knows when Richard will come around? I can't count on him. . . ."

"No," Chris said. "You can't. You've done too much for him, by the way."

"All I did was call his lawyer," Neve said. She knew that Jim Swenson had contacted Alyssa, who was posting bail. Neve supposed that Richard would be out by now; he was probably running through the litany of promises and mea culpas that would buy him time and good graces.

She had long stopped hoping that Richard would change, even for Mickey. His love for her was unassailable—Neve knew that he would stop drinking if he could. It's just that love could motivate a person only so far. Standing among all of Berkeley's paintings, she felt that she was standing in a temple of hope—surely to the man who had made such transcendent art, anything would be possible.

Yet it wasn't. War had devastated him, and he'd never painted again. Looking around, she noticed several old men and their wives. She was quite sure she'd never seen them at the gallery before. Squeezing Chris's hand, Neve made her way over to where they stood.

"Hello," she said. "Are you enjoying the exhibit?"

"We are," one of the men said. "Beautiful pictures."

"Yes, Berkeley was extremely gifted," she said.

The tallest of the old men laughed gently. He shook his head, staring at the canvas of two screech owls on the same branch.

"What's so funny?" she asked.

"We never called him Berkeley," he said. "We called him Damien."

"You knew him as Damien O'Casey?" she asked.

"Yep," the man said. "We were crewmates, from our first day—492nd Bomb Group, in World War II." He introduced himself as George Heyer, along with his wife, Sally, and two other crewmates and their wives.

"My husband and Damien flew together," said Sally, a trim white-haired woman dressed in a rose-colored suit, her accent pretty and Southern. "George and I were already married, and I used to get letters all about his great friend Damien. . . ."

"You had no idea he was an artist?" Neve asked.

"We knew he could draw up a storm," Gerry McGovern said. "On days when we didn't fly, he'd write letters home—to his mother and father, or his brother Joe—and he'd fill the pages with pictures."

"Birds, as a matter of fact," George said. "We tried to call him Birdman, but the nickname wouldn't stick. He was the Silver Shark. And damned if that didn't become the name of our plane."

"We were one of the first silver planes, see," Gerry said.

"Meant as a way to elude German radar," Simon Clark said. "We flew deep into Germany, and being the Silver Shark gave us that extra toughness we needed. Made us feel like no one could get us, you know? Especially with that shark Damien painted on for nose art."

"Where is Joe?" George asked.

"Yeah," Simon said. "We weren't even sure he was still alive, but once we read the news story, we figured we had to fly out to see Damien's paintings—and meet his brother."

"They're all like family, you see," Sally said. "They spent so many hours together, during such trying times; they all knew each other's parents, and brothers, and girl-friends, and wives . . ."

"So where's Joe O'Casey?" Gerry asked. "I know he's the most famous WWII vet around here—sank that U-boat we keep reading about. Even out in San Francisco, where Mary and I live, the story's made the papers."

"How could it not, with Cole Landry in the picture? Damn fool," George said. "Where's Joe? I came a long way to meet him. . . ."

"I invited him," Neve said quietly. She didn't want to share the rest of the O'Casey family story with these people—as much as they loved Damien, some of it was too private, just for Joe, Tim, and Frank.

"I can't believe he wouldn't show up for his own brother's exhibit," George said, frowning.

"Come now, darling," Sally said, taking his arm. "You know how difficult you expected it to be—walking into this gallery and seeing all these paintings come alive . . . done by your dear, dear friend; it has to be a hundred times harder for his own brother."

"I guess," George grumbled.

"Well, it'll just be the most disappointing thing in the world," Simon said. "To have come all the way from Chicago . . ."

"From Alabama," George added.

"The most disappointing thing in the world," Simon said again as they all stared at the painting of two screech owls on the same branch.

Mickey was sitting at the desk, trying to ignore all the voices buzzing about the exhibit, arranging all the letters she'd received. If only the timing worked out, she could hand them to Senator Sheridan. She cringed, thinking of how her father had made his single phone call to him—what had he said? Mickey knew he'd probably begged his old friend to get him out of jail—and he hadn't. Her father had still been in custody when her mother had dragged her away. Mickey would have stayed all night, but the desk sergeant had told her she had to leave, that he wasn't a babysitter.

Babysitter! As if she was a kid. She was working like crazy to save a landmark, to create a memorial. And that cop had treated her like a sniveling little jerk. Just because she was upset about her father being taken into custody! Wouldn't anyone be?

And who would, who *could* think it was all Shane's fault? What had made him do it—drop a dime on Mickey's dad? If her father had been drinking, that would be one thing. But he wasn't—he hadn't had a drink all day. And now he was locked up, at the mercy of the court, just because he'd had a run of bad luck.

"You okay?" Chris asked now, coming to stand with her.

"I'm fine," Mickey said.

"Would you like a soda? Maybe some cheese and crackers?"

"I'm not hungry."

"No appetite?"

"Nope."

"Guess it's because you're upset about your dad."

Mickey nodded. "I should be down there at the station. But the cops wouldn't let me stay, and Mom made me come here."

"Your dad'll be fine," Chris said.

"I doubt it," Mickey said. To her great consternation, her chin began to wobble. Tears hadn't been far away all day—or at least ever since her father had picked her up at school. It had been so wonderful to be with him—just sitting there in the car, riding through town, like any other father and daughter. Yes, he had smelled of gin—but it was old gin. Why couldn't Shane have left well enough alone?

"You doubt what?"

Looking up, Mickey saw old Mr. O'Casey standing there. She almost didn't recognize him—he was wearing an old Navy uniform, hat and all.

"How's the owl?" she asked.

"He's fine, making friends," he said. "He's doing well, improving every day. Now answer me—you doubt what?"

"That my dad'll be fine," Mickey said, dropping her voice.

Old Mr. O'Casey stared at her thoughtfully. She had the feeling he had many questions he wanted to ask about her father, and the funny thing was, she might not even mind answering them. Just looking into his watery blue eyes, she knew that he knew about mistakes and suffering; she somehow knew that he wouldn't look down on her father the way Chris, as much as Mickey loved her, did.

"I'm Christine Brody," Chris said now. "Neve and Mickey's friend."

"I'm Joseph O'Casey," he said.

"Tim's father," Chris said, twinkling as if she knew something. Mickey looked up, wondering whether her mother's best friend hadn't noticed that Tim hadn't exactly been around lately.

"Yes," he said, turning back to Mickey. "What's the matter with your father?"

Mickey just shook her head. She wasn't going to go into it here, now. Instead she stared up at old Mr. O'Casey. "Why are you wearing your uniform?" she asked.

"To honor my brother," he said.

People had started to notice him. Dominic

and the reporters had caught sight of the old man in uniform, and so had Mickey's mother and the white-haired people she was talking to. The room had been buzzing, but suddenly it fell silent. Mickey heard someone whisper, "That's Joe O'Casey."

"Joe O'Casey, Damien's brother?" called one of the white-haired old men.

"That's right," Joe said, starting to walk over. "Who are you?"

"I'm George Heyer," he said. "Damien's . . ."

Joe just stood there, unable to speak for a moment. "Damien's radioman," Joe said quietly.

"We're what's left of Damien's old crew," one of the others said.

"From the 492nd," Joe whispered.

"We loved your brother," George said. "Loved him a lot."

Mickey watched as Joe drew himself up. He walked over to the group of men, and with his hand shaking, he drew it up in a salute. The other men stood tall, faced him, and saluted back. She watched as her mother put her hand over her mouth—but she wasn't looking at old Joe, not at all. She was facing the gallery door, where

Shane was walking in, just ahead of Ranger O'Casey.

"Damien's brother," George said, reaching out to take Joe's hand.

"You're Damien's brother, too," Joe said, hugging him. "Don't think I have any doubt. You all are."

Neve walked over to Tim. The rest of the room fell away, and she looked straight into his eyes. He'd been just behind his father, and she knew he'd seen the exchange between Joe and Damien's crewmates. She thought of how he felt about his father and Damien's war service, how he believed it had led to Frank's deciding to enlist.

"I've never seen him in his uniform," he said, gazing past Neve. "I didn't think he still had it."

"Why do you think he's wearing it tonight?" Neve asked.

"For Damien," Tim said, watching his father a few more seconds, then meeting Neve's eyes. She saw an old spark there, and she felt him taking her in, looking her over. She'd worn a black cocktail dress and high heels; her shoulders and arms were bare; she wore a simple silver chain that dipped down between her breasts. She'd dressed in the almost nonexistent hope that Tim would come, and now he was here.

"You came," she said. "I'm so glad."

"When it got right down to it," he said, "I couldn't stay away."

"Let me show you the exhibit," she said. "Would you like a glass of champagne?"

He nodded, so Neve called over a waiter circulating with flutes on a silver tray. Neve took one for her and one for Tim. They walked through the gallery, among the throngs of people. Neve wished they could be alone so Tim could have privacy to look at his uncle's work—not that he wasn't familiar with it, but just to take in the enormity of such a large group of his paintings all in one place, and to feel the stillness incorporated in every single one.

The room was anything but still. Neve and Tim made their way around the room, pausing in front of every painting, saying hello to people they knew from town. Feeling people's eyes on them, hearing them whisper, Neve blushed slightly.

"They're talking about us," Tim said.

"I think you're right."

"It's our first time out together, not counting Newport."

"Takes two bridges to get to Newport," she said, smiling hesitantly. "I guess we escaped detection."

"Well, we haven't now," he said. "The word is out."

"I wasn't sure you wanted to see me again; I hoped you'd come tonight, but I honestly didn't expect you to."

"I didn't expect to either," he said. He glanced over to the front desk, where Shane and Mickey were in fierce discussion. Neve followed his gaze.

"Mickey's upset with him for calling the cops on her father," she said.

"He did the right thing," Tim said.

"I know. Mickey's father needs every wake-up call he can get. Right now he's down at the police station, or maybe his girlfriend has already bailed him out. He's such a good talker, he's probably figured out a way to stave off this latest onslaught. I almost wish he *had* been drinking—they'd send him to rehab."

Joe O'Casey had been standing with Damien's old crewmates, but at the sight of Tim, he excused himself and made his way over. Neve watched the two O'Casey men staring at each other, not speaking.

"Well," Joe said, putting his arm around Neve's shoulder but facing Tim. "Didn't Neve do a fine job?"

"Of hanging the show?" Tim asked. "She did."

"Yes," Joe said. "You've done our family proud, Neve."

"You have," Tim said, gazing down at her.

"It's not how I planned everything to happen," she said. "It was an accident, my boss finding out that Berkeley was really Damien. I should never have said anything."

"Well, it's not your fault," Joe said. "As I said once before, you didn't learn Berkeley's identity all on your own, after all."

"Dad," Tim said, "I'm sorry. I told her . . ."

"Don't be sorry," Joe said, waving his hand. "If you hadn't said something, Neve wouldn't have told her boss, and he wouldn't have called the press, and Damien's crew wouldn't have found out about the exhibit and flown in to see it."

"It must be amazing to meet them," Neve said softly.

"You have no idea," Joe said. "Damien talked and wrote about them all the time.

They really were his other brothers. They're staying overnight in town; tomorrow they're going to meet me down at the beach, so I can show them where U-823 went down. In fact, I'd better go home and get some rest now, so I'm ready for it."

Neve held his hands. He looked tired, and his eyes were glittering, as if the night had been too much for him—as well it must have been, surrounded by so many of his brother's paintings, meeting his surviving crewmates.

"Thank you for coming," she said. "It means so much."

"You're welcome, Neve," he said. "Now, since you've gotten so deeply into our family, I'm going to ask you something personal about yours."

"Sure," she said. "Anything; what is it?"

"What's Mickey upset about?" he asked. "She said that her father 'won't be fine.' "

"Oh," Neve said, her heart falling. "The police took Mickey's father into custody today. It's for child support issues, but they initially thought he'd been drinking."

"Had he?"

"Surprisingly not," Neve said. "I guess he's trying to quit again."

Joe nodded, as if he had some idea about that.

"You know how Mickey feels, don't you, Tim?"

"To see her father drinking himself to death?" Tim asked. "Yeah, I do." Neve was aware of Tim staring at Joe intently, and a hard look passed between father and son. It ended with something like a smile, an acknowledgment that something had changed. Neve didn't know the whole story, but she thought she could piece together most of it.

"I wish Mickey's father could stop," Neve said to Joe. "The way you have."

"So do I," Joe said.

Then Joe hugged Neve; he made a move to hug Tim, but the two men shook hands instead. Joe left the gallery, and Neve heard George and Sally say they'd see him at the beach tomorrow. She glanced over at Mickey, saw her head buried in Shane's shoulder.

"Looks as if they've made up," Tim said.

"I'm so glad about that," Neve said, staring up into his eyes. "But have we?"

"Yes, Neve," Tim said. "It took me a while. . . ."

"I'm just so sorry about what I did. I care about you so much," Neve said. "Your whole family. I've just been so swept away, and it's been so long since that has happened."

"Like my father just said: there's no need to be sorry."

Neve nodded. Tim had opened his mouth to say something else, but suddenly he stopped. His gaze was directed at the gallery door. Wide open, it was letting in the fresh spring breeze behind a whole group of young people. A few years older than Mickey and Shane, by the looks of them.

Dominic would be so happy—he loved attracting a young crowd. Sometimes he'd advertise in *Chelsea* magazine, hoping young artists would take the train out from New York, or down from Boston. Neve wondered who these kids might be—an art class from Brown or RISD or URI maybe? But as she stared, she saw that they weren't all art school hip. Some looked pretty solidly middle class, some single, some in couples, and one with a toddler in tow.

"More Berkeley lovers," she said, watching them enter the gallery, stop to get their bearings.

"No," Tim said, standing still, watching as some of the kids saw him standing there.

"Who are they?" Neve whispered.

"They're Frank's friends," Tim said.

And suddenly he was surrounded by ten young men and women, some of them crying, all of them thronging around so they could give him a hug. They wore dresses, jackets and ties; they were in their mid-twenties, older than Neve had first thought. She saw them smiling, leaning close to their friend's father, saying hello.

She saw Tim's face, too. It was weathered and lined, a face so much more comfortable outside on the beach than here in the stuffiness of the Dominic di Tibor Gallery. He greeted all the kids, hugged them, nodded and said how surprised he was to see them, how much he'd missed them, how wonderful it was of them to come. Neve watched. She saw Tim's face smiling.

His face was covered with tears, but he was smiling.

25

There was no place worse for detoxing than a lockup. Richard had done it more than once—right here within these same four walls. He felt the poison swirling around his system; his head was dizzy, and his stomach ached. He had dry-mouth like crazy. He had the shakes. The cops didn't care. They probably thought it was funny—they'd picked him up for a DUI, and even though he technically wasn't drunk, they got to hold him on failure to pay child support.

Noises were amplified by the cinder block walls, giving Richard a wicked headache—to go along with everything else. The desk sergeant had brought him a sandwich, but he felt too sick to eat it. He sat on the floor of his cell, slumping against the wall because it felt cool against his back. He felt as if his skin were on fire.

He hung on with all he had to the knowledge he'd gotten through to Senator Sheridan. He'd made the call and talked to Sam, explained the situation—finally he'd done something for Mickey. He just hoped the senator would follow through. Otherwise the despair Richard felt would become so unbearable, he was sure it would kill him.

"Hey," the sergeant said, coming down the corridor. "There's someone here to see you."

"Well, I don't want to see them," Richard said. So far his visitors that day hadn't worked out. Neve had been furious about him driving "drunk" with Mickey; Richard's divorce lawyer was pissed about not being paid, and besides, now Richard was looking at charges, and would need a criminal attorney; and Alyssa had just stood there crying, cradling her belly, asking why he had done this, what she had done wrong.

"Tough shit if you don't want to see anyone," the sergeant said. "You know who this is?"

Richard squinted into the fluorescent light, tried to shield his eyes. He saw a naval officer standing there—the white coat and hat of a commander, stripes and all. Jesus Christ, Richard had the D.T.'s. Next he'd be seeing flying pink elephants.

"What, am I under military arrest, too?" he asked.

"This is Commander Joseph O'Casey," the cop said.

"Who sunk the U-boat?" Richard asked. Everyone who'd grown up in Rhode Island had heard that name.

"For some reason, he wants to see you," the cop said. "So why don't you get your sorry ass off the floor and show a little respect?"

Richard nodded; he wanted to. Joseph O'Casey had been Richard's hero when he was a boy; besides, hadn't Mickey mentioned something about him earlier today? About the owl? The name had only semi-registered. Richard tried to push himself up, but his legs were rubber.

"That's okay, Officer," the naval commander said. "You can leave us now."

"Sir, look at him, down on the floor like that. You sure you want to do this?"

"I'm sure."

Richard hid his eyes. When he looked up, the commander had crouched down—was sitting on the other side of the bars, right on the dirty floor in his white uniform.

"Richard," he said, "I'm Joe O'Casey."

"Hello, sir," Richard said. He stuck his hand through the bars, but it was shaking so hard, he felt too ashamed and pulled it back. "I'm Richard Halloran; are you sure I'm who you want to see?"

"You're Mickey's father, right?"

"Right," Richard said, swallowing with shame. Mickey; she'd seen him in handcuffs, hauled away in a police car.

"Then you're the right Richard Halloran."

"What can I do for you, Mr. O'Casey?"

"Call me Joe. From the sounds of it, you've had a tough day."

"Yeah. It hasn't been too hot."

"Why don't you tell me about it?"

Richard looked through the bars. Was he kidding? Richard tell a great state hero about getting arrested? Suddenly the reality of who he was talking to kicked in. Richard wouldn't be in jail forever—he'd be out soon, and he'd have real estate to sell, deals to make. Joe O'Casey was potentially a great contact—right up there with Sam Sheridan.

"Do you know Sam Sheridan?" he heard himself asking now.

"Senator Sheridan? I voted for him. But forget that. Tell me about your day."

Richard frowned. If only he could stand; if only he could convince the desk sergeant to let him and the commander talk in a private room. This was so ugly, so humiliating. Richard Halloran went first class or he didn't go at all; that was the message he wanted to give Joe O'Casey.

"Well, I'll tell you, Joe," Richard chuckled, patting his pocket. That's right—the cops had taken his cigarettes and lighter. "It's been a bitch of a day."

"Yeah? Why?"

"Well, my daughter's friend. Nice enough kid, but a little flaky. You know? One of those surfer types, all peace and love and the beach. He meant well, I'm sure, but he misunderstood something."

"What's that?"

"Well, he thought he smelled alcohol on my breath—which is ridiculous, considering

I haven't had a drink all day—and he called the police to report me. Now, what I think is that my daughter must have given him the brush-off, and he wanted to retaliate in some—"

"You do stink," Joe said. "You realize that, don't you?"

"Excuse me?" Richard asked, thinking he had to have misheard. A classy guy like Commander Joe O'Casey speaking to him that way?

"You reek of alcohol. Didn't you know that?"

"Joe!" Richard said, shocked and offended. "I told you—I haven't had a drink all day!"

"Do you think that matters, son? You've got so much booze in your bloodstream, you'll be sweating it out for days to come. Next you'll be telling me you drink vodka, that it doesn't have any smell."

"I do," Richard said. "And it doesn't."

"Oh, Richard," Joe said. "I used to think that, too."

"What do you mean?"

"Well, it gets metabolized, and, well—people can smell it. Neve smelled it on you every time you came home drunk and hoped she wouldn't know. Your girlfriend—what's her name?"

"Alyssa," he said.

"Yes. Alyssa. She smells it, too. Hopes against hope she won't—hopes that this time you're going to keep your promise. Wants to believe that this time you get it, this time you're going to put her and your family first. Mickey, and I hear you have a new one on the way."

"I know," Richard said, suddenly miserable, beset with such anguish he thought and wished he would die. The kids. Not just his beloved Mickey, already almost through high school, but a new baby—a child he'd never even met yet.

"You do know, right?"

Richard nodded. "I will quit this time. For them, Joe. I swear I will."

But Joe sat on the other side of the bars, arms draped around his knees, shaking his head. "Nah," he said. "You won't."

Richard was in shock. How could this guy judge him?

"Joe. How dare you! I love Mickey, and I'm going to love the new baby. I do already!"

"I know you want to," Joe said.

"I don't just *want* to," Richard said, feeling desperation growing. "I do. I love them."

"I know how hard it is," Joe said quietly.

"It's not hard," Richard said. "Loving Mickey's the easiest thing in the world."

"Ask me why I sat down here on the floor," Joe said. What was he doing, constantly throwing Richard off balance? Christ, what a nightmare—Richard would just think he had a handle on it, had this guy's number, and he'd change course.

"Are you messing with me?" he asked.

"Ask me why I sat down here on the floor," Joe said again.

"Fine," Richard said, exhaling. "Why?"

"Because I know what you're going through," Joe said. "I know your legs are worthless right now—two rubber hoses. Your stomach is in knots—you'd throw up, but there's nothing left in there. Your head has iron bands around it, and you think it's going to explode. You can't stand up, Richard—that's why I sat down."

"How do you know I can't stand up?"

Joe tilted his head and gave Richard a long, fatherly look that almost brought tears to Richard's eyes. "Because I'm a drunk, too," Joe said.

"You're no drunk," Richard said.

"I was," Joe said. "So was my brother. The two of us. We went into the service two nice, innocent young boys—and we came back something else. We were numb inside, so we drank to feel—and then we drank more to stop feeling. Sound familiar, son?"

"I never went to war," he said.

"The reasons don't matter," Joe said, staring at Richard through the bars.

Richard shrugged, because it seemed to him they did; war heroes drinking too much was one thing. A guy with every comfort possible—that seemed something else.

"Alcoholism is a disease," Joe said.

"It's a shortcoming," Richard said.

Joe shook his head slowly. "No one knows who gets it or why. People joke about us Irish being predisposed. I don't know about that. I just know I've got it, and it seems to me you do, too."

"At least you have an excuse," Richard said.

Joe laughed. "Oh, come on. You have excuses, too. Right? The real estate market is in the toilet; the real estate market is going crazy; she doesn't understand you; your best friend's dog died. Richard, there's always a reason to drink."

"Yeah, but the kids," Richard said. "They're the reason I'm going to stop."

"How many times have you told yourself that before?"

"I don't know," Richard said, shrugging.

"A hundred? Five hundred? A thousand? You know the dialogue that goes on in your mind? I won't drink today . . . well, maybe just one . . . I'll stick to beer . . . I'll quit for Lent . . . I'll just drink on the weekends . . . this is the last one. For me, it was probably a hundred times a day until Tim turned sixteen. That's the year I got sober. And you know what?"

Richard shook his head.

"I didn't do it for Tim."

Peering through the bars, Richard wondered: what kind of father was this asshole?

"I wanted to, and once I stopped, he was a big reason I stayed sober. But I had to do it for myself. That's the only way."

Richard lowered his eyes, shook his head. Didn't the old man have eyes? Richard was a piece of shit in the local lockup. He'd lost his wife and child—now he was on his way to doing it again. Why would he think he was worth anything?

"Only you can say whether you've had enough," Joe said.

"I had enough a long time ago," Richard said. "But I can't stop. I don't know why. My life was never so bad. I never lacked for love, or a roof over my head, or enough to—"

"You can't stop because you're an alcoholic," Joe said.

"Yeah," Richard said. He got no relief from hearing the truth spoken. In fact, he just wished it would go away, that Joe would go away.

"You been to the meetings?"

"AA? Once or twice. Doesn't seem like my type of people," he said, thinking of the hard-luck cases he'd seen, burning to tell this old guy that people like Sam Sheridan took his calls.

"I go," Joe said. "Once a week, Saturday mornings, over in Jamestown. Once you get out of this place, why don't you stop in? I'll save a seat for you."

"Maybe," Richard said.

Joe started pushing himself up, then sank back down. "You say it's not your kind of people. We take all kinds, and we have a saying in the rooms: 'From Yale to jail, from Park Avenue to a park bench.' It doesn't matter. For people like us, one drink's too many and a thousand isn't enough."

Richard nodded; that sounded exactly right.

"Like I said, I'll save you a seat."

Richard stared through the bars.

"Why did you come here today, anyway?" he asked. "How do you even know me?"

"I know Neve and Mickey," he said. "I look at them, and I think of how much time I wasted with my wife and Tim."

"Mickey said she brought the snowy owl to you," Richard said bitterly. "Do you make it a habit, taking care of broken things?"

"It's my honor and my privilege, taking care of that owl," Joe said. "Taking care of you? Only you can do that, Richard. Only you can get better. And I wish you luck. More than you can know."

Joe reached through the bars and patted Richard's shoulder. He didn't reach for his hand, as if he'd seen how badly it was shaking. Richard felt the weight of the old man's hand on his shoulder, and he thought of his own father. His dad had used to do that, a long time ago. Pat Richard on the back for a job well done.

He wouldn't do that now, not if he could see what had become of his son. Richard bowed his head, just hoping it would all end soon. But he loved Mickey so much, and he had the new baby coming.

Only you can do that, Joe had just said. *Only you can get better.*

Richard felt his whole body start to shake—not tremors like before, but something else, quiet sobs—and he sat in the corner of his jail cell and wept.

26

That night Mickey felt the world change again. It had started about two hours ago while she was sitting at her mother's desk at the gallery, with strangers strolling past the paintings, drinking champagne. So many people had come from such great distance to see Berkeley's art, and sitting very still at the desk, Mickey watched the emotions in all of their faces, everyone moved by the delicacy of the work.

The lights were warm and glowing; the buzz of conversation was exciting. The old members of Damien O'Casey's crew were so happy to be together, here to celebrate their friend's great talent. But as Mickey watched them move slowly around the gallery, two of them on canes, her heart opened to the fact that he wasn't here anymore. Damien wasn't here to see all this—all the people who loved him.

But they loved him anyway! Whether he was in the room or not, whether he lived on earth or in heaven, their love followed him. She'd heard from her mother that he had had problems after coming home from the war. Bad problems, enough for him to stop painting—but they didn't matter. People loved him anyway.

It was probably just two minutes after that revelation that Shane walked in. He was with Mr. O'Casey; they were both dressed in jackets and ties, a sight that in and of itself made Mickey smile. Shane in a tie? She'd never thought she would see the day. When he saw her, he came right over. His long hair was damp, as if he'd just taken a shower. His blue eyes were solemn, and his shoulders came forward, as if he was ashamed or afraid of something.

"Hi," he said.

"Hi," Mickey said. She stared at him. If he had arrived two minutes earlier, before her great realization, she might still have been too upset to talk to him. She was still mad at him, but the worst of it, the hot rage, had spiraled out of her like a ghost.

"Mickey, I'm really sorry about what I did."

"It's okay," she said.

"No, it's not," he said. "I know how much you love your dad, and it must feel rotten to have seen him taken away like that."

"Almost the worst thing ever," Mickey said. Just thinking about it made some of the anger and hurt come back, and in spite of how glad she'd been to see Shane walk in, she had to turn away now.

He came up behind her, put his hand on the small of her back. She shivered to feel the pressure of his fingers, but still she wouldn't look at him. He steered her gently away from the desk, to stand by a painting of a flock of swans. She glanced at the painting, recognized the location, looked down at her shoes.

"You look so pretty," he said.

"I didn't even change," she said. Even though her mother had rushed her home from the jail, Mickey had stayed dressed in the clothes she'd worn to school: black capri pants, pink shirt, jean jacket. She glanced up at Shane, who looked amazing.

"It doesn't matter what you wear," he said. "You're beautiful no matter what."

She shook her head, and tears welled up. If she was so beautiful, why did her father drink? Why did he abandon her? Fathers with lovable, pretty daughters didn't do that.

"What's wrong?" Shane asked.

"I didn't want you to see him that way," Mickey whispered.

Shane didn't reply right away, and Mickey was glad. She didn't want him to pretend he hadn't seen anything, or that it wasn't as bad as it was. She shuddered slightly, and she felt his arms come around her. They stayed like that in spite of all the people standing around.

After a while they broke apart. Old Mr. O'Casey came over to talk to them, and then he left. A bunch of Frank O'Casey's friends from high school showed up, and Mickey watched her mother and Ranger O'Casey talking to them. The crowds began to dissipate. Chris Brody went home. Even Dominic di Tibor left—sweeping away in his cape, calling Mickey's mother "Bella" and congratulating her on a great show.

Now, at the end of the night, Mickey and

Shane began to move around the exhibit. Not talking, but just looking at the paintings. They looked at all the birds: egrets, blue herons, kestrels, sharp-shinned hawks, barn owls, screech owls, and then, the most beautiful and disturbing painting of all, the snowy owl.

It was almost horrible to behold: the owl had just swooped down on a brown bird— beak hooked, claws extended, blood dripping on the snow from the kill. It was the most fierce and brutal of all Berkeley's paintings.

"This one seems different," Shane said, stepping closer to look.

"In so many ways," Mickey murmured.

"Why do you think he's showing the owl that way?"

"Because it's real," Mickey said. "Because owls are predators."

"The place looks far away."

"It does," Mickey agreed. All of Berkeley's paintings seemed so local—there were many defining Rhode Island landmarks in the background. The Point Judith Lighthouse, Hanging Rock, Cliff Walk, Mansion Beach, the jetty at Refuge Beach. But the painting of the snowy owl was clearly of the arctic tundra.

"Do you think Damien went there?" Mickey asked. "Traveled to the Arctic?"

"He must have," Shane said. "That's definitely a snowfield, not a beach."

"I don't even recognize that species of bird that it's holding," she said, moving closer, so her face was right beside Shane's. The snowy owl had captured prey, a small grouselike bird—and was flying over the snow with it in its talons.

"I don't either," Shane said, but when Mickey glanced up, he wasn't even looking at the painting—he was staring at Mickey with such intensity, it made her shiver. "I wish I could find out for you," he whispered.

Mickey nodded. She thought she knew a way. She looked across the room at her mother, standing with Mr. O'Casey. Her heart had felt so hard all night—especially toward her mother and Shane, the two people she loved most in this room. She knew that it had been because of what happened with her father: they had seen him in such terrible circumstances. And although those circumstances weren't exactly their fault, Mickey couldn't quite separate them out.

Shane had called the police on her father, and her mother had left him at the police station.

Mickey's mother was watching her now. In fact, with all the evening's excitement, Mickey knew there hadn't been a five-minute stretch where she hadn't been. Holding Shane's hand, Mickey took a deep breath and started pulling him across the room. When she got there, she saw that her mother had the tired, excited glow of knowing it had been an amazing opening, or maybe it was the fact that Mr. O'Casey was right there with her.

"Hi, honey," her mother said, hugging her. Mickey let her, too. It felt good to make up. "Hi, Shane."

"We had a question," Shane said. "About the snowy owl painting."

"We did," Mickey said. "What's the other bird—the one the owl is carrying away?"

The four of them drifted over to the painting. By now the gallery was really clearing out. The last viewers called their goodbyes, and the caterers were busy cleaning up in the kitchen. Mickey stood between her mother and Shane, as they all stared at the canvas.

"I think it's a ptarmigan," Mr. O'Casey said. "But I'm not sure."

"They're not native to Rhode Island," Mickey said. "And besides, doesn't the landscape look like the tundra?"

"I believe it is," her mother said. "When I was researching this painting for the catalogue, I noticed that this was the only setting that wasn't obviously local. What do you think, Tim?"

"I think there's only one person who would know," he said.

Mickey watched as he pulled out his cell phone and dialed a number. It took a few rings, and he must have gotten an answering machine, because he started leaving a message:

"Hi, Dad. We're still at the gallery, looking at the snowy owl painting. Mickey wanted to know whether it was done in the Arctic—and we were wondering what species the prey—" A look of surprise crossed his face, and he said, "Oh, hi, Dad—did I wake you?"

He listened a few moments, starting to smile, his eyes widening.

"Wow," he said. "Really? Okay—we'll be right there." He hung up the phone, turned to everyone's expectant faces.

"It's a ptarmigan," he said. "And the painting is of the Arctic, a spot up near Hudson Bay."

"But why did you say 'wow'?" Mickey asked. "What happened?"

Mickey saw the look that passed between him and her mother. Mickey's heart bumped; she felt as if she'd just gone over a cliff, was free-falling through the air. This day had been a shock to her, and she was afraid if someone didn't catch her now, she'd crash and never be the same again.

"Is it the owl?" she asked, grabbing Mr. O'Casey's sleeve. Her father was in jail; if the owl had died, she would die herself.

"My father says it's a miracle," Mr. O'Casey said. "And he doesn't use that word lightly."

"What kind of miracle?" Mickey's mother asked.

"The owl is flying," Mr. O'Casey said.

So of course they had to go see. Mickey's mother paid the caterers, locked up the gallery. Mr. O'Casey's truck didn't have enough seats, so they all piled into the Volvo. Mickey's mother drove north, along the windy, wooded road that led to the barn.

Mickey and Shane sat in back. They

pressed close together, holding hands. Thick trees lined the roadsides, their branches meeting overhead. Blotches of orange streetlight splashed on the narrow road at quick intervals. Shadows fell into the car, making everything dark and quiet. Looking between the two front seats, Mickey saw Mr. O'Casey take her mother's hand; the sight made Mickey happy and sad, all at once.

When they got to the barn, Mickey's mother parked where she had that first day, when they'd delivered the owl here. He had been so badly injured—his beak broken, his wing dangling as if it would never work again. Mickey felt the weight of so much pain—not just the owl's, but her mother's and father's, the solemn mystery of the U-boat, and her own. Holding Shane's hand, she realized that she didn't believe that anything really good could happen anymore—the owl couldn't possibly fly, the U-boat would be taken away by the big yellow crane.

The four of them entered the barn. The space was completely dark, just as it would be in the wild. Old Mr. O'Casey greeted them, an enormous grin on his face. He led them in without a word—and no words were necessary, and no words could explain what Mickey was seeing.

The owls were flying.

It was night—Mickey's first time here in the darkness, the time when owls were awake and came to life. The flight corridors leading between cages had been empty and quiet before, and Mickey had believed they were probably forever unused, just an optimistic architectural detail. But tonight the corridors were alive with owls.

Their yellow eyes flashed like shooting stars. Great wings beat with such a rush of energy, everyone ducked, momentarily forgetting the owls were contained in wire mesh. Mickey looked overhead, seeing brown feathers everywhere. She saw screech owls swooping in one corridor, the barn owls in another, the great horned owl diving down to a lower branch. And there, in the last corridor, high above the cage where it had appeared so close to death just weeks before, the snowy owl was soaring.

"He's flying," Mickey whispered.

"How did he heal so fast?" her mother asked.

"What's that other snowy owl in there, flying with him?" Shane asked.

"That's his mate," Joe said.

"His mate?" Mickey asked. "He didn't have one. . . ."

"He met her here," Mickey's mother said quietly.

"Someone found her hurt on Block Island," Joe said. "Brought her to me a while back. She was surviving, that's certain, but now she's like a wild bird again. And so is he."

Mickey gazed up. The female's plumage was duller, not so brilliantly white as the male's. But she flew with such zeal, she exhibited such ferocity, it was as if she was wearing her heart on her wing. The male owl had brought her back to life, and vice versa. She knew, staring into the sky of the barn, that this was what Joe had meant earlier by "miracle."

"What will happen now?" Mickey asked.

"I never would have thought this," Joe said. "But we might be able to release them."

"Do you really think so?" Tim asked.

"I think it's possible."

The five of them stood still, watching the owls fly with such force and energy, Mickey was afraid they might reinjure themselves against the sides of the corridor. It ran like an open heating duct along the ceiling, the entire width of the barn, then took a turn and continued the length. Mickey saw that it was the biggest flight corridor in here, but even so, the snowy owls were almost thrashing with the sheer joy of even restrained flight.

"Let them out now," Mickey said suddenly.

"Mickey," her mother said.

"Please," Mickey begged, turning to Joe. She felt almost desperate, thinking of beautiful beings locked in a cage, thinking of her father in a jail cell, thinking of the German ghosts in the U-boat. "Please, let them go."

The old man looked deeply into her eyes. His face looked so like his son's, but with even more wisdom and sadness etched into the sun-weathered lines and angles. He had changed out of his uniform, into jeans and a plaid shirt.

"Mickey, we have to observe them long enough to make sure that would be a wise decision, that they can survive."

"I can't bear to see them flying in captivity!" she cried.

The old man hugged her. She felt the energy of someone who really understood, and she let herself cry against his shoulder.

"I think I know what you're feeling right now," he said. "I saw your father tonight."

"My dad?" she asked, pulling her head back to look at him.

"Yes," he said.

"At the police station?"

"Yes," he said again.

"I didn't want to leave him there," Mickey cried. "I just thought if I could have waited with him, been there when he got out, then maybe he would be all right. I thought maybe he'd go home and be safe!"

"Mickey," he said, "we want to help the ones we love so much. And it isn't always easy. Sometimes the best thing we can do is wait. That's what Tim had to do for me."

"He's right," Tim said. He was standing so still, his arm around Mickey's mother. Mickey looked over with tearstained eyes and saw him gazing at her with such care, it was almost as if they were part of the same family.

"When I was your father's age," the old man said, "I was in bad shape. I was trying to drink the war away, drink my brother's downfall away. Wouldn't come home, wouldn't talk when I got there. I put Tim and his mother through the wringer."

"Not you," Mickey whispered, not wanting to believe that such a wonderful man as Joe O'Casey could ever have done that.

"Yes, me. Good people do stupid things, Mickey. Sometimes they grow out of it. Let's count on your father finding his way, all right? You couldn't wait at the police station all night, but maybe—if your mother says it's okay, and if Shane calls home and his mother says it's okay—the two of you can wait here with me."

"With you and the snowy owls?" Mickey asked.

"Yes," he said. "We'll observe them through the night, and consider the possibility of release. Shane, will you call your mother?"

"Sure," he said, and Mickey's mother handed him her cell phone.

The call was made. Mickey's mother made her promise to call her cell if she needed anything. Tim went with his father into the house to dig out some old sleeping bags. Overhead the squawking and tumult continued, and Mickey hugged her mother.

By the time Shane hung up, they all knew

he'd gotten the go-ahead. He was grinning as if he'd never been happier.

"She said it's fine," he said. "She's leaving for North Carolina next week, and she said she likes knowing I have friends; makes it easier to leave for a while."

"How long will she be away?" Mickey's mother asked.

Shane shrugged. "I guess she's going to see how things go with the major."

And then it was time for Mickey's mother and Tim to leave. Mickey kissed her mother goodbye, and she gave Tim a hug. They took a last look up at the owls, then walked out to the Volvo. Mickey waved as it drove away, then returned to Shane and Joe.

"Can I ask you a question?" she asked Joe. "Your brother's painting of the snowy owl: why did he make it so terrible and bloody?"

"That's a very good question," Joe said. "And as far as I know, you're the only one ever to have asked it."

"But what's the answer?"

Joe was silent. He gazed up into the barn's ceiling, at the two snowy owls flying back and forth along the corridor. For a moment, Mickey imagined him watching airplanes, and she remembered the long flights his brother had taken from England to Germany, while Joe was patrolling the New England shore.

"It's my brother's antiwar painting," Joe said quietly. "It shows the brutality of death in the sky."

"But he was such a brave airman," Shane said. "Such a war hero, just like you . . ."

"A war hero who lost everything," Joe said. "He has daughters, you know. I'd hoped they would be at the show tonight, but they weren't. My brother stopped painting, and he stopped being able to love his family."

"How could a man who painted like him stop loving?" Mickey asked.

"I think because he knew what could happen," Joe said. "The terrible things that people in this world can do to each other. It made him give up hope."

And that was all he said. He walked away, to stand by his workbench, where the single Berkeley painting hung. Mickey imagined him thinking of his brother. She huddled closer to Shane. If she held on tight enough, could she stop terrible things from happening to him?

"Mickey," he whispered, so softly she had to tilt her face up, feel his kiss, pour herself into him.

"Shane, I'm so sorry about before," she said when they stopped.

"What do you mean?"

"Getting so mad at you about my father," she said. "It wasn't your fault, and I'm so sorry."

"Love means never having to say . . ." he said, smiling, starting to quote from an old movie.

But Mickey reached up, touched her finger to his lips. The night was as miraculous as Joe O'Casey had said, and Mickey knew it all had to do with forgiveness. People made mistakes, took wrong turns, made horrible decisions. But as long as there was love and hope, they could talk about it, see everything in a new light, forgive each other. Look at Tim and his father; look at him and Mickey's mother. Even, especially, Mickey and Shane—and it was all because of forgiveness.

"Love means *always* having to say you're sorry," she whispered, kissing him again as the snowy owls flew in reckless pathways overhead.

27

As Neve drove Tim back to the art gallery so he could get his truck, she felt the spring air coming through the Volvo's open window. The night was cool, but it held a promise of the warmth to come, the melting of the winter's last snows. Spring peepers called from the woods. And the image of the snowy owls flying through the mesh corridors seemed like the greatest hope of all.

"Do you think your father will really be able to release the owls?" Neve asked as she drove.

"I think it's possible," Tim said. "I'd never have believed it."

"No," Neve said. "Neither would I."

As they drove through downtown, she skirted the seawall. The moon was in its last quarter, settled low in the sky, illuminating a slice of yellow in the harbor. The crane, floating on the barge. Just seeing it felt like a knife, cutting through all the goodness. Turning into the gallery's driveway, she felt Tim's hand on her arm.

"Don't stop," he said. "Come down to the beach with me. . . ."

"It's so late," she said, stopping on the side of the road.

"I know. But Mickey's staying at the barn. You have your cell phone—she'll call if she needs you." Tim leaned over, kissed her. "Tonight we need each other."

Neve nodded. She knew that was true. They decided he'd take his truck, so she waited while he backed out, then followed him down the shore road. The night air felt sharper and crisper than before. The yellow crane was still there, rocking as the protected waters of the harbor rose and fell, but Neve didn't even see it. All she could think about was where she and Tim were going, and that brought the sense of goodness back.

When they got to the ranger station, Neve pulled in beside Tim. She was still wearing the black dress she'd worn to the opening. The sound of the breakers filled her ears, and their salt mist carried over the beach and dunes, brushing the skin of her bare arms.

Tim unlocked the door; he stood back, let her pass in front of him. He started to turn on a light, but she turned around, pressed herself into his arms, led him into the living room. The quarter moon tipped over the water, splashing a sparkly net across the waves. Her heart caught in her throat as she thought of everything this beach meant to them, and she stood on tiptoes, kissing Tim to let him know how she felt.

He had a message of his own. She felt it coming through his hands and lips, telling her with everything he had. They held hands, walking into his bedroom. She'd never been in here before; she had the feeling very few people had. It was all Tim: just the bed and dresser, a shelf full of marine books, a chart of the Rhode Island shore, some photos of shorebirds.

And a picture of Frank.

It wasn't like the one Joe had—of Frank in his dress uniform, looking solemn and dignified for the camera. No, it showed a young man in camouflage gear, sunglasses, and a big floppy hat, grinning from ear to ear. Neve stared at it, seeing the tremendous life in Frank's face and smile, and she noticed that Tim kept it right by his bedside. It had to be the last thing he saw when he fell asleep, the first thing he saw when he woke up.

"What a wonderful picture," she said.

"I love it because it looks like him," Tim said. "Not many of the pictures I have do."

"So vibrant, and handsome . . . and right *there*."

"That was Frank," Tim said. "Right there. He was so present, always in the moment. No matter what was happening, he had his eyes open, he just took it all in."

"Was it good to see his friends tonight?" Neve asked.

"Better than anything that's happened in a long time," he said. "Except you. Nothing's been better than meeting you."

They stood by the bed, kissing for a long time. Neve felt so conscious of the bed's nearness, and she figured Tim did, too. She felt magnetized to him, with such crackling energy that when he pulled away, she leaned in his direction.

Neve watched as Tim rummaged through his bedside drawer, came out with an envelope. It was big and square, as if it held a card. He sat on the bed, smoothing it on his lap. Neve sat beside him. He looked over at her, tried to smile.

"I've never shown this to anyone," he said.

She couldn't speak, her mouth was so dry. Instead, she just took his hand. When he passed her the envelope, she knew he wanted her to read what was inside. She pulled it out, trying to keep her hands steady. The card showed two people, a man and a little boy, both wearing dive gear, standing at the bottom of the ocean. A submarine had been hand-drawn in the background. Fish swam all around. Bubbles were coming from the boy's mouth, and the words *Happy Father's Day!* were printed above the waves overhead.

Opening the card, a sheet of paper fell out. Neve unfolded it and began to read.

Dear Dad,

Happy Father's Day! I know this card is late, and I really have no excuse except to say it's been a little busy over here. Also, I apologize in advance for the sand. There's been crazy wind the last few days, and our tents are full of sand.

It kind of reminds me of the beach during summer storms—except over here the sun is always shining, and the wind never stops blowing.

I wish we could go for a dive. I miss the ocean so much; the river isn't quite the same. Even though I can't tell you much about where I am and what I'm doing, I'm sure you understand. That's one thing about coming from a family where lots of us have been to war; some things just don't need to be said.

Grandpa talked to me about it more than he did to you. Maybe I'm figuring that out a little. It's something you don't want to talk about—maybe not until fifty years go by. But I will say that my buddies are great, the best friends I've ever had. We'd do anything for each other, you can count on that. I'm just one of the crew. But sometimes I imagine what I'd do if I had to lead—if it all fell on me. And you know, Dad, when I imagine that happening, I think of you.

I think about you staying calm. No matter what happens, no matter how loud or close it gets, I just think about you. That time we went diving, and when we came

*up we were in a thunderstorm—man, all
those lightning bolts hitting the beach and
the boat and everything around us, and
our air nearly out, and how you just held
my hand and eased me underwater, how
you taught me to conserve my air and
breathe calmly instead of as if I was
scared to death, how you taught me
something and saved my life.*

*I think of the time we went ice fishing in
New Hampshire, and how we were way
out in the wilderness and our car
wouldn't start. And how it was before
you had a cell phone, and we were stuck
in the middle of nowhere, on the frozen
lake. We'd gone up more to watch
eagles and hawks than to fish, but that
day you became the greatest fisherman
in the world. Cut a hole in the ice,
showed me how to drop my line in, wait
for the tug. We ate like kings that night,
Dad, and even though we nearly froze in
our tent, when the ranger came by the
next morning—I didn't even want to
leave!*

*The sand in my tent here reminds me
a little of the snow in our tent up there,
so it doesn't seem as bad. I remember*

*you laughing about it, no matter how
cold it got. So I try laughing about it
now, no matter how hot it gets. My
buddies have started doing the same.
We just have a blast, Dad. Even Major
Wrentham chuckles, sort of.*

He's not a bad guy.

*Anyway, there were just a few things I
wanted to say for Father's Day. I know
you and I went at it before I came over
here. I just want to say—I didn't get it
then, but I do now. We don't have to go
into it here, but I want to tell you I
appreciate what you were trying to do.
We'll talk about that when I get home.*

*Mainly, more importantly, I want to tell
you how much I love you. I couldn't ask
for a better dad. And I'd better not even
try, because you're what they'd give me.
You're my hero, Dad. I'm not a Marine
because of you. But I'm a diver, a
fisherman, a joker, a beach bum, and a
bird freak because of you.*

THANKS A LOT!

*Just kidding. I'm proud to be your son.
In all the ways I can think of and probably
about a million I can't. Say hello to the
beach for me? There's all this damn*

sand, but not a speck of salt water! My buddies call the blowing sand "Desert Music," but I tell them they're nuts. It's "Beach Tunes," and that's all there is to it.
                    Love,
                    Frank O'Casey

Neve finished reading the letter, unable to breathe. She touched his name. Outside the house, she heard the waves crashing and sharp grains of sand blowing against the wood shingles.

"I got that letter two days after his funeral," Tim said. "He and his unit were crossing the Euphrates, west to east, sixty miles south of Baghdad. Insurgents had forced a gap in the embankment, flooding the terrain—it must have weakened the ground, because the bank gave way beneath Frank's tank. He never got out."

"Oh, Tim!"

Tim nodded. He took the card from her, held it in his hands. She knew that he was trying to feel Frank; Frank had touched the paper, and that meant something.

"We knew that he was in a dangerous situation," Tim said. "His mother and I, and my father. I don't think there was a moment that we didn't have CNN or news radio on. We'd been following troop movements. So when I got the call . . ."

"They called you?" she asked, surprised they would deliver that news in a phone call.

"*Beth* called me," he said. "I picked up the phone, and she said, 'They're here.' "

"I asked her—'Is it two of them?' Because the military always sends two to notify you; one of them is a chaplain. I thought, if there's just one, then we're okay. I thought, damn her—why was she home? Why's she looking out the window? If she didn't see them, if she didn't answer the door, then Frank would be okay."

Neve listened, gazing at the card. At first she'd thought Frank had bought it some-where, but the more she looked, the more she realized that he had drawn the whole thing—not just the U-boat. He was a good artist, had some of his great-uncle's talent; he'd really captured the affection between the father and son divers—she thought it was so achingly sweet that a Marine had made the son such a small boy.

"She said the tap on the door was so light, she almost didn't hear it," Tim said. "She said if she'd closed her eyes, she might not have heard it at all. But she did hear, and she did open the door. I was on the phone the whole time, so I heard what they said. And that was the end of it."

Neve held him. She couldn't believe that it could be the end—her eyes fell on Frank's picture. His smile held such light and life; could it really be over in an instant, a tank plunging into the river where human life first began?

Frank was in his father's heart, and his mother's and grandfather's, and even though she'd never met him, in Neve's. But for Tim, knowing he'd never see or hear or touch his beautiful son again was a grief beyond knowing. Did the sound of sand blowing give Tim comfort or drive him mad? Neve held him and rocked him, letting the sounds of the sand and the ocean from which it came reverberate around them, wash through the walls and surround them.

After a while, he pulled her down on the bed. She knew that he wasn't putting anything behind him. Instead, he was bringing Neve into his life with Frank, into their family. She felt it, and was honored. Their arms were around each other. Waves kept breaking on the beach, but the house was solid.

Neve closed her eyes and kissed him. The sound of the sand and waves continued with no sign of letting up. She kissed him, and she didn't stop.

Tim lay with his eyes open. His life had been destroyed that day when the two men showed up at Beth's door. Until just a few hours ago, he'd never talked about it, never shown anyone Frank's card, never let another soul read Frank's letter.

They'd fallen asleep on his bed. Neve rested in the curve of his arm, her chest rising and falling in deep sleep. Tim lay as still as he could, listening to the waves pound the beach. His heart was racing—could it be from the dreams?

His dreams had been the same for weeks: writing Frank's name in the sand, the German sailors peering out of the U-boat at him. Holding Neve now, he realized that tonight's dream had been different. Frank was alive—all those nights of scrawling his name had brought him back. He stood beside Tim and Neve on the beach, and said one word: *Remember.*

Just thinking of the dream, hearing that

word in Frank's voice, made Tim's eyes flood. *Remember*? How could he think Tim would ever forget? But then he realized something else—the German sailors were gone. The waves had died, and the dream sea had been as flat as a lake. Somehow Tim knew that the U-boat had been taken away, that the evidence of war, of its trail of attack and death so close to their beloved home, had been erased.

That's what Frank had meant in the dream: *Remember.*

Tim's arms were around Neve. He felt such a surge of life, feeling her lying beside him. She was on her side, bottom pressed into his groin. Her sleeveless black dress had bunched up to her hips; he leaned over, kissed her bare shoulder. His lips brushed her skin.

Her auburn hair spilled over her face. He reached over, moved it away. Easing her toward him, onto her back, he kissed her lips. She slid her arms around his neck, pressing her body against his. He felt the swell of her breasts against his chest, heard her moan gently as he slid his hand beneath her, held her close.

Their heads were together on the pillow.

Kissing tenderly, then suddenly the opposite. He felt her holding him so tight, wanting to make love, something neither of them had done in a long time. That made it as amazing as anything else—made the desire more explosive than the ocean waves pounding the beach outside.

When they were finished once, they made love again. A long time passed, because all of a sudden, gray morning light was coming through the window. It was silver, tinged with the pink of dawn. Birds, migrants from the south, filled the thicket along the dunes. Their song nearly obliterated the sound of the waves.

"Good morning," Neve whispered.

"Morning, Neve," he said.

"I woke up in the middle of the night and thought I was dreaming," she said. "Being here with you."

"I dreamed of you," he said, the dream coming alive again. *Remember . . .*

"Were we doing this?" she asked, smiling and kissing him, reaching down.

He smiled, kissed her for a while, then shook his head.

"We were doing something else," he said. "Do you have to work today?"

"In theory, yes," she said. "But if Dominic doesn't owe me a day off after last night, then he really needs to find someone else. Why?"

"I want you to come to the beach with me."

"I have to get home, then go pick up Mickey and Shane. Thank heavens it's Saturday, because I'm not sure they'd feel like going to school."

"Bring them back here, okay?" he asked, kissing her again. "Shane and I are making a dive."

"Like . . ." she began.

"Like me and Frank," Tim said.

"I'll get the kids right away," Neve said, giving him one more kiss before getting up.

The wind was always calm first thing in the morning, and today was no exception. The only sounds were the birds and the waves. Tim wouldn't say this out loud—not yet, anyway—but early mornings he missed the sound of the sand blowing.

He missed hearing what he knew Frank had heard in his tent, halfway around the world, the music of, not desert music, but beach tunes, when he'd written that last letter to the father who still and forever loved him so much.

28

Mickey and Shane had watched the owls last night, until they were too tired to stay awake anymore. They fell asleep in sleeping bags on the barn floor, and they woke to Mickey's mother shaking them gently, asking Shane if he wanted to go diving. He'd jumped up, eager from the first moment. And old Mr. O'Casey was going to go, too—he'd agreed to meet Damien's old crew members down on the beach, to show them the site of U-823, but first he was going to drive the dive boat.

Driving to the beach, they had passed through town. Both Mickey and Shane had been born here. They were natives, and they knew every inch of every street. So when the car swung along the big seawall near the boat launch, Mickey got a knot in her stomach—because there was the huge underwater engineering barge, with the yellow crane sitting on top.

"Look at it out there, just waiting," Shane said.

"It's as if Mr. Landry moored it there just so it would be in our faces," Mickey said.

"Seems as if people are excited about it being there," Shane said. "They're all looking."

And it was true. Mickey noticed many cars parked by the seawall, the people standing around in groups with coffee and doughnuts from the bakery, staring out at the crane and talking. Others came by boat; they circled the barge in wide, slow circles, curious about such big machinery and trying to get a better look.

"Why can't they realize how wrong this is?" Mickey asked.

"Maybe they will," her mother said.

"But there's no time!" Mickey said. "The crane's going to pick up the U-boat in such a short time, and it will be gone forever."

"A lot can happen in a short time," her

mother said quietly. "Just think of the snowy owl."

Mickey fell silent. She glanced over at her mother, who looked happy, glowing, as if she had a secret. Maybe it had to do with such a successful opening last night, or maybe it was because she and Mr. O'Casey were friends again. Either way, Mickey didn't believe that enough would happen in a short time; not to save the U-boat, anyway.

"This came for you," her mother said, sliding a blue envelope across the seat.

Mickey took it; the mail must have come after they'd left for the gallery yesterday— the return address was Berlin.

"Is it another one?" Shane asked from the back seat.

"Yes," she said, handing it to him.

"Another letter from Germany?" her mother asked.

"It's the eleventh I've gotten," Mickey said.

"Mickey sent out fifty-five letters, to all the families who had relatives aboard the U-boat," Shane said.

"I know," her mother said softly. "I remember you telling me that; I just didn't know they'd really write back."

Mickey felt her mother's eyes on her. It didn't happen often—they were so close; but every once in a while Mickey surprised her mother. Maybe it was because they lived alone—Mickey's father hadn't lived with them for such a long time. Her mother was vigilant—it was as if she'd read all the books, as if she *lived* the TV commercial that asked "It's ten o'clock—do you know where your children are?"

Yes, and at eight and six and three and one o'clock, too. Mickey's mother paid attention, to Mickey's undying frustration and consternation. Mickey's mother followed all the good-parent advice: she talked to her about drugs; she told her about the dangers of smoking; she patrolled her Internet use for online predators. So when a moment like this occurred, and Mickey managed to reach a goal without her mother's help, she couldn't help but feel a big surge of triumph.

"It must have been such hard work, finding their current addresses," Mickey's mother said, her grin filled with admiration.

"Research," Mickey said proudly. "It's one good thing about being your daughter—with all those catalogues you've written on elusive artists over the years, I've learned how to track things down."

"And you found all fifty-five?" her mother asked.

"I wrote to the U-boat archive," Mickey said. "And explained that I wanted to write to any surviving family members of U-823. The archive provides a service for any family members who want to be in touch with people who want to know about their relatives."

"At first Mickey thought they might not want to," Shane said. "Because she's American, and the men died over here."

Mickey nodded, trying to smile. She'd told him everything last night; watching the owls, thinking of what Joe O'Casey had told them about his brother and the war, it had all come pouring out.

"But they did write back!" her mother exclaimed.

Mickey nodded. "So much time has passed; they just seemed happy to know that someone was asking."

"Who are they?" her mother asked.

"Daughters, sons, a couple of grandchildren; I wrote in English, and the ones who wrote back did it in English," Mickey said.

Her plan had been to collect as many letters as she could and then deliver them to Senator Sheridan. It had seemed like such a good plan at the time. But now, with everything moving so fast, the crane already here and ready to go, the next step seemed unattainable.

"It must be weird," Shane said. "Going about your life, just hanging out, and getting a letter like that out of the blue. Some people would probably just rather forget all about it."

"Like Damien's daughters," Mickey said sadly. "Mom, why do you think they didn't come to the exhibit?"

"I don't know, honey," her mother said. "Every family is different."

Yes, Mickey thought, but every family is the same, too. She sat in the front seat, looking out the window as they neared the beach. She thought she knew, maybe, why they hadn't come. Some things were too hard; she thought of her father in jail, and shivered. Maybe Damien's daughters had loved their father so much, and maybe he'd broken their hearts one time too many. Thinking of the letters she had gotten from Germany, she knew that children loved their

parents in such different ways. It didn't matter how old any of them were.

Her mother pulled into the parking lot at
the ranger station, and Mr. O'Casey was
waiting. Joe had arrived, too, and he was
out of his car, talking to his son. Mickey held
her breath, looking around for another car.
She had hoped that Mrs. West would be
here, too. Mickey's mom had made Shane
call to ask permission to dive: he'd woken
his mother up with his call. She'd said yes,
but be careful.

Shane hadn't said, but Mickey knew that
he hoped she'd come to watch. She'd be
leaving for North Carolina soon, figuring that
with summer coming, Shane would be busy
on the beach all day anyway. Mr. O'Casey
had offered him a job raking the beach—
even after his ninety-day community service
was up. Of course he'd accepted; a beach
job was even better than the surf shop. So
it would have been nice, meant a lot to
Shane, if his mother had come down today.

"I'm sorry she's not here," Mickey said to
him, holding his hand as they walked
toward the ranger station.

"She doesn't like the beach," he said.
"Reminds her too much of my dad."

"I guess I can understand that," Mickey said. Even though she didn't, not exactly—she was having one of those, "It's ten o'clock, do you know where your children are?" moments. Except she would have substituted "parents." People needed to keep track of each other, the ones they loved.

Otherwise, they could just slip away. Just like Damien had from his daughters, just like Mickey's father had from her. And just like it seemed Shane's mother was about to do.

"I'm here," she said, holding his hand hard.

"I know," he said, smiling.

"Go down there, take a bunch of pictures, so no one ever forgets what once was here."

"The Battle of Rhode Island," Shane said, looking out at the sea. "Right here on our shore. It's going to be pretty awesome, diving the wreck with the guy who sank it up above."

"Joe."

"Yeah," Shane said, gazing at the two O'Casey men standing together. Did seeing fathers make him miss his as much as it made Mickey miss hers?

"This'll be a big day for him, too," Mickey said.

"It would have been bigger if the owl . . ."

Mickey nodded; he didn't have to finish his thought. Midway through the night, the snowy owl had stopped flying. He had gone to the corner of his cage, his wing trailing slightly, as if the flight had been too much too soon. The female had landed beside him, grooming him quietly. Joe had told them not to consider it a setback, but to realize that healing happens for a reason.

"Everything in its own time," she said to Shane, echoing Joe. "Today, you're going diving."

"I'll get good pictures," he promised, kissing her.

Mickey held him, thinking of battles big and small, battles won, and the fight for the U-boat that felt already lost. Then she watched Shane as he ran into the station to change into his wetsuit and, instead of riding the waves on top, prepared to dive right down to the wreck of the vessel U-823.

The day was fresh and clear—the wind low, and the sea calm. Joe sat at the helm of the big inflatable, navigating Tim and Shane out to the wreck. He wore his old hat, the one he'd worn on the bridge of the USS *James* the day he'd battled U-823. It made him feel young again, filled his mouth with the taste of the sea, and of commanding a ship. Only today, the question was who was commanding whom.

"Here we are," Joe said, when he got to the spot.

"Dad, the wreck's a hundred yards east," Tim said.

"No, man," Shane said. "Your dad's right."

Tim shot the kid a dirty look. Joe tried not to smile. Joe had been shocked to get Tim's call this morning, asking him to man the dive boat. It had been such a long time since they'd been out on the water together. When Frank was a young teenager, first starting to dive, they'd come out here together all the time—three generations of O'Caseys, all water dogs.

As Frank got older, and he and Joe had started getting closer—talking about U-823 and the Battle of Rhode Island—Tim had started backing away. Maybe he'd resented all the early years, when Joe should have been talking to him; whatever it was, a small rift had turned into the Mariana Trench—the deepest ocean canyon in the world. So that's why today was all the more important to Joe.

Not to mention seeing Tim with Shane. Not that anyone could ever replace Frank— to think so would be a gash in Joe's soul. But just to see his son reaching out to another young man, sharing with him his great knowledge of and love for the sea, gave Joe some ease. So he listened to the bickering with a hidden smile.

"I'm the park ranger," Tim was saying. "I think I know where the U-boat is located, especially since my father's the one who sank it."

"Mr. O'Casey, with all due respect, I surf out here every day," Shane said. "It's the wedge, man—the wave rises up right off the conning tower, falls back on itself, and blows out off the jetty." He shielded his eyes, getting his bearings, nodded as if he was sure.

"He's right, Tim," Joe said, throttling back so the engine idled, holding them relatively steady over the spot. Although both were available, he didn't have to rely on electronics or check coordinates on the chart: he just knew. He felt it, as if U-823 were exerting an intense pull on him. The feeling spread through his legs and up his spine, electric and compelling. This was it, right under the water in this spot.

"Okay, we'll dive here," Tim said.

"Sorry, Mr. O'Casey," Shane said.

"I guess I know the refuge better than I do the water," Tim said. Then, looking at Shane, "Look, if we're going to be dive partners, you'd better call me Tim, okay?"

"Okay," Shane said, grinning.

Then Joe heard Tim running through the rules. Stay together; the water was clear today, and they wouldn't be going deeper than one hundred feet. They'd dive around the conning tower, take some pictures. They wouldn't enter the wreck, and they wouldn't even get close enough to get tangled in any of the fishing lines or nets that had snagged on the U-boat over the years.

"You got that?" Tim asked.

"Sure do," Shane said.

Joe dropped anchor; he knew the two men would use the line to guide themselves down to the U-boat and back to the surface. He heard Tim reminding Shane about the bends—every thirty-three feet of depth, the pressure increased to twice what it was at the surface. Nitrogen built up in the lungs, traveled into the bloodstream, and created a narcotizing effect on the diver.

"Man, I'm certified, remember?" Shane asked.

"I remember, but just in case," Tim said. "You start hearing fish talking to you, or seeing men come out of the U-boat with machine guns, you let me know—and we'll head back up. And we'll take it slow; we'll hang out on the anchor line on the way up, okay?"

"Right."

"So the atmospheric pressure in our bodies can decrease gradually."

"Got it," Shane said. He was polite, but Joe could hear his impatience. Was Tim hearing echoes of Frank, as Joe was? Young men being told how to do things . . . it never changed. Joe had experienced it with the men under his command, with his own son, and with his grandson.

While Shane busied himself, adjusting his weight belt and fins, his mask and dive knife, Joe checked the walkie-talkie. Tim had given one each to him and Neve—standard park ranger issue—just in case. While

Joe clicked the button, made a test call, heard Neve's voice loud and clear, he looked up and saw Tim standing there.

"Dad," Tim said, "is there anything in particular you want to say?"

"Say?" Joe asked, frowning.

"Yes," Tim said. "Anything you want me to do while I'm down there? Any specific pictures you want me to take?"

Joe narrowed his eyes, felt the boat rocking beneath them, wondered how his son had managed to read his mind. Over the years, he had brought wreaths of flowers to the beach on April 17, the date of battle. He'd done it to commemorate the deaths of Johnny Kinsella and Howard Cabral, his two crew members who had died here; although their bodies had been recovered and were buried in their home states, to Joe, this was their grave.

"I brought something," he said. "I'd planned to drop it myself, after you and Shane went down."

"What is it?" Tim asked.

Joe reached into the pocket of his windbreaker, pulled out a small miraculous medal, sterling silver, depicting the Virgin Mary, given to him by his mother when he'd made his first communion. He'd had it with him every day of the war; he believed it had kept him alive, made him a good commander. He'd been wearing it that April 17, and he'd always prayed that Mary would bless the souls of Johnny and Howie.

"It's this," he said, handing it to Tim.

"Your medal," Tim said, looking at it; Joe knew it was a family talisman, along with his Navy hat and medals awarded to mariners in World War II: the Navy Cross, Distinguished Service Medal, Silver Star, and Bronze Star.

Back when Tim was young, Joe had kept them all hidden. Up in a drawer in the storage room, out of sight and out of mind. He'd come home from work or the bar some days, find Tim burrowing through the drawer, trying on the medals, reading the commendations. The only medal that had been out in the open had been this one, the miraculous medal, and only because Joe had never taken it off.

"Why are you throwing it in?" Tim asked now.

"Because it belongs here," Joe said.

"For your crew? Johnny and Howard?"

Joe stared at the surface. He thought

back to the battle, sixty-one years ago this month. To Joe, it felt like yesterday. He could still feel the adrenaline, that powerful mixture of fear and courage. He could smell the gunpowder, see the black conning tower—in that one moment the U-boat had surfaced. He had been face-to-face with his enemy, and the guns had fired, and Johnny and Howie were slaughtered.

"Dad?"

Joe had never been more filled with rage and grief. His men were dead, and the U-boat had attacked his home shore. He'd watched the black monster descend, bubbles rising to the surface, as if to mock the USS *James*. Those air bubbles had inflamed him—to think of the Germans breathing while two of his men were killed.

Everything America stood for surged through him, and he'd known he would fight back and destroy the U-boat and every man aboard. He felt it personally, as if he were avenging murder. They were his adversary, the foe of everything good and decent and innocent in the world, the enemy of all that was sacred, not just here in Rhode Island, but abroad in the world.

So he'd ordered the attack, and it had

been monstrous and righteous. Hedgehogs, depth charges, everything he and the *James* had, every ounce of firepower, and every fiber of courage in each of his men. These Nazi sea lords had crossed the Atlantic in 1942 to pick off merchant ships, to destroy shipping and massacre American crews, and right now, April 17, 1944, Commander Joseph O'Casey was going to put an end to it.

And he had.

The oil slick had been the telltale. Done deal. The German officer's hat and the shattered bits of chart table had just been more confirmation. But not enough for Joe—with Johnny and Howie on his mind, with Damien flying missions over Germany, with the very fate of the world in his heart, Joe had kept bombing.

One more, he'd think, dropping another depth charge. And another. The circular pattern of explosions, of water boiling up to the surface, the oil slick spreading. Another depth charge. Joe had wanted to empty his hold, give the devils more than their due.

The spring day had brought strange weather. Clear skies at dawn, then clouds scudding in and dumping snow on the sea and beach. Joe had looked up—after hours of fighting and bombing—to see aimless flakes falling. Thick snow covering the beach, as if with a blanket. And a flock of swans—that's what had woken him up.

Swans swimming at the water's edge. Oblivious to what was going on just a hundred yards out, feeding in the shallows, their feathers radiant, whiter than the snow. Joe had thought of his brother: if only Damien were here to paint that. Berkeley—his sweet, sensitive, gentle brother. Why weren't they together at Hanging Rock? Or even here, on Refuge Beach.

Refuge Beach . . . the name occurred to him, and he literally stepped back from the helm. In that one instant, his ship was without a commander. It all flooded his mind: the swans, the shore, the snow. And that's when he'd heard the pinging.

That sound he never forgot. The tap, tap, tap . . . Coming from down below, audible on sonar and even—was it possible—to anyone with ears? Joe swore he'd heard the sound emanating through the waves, as if amplified by the water itself.

The sound of Germans, trying to get out. Begging for help, for mercy, asking to be rescued. And there, just a hundred yards off Refuge Beach, Joe had declined to give them refuge. He knew right now, hands on the wheel of the dive boat, that if he could personally have dived down, opened the hatch of U-823, he wouldn't have done it.

He let those German sailors die. Their leader, Oberleutnant Kurt Lang, had been just twenty-four, the same age as Joe; he had killed Lang and his men, every last one of them, and he'd taken pride in doing it.

"Dad?" Tim asked now.

"Do you know how much I don't want the U-boat taken away?" he asked fiercely. "Do you know how wrong I think it is?"

"I do," Tim said, and in the gravity of his voice and the steadiness of his eyes, Joe knew his son was appreciating the honor of the USS *James.*

"Will you take this down there?" Joe said, looking into his son's eyes. "Leave my medal somewhere on the wreck?"

"Of course," Tim said, his hand closing over the silver medal. "For Johnny and Howard."

Joe shook his head, his eyes filled with tears. He had paid respect to his men every April for sixty-one years, and he knew he would never stop. But today was different; there was something else to be done. "For Kurt Lang," he said. "And his crew. The men of U-823."

"I will, Dad," Tim said.

And he kissed his father, and held the miraculous medal in his closed hand, and then he tapped Shane on the shoulder, and they put on their air tanks, and they went into the water.

The water was clear, and visibility was decent. Tim heard his own breath in his ears, and he looked over at Shane, and his heart pounded as he swam down, clasping his father's medal. He had seen the pain in his father's eyes, and as he swam downward, he was determined to do all he could to put that to rest.

The currents were strong down here, but Tim and Shane used the anchor line to guide them. The wreck appeared almost instantly. Seeing it filled Tim with emotion, but he fought the feelings, knowing that he had to stay calm in order to stay safe.

Just yesterday, wanting to dive here alone, everything had been different. He and Neve hadn't been speaking; his dreams had been of missing Frank with such anguished intensity, he'd seen no way he could continue living and be able to stand it. Deciding to dive on the wreck, take photos in order to document its importance as a Rhode Island battle site, had been reckless at best. When Shane had caught him on the beach, Tim had been thinking it just might be easier if he didn't come up.

Now, glancing up the anchor line, he saw the sun slipping across the water's surface. He knew his father was waiting in the boat, and he knew that Neve and Mickey were standing on the beach. Frank had come to him in his dream last night—instead of being reduced to just a name in the sand, he'd actually appeared to Tim.

It had just been a dream, but dreams could mean everything. Tim clutched his father's medal, knowing that was true, leading Shane toward the dark hulk. He was the father of a drowned boy, and Shane the son of a drowned father. Water was their medium; he wondered whether Shane felt as much peace, as close to the man he loved, as Tim did now.

The hiss of the regulator and the thud of

every exhalation rang in Tim's ears. The sight of U-823, his first in many years, was as shocking as ever. The long black hull was cracked and broken, encased in a tomb of snagged, ruined fishing nets. Skeletal remains of tautog, flounder, bluefish, and something larger—maybe a young whale—caught in the nets long ago, now drifted in the current.

Behind the nets lay the U-boat itself. It had come all the way from Germany, a feared predator; now its menace was gone. He stared down at the pipes and wires spilling from cracks, at the holes torn by bombs and the disastrous descent, at the propeller half-submerged in sand, at the rudder crumpled under the hull.

Shane swam carefully, right beside him. They took pictures from every angle. The young man was a good diver; he'd paid attention to his instructor, staying away from the nets, from the wreck itself. The only exception was when they swam over the conning tower and Shane reached out to touch the periscope.

What was Shane thinking? Was he thanking the U-boat, for all the magnificent waves it had provided, all the great, mystical rides

Shane—and his father before him—had taken over the years? Or was he imagining Oberleutnant Kurt Lang staring through the periscope, watching Commander Joseph O'Casey as he fought back and fought hard for his ship and his country? Was he thinking of all the loss, all the death, how the path of destruction never seemed to end? Was he thinking of Frank?

Because Tim was. Diving on U-823, he could almost feel his son at his side. Every flip of his fins stirred the silt a little more, made visibility just a little worse. He thought of the sandstorms Frank had written about, the sand in his tent, the beach tunes. Hearing his own breath in his ears, Tim imagined it was Frank's.

Motioning to Shane, Tim knew he had to go down a little deeper. Shane hesitated, not wanting Tim to go. But Tim indicated he'd be right back, so Shane hovered by the anchor line, waiting.

Tim held the medal. The sound of breathing was so loud and constant, and he couldn't stop thinking it was Frank's. He knew that wearing a regulator created this percussion of breath, but he imagined it might have been very similar for Frank, in his tank, underwater.

His father had told him to place the medal on the wreck, and Tim did. Wriggling down, close to the conning tower, he reached through the nets and stuck his hand out. He remembered just hours ago, showing Frank's card to Neve. His son's drawings and writing, the last letter he ever wrote. Somehow, hovering over U-823, the murky water full of silt and rust flakes, Tim knew that Frank would want him to do this.

Tim thought of Neve, felt her love. He thought of all the women who had loved the men trapped inside U-823. The mothers and daughters, wives and sweethearts waiting at home, an ocean away. He thought of Beth, who had loved Frank so much, and imagined all the mothers who'd lost sons in this wreck. He thought of his own mother, who had stayed with his father through all the torment, and he thought of his uncle Damien's wife and daughters, of how in their own ways, they were war casualties, too.

Gazing down, through the fishing nets and past the fast-moving current, Tim saw the hull captained by his father's old enemy, the

German Oberleutnant Kurt Lang. He remembered his days as a medic, those he had saved and those he had lost. His own war service had given him some frame of reference to imagine what Kurt Lang must have felt—such a young man, with so much responsibility, about to lose his own life—and those under his command.

"For you, Kurt," Tim thought.

And he opened his fingers, watched the silver medal drift down, settle on the moss- and barnacle-encrusted wreck of the U-boat. How could anyone think of moving this ship, this grave? Tim closed his eyes, said a prayer for them all. Everyone: the Oberleutnant and his men, the families they had left behind, his father and the crew of the USS *James*. And that brave boy who'd died in the distant waters of another war, Frank.

Feeling a bump against his shoulder, Tim startled. It was Shane, eyes behind his mask full of worry. Tim realized he must have thought Tim had gotten tangled in the nets. Slowly Tim withdrew his arm, gestured to Shane that he was fine.

They gave one last look at U-823. Already, Tim's father's medal was being covered over with silt. Soon it would be disturbed forever, when the crane came to lift the wreck and carry it away. Perhaps the silver medal would be left behind, all that would remain of what had happened here.

Tim tapped Shane's arm, and they began to ascend. He knew they had to remember to stop along the way, take time for the nitrogen to leave their bloodstream, for the pressure to stabilize. But Tim couldn't wait to get to the surface. He could hardly wait for the blue sky, for the birds flying north, for the beach, for Neve.

For life.

29

"Mom, who are those people?" Mickey asked, glancing down the beach.

Neve looked over, saw two cars parked up along the road. Three elderly couples were climbing out, and she recognized them from last night's opening at the gallery.

"Those three men were in Damien O'Casey's old crew," Neve said, watching as they stood by the car in the bright sun, raising binoculars to their eyes, pointing out Joe in the dive boat. Because she knew he'd want to know, she raised the walkie-talkie to her mouth and called him.

"Joe, they're here," she said. "George, Simon, Gerry, and their wives."

"Thanks, Neve," he said. "Let them know I'll be in shortly, okay?"

"Any sign from below?" she asked.

"Yes, they're on their way up. It'll take a while, because they're decompressing. Don't worry . . ."

"I won't," she said.

Mickey had heard, and offered to run up the beach to tell the three couples what was going on. Neve leaned against the jetty, watching her daughter. She flew across the sand, across the dunes, and started talking animatedly. Watching, Neve felt so relieved. Mickey had such deep feelings, such sensitivity for her father—but she also had powerful optimism and resilience, and for that, Neve felt grateful.

A call to the police station that morning had revealed that Alyssa had bailed Richard out during the night. So Neve had called Richard at her house, and he'd actually come to the phone. Usually, he'd sound so contrite the day after, when the heat was on. He would always promise to go to rehab, to become more regular in his visits to Mickey, to pay all his back child support, to go to AA. But today, something had been different. He had just sounded tired.

"Are you all right?" Neve had asked.

"Not really," he'd said, and that was different. Where were the bravado, the promises, the grand gestures?

"Why?" she asked. For anyone else it would be obvious, but for Richard, always looking for the angle, the rationalization, the way to blame anyone but himself, even a night in jail didn't always drive the point home.

"I'm just sorry," he said. "That's all I can say right now. Sorry to you, sorry to Alyssa. Especially sorry to Mickey." He'd paused, and she'd felt him wanting to say something more.

"What is it, Richard?" she'd asked.

"Did you send someone to see me last night?" he'd asked. "An old guy in a Navy uniform?"

Joe. Neve smiled in spite of herself. "No," she said.

"Damn if I didn't have a visitation," he said. "I didn't feel shitty enough, you had to send the U.S. Navy after me. My goddamn childhood hero, coming to see me in the drunk tank."

"I told you, I didn't. He went for Mickey."

"Fuck it, Neve."

What did he mean by that? She couldn't

even begin to know, so she just did what she always did on the phone with Richard, focused on staying calm. She'd spent years begging him to be a decent father, to pay his debts, to take care of their daughter. That hadn't happened so far, and she didn't hold out much hope that even a visit from Joe O'Casey would do the trick.

"I'll pay you," he said. "And not just because the courts are on my case. Because it's the right thing to do."

"Yes, it is," she said. And she took the promise with an extra grain of salt; she'd heard it all before. Besides, Dominic had given her a bonus for the great job she'd done on the Berkeley exhibit, so now she didn't have to worry about Mickey having a little extra spending money for her trip to Washington.

"And I did my best with Sam Sheridan," Richard said. "He'll see Mickey when she heads to D.C. Maybe I didn't have the money yet, to help you out with the trip, but I'll work on it. And meanwhile, the senator is expecting her visit."

"Really?" Neve asked, skeptical.

"Yeah. I used my phone call for that," he said. "You know, from jail."

"Instead of calling your own lawyer."

"You took care of that for me," he said. "Thank you, Neve. You're too good to me. . . ."

"Yep. I am. You've got that right."

They laughed. Not hard, but just a little chuckle—two people who knew each other well, who had a daughter they loved. So what if one of them was an idiot most of the time? They still loved Mickey.

"It's Saturday morning," he said. "I'm going to a meeting. Joe said it's a good one."

"Well, Joe's busy today," she said. "He's not going to be there this morning."

"Yeah, just as well. I've got to do this on my own," he said.

"Good luck, Richard," Neve said. She'd hung up feeling not quite overflowing with hope—maybe just simmering with it. Even after all his years of missteps, she knew Richard's heart was mostly in the right place. Mostly.

Now, standing on the beach, she felt the wind start to pick up. As the sun grew warmer the offshore breeze began to blow. She was glad the dive was almost over, that Joe would soon be ferrying Tim and Shane back to shore. She wondered what they had

seen, whether they had gotten any pictures
that would prove persuasive.

Just then, she heard another vehicle up on
the road: strangers here to walk on the
beach, maybe take a last look at the water
before the wreck was gone. Rhode Is-
landers all had a relationship with U-823,
and the news stories had brought people
from all over the state and beyond. As Neve
watched, some of the onlookers drifted over
to Damien's old crew and started talking.

A few moments later, Mickey came trudg-
ing down the path from the dunes. She
looked thoughtful, sad. Walking over to
Neve, she leaned beside her on the jetty. Her
reddish hair glinted in the sun, freckles sprin-
kled lightly across her cheeks. Neve looked
at her freckles and fought the urge to kiss
them, as she had when Mickey was little.

"When are Shane and Mr. O'Casey coming back in?" she asked.

"Soon," Neve said, putting her arm around
her.

"This feels like the end," Mickey said,
glancing up at the road. "All these people
coming to say goodbye."

"I know," Neve said. She had long ago determined not to lie to Mickey, even to make

her feel better. Honesty had been the way they handled everything, every disappointment and sorrow; she couldn't start to change that now. "I'm so sorry, honey."

Just then, a young woman began making her way down from the top of the sand dune. Blonde and pretty, wearing jeans and a red sweater, she gazed straight at Mickey. She was wearing sneakers, but as if she was an old beach hand, she quickly kicked them off and carried them in her hand, coming barefoot toward Mickey and Neve.

"Mrs. West!" Mickey said suddenly. "Shane's mother?"

"Yes," the woman said. "I'm Talia West. You must be Mickey . . ."

"Hi," Mickey said. "And this is my mother."

"Neve," Neve said, shaking Talia's hand.

"Where is he?" she asked, looking borderline panicked. "I thought he'd be back up by now."

"They're on the way," Mickey assured her. "That man in the boat said so."

"Oh God," Talia said. "Please let that be true. I can't stand to come to the beach and watch him surf. The waves are so violent—it kills me to think of him going out every day, doing what his dad did. Somehow I thought diving, especially with an experienced older man, would make me feel better."

"Tim O'Casey is the best," Neve said.

"I know, but so was Shane's father. God, I really did think diving wouldn't bother me in the same way, but turns out it felt worse; I was sitting home, just thinking about how Mac drowned, and how Shane was under-water, and I just thought I'd crawl out of my skin. Where is he?"

Neve picked up the walkie-talkie. She could see Joe from here, watched him re-spond to the call. Asking where Tim and Shane were, for Talia West, hearing Joe's re-ply: "Right here."

And they were. As if Shane heard his mother's request himself, his head popped up on the surface, right beside Tim's. Neve felt flooded with relief herself—there was nothing like another mother's anxiety to get her own going in overdrive. The men climbed into the boat, they hauled in the an-chor line, and Joe started the engine. Mickey ran down to the waterline, to help them beach the boat.

"Oh, thank heavens," Talia said. "When I think of going away for two straight weeks, I must be out of my mind."

Neve smiled. "That must feel like a long time."

"He's seventeen," Talia said.

"I know," Neve said, hearing the defensiveness in her voice.

"Old enough to take care of himself—especially because he thinks I'm just in the way anyway. I'm just a big inconvenience to Shane. I swear, he grew up all at once, the year his father died; three years old, and acting like the man of the family. You'd have thought seeing him drown would've scared Shane off surfboards for life—nope. He bought his first surfboard as soon as he could shovel driveways and mow lawns, earn his own money."

"He loves the water," Neve said. "So does Mickey."

"I just hope . . ." She paused. "I just want him to be okay while I'm gone. Thank you for letting him stay with you after he got into the fight with that Landry kid. That's what I'm afraid of—that he'll get in trouble again while I'm gone."

"He seems like a really good kid," Neve said.

"He is. But he's still a boy." She looked into Neve's face, and Neve thought that

Talia looked almost like a kid herself; she must have had Shane very young. Neve thought of all the mistakes she'd made, of how much learning it took to be a parent. People weren't born being good mothers and fathers.

"He is," Neve said.

"Am I being selfish?"

Neve smiled, waiting for her to continue, not quite knowing what she meant.

Talia hesitated. "I met someone down in North Carolina. He lives on the base, near my sister. I've been alone for so long. . . ."

Neve nodded; she could relate to that.

"I've been going back and forth, leaving Shane alone a lot. Jack wants to come up and see me here, but I don't want to introduce him to Shane too soon." She shook her head, exhaling. "I don't know. Is it wrong for me to want to be happy?"

Neve paused, thinking about her own life. "I don't know the right answer," she said. "Whether you should go for the whole two weeks, whether it's a good or bad idea. You're Shane's mother, and you have to take care of him." She paused, watching Tim jump off the boat as it pulled onto the beach, seeing the sun glint on his wetsuit, muscles straining as he pulled the boat higher on the sand, flashing her a smile when he saw her watching. "But I do know that happiness is a gift," she said. "I guess, for me, it's a balance. I'm only really happy when I know Mickey is, too."

"I was thinking," Talia said. "A way to make Shane happy, and also shorten the time I'd be away from him."

"What's that?" Neve asked.

"Well, that trip to Washington. I've felt so guilty, going back and forth to see my sister, meet my friend, and it gets expensive. Shane's so good about not asking for extra money, but I know he'd love to go on the school trip. The thing is, I think there's a way I could afford both."

"What do you mean?"

"I thought maybe I could drive Shane and Mickey down. Drop them off in Washington—it's on my way to North Carolina. And pick them up on the way home. That way, I'd only have Shane's hotel and food bills to worry about. You know?"

"I know," Neve said, smiling. "I'm sure that would make both Shane and Mickey very happy."

Joe and Tim secured the inflatable, setting

the anchor right by the jetty. They all came up the beach, exhausted and exhilarated. Tim put his arms around Neve and kissed her. His lips were salty, and when his body pressed against hers, she felt the freshness of the sea.

They stood there, in a circle on the sand, gathered together. Shane talked excitedly about what he'd seen down below, and Neve knew the extra sparkle in his eyes was because his mother had come down to see him. She listened to the stories. Tim's arm was around her, and she couldn't help thinking of the time they'd been here, right in this spot on the beach, when it had been so much colder.

Winter's ice and snow had covered the sand; her skin had felt numb, partly from the cold, partly from her frozen heart. The snowy owl had been on its sharp, swift flight out from the weather-silvered driftwood log. This beach bore the tracks and footprints of so many that Neve loved—some gone forever, others being made right now.

"Are you okay?" she asked Tim in a low voice, so no one else could hear.

"I am," he said. "Better than I thought."

"How's your father?"

"He's all right. I guess we're getting accustomed to the idea of this really happening. I never thought I'd see the day, but the wreck will be gone soon."

Another car pulled up, stopped on the road beyond the dune. Neve looked up, saw the door open. Several people got out, and a very old lady was helped from the back seat. She had white hair, and she was dressed in black. Standing very straight and tall, she faced the water.

As Neve and Tim watched, the wives of Damien's crew drifted over to her and the people she'd come with. Perhaps she's another wife, Neve thought. Another of Damien's flight crew, attracted to Secret Harbor by the news of the Berkeley show. Voices carried over the sand, scraps of conversation. Neve saw Mickey and Shane look at each other.

"They're speaking German," Mickey said, and she and Shane ran up the beach.

Talia went behind them, followed by Joe, Tim, and Neve. Neve watched the way Tim supported his father as he made his way across the sand. It gave way beneath his legs, and the dune was steep, and as sure-footed as he seemed in the boat, on the water, right now there was no mistaking that he was an eighty-five-year-old man.

Once they got up on the road, Mickey turned to them. She had been talking to the new arrivals—the very old white-haired woman, and the four people with her.

"They got my letter," Mickey said, her eyes gleaming.

"Yes, my mother appreciated it very much," one of the women said—she looked to be about sixty-five, but very trim and beautiful, with chic gray hair and a slim black suit. "My brother and I, and our spouses, wanted to come for ourselves. And she, of course, has wanted to make this trip for a very long time."

The old woman spoke in German, and her daughter translated.

"Many years I have wanted to come here, yet also dreaded it. Because I knew that once I stood on this shore, I would be so close to him, that he would seem even farther away."

"Your husband?" Joe asked, stepping forward.

Neve watched Tim hold on to his father's elbow, steadying him, before Joe pulled away.

The woman translated to her mother, then listened to the reply.

"Yes," she said. "He died here, just off this beach, aboard a U-boat."

"U-823," Joe said.

"Yes."

"April seventeenth, nineteen forty-four," Joe said. He faced the old woman, not her daughter. "I am Joseph O'Casey; I was the commander of the USS *James*, the destroyer escort that sank your husband's U-boat."

"My father was only twenty-four years old," the daughter said.

"So was my father," Tim said.

"They were enemies," one of the men said, stepping forward. He was tall and dark, with blue eyes behind wire-rimmed glasses. "The war took our father from us."

Neve watched Tim battling with himself; perhaps he wanted to say it had taken his from him, too. But his father stood there now, and she knew what a blessing it was, for people to have a whole lifetime together to work out their worst hurts.

"I'm so sorry," Joe said. "I would do anything to change it if I could."

"He would," Tim said. "He's lived with the

responsibility of this battle every day. You have to understand, he was defending our country."

But Joe shook his head. The reasons didn't matter right now. The battle seemed ancient history; there were just people, human beings, families scarred by war, facing each other now. Neve watched as he took a step closer to the old woman.

"I'm sorry," he said, the words so simple.

Everyone was silent. The two oldest people stared into each other's eyes. The daughter didn't even translate; it was unnecessary. The old woman's eyes clouded, filled with tears. She nodded as they streamed down her cheeks.

"Es war Krieg," she said. *It was war. . . .*

"Who was your husband?" Joe asked, and when he took her hand, Neve saw that his eyes were flooded, too.

"Oberleutnant Kurt Lang," she said.

And Neve had to bury her face in Tim's shoulder as she saw Joe reach for the old woman, saw their shoulders shaking in silent sobs.

Epilogue

It was just three weeks later, on the same beach.

The trip to Washington had been a blast. Cherry blossoms seen, Lincoln Memorial visited at night, Smithsonian toured, postcards sent: *Having a great time, Senator Sheridan was wonderful! Thanks, Dad!*

Mickey's father hadn't been kidding when he said he'd called.

The Senate office building had been so austere, so grand, that Mickey and Shane had felt tiny and unimportant, unable to believe that their being there could ever make any kind of difference.

Of course, their being there *had* rankled

Josh Landry, which in itself was almost worth it. He'd had huge visions of taking the whole class up to see Senator Sheridan, but ha! They'd all been stopped at the security checkpoint—all except Mickey and Shane.

The senator had been so gracious. Tall, handsome, Irish American, a photo op waiting to happen. He'd gone on a bit about how Mickey's dad had sold him his house on Rumstick Point, and what a great golf swing he had, and how he sure could tell a great story, and a bunch of other stuff.

But Mickey, knowing that the senator had probably allotted just so much time to be nice to the constituent's daughter, had reached into her satchel, pulled out the letters, and plunked them down on the big mahogany desk, right beside the picture of John F. Kennedy.

"We want the U-boat to stay in Rhode Island," she'd said.

"Ah, yes, the U-boat," Senator Sheridan had said, a little shocked.

"These are pictures we took underwater," Shane had said. He'd pulled out the album he and Mr. O'Casey had put together—the one he'd almost left in his mother's car as she'd dropped them off at the Capitol Hill

Holiday Inn. Thank God he'd had Mickey with him to remind him.

"And these are pictures we took of Joseph O'Casey with the widow of Oberleutnant Kurt Lang," Mickey had said, turning to the right page.

"You mean the commander of U-823?" Senator Sheridan had asked, clearly a student of his state's history.

"That's the one," Mickey had said.

Now, standing on the beach, she felt the very late-day sun on her face. Shane had spent the afternoon surfing—the waves as big and mighty as ever, because the topography down below hadn't changed.

The U-boat was staying.

Oh, Senator Sheridan, Mickey wanted to say to the sky. *Thank you. Thank you for reading the letters, looking at the pictures, having a heart, and even more—having a soul. Thank you for saying no to Cole Landry, thank you for saying yes to Richard Halloran.*

Mickey's dad was the hero here—she'd never believe otherwise. If he hadn't pulled strings, would Mickey and Shane have gotten their audience with Senator Sheridan? See? Case closed.

Right now, while Shane dried off, Mickey let the sun warm her face. He came over, put his arm around her. Together they went over to the jetty, where Jenna and Tripp were standing. Mickey smiled at Jenna—it meant so much that she had come today.

"When are they getting here?" Jenna asked.

"Any second now," Mickey said.

"Man," Tripp said to Shane, "you can really surf."

"Yeah," Shane said modestly.

"You been doing it awhile?"

"Only my whole life."

"You must love it."

"Yeah," Shane said.

Mickey smiled, and she and Jenna exchanged a look. They'd been bird-watching their whole lives, and if this whole episode had taught them one thing, it was that you don't outgrow the things you love.

A few minutes later, they heard the truck, and together they all hurried up the beach, to meet Joe, Tim, and Mickey's mom. Tim and Shane reached into the back of the truck bed, hauled the big cage forward. Mickey remembered back to the night Mr. O'Casey had dug it out of the ranger station shed—all filled with cobwebs and dead moths.

They had used the cage to take the injured snowy owl over to the raptor barn, and tonight they were delivering him back to the beach—to the weathered driftwood log that they hoped would be his runway, his launching pad to return home, northward to the Arctic.

"Oh my God," Jenna said, when she looked in the cage. "There are two of them."

"He has a mate," Mickey said.

"She was badly wounded herself," Joe explained to Jenna and Tripp. "I've been caring for her for a year now, and she never flew until this spring."

"Because she found love," Mickey said. "With our snowy owl."

"That's right," Mickey's mother said. "And it healed them both."

Mickey glanced over at her and Tim. They were holding hands, standing on the beach road like two kids. Sometimes it still hurt Mickey, pierced her heart to think of her mother being happy with someone else, not her father. And it made Mickey ache to know that her father had disappeared again.

She looked up at Joe, saw him watching

her. Why did she feel he could read her mind? It was as if he knew the best of her father, and the worst, and was encouraging her to love him for all of it—especially for the hero he was, in helping keep U-823 here in Rhode Island.

We couldn't have done it without your father, he'd said to her, as soon as the decision had been announced. He gazed at her now with such stern love, she could almost believe he'd magically become her grandfather. She felt him willing her to have faith, to stay strong, to see the best in her father. He had shown her a picture of his brother and his daughters when they were little, as well as a sepia-toned photograph of an old farmhouse, and a 1940s map of the mountains near Alsace-Lorraine, when it had been occupied France.

"Damien's daughter Aimée once asked me to tell her something about her father," he had said to Mickey. "Something to explain the way he was."

"What did you tell her?" Mickey had asked, wishing he, or someone, could do the same for her.

"I told her it's a love story," he'd said. "It's difficult, and it doesn't have a happy ending.

But it's about how brave her father was, and it's about the courage of some women who believed in goodness even while the world around them seemed to be ending."

"What did she say after you told her?" Mickey had asked.

"She never stayed to listen," he'd said, staring at the cracked photo of the farmhouse. "She walked away that day, and she's never come back since. Even though the story is waiting. And it's as magical and true as any story I know."

"Maybe she will come back," Mickey had whispered, her own heart broken again. "No matter how much time goes by, he's still her father."

Joe had nodded, looking at her as if he thought her very wise. Mickey didn't know about that, but she did know about love. She felt it, all the way through, for everyone here right now—and for her father, wherever he was. Love was like a silver cord with a bright red core, running through the center of her spine, the part of her that was most alive.

Watching Tim and Shane carry the cage onto the beach, she noticed how much later it stayed light now. It was nearly seven, and the sun was setting behind the thicket. The day's last light spread across the pine trees, turning their sharp green needles golden. It poured onto the dunes, making them gleam with pink and gold. Spreading into the sea, it slicked across the boldly breaking waves, exploding into sparks of foam. If Berkeley were here now, he'd paint something extraordinary.

Because as the sun set, the moon rose. The moonlight chased the gold away, replaced it with silver. Mickey thought of the miraculous medal Shane had told her about, the silver disc showing Mary crushing the serpent, that Tim had laid on the broken hull of U-823. Mickey imagined the medal blessing the men who had died inside the wreck, and those who had died on the surface. Those who were still alive . . .

Shane's father, and her own father. Everyone's families. Damien and his daughters, and the love story still untold. Mickey looked around the circle now, saying a silent prayer for her mother and Tim, Joe, Jenna and Tripp, Shane, his mother and the major, Beth, and Frank.

And, of course, the snowy owls.

This was Joe's area of expertise. Everyone

stood back, right against the dunes. Joe crouched alone beside the cage. The birds rustled inside, turning their heads, already testing their white wings. Mickey stared at the male, the one she'd found here on the beach, the very first snowy owl she'd ever seen. She held her breath as Joe opened the cage door.

He stayed very still. It took a few minutes; the moon rose perceptibly higher, a white disc over the sea. While time ticked by, one owl emerged from the cage, followed by the other. When they were both on the sand, Joe inched back with the cage.

But he didn't go too far. It was as if he wanted to be sure it was safe—Mickey watched him kneel down on one knee, eyes sharply riveted on the owls. She heard the cry—joyous, hungry for the tundra, ready for ice. One owl lifted off, and instantly so did its mate.

They flew in a straight line off the end of the jetty, over the water, toward the moon. Its bright path traced the waves, breaking over the sunken remains of U-823. Mickey watched the owls veer, just like aircraft, just like the Silver Shark. They tilted suddenly, as if too unstable to fly. Mickey's heart jumped, and she wanted to catch the owls, bring them back, and she tore onto the beach, her arms out.

Joe caught her, held her while she reached up, into the sky.

"Let them go," he said. "It's time."

"What if they can't make it? If they get hurt, or if they fall?" she cried, thinking of how far they had to go, of all the dangers they'd face on the way.

"Just look at them," he said as they grew more distant. "They're not hurt or falling right now, are they?"

She couldn't speak. Standing there, she just stared after the owls, her heart pounding. She thought of all the awful things that could happen to two creatures, all the trials they would have to go through before they reached their home.

"What if they don't make it?" she asked. "What if they aren't ready? Or if they're too weak? Or they can't find food? Or someone attacks them, like what happened to them here?"

"There's goodness in the world, Mickey."

"But not enough," she whispered, hot tears in her eyes.

"There's you," he said.

"Me?"

"You did your part, and things changed."

Mickey blinked, wiped her eyes. Her part; all she had done was try to help, just the smallest way she could. She wanted to believe that he was right, that the world was full of good. And when she glanced around, saw the people she loved standing there, smiling at her with encouragement, as if she were the one who had spread her wings, was trying to fly, she could almost believe that Joe was right.

"Just trust, Mickey. Believe in peace, okay?"

They stood together, the old man and the teenaged girl, and she tried to take his words in, tried to feel the possibility.

Mickey breathed the salt air, watching the owls bank over the sea, adjust their course. Their wings gleamed in the moonlight, and Mickey knew that Joe was seeing his brother's silver plane. But then one snowy owl let out a cry—a deep, hollow hoot—and the other answered, as if to let each other know that it was really time to go, that they were on their way; and the snowy owls beat their strong white wings, flying north over the beach and the thicket, finally heading home.

Joe took Mickey's hand, and together they grabbed the cage, and they walked up the beach. Spring was really here. The night was warm, and the waves broke over the old hull, eleven fathoms down, that had once brought war to this beloved shore. The moon shone on the waves and this beach, making its nightly transit all around the world. And Mickey held tight to the peace.

About the Author

LUANNE RICE is the author of twenty-two novels, including *Sandcastles, Summer of Roses, Summer's Child, Silver Bells, Beach Girls,* and *Dance With Me*. She lives in New York City and Old Lyme, Connecticut.